Return To Banksia Bay

RETURN TO BANKSIA BAY © 2025 by Harlequin Books S.A.

NIKKI AND THE LONE WOLF
© 2011 by Marion Lennox
Australian Copyright 2011
New Zealand Copyright 2011

First Published 2011
Third Australian Paperback Edition 2025
ISBN 978 1 038 95300 1

MARDIE AND THE CITY SURGEON
© 2011 by Marion Lennox
Australian Copyright 2011
New Zealand Copyright 2011

First Published 2011
Third Australian Paperback Edition 2025
ISBN 978 1 038 95300 1

Except for use in any review, the reproduction or utilisation of this work in whole or in part in any form by any electronic, mechanical or other means, now known or hereafter invented, including xerography, photocopying and recording, or in any information storage or retrieval system, is forbidden without the permission of the publisher.

This book is sold subject to the condition that it shall not, by way of trade or otherwise, be lent, resold, hired out or otherwise circulated without the prior consent of the publisher in any form of binding or cover other than that in which it is published and without a similar condition including this condition being imposed on the subsequent purchaser.

All rights reserved including the right of reproduction in whole or in part in any form. This edition is published in arrangement with Harlequin Books S.A. Cover art used by arrangement with Harlequin Books S.A. All rights reserved.

This is a work of fiction. Names, characters, places, and incidents are either the product of the author's imagination or are used fictitiously, and any resemblance to actual persons, living or dead, business establishments, events, or locales is entirely coincidental.

Published by
Mills & Boon
An imprint of Harlequin Enterprises (Australia) Pty Limited
(ABN 47 001 180 918), a subsidiary of HarperCollins
Publishers Australia Pty Limited (ABN 36 009 913 517)
Level 19, 201 Elizabeth Street
SYDNEY NSW 2000
AUSTRALIA

® and ™ (apart from those relating to FSC®) are trademarks of Harlequin Enterprises (Australia) Pty Limited or its corporate affiliates. Trademarks indicated with ® are registered in Australia, New Zealand and in other countries. Contact admin_legal@Harlequin.ca for details.

Printed and bound in Australia by McPherson's Printing Group

MARION LENNOX

Return To Banksia Bay

MILLS & BOON

Marion Lennox is a country girl, born on an Australian dairy farm. She moved on—mostly because the cows just weren't interested in her stories! Married to a "very special doctor", Marion writes for the Harlequin Medical™ Romance and Harlequin Romance lines (she used a different name for each category for a while—so if you're looking for her past Harlequin Romance titles, search for author Trisha David, as well). She's now had more than seventy-five romance novels accepted for publication.

In her non-writing life, Marion cares for kids, cats, dogs, chooks and goldfish. She travels, she fights her rampant garden (she's losing) and her house dust (she's lost).

Having spun in circles for the first part of her life, she's now stepped back from her "other" career, which was teaching statistics at her local university. Finally she's reprioritized her life, figured out what's important and discovered the joys of deep baths, romance and chocolate.

Preferably all at the same time!

Books by Marion Lennox

MISTY AND THE SINGLE DAD*
ABBY AND THE BACHELOR COP*

*Banksia Bay

Other titles by this author available in ebook

CONTENTS

NIKKI AND THE LONE WOLF — 7

MARDIE AND THE CITY SURGEON — 215

Nikki And The Lone Wolf

Dear Reader,

Every night around five o'clock my dog, Mitzi, starts pacing. She starts with a mournful sigh, then trudges to the door where her lead hangs, then back to me. Over and over. Finally, I relent. Snow, sleet or baking sun, off we go to our local lake, where I let her off the lead and she can run.

And she does run—a black-and-silver mini-schnauzer, the runt of the litter, a huge dog in a little dog's body, mixing with all the other dogs who've had similar success getting their lead-holders out of their houses. We love it.

Mitzi's best mates are wolfhounds—two vast mutts who play with her as if she's an equal. She does doughnuts through their legs while I chat to their owner, Wolfhound Man, their equal in the large department—though a lot better-looking. *A lot!*

So for this story, when I needed a dog and a hero, there they were in my head—my wolfhound, Horse, and the man who loves him. Wolfhound Man has become Gabe, a sea captain and all-round hero, and of course there's Nikki, a heroine deserving of both man and dog. I'm imagining you, my reader, as my heroine, and I hope you do, too. And you don't even have to feed a wolfhound to do it.

I love the dogs in my life. I love the dogs in my books. But what I love most is when they come together with passion and laughter, and write themselves into love stories for you to enjoy with me.

Happy reading!

Marion

To Gail and to Charles, for Bob,
a gentle giant with a heart as big as he was.

CHAPTER ONE

A WOLF WAS at her door.

Okay, maybe it wasn't quite at her door, Nikki conceded, as she came back to earth. Or back to the sofa. The howl was close, though. Her hair felt as if it was spiking straight up, and for good reason.

It was the most appalling, desolate sound she could imagine—and she wasn't imagining it.

She set her china teacup onto the coffee table with care, absurdly pleased she hadn't spilled it. She was a country girl now. Country girls didn't get spooked by wolves.

Yes, they did.

She fought for logic. Wolves didn't exist in Banksia Bay. This was the north coast of New South Wales.

Was it a dingo?

Her landlord hadn't mentioned dingoes.

He wouldn't, she thought bitterly. Gabe Carver was one of the most taciturn men she'd ever met. He spoke in monosyllabic grunts. 'Sign here. Rent first Tuesday of the month. Any problems, talk to Joe down at the wharf. He's the handyman. Welcome to Banksia Bay.'

Even his welcome had seemed grudging.

Was he at home?

She peered nervously out into the night and was absurdly comforted to see lights on next door. Actually, it wasn't even next door. This was a huge old house on the headland at the edge of town. Three rooms had been split from the rest of the house and a kitchen installed to make her lovely apartment.

Her landlord was thus right through the wall. They shared the entrance porch. Taciturn or not, the thought that he was at home was reassuring. The burly seaman seemed tough, capable, powerful—even vaguely scary. If the wolf came in...

This was crazy. Nothing was coming in. Her door was locked. And it couldn't be a wolf. It was...

The howl came again, long, low and filling the night with despair.

Despair?

What would she know?

It was just a dog, howling at the moon.

It didn't sound like...just a howl.

She peered out again, then tugged the curtains closed. Logical or not, this was scary. Barricade the door and go to bed. It was the only logical thing to do.

Another howl.

Pain.

Desolation.

Did pain and desolation make any kind of sense?

Step away from the window, Nikkita, she told herself. This is nothing to do with you. This is weird country stuff.

'I'm a country girl.' She said it out loud.

'Um, no,' she corrected herself. 'You're not. You're a city girl who's lived in Banksia Bay for all of three weeks. You ran here because your low-life boss broke your heart. It was a dumb, irrational move. You know nothing about country living.'

But her landlord was right next door. Dogs? Wolves? Whatever it was, he'd be hearing it. He could deal with it himself or he could call Joe.

She was going to bed.

The howl filled the night, echoing round and round the big old house.

There was a dog out there, in trouble.

It was not Gabe's problem. Not.

The howl came again, mournful as death, filling his head with its misery. If Jem had been here she'd be off to investigate.

He missed Jem so much it was as if he'd lost a part of him.

He was settled in his armchair by the fire. Things were as they'd always been, but the place at his feet was empty.

He'd found Jem sixteen years ago, a scrappy, half grown collie, skin and bones. She was attacking a rotting fish on the beach.

He'd lifted her away, half expecting the starved pup to growl or snap, but she'd turned and licked his face with her disgusting tongue—and sealed a friendship for life.

She passed away in her sleep, three months back. He still put his hand down, expecting the warmth of her rough coat. Expecting her to be...there.

The howl cut across his thoughts. Impossible to ignore.

He swore.

Okay, he didn't want to get involved—when had he ever?—but he couldn't bear this. The howl was coming from the beach. If a dog was trapped down there... The tide was on its way in.

Why would a dog be trapped on the beach?

Why would a dog be on the beach?

The howl…again.

He sighed. Abandoned his book. Hauled on the battered sou'wester that, as a professional fisherman, was his second skin. Tugged on his boots and headed for the door.

There wasn't a lot of use staring at the fire anyway. He'd made a conscious decision when his wife walked away to never live with anyone again. Emotional connection spelled disaster.

That didn't mean he had to like his solitary life. With Jem it had been just okay.

Not any more.

Her silk pyjamas were laid out on her pretty pink quilt, waiting for her to climb into her brand new single bed. But the howling went on.

She couldn't bear it.

She might not be a country girl but she'd figured whatever was out there was distressed, not threatening. The howl contained all the misery in the world.

Her landlord lived next door. He should fix it, but would he?

The first day she'd been here she'd worried about pipes gurgling in her antiquated bathroom. The bathroom was vast, the bathtub was huge, and the plumbing looked as if it had come from a medieval castle. The gurgling had her thinking there was no way she was using the bath.

Gabe had been outside, chopping wood. She'd hesitated to approach, intimidated by his gruffness—and also the size, the sense of innate power, the sheer masculinity of the man. Chopping wood…he'd looked quite something.

Actually...he'd been stripped to the waist and he'd looked *really* something.

She was being stupid. Hormonal. Dumb. She'd plucked up courage and approached, feeling like Oliver Twist asking for more gruel. 'Please sir, could you fix my pipes?'

'See Joe,' he'd muttered and promptly disappeared.

She'd been disconcerted for days.

She'd seethed for a bit, tried to ignore the gurgling for a few days, had showers, and finally gone to find Joe.

Joe was an ancient ex-fisherman living on a dilapidated schooner that looked as if it hadn't been to sea for years. He'd promised to fix the gurgling that afternoon. He did—sort of—thumping the pipes with a spanner—but while she'd been explaining the problem, a fishing boat swept past. Huge. Freshly painted. Gleaming clean and white. The deck was stacked with cray-pots. The superstructure was strung with scores of lanterns that Joe explained were to attract squid.

Her landlord had been at the wheel.

Still disconcerting. Big, weathered, powerful.

Still capable of doing things to her hormones just by... being.

'Turns his hand to anything, that one,' Joe told her as they watched Gabe go past. 'Some of the guys here just fish for squid. Or crays. Or tuna. Then there's a drop in numbers, or sales go off and they're in trouble. I've been a fisherman all my life and I've seen so many go to the wall. Gabe just buys 'em out and keeps going. He went away for a while, but came back when things got bad. Bailed us out. Six of the boats here are his.'

At the wheel of his boat, Gabe looked an imposing figure. His sou'wester might have once been yellow, but that time was long past. He wore oversized waterproof trousers with braces, rubber boots and a faded checked shirt rolled up to reveal arms maybe four times the width of hers. His eyes were creased against the elements, and his face looked almost grim.

After days at sea, his stubble was almost a beard. His thick black hair—in need of a cut—was stiff with salt.

His boat passed within yards of Joe's, and he gave Joe a salute. No smile, though.

He didn't look as if he ever smiled.

He bought up other fishermen when they went broke? He made money out of other people's misery?

Her hormones needed to find someone else to fantasise about, fast.

'I'd guess he's not popular,' she'd ventured, but Joe had looked at her as if she was crazy.

'Are you kidding? Without Gabe, the fishing industry here'd be bust. He buys out the guys who go broke, gives 'em a fair price, then employs 'em to keep working. He's got thirty men and women working for him now, all making a better living than they ever did solo, and there's not one but who'd lay down their lives for him. Not that he'd ask. Never asks anything of anyone. Never lets anyone close. If anyone's in trouble Gabe's first on hand, doing what needs doing, whatever the cost. But he doesn't want thanks. Backs off a mile if you try and give it. He keeps to himself, our Gabe. Apart from that one disaster of a marriage, he always has and he always will. The town respects that. We'd be nuts not to.'

He paused, watching as Gabe expertly manoeuvred his boat into a berth that seemed way too small to take her. He did it as if he was parking a Mini Minor in a paddock, as if he had all the room in the world. 'But now his dog's died,' Joe said slowly, reflectively. 'I dunno... We've never seen him without her; not since he was a lad, and how he's handling it...' He broke off and shook his head. 'Yeah, well, about those pipes...'

That was two weeks ago.

Another howl jerked her back to the present. A dog in trouble.

Desolation?

She had to do something.

There was nothing she could do. This was something her landlord had to cope with.

The howl came again, long, low and dreadful.

She'd tugged on her pyjama top. Almost defiantly.

Another howl.

She paused, torn.

What if her landlord wasn't at home? What if he'd left the light on and was gone?

There was a dog out there in trouble.

Not your problem. NYP. NYP. NYP.

She closed her eyes.

Another howl.

She hauled off her pyjamas and tugged on jeans. Designer jeans. She should do something about her clothes.

She should do something about a dog.

Where was a torch?

What if it was a dingo?

She grabbed her mobile phone. Checked reception. Checked she had the emergency services number on speed dial.

There was a heavy metal poker by the fireside. So far she hadn't lit the fire—or she had once but it had smoked and what did you do about a fire that smoked?

You bought a nice clean electric fire.

Another howl—they were now almost continuous.

Enough.

Poker in one hand, torch in the other, country-girl Nikki—or not—went to see.

The beach beneath the headland was bushland almost to the water's edge. Gabe strode down the darkened track with ease. He'd lived here all his life—he practically knew each twig. He didn't need a torch. In moonlight, torchlight stopped you seeing the big picture.

He reached the beach and looked out to the water's edge. Following the howl.

A huge dog. Skinny. Really skinny. Standing in the shallows, howling with all the misery in the world.

Gabe walked steadily forward, not wanting to startle it, walking as if he was strolling slowly along the beach and hadn't even noticed the dog.

The dog saw him. It stopped howling and backed further into the water. Obviously terrified.

A wolfhound? A wolfhound mixed with something else. Black and shaggy and desolate.

'It's okay.' He was still twenty yards away. 'Hey, boy, it's fine. You going to tell me what's the matter?'

The dog stilled.

It was seriously big. And seriously skinny. And very, very wet.

Had it come off a boat?

He thought suddenly of Jem, shivering on the beach sixteen years back. Jem, breaking his heart.

This dog was nothing to do with him. *This was not another Jem.*

He couldn't leave it, though. Could he entice it up the cliff?

If he could get it into his truck he'd take it to Henrietta who ran the local Animal Welfare shelter.

That was the extent of his involvement. Dogs broke your heart almost worse than people.

'I'm not going to hurt you.' He should have brought some steak, something to coax him. 'You want to come home and get a feed? Here, boy?'

The dog backed still further. For whatever reason, this dog didn't want company. He looked a great galumphing frame of terror.

It'd have to be steak. There was no way he'd catch him without.

'Stay here,' he told the dog. 'Two minutes tops and I'll be back with supper. You like rump steak?'

The dog was almost haunch-deep in water. Was he dumb or just past acting rationally?

'Two minutes,' he promised. 'Don't go away.'

The dog was on the beach. As soon as she walked out of the front door she figured it out. The house was on the headland and the howls were echoing straight up.

Should she knock on her landlord's side of the house?

If he was home he must be hearing this, she thought, and if he'd heard it and done nothing, then no amount of pleading would make a difference. Joe said he helped people. Ha!

He must have heard and decided to ignore it. He was like Joe said, a loner.

Knock and see?

What was worse, the Hound of the Baskervilles or her landlord?

Don't be stupid. Knock.

She knocked.

Nothing.

She didn't know whether to be relieved or not.

Another howl.

What next? Ring the police?

What would she say? Excuse me but there's a dog on the beach. What sort of wimpy statement was that?

She needed to see what was happening.

Cautiously.

There was a narrow track from the house to the beach but she'd only been on it a couple of times. It was a private track, practically overgrown. Where did the track start?

She searched the edge of the overgrown garden with the torch but she couldn't find it.

So was she going to bush-bash her way down to the cove?

This was nuts. Dangerous nuts.

Only it wasn't dangerous. There was only about fifty yards of bush-land between the house and the beach. The bush wasn't so thick she couldn't push through.

And that howl was doing things to her insides. It sounded like she imagined the Hound of the Baskervilles would sound, howling ghostly anguish over the moors. Or over her beach.

The animal must be stuck in a trap or something.

If it was stuck, what could she do?

Go to the beach, figure what's wrong and then ring for help.

You can do this. You're a big girl. A country girl. Or not.

She wanted, suddenly and desperately, to be back home in Sydney. In her lovely life she'd walked away from.

Face that tomorrow, she told herself harshly. For tonight… go fix a howl.

* * *

He was striding up the track, moving swiftly. With a slab of meat in his hand he could approach the dog slowly, letting it smell the meat before it smelled him. He'd intended to have the steak for breakfast—he needed a decent meal before heading to sea again—but he could cope with eggs.

Don't get sucked in.

'I'm not getting sucked in,' he told himself. 'I'm hauling the thing out of the water, feeding it and handing it over to Henrietta. End of story.'

It was dark.

The bush was really thick. Her torch wasn't strong enough.

She was out of her mind.

The howls stopped.

Why?

The silence made it worse. Where had the howls been coming from? Where were the howls now?

Anything could be in here. Bunyips. Neanderthals. The odd rapist.

She was losing her mind, and she was going home now! She turned, pushed forward, and a branch slapped her forehead with a swish of leaves. She almost screamed. She was absurdly pleased that she didn't.

But still no howl.

Where was it?

She was going back to the house. There was no way she was going one inch further.

Where was the thing behind the howl?

She shoved her way around the next bush, pushing herself against the thick foliage. Suddenly the foliage gave way and she almost tumbled out onto the track.

Hands grabbed her shoulders—and held.
She screamed and jerked back.
She raised her poker and she hit.

CHAPTER TWO

SHE'D KILLED HIM.

He went down like felled timber, crumpling from the knees, pitching sideways onto the leaf-littered track.

She had just enough courage not to run; to shine the torch at what she'd hit.

She'd hit someone—not something. She didn't believe in werewolves. Therefore...

Sanity returned with terrifying speed. She had it figured almost before she got the torchlight on his face, and what she saw confirmed it.

She whimpered. There seemed no other option.

This was ghastly on so many levels her head felt it might explode.

She'd knocked out her landlord.

The howling started up again just through the trees, and she jumped higher than the first time she'd heard it.

A lesser woman would run.

There wasn't room for her to be a lesser woman.

She knelt, shining the torchlight closer to see the damage.

Gabe's dark face was thick with stubble, harsh and angular.

A thin trickle of blood was oozing down the side of his cheek. A bruise with a split at its centre was rising above his eye.

He seemed totally unconscious.

To say her heart sank was an understatement. Her heart was below her ankles. It was threatening to abandon her body entirely.

But then… He stirred and groaned and his fingers moved towards his head.

Conscious. That had to be good.

What to do? Deep breath. This was no time for hysterics. He looked as if he was trying to focus.

She placed the poker behind her. Out of sight.

'Are you… Are you okay?' she managed.

He groaned. He closed his eyes and appeared to think about it.

'No,' he managed at last. 'I'm not.'

'I'll find a doctor.' Her voice wobbled to the point of ridiculous. 'An ambulance.'

He opened his eyes again, touched his head, winced, closed his eyes again. 'No.'

'You need help.' She was gabbling. 'Someone.' She went to touch his face and then thought better of it. She definitely needed help. Someone who knew what they were doing. She reached inside her jacket for her cellphone.

His eyes flew open, he grabbed her wrist and he held like a vice.

'What did you hit me with?' His voice was a slurred growl.

'A…a poker.' His voice was deep. In contrast, her voice was practically a squeak.

'A poker,' he said, almost conversationally. 'Of course. And now what?'

'S…sorry?'

'You have a gun in your jacket? Or is only your poker loaded?'

Her breath came out in a rush. If he was making stupid jokes, maybe she hadn't done deathly damage.

'There's not…that's not funny,' she managed. 'You scared the daylights out of me.'

'You *hit* the daylights out of me.'

Reaction was making her shake. 'You snuck up.' Her voice was getting higher. 'You grabbed me.'

'Snuck up…' He sounded flabbergasted. 'I believe,' he said through gritted teeth, 'that I was running up the track. On *my* land. Back to *my* house. And you burst out of the undergrowth. Bearing poker.'

He had a point, she conceded. She'd almost fallen as she lurched onto the cleared track. She might indeed have fallen into his path.

It might even have been reasonable for him to grab her to stop them both falling.

And he was her landlord. Hitting someone was bad enough, but to hit Gabe…

It hadn't been easy to find decent rental accommodation in Banksia Bay and she'd been really lucky to find this apartment. Apart from howling dogs, it had everything she needed. 'Just be nice to your landlord and respect his privacy,' the woman in the rental agency had advised. 'He's a bit of a loner. You leave Gabe in peace and you'll get along fine.'

Leaving him in peace wouldn't include hitting him, she conceded. Mentally she was already packing.

'I need steak,' he said across her thoughts.

She blinked. 'Steak?' She groped for basic first aid; thought of something she'd once read. 'To stop the swelling?'

She tried to look wise. Tried to stop gibbering. 'I don't... I don't have steak but I'll get ice.'

'For the dog, dummy.' He'd raised his head but now he set it down again, staying flat on the leaf litter. Gingerly fingering the bruise. 'The dog needs help. There's steak in my fridge. Fetch it.'

'I can't...'

'Just fetch it,' he snapped and closed his eyes. 'If you run round in the middle of the night with pokers, you face the consequences. Get the steak.'

'I can't leave you,' she said miserably, and he opened one eye and looked at her. Flinching.

'Turn the torch around,' he said, and she realised that just possibly she was blinding him as well as hitting him.

'Sorry.' She swivelled the light so it was shining harmlessly into the bush.

'No, onto you.'

He reached out, grabbed the flashlight and turned it onto her face. Then he surveyed her while she thought ouch, having a flashlight in her eyes hurt.

'There's no need to be scared,' he said.

'I'm not scared.' But then the dog howled again and she jumped. Okay, maybe she was.

'You can't afford to be,' he said, and she could tell by the strain in his voice that he was hurting. 'Because the dog needs help. I don't know what's wrong with him. He's standing on the beach howling. You were heading down with a poker. I, on the other hand, intend to try steak. I believe my method is more humane. It might take me a few moments to stop seeing stars, however, so you fetch it.'

'Are you really seeing stars?'

'Yes.' Then he relented. 'It's night. There are stars. Yes,

I'm dizzy, but I'll get over it. I won't die while you're away, but I do need a minute to stop things spinning. My door's open. Kitchen's at the back. Steak's in the paper parcel in the fridge. Chop it into bite sized pieces. I'll lie here and count stars till you come back. Real ones.'

'I can't leave you. I need to call for help.'

'I'm fine,' he said with exaggerated patience. 'I've had worse bumps than this and lived. Just do what I ask like a good girl and give me space to recover.'

'You lost consciousness. I can't...'

'If I did it was momentary and I don't need anyone to hold my hand,' he snapped. 'Neither do you. You're wasting time, woman. Go.'

She went. Feeling dreadful.

She tracked the path with her torch, trying to run. She couldn't. The path was a mass of tree roots. If Gabe had been running he must know the path by heart.

She didn't have the right shoes for running either.

She didn't have the right shoes at all, she thought. She was wearing Gucci loafers. They worked beautifully for wandering the Botanic Gardens in Sydney after a Sunday morning latte. They didn't work so well here.

She wanted so much to be back in her lovely apartment overlooking Sydney Harbour. Back in her beautifully contained life, her wonderful job, her friends, the lovely parties, the coffee haunts, control.

Jon's fabulous apartment. A job in a lovely office right next to Jon's. A career that paid...extraordinarily. A career with Jon. Friends she shared with Jon. Coffee haunts where people greeted Jon before they greeted her.

Jon's life. Or half of Jon's life. She'd thought she had the perfect life and it had been based on a lie.

What to do when your world crumbled?

Run. She'd run to here.

'Don't think about it.' She said it to herself as a mantra, over and over, as she headed up the track as fast as she could in her stupid shoes. There'd been enough self-pity. This was her new life. Wandering around in the dark, coshing her landlord, looking for steak for the Hound of the Baskervilles?

It was her new life until tomorrow, she thought miserably. Tomorrow Gabe would ask her to leave.

Another city might be more sensible than moving back to Sydney. But it was probably time she faced the fact that moving to the coast had been a romantic notion, a dignified way she could explain her escape to friends.

'I can't stand the rat race any longer. I can deal with my clients through the Internet and the occasional city visit. I see myself in a lovely little house overlooking the sea, just me and my work and time to think.'

Her friends—Jon's friends—thought she was nuts, but then they didn't know the truth about Jon.

Scumbag.

She'd walked away from a scumbag. Now she'd hit her landlord.

Men! Where was a nice convent when a girl needed one? A cloistered convent where no man set foot. Ever.

There seemed to be a dearth of convents on her way back to the house.

Steak.

She reached the house, and headed through the porch they shared, where two opposite doors delineated His and Hers.

She'd never been in His. She opened his door cautiously as if there might be a Hound or two in there as well.

No Hounds. The sitting room looked old and faded and comfy, warmed by a gorgeous open fire. There was one big armchair by the fire. A half-empty beer glass. Books scattered—lots of books. Masculine, unfussed, messy.

All this she saw at a glance as she headed towards the kitchen, but strangely…here was the hormone thing again. She was distracted by the sheer masculinity of the place.

As she was…distracted…by the sheer masculinity of her landlord.

Stupid. Get on with it, she told herself crossly, and she did.

His fridge held more than hers. Meat, vegetables, fruit, sauces—interesting stuff that said when he was at home he cooked.

She needed to learn, she thought suddenly, as she caught the whiff of meals past and glanced at the big old firestove that was the centrepiece of the kitchen. Enough with 'Waistline Cuisine'.

It was hardly the time to be thinking cooking classes now, though. Or hormones.

Steak.

She had it. A solid lump, enough for a team of Hounds. She sliced it into chunks in seconds, then opened the freezer and grabbed a packet of frozen peas as well.

First aid and Hound meat, coming up.

Men and dogs. She could cope.

She had no choice. Convents had to wait.

What did you do with hormones in convents?

He'd terrified her.

Gabe lay back and looked at the sky and let his head clear.

She'd packed a huge punch, but any anger he felt had been wiped by the look on her face. She'd looked sicker than he felt.

What was he about, letting the place to a needy city woman?

It was the second time he'd let it. The first time he'd rented it to Mavis, a spinster with two dogs. The moment she'd moved in she decided he needed mothering. Finally, after six months of tuna bakes, her mother had 'a turn' and Mavis headed back to Sydney to take care of her. Gabe had been so relieved he'd waived the last month's rent.

And now this.

Dorothy in the letting agency had made this woman sound businesslike and sensible. Very different to Mavis.

'Nikkita Morrissy. Thirty years old. She designs air conditioning systems for big industrial projects. Her usual schedule is three weeks home, one week on site, often overseas. She's looking for a quiet place with a view, lots of natural light and nothing to disturb her.'

A woman who worked in industrial engineering. She sounded clever, efficient and non-needy.

His house was huge. He should move into town but he'd lived in this place all his life. *His mother was here.*

He'd lost his mother when he was eight years old, and this was all that was left. The garden she'd loved. The fence she'd almost finished. He walked outside sometimes and he could swear he saw her.

'I'll never leave you...'

People lied. He'd learned that early. Depend on no one. But here...in his mother's garden, looking out over the bay she'd loved, this was all that was left of a promise he'd desperately wanted to believe in.

Emotional nonsense? Of course it was, he knew it, but his

childhood house was a good place to crash when he wasn't at sea. He had the money to keep it. If he could get a reasonable tenant for the apartment, then there'd be someone keeping the rooms warm, used.

Go ahead, he'd told Dorothy.

And then he'd met Nikkita. Briefly, the day she'd moved in.

She didn't look like an industrial engineer. She looked like someone in one of those glossy magazines Hattie kept leaving on the boat. She was tall, five nine or so, slim and pale-skinned, with huge eyes and professionally applied make-up—yes, he was a bachelor but that didn't mean he couldn't pick decent cosmetics a mile off. Her glossy black hair was cut into some sort of sculpted bob, dead straight, all fringe and sharp edges.

And her clothes... The day she'd arrived she'd been wearing a black tunic with a diagonal slash of crimson across the hips. She'd added loopy silver earrings, red tights and glossy black boots that were practically thigh high. Low heels though. It was her moving day. She'd obviously thought low heels were workmanlike.

Tonight she'd been wearing jeans. Skin-tight jeans and a soft pink sweater. She must be roughing it, he thought, and his thoughts were bitter.

His head was thumping. He was trying hard not to think critical thoughts about ditzy air conditioning engineers who bush-bashed through the night with pokers.

And suddenly she was back again—practically running, though if she'd tried to run in those shoes she would have run right out of them. She was panting. Her eyes were still huge and the sculpted hair was...well, a lot less sculpted. She had a twig stuck behind one ear. A big twig.

'Are you okay?' she demanded, breathless, as if she'd expected to find him dead.

'I'm fine,' he growled and struggled to stand. Enough of lying round feeling sorry for himself. He shook away the hand she proffered, pushed himself to his feet—and the world swayed. Not much, but enough for him to grab her hand to steady himself.

She was stronger than he thought. She grabbed his other hand and held, hard, waiting for him to steady.

'S...sorry.' For a moment he thought he might throw up. He concentrated for a bit and decided no, he might keep his dignity.

'Let me help you to the house.'

'Dog first,' he said.

'You first.'

'The dog's standing up to his hocks in the water, howling. I'm not even whinging. I'm prioritizing.' He made to haul his hands away but she still held.

He stopped pulling and let her hold.

Two reasons. One, he was still unsteady.

Two, it felt...not bad at all.

He worked with women. A good proportion of his fishing crews were female. They mostly smelled of, yeah, well, of fish. After a while, no matter how much washing, you didn't get the smell out.

Nikkita smelled of something citrussy and tangy and outright heady. It didn't make the dizziness worse, though. In truth it helped. He stood still, breathing in the scent of her, while the night settled around him.

She didn't speak. She simply held.

Two minutes. Three. She wasn't a talker, then. She'd figured he needed time to make the ground solid and she was giving it to him. It was the first decent thing he'd seen of her.

Maybe there were more decent things.

Her hands felt good. They were small hands for a tall woman. Soft…

Yeah, well, of course they'd be soft. For the last ten years any woman he'd ever gone out with was a local, one of the fishing crews, women who worked hard for a living. The only woman he'd ever gone out with who had soft hands…

Yeah. Lisbette. He'd married her.

So much for soft hands.

'I'm right now,' he said, finally, as another howl split the night. 'Dog.'

'Please let me take you home first.'

'Are you good with dogs?'

'Um…no.'

'Then we both do the dog,' he said. 'Sure, I'm unsteady, so you do what I tell you. Exactly what I tell you. After the poker, it's the least you can do.'

Was she out of her mind?

She was acting under orders.

Gabe was sitting in the shadows, watching, as she approached the dog with her hands full of steak. Upwind, according to Gabe's directions, so he could smell the meat.

The dog was huge. Soaking wet, its coat was clinging to its skinny frame, so it looked almost like a small black horse.

Talk gently, Gabe had said. Soft, unthreatening.

So… 'Hey, Horse, it's okay,' she told him. 'Come out of the water and have some steak. Gabe's gone to a lot of trouble to get it for you. The least you can do is eat it.'

Take one small step after another, Gabe had told her. Stop at the first hint of nervousness. Let the dog figure for himself that you're not a threat.

'Come on, boy. Hey, Horse, it's okay. It's fine. Come and tell me what your real name is.'

What was she doing, standing in the shallows with her hands full of raw meat? She'd tugged off her shoes but her jeans were soaked. To no avail. The dog was backing away, still twenty feet from her.

His coat was ragged, long and dripping. Fur was matted over his eyes.

He wasn't coming near.

If Gabe wasn't in the shadows watching she might have set the meat down on the sand and retreated.

But her landlord was expecting her to do this. He'd do it himself, only, despite what he told her, the thump on the head was making him nauseous. She knew it. He wasn't letting her call for help but she knew it went against the grain to let her approach the dog. Especially when she was so bad at it.

'Here, Horse. Here...'

A wave, bigger than the rest, came sideways instead of forward. It slapped into another wave, crested, hit her fair across the chest.

She yelped. She couldn't help herself.

The dog backed fast into the waves.

'It's okay,' she called and forgot to lower her voice.

The dog cast her a terrified glance and backed some more. The next wave knocked him sideways. He regained his footing and ran, like the horse he resembled. Along the line of the surf, away, around the bed in the headland and out of sight.

* * *

'It's okay.'

It wasn't, but she hadn't expected him to say it. She'd expected him to yell.

She'd coshed him. She'd scared the dog away.

A little voice at the back of her mind was saying, *At least the howling's stopped.*

NYP, the same little voice in the back of her head whispered. Not your problem. She could forget the dog.

Only... He'd looked tragic. Horse...

Gabe was sitting where the sand gave way to the grassy verge before the bush began. At least he looked okay. At least he was still conscious.

'You did the best you could.' *For a city girl.* It wasn't said. It didn't have to be said.

'Maybe he's gone home.'

'Does he look to you like he has a home?' He flicked his cellphone from his top pocket and punched in numbers. Then he glanced at her, sighed, and hit loudspeaker so she could hear who he was talking to.

A male voice. Authoritative. 'Banksia Bay Police,' the voice said.

'Raff?' Gabe's voice still wasn't completely steady and the policeman at the end of the line obviously heard it. Maybe he was used to people with unsteady voices calling. He also recognised the caller.

'Gabe? What's up?' She heard concern.

'No problem. Or not a major one. A stray dog.'

'Another one.' The policeman sighed.

'What are you talking about?' Gabe demanded.

'Henrietta's Animal Welfare van was involved in an accident a few days back,' the policeman explained. 'We have stray dogs all over town. Describe this one.'

'Big, black and malnourished,' Gabe said. He was watching Nikki as he spoke. Nikki was trying to get the sand from between her toes before she put her shoes on. It wasn't working.

She was soaking. She sat and the sand stuck to her. Ugh.

She was also unashamedly listening.

'Like Great Dane big?'

'Yeah, but he's shaggy,' Gabe said. 'I'd guess Wolfhound with a few other breeds mixed in as well. And I don't have him. He was down the beach below the house. We tried to catch him with a lump of steak but he's headed round the headland to your side of town.'

'We?' Raff said.

'Yeah,' Gabe said dryly. 'My tenant's been helpful.'

'But the two of you can't catch him.'

'No,' Gabe said, and Nikki thought miserably that he sounded as if he could have done it if he was by himself. Maybe he could, but at least he didn't say so.

'I'll check from the headland in the morning,' Raff was saying. 'You okay? You sound odd.'

'Nothing I can't handle. If he comes back...you want me to take him to the shelter?'

'You might as well take him straight to the vet's,' Raff said. 'He was on his way there to be put down. If he's the one I think he is, someone threw him off a boat a couple of weeks back. We found him on the beach, starving. He's well past cute pup stage. He's huge and shabby. Old scars and not a lot of loveliness. He looks like he's been kicked and neglected. No one will rehouse a dog like that, so Henrietta made the decision to get him put down. But if he doesn't come back to your beach it's not your worry, mate. Thanks for letting me know. 'Night.'

''Night.'

Gabe repocketed his phone.

Nikki flicked more sand away.

A starving dog. Kicked and neglected. Thrown from a boat. She hadn't even managed to give him a meal, and now he was lost again.

Plus a landlord who was still sounding shaken because she'd thumped him.

Was there a scale for feeling bad? Bad, terrible, appalling.

'Leave the steak just above the high tide mark,' Gabe said, his voice gentle. 'It's not your fault.'

'Nice of you to say so.'

'Yeah, well, the bang on the head was your fault,' he conceded, and he even managed a wry smile. 'But there's nothing more we can do for the dog. He's gone. If he smelled the steak he might come back, but he won't come near if he smells us. We've done all we can. Moving on, I need an aspirin. Do you have those toes sand-free yet?'

'I...yes.' No. She was crusted in sand but she stood up and prepared to move on.

She glanced along the beach, half hoping the dog would lope back.

Why would he?

'Raff'll find him,' Gabe said.

'He's the local cop?'

'Yes.'

'He won't look tonight?'

'There's no hope of finding him tonight. The beach around the headland is inaccessible at high tide. We'll find him tomorrow.'

'You'll look, too?'

'I'm leaving at dawn,' he said. 'I have fish to catch, but you're welcome to look all you want. Now, if you want to stay here you're also welcome, but I need my bed.'

She followed him up the track, feeling desolate. But Gabe must be feeling worse than she was. Maybe he was walking slowly to cater for her lack of sensible shoes, but she didn't think so. Once he stumbled and she put out a hand. He steadied, looked down at her hand and shook his head. And winced again.

'I hit you hard,' she muttered.

'Women aren't what they used to be,' he said. 'Whatever happened to a nice, tidy slap across the cheek? That's what they do in movies.'

'I'll remember it next time.'

'There won't be a next time,' he said, and she thought uh-oh, was her tenancy on the line?

'I'm not about to evict you,' he said wearily, and she flinched. Beside being clumsy and stupid, was she also transparent?

'I didn't think…'

'That I was about to evict you for hitting me? Good.'

'Thank you,' she said feebly and he went on concentrating on putting one foot in front of the other.

He didn't stop until they reached the house. The lights were still on. He stood back to let her precede him into the porch. Instead of going straight into her side of the house, she paused.

Under the porch-light he looked…ill. Yes, he still looked large, dark and dangerous, but he also looked pale under the weathering, and the thin trickle of blood was at the centre of a bruise that promised to be ugly.

He staggered a bit. She reached out instinctively but he grabbed the veranda post. Steadied.

She could have killed him. He looked so...so...

Male?

There was a sensible thought.

'You could have me arrested,' she managed. 'I'm so sorry.'

'But you weren't planning to hit the dog.' It wasn't a question.

'N...no.'

'That's why I won't have you arrested. You meant well.'

'You need to see a doctor.'

'I need to go to bed.'

'But what if it's terrible?' she said before she could stop herself. 'I've read about head wounds. People get hit on the head and go to bed and never wake up. You should get your pupils looked at. If one's bigger than the other...or is it if one doesn't move? I don't know, but I do know that you should get yourself checked. Please, can I drive you to the hospital?'

'No.' Flat. Inflexible. Non negotiable.

'Why not?'

'I've spent my life on boats. Believe it or not, I've been thumped a lot worse than this. I'm fine.'

'You should be checked.'

'You want to look at my pupils?'

'I wouldn't know what to look for. But if you go to bed now... It could be dangerous. Please...'

He was too close, she thought. He was too big. He smelled of the sea. But maybe it wasn't just the sea. He smelled of diesel oil, and fish, and salt, and other incredibly masculine smells she'd never smelled before.

The only man she'd been this close to in the last few years was Jon. Jon of the sleek business suits, of expensive aftershave, of cool, sleek, corporate style.

Compared to Jon, Gabe was another species. They both might be guys at the core, but externally Gabe had been left behind in the cave. Or at sea.

Beside Gabe she felt small and insignificant and stupid. And he made her feel...vulnerable? Maybe, but something more. Exposed. It was a feeling she couldn't explain and she didn't want to explain. All she knew was that she didn't want to be beside him one moment longer, but she was still worried about him. That worry wouldn't be ignored.

'You should be checked every couple of hours,' she said, doggedly now. Once upon a time, well before Jon, she'd dated a medical student. She knew this much.

'I'm fine.' He was getting irritated. 'In eight hours I'll be out at sea. I need to go to bed now. Goodnight.'

'At least let me check.'

'Check what?'

'Check you. All night.'

He stilled. They were far too close. The porch was far too small. Exposed? It was a dumb thought, but that was definitely how he made her feel. His face was lined, worn, craggy. He couldn't be much over thirty, she thought, but he looked as if life had been hard.

It could get harder if she didn't check him. If he was to die...

'What are you talking about?' he demanded.

'I need to check you every two hours,' she said miserably, knowing her conscience would let her off with nothing less. 'I'll come in and make sure you're conscious.'

'I won't be conscious. I'll be asleep.'

'Then I'll wake you and you can tell me your name and what day it is and then you can go back to sleep.'

'I won't know which day it is.'

'Then tell me how much you dislike the tenant next door,' she said, starting to feel desperate. 'For worrying. But I need to do this.' Deep breath. 'It's two-hour checks or I'll phone your friend, the cop, and I tell him how badly I hit you. I wouldn't be the least bit surprised if he's the kind of guy who'll be up here with sirens blazing making you see sense.'

Silence.

Her guess was right, she thought. In that one short phone conversation she'd sensed friendship between the two men, and maybe the unknown cop was as tough as the guy standing in front of her.

'I'm serious,' she said, jutting her jaw.

'I'll be on the boat at dawn. This is nonsense.'

'Being on the boat at dawn is nonsense. After a hit like that you should stay home.'

'Butt out of my life!' It was an explosion and she backed as far as the little porch allowed. Which wasn't far, but something must have shown in her face.

'Okay, sorry.' He raked his hand through his thatch of dark, unruly hair. He needed a haircut, Nikki thought inconsequentially. And then she thought, even more inconsequentially, what would he look like in a suit?

Like a caged tiger. This guy was not meant to be constrained.

That was what she was doing now, she thought. She was constraining him, but she wasn't backing down. There was no way she could calmly go to bed and leave him to die next door.

She met his gaze and jutted her chin some more and tried to look determined. She was determined.

'Every two hours or Raff,' she said.

'Fine.' He threw up his hands in defeat. 'Have it your way. You can sleep tomorrow; I can't. I'm going to bed. If you shine your torch in my eyes every two hours I might well tell you what I think of you.'

'Fine by me,' she said evenly. 'As long as you're alive.'

'Goodnight,' he snapped and turned away. But as he did she saw him wince again.

She really had hurt him.

She showered and tried not to think about dead landlords and starving dogs. What else?

Live landlords. Two-hourly checks. Pupil dilation?

Maybe not. Questions would have to do.

Her pipes gurgled.

She thought briefly about discussing antiquated pipes every two hours but decided, on balance, maybe not. Name and date. Keep it formal and brief.

She set her alarm for two hours on but she didn't sleep. Two hours later she tiptoed in next door.

She'd forgotten to ask which was his bedroom. It was a huge house.

There was a note on the floor in the passage, with an arrow pointing to the left.

'Florence Nightingale, this way.'

She managed a smile. Her first smile of the night. Okay, he'd accepted her help.

She tiptoed in.

He was sprawled on a big bed, the covers only to his waist. Face down, arms akimbo.

Bare back. Very bare back.

She was using her torch. She should quickly focus on his head, wake him, make sure he was coherent, then slip away.

Instead, she took just a moment to check out that body.

Wow.

Double wow.

His shoulders were twice the size of Jon's, but there was no hint of fat. This was pure muscle. A lifetime of pulling in nets, of hauling cray-pots, of hard manual labour, had tuned his body to...

Perfection.

It wasn't often that Nikki let herself look at a guy and think sheer physical perfection but she did now.

The weathering of the man...a life on the sea...

There was a scar on his shoulder, thin and white. She wanted, quite suddenly, to reach out and trace...

'I'm alive,' he snapped. 'Gabriel Carver, Tuesday the fourteenth. Go away.'

She almost yelped again. Habit-forming?

'Your...your head's hurting?'

'Not if I close my eyes and think of England. Instead of thinking of women with pokers. Go away.'

She went.

At least he was alive.

And at least she hadn't touched him. She hadn't traced that scar.

She still wanted to.

Nonsense.

She didn't sleep for another two hours. She checked again. He was sprawled on his back. He looked as if he'd been fighting with the bed.

He was deeply asleep this time, but he looked…done. The bruise on his face looked awful.

She couldn't see the scar on his back. All she could see was his face, exhaustion—pain?

Something inside her twisted. A giant of a man.

Just a little bit vulnerable?

He wouldn't thank her for thinking it but, stupid or not, the thought was there.

It was two in the morning. She glanced at his bedside clock. His alarm was set for four.

She hesitated. Then, carefully, she removed the clock, flicked the alarm off and slipped it in her pocket. His phone was on the bedside table. Why not go all the way? She pocketed that, too.

Then she touched his face. The good side.

His eyes opened. He looked a bit dazed, but he did focus. This was nothing more than someone waking from deep sleep.

'I'll live,' he said, slurred.

'Say something bitter.'

'I'm removing all fireside implements from rental properties.'

'That'll do,' she said and let him go back to sleep.

At four she checked him again. Another slurred response but just as together. Excellent. One more check would get her in the clear, she thought. No more inspections of semi-naked landlords.

She wasn't sure whether to be glad or sorry.

Glad, she told herself, astounded where her thoughts were taking her. Of course, glad.

She went back to bed. Tried not to think of half naked landlords.

Didn't succeed.

At five-thirty Gabe's phone rang. She was on her side of the wall with Gabe's phone beside her bed. She answered. A woman's voice. 'Gabe? Where are you?'

'Hi,' she said cautiously. 'This is Nikki, Gabe's next door neighbour.'

'The city chick,' the woman said blankly.

'That's me.'

'Where's Gabe?'

'I'm sorry, but Gabe had a bit of an accident last night. He won't be in this morning.'

'He won't be in...'

'He can't come to work.'

'What sort of an accident?'

'He fell. He almost knocked himself out. He's got a headache and a badly bruised face.' No need to mention he had the bruised face before he fell.

'Gabe turns up for work when he's half dead.' The woman sounded stunned. 'How bad is he?'

'Determined to come in but I've taken his alarm and his phone and he hasn't woken up.'

There was a moment's awed silence. Then... 'Well, good for you, love. You've got him in bed, you keep him there. When he wakes up, tell him Frank's rung in and his head cold's worse, so it would have only been me on board with him. The *Mariette*'s short a crew member as well, so I'll go on the *Mariette* and the *Lady Nell* can stay in port. That'll play into your hands as well. He no longer has a crew. You keep him in bed with my blessings, for as long as you want. Go for it, girl.'

She disconnected. Laughing.

Nikki stared at the phone as if it stung.

This was a small town. This'd be all over town in minutes.

How would Gabe react?

Um...what had she done?

Whatever. It was done now. She had an hour before the next check.

She really was incredibly tired.

She put her head on her pillow and closed her eyes.

She forgot to set the alarm.

Gabe woke and sunshine was flooding his bedroom. This on its own was a novelty. If the weather was decent he was out fishing, as simple as that.

He opened one eye and tried to figure it out. Why the sunbeams?

His head hurt a bit, not too much, just a dull ache. If he lay still and only opened the one eye it didn't hurt at all.

The sun was streaming through his window. He felt...

Suddenly wide awake. He turned to the bedside table, looking for his clock in disbelief.

No clock.

He groped for his phone.

No phone.

What the...?

His watch.

It was eight o'clock. Eight! He'd slept for ten hours.

The boat. The crew. They'd be waiting.

Where were his...?

Nikkita.

Hitting him on the head was one thing; making him miss a day's fishing was another. She was so out of here.

He threw back the covers and headed for the door, thumping the wall as he went, just to make sure she was awake.

Anger didn't begin to describe what he was feeling. Women!

The thump on her bedroom wall was loud enough to wake the dead. She sat bolt upright. Stared at the clock.

Uh-oh. Uh-oh, uh-oh, uh-oh.

Eight o'clock. She might just have slept in.

She'd missed a check.

At least he wasn't dead, she thought. He should be grateful.

By the sound of the thump on her wall, he wasn't grateful.

By the sound of the thump, he wished for her undivided attention.

Her door was locked. A lesser woman might have tugged the duvet over her head and stayed where she was.

There were a lot of things a lesser woman might do. After today she was going right back to being a lesser woman, but right now...

There wasn't a lot of choice.

She grabbed her robe and headed next door to face Gabe.

She opened her door right as he opened his.

The dog was lying right across the porch.

Her Hound of the Baskervilles.

Horse.

CHAPTER THREE

NIKKI ALMOST TRIPPED and so did Gabe. They were focused on each other. Gabe's face was dark with anger, and Nikki was just plain terrified. Gabe was still only wearing boxers and that didn't help. Neither was looking at their feet and the dog was sprawled like a great wet floor mat.

Both of them stumbled and both had to grab the door jambs to keep their balance.

Both stared down in amazement.

The dog was even bigger than Nikki had thought last night. Four feet high? It was impossible to tell. All she knew was that, prone, he practically covered the small porch.

He was almost as flat as a doormat. He lay motionless, only the faint rise of his chest wall telling her he was alive.

'It's Horse,' she said blankly.

The big dog stirred at her voice. He hauled his great head off the floor, as if making a Herculean effort. He gazed up at her and all the misery of the world was in that gaze. It was a 'kill me now' look.

She didn't know a thing about dogs. If she'd been asked,

she'd confess she probably didn't like them much. But that look…

Her heart twisted. In the face of that look, she forgot her landlord and she sank to her knees. 'Oh, my… Oh, Horse…'

'What do you think you're playing at?' Her landlord's voice was like a whip above her. 'You've brought him in here…'

She wasn't listening. The big dog was so wet he couldn't get any wetter. While she watched, a shudder ran though his big frame and she thought…she thought…

She had to help. There was no way she could walk away. Not your problem? Ha.

'Hey, it's okay.' She ignored Gabe. She could only focus on the dog. She could only think about the dog.

'You caught him.' Gabe's voice had lost its edge as he took in Horse's condition.

'I didn't catch him. Maybe he found the meat and followed our scent. Pushed into the porch. Do you think he wants more?'

'Has he been here all night?'

'Are you nuts? Look at him. He's soaking. Why doesn't he move? Should we take him to the vet? Will you help me carry him to the car?'

'Fred will put him down,' Gable said bluntly.

'Fred?'

'The vet.'

That brought her up short. Last night's phone conversation was suddenly replaying in her head.

This dog had been on his way to be put down when he'd escaped. If they took him to the vet, that was what would happen.

'No,' she said. It was all she could think of to say.

'Do you want a dog?'

'I…'

She swallowed. Did she want a dog?

She didn't. She couldn't. But she wasn't thinking past now.

'I'll think about that later,' she said. 'He's not going anywhere until he's dry and warm and fed. Can you help me take him into my place?' She looked up at Gabe, and then she thought…

Anger. Uh-oh.

Maybe there were a few unresolved issues to be addressed before he'd help her.

She was aware again of his body. That chest. Those shoulders.

Hormones.

Anger.

'I slept,' he said, carefully neutral. 'Through my alarm. That might be because it was moved from my bedside table.'

'I slept through it too,' she confessed. 'That's because I forgot to set it.'

'My crew…'

Act efficient, she decided. Brisk. As if she knew what she was doing. 'Hattie's on the…let me think…on the *Mariette*,' she told him. 'Because they're short a crew member. Frank called in sick so the *Lady Nell*'s staying in port. You have the day off.'

He didn't answer. He looked speechless.

'So can you help me with the dog?' she asked.

'You took my alarm.'

'You were sick. I thought I'd killed you. It was the least I could do.'

'You took my phone.'

'Yes, and I talked to Hattie. She agrees you need a day off.'

'It's not her business. It's not your business.'

'No,' she snapped. 'And neither is this dog but he's freezing. Get over it and help me.'

Her gaze locked with his. She could feel his anger, his frustration, his shock.

His body...

His body was almost enough to distract her from his anger, his frustration, his shock.

But she couldn't think of it now. She had the dog to think of. And, while she was chiding herself, Gabe stooped and touched the dog's face.

The dog tried to raise his head again. Failed.

'Don't think you've heard the last of this,' he said grimly. 'But this guy's done.'

'Done.' Nikki cringed. 'He's not dying.'

'Close to.' He'd moved on, she thought. All his attention was now on the dog. He seemed hesitant, as if he didn't want involvement, but the dog stirred and moaned, and something in Gabe's face changed. 'All right,' he said. 'If you're serious, let's get him into my place. The fire's going. Did you stoke it?'

'Yes. I did it for you.' Or not exactly. In her night-time prowls she'd tossed a couple of logs on the fire at each pass. It had seemed comforting. She'd been in need of comfort, and the thought of taking the dog in there now was a good one.

'Can you get up, big boy?' Gabe asked. 'Come on, mate, let's see you live.'

Gabe was fondling him behind the ears, speaking softly, and the dog responded. He gave Gabe another of those gut wrenching looks, another moan, then heaved. He managed to stand.

Standing up, he looked like a bag of bones with a worn rug stretched over him. Only his ears were still full fur. They hinted at a dog who'd once been handsome but that time was long past.

He swayed and Gabe stooped and held him, still fondling him, while the dog leaned heavily against him.

'So you decided to come and find some help?' he said softly. 'Great decision. You're safe here. You even seem to have found a friend. Mind, you need to beware of pokers.' But he wasn't glancing up to see how she took the wisecrack; he was totally focused on the dog. 'Let's get you warm. Miss Morrissy, could you fetch us some towels, please? A lot of towels. Put some in the tumble dryer to warm them.'

'It's Nikki,' she said numbly.

'Nikki,' he repeated, but he still didn't look up.

The dog took a staggering step forward and then stopped. Enough. Gabe lifted him into his arms as if he were a featherweight, and the dog made no objection. Maybe he knew he was headed for Gabe's fireside.

Nikki headed for towels.

But, as she went, she carried the image of Gabe, a big man with his armful of dog.

He was making her heart twist.

It was the dog, she told herself fiercely. Of course it was the dog.

Only the dog. Anything else was ridiculous.

She did not need hormones.

Horse was freezing. It hadn't been raining, yet he was soaked—had he been standing in the water all night?

Nikki fetched her hairdryer. Gabe sponged the worst of the salt crust from his coat, then towelled him dry as she ran warm air over his tangled fur. The big dog lay passive, hopeless, and Nikki felt an overwhelming urge to pick him up and hug him.

He was so big... She'd have to hug him one end at a time.

She also wanted to kill whoever had abandoned him. To do something so callous...

'Your cop friend said he was thrown from a boat.'

'He'll still feel loyal to the low-life who did it to him,' Gabe said grimly. 'I'd guess that's why he's been standing in the shallows howling.'

She sniffed. She sniffed more than once while she wielded her hairdryer, and she had to abandon her work for a bit to fetch tissues. She couldn't help herself. The emotions of the night, the emotions of the past two months, or maybe simply the emotions of now, were enough to overwhelm her. This gentle giant being betrayed in such a way...

She'd set towels by the fire for Gabe to lay him on. With her hairdryer and Gabe's toweling, they dried one side of him. Then Gabe lifted him. She replaced the sodden towels with warm ones and they dried his other side.

Gabe spoke to him all the time. Slow, gentle words of comfort. While Nikki sniffed.

Gabe's words were washing over her, reassuring her almost as much as the dog. His kindness was palpable. How could she ever have thought he'd ignore a dog in trouble on the beach? His hands stroking the dog's coat...his soft words...

He was a gruff, weathered fisherman but he cared about this dog.

He'd been rude and cold to her the day they'd met. Where was that coldness now?

She tried to imagine Jonathan doing what Gabe was doing now, and couldn't. And then she thought...what was she thinking? Comparing Gabe and Jon? Don't even think of going there.

Um...she was going there. Gabe's body was just a bit too close.

Gabe's body was making her body feel...

No. Stupid, stupid, stupid.

Focus on dog.

The big dog's body had been shuddering, great waves of cold and despair. As the warmth started to permeate, the shaking grew less. Gabe was half towelling, half stroking, all caring.

'It's okay, mate. We'll get you warm on the inside as well.'

'Do you think he got the steak?'

'I'm guessing not,' he said. 'Not in the state he's in—the food would have warmed him and he wouldn't be so hopeless. There's all sorts of predators on the beach at night—owls, rats, the odd feral cat. I'm guessing that's why he's here. He came back round the headland looking for the steak, then when we were gone he followed our scent. There was nowhere else to go.'

'Oh, Horse.'

Grown women didn't cry. Much. She concentrated fiercely on blow-drying—and realised Gabe was watching her.

'Horse?' he said.

'I've been thinking of him all night,' she said. 'In between worrying that I killed you. A dog that looks like a horse. A landlord who might have been dead.'

'Happy endings all round,' Gabe said wryly and she cast him a scared look. She knew what he was going to say. She was way in front of him.

The vet.

'Do you have any more steak?' She couldn't quite get her

voice to work. She couldn't quite get her heart to work. But she wasn't going to say the vet word.

'No. You?'

'I have dinners for one. Calorie controlled.'

'Right, like Horse needs a diet.'

'I'll bring four.'

They worked on. Gabe hauled on a T-shirt and jeans and so did she, but the attention of both was on the dog. Hostilities were suspended.

The dog was so close to the edge that the sheer effort of eating seemed too much. By the look of his muzzle, he'd been sick. 'Sea water,' Gabe said grimly as he cleaned him. 'There's little fresh water round here. If he's been wandering since the van crashed he's had almost a week of nothing.'

That was a lot of speech for Gabe. They should take him to the vet, Nikki thought, but with the vet came a decision that neither of them seemed able to face. Not yet.

Save him and then decide. Dumb? Maybe, but it was what her gut was dictating, and Gabe seemed to be following the same path.

Gabe was encouraging the dog to drink, little by little. He found some sort of syringe and gently oozed water into the big dog's mouth. Once they were sure he could swallow, Nikki shredded chicken, popping tiny pieces into Horse's slack mouth and watching with satisfaction as he managed to get it down.

Slowly.

'If we feed him fast he'll be sick and we'll undo everything,' Gabe said. He sounded as if he knew what he was doing. How come he had a syringe on hand? Had he coped with injured animals before?

He was an enigma. Craggy and grim. A professional fisherman. Broad, but with muscles, there was not an inch of spare flesh on him.

He flashed from silence and anger, to caring, to tender, just like that. His hands as he cared for the big dog were gentle as could be; rough, weathered fisherman's hands fondling the dog's ears, holding the syringe, waiting with all the patience in the world for Horse to open his mouth.

Horse.

Why name a stray dog?

Why look at her landlord's hand and think...and think...?

Nothing.

She should be back on her side of the house right now, enmeshed in plans for the air conditioning system for a huge metropolitan shopping centre. The centre had been the focus of an outbreak of legionnaires' disease. Their air conditioning system needed to be revamped, and the plans needed to be finalised. Now.

Her plans were urgent—even if they bored her witless.

And Gabe should be fishing. He obviously thought that was urgent.

But nothing seemed more important than sitting by the fireside with Gabe and with Horse, gradually bringing the big dog back to life.

They were succeeding. The shuddering ceased. The dog was still limp, but he was warm and dry, and there was enough food and water going in to make them think the worst was past.

So now what?

The dog was drifting into sleep. Nikki glanced briefly at Gabe and caught a flash of pain, quickly suppressed. His head? Of course it was his head, she thought. That bruise looked horrible. What was she doing, letting him work on the dog?

'You need to sleep, too,' she told him.

'We should make a decision about this guy. Take him...'

'Let him sleep,' she said, cutting him off. 'For a bit. Then... maybe we could clean him up a bit more. If we take him back to the shelter looking lovely, then he has a better chance...'

'He's never going to look lovely,' Gabe said. 'Not even close.'

Maybe he wouldn't. The dog was carrying scars. Patches of fur had been torn away, wounds had healed but the fur hadn't grown back. An ugly scar ran the length of his left front leg. And what was he? Wolfhound? Plus the rest.

'It's drawing it out,' Gabe said and Nikki flinched. She looked down at the dog and felt ill—and then she looked at Gabe and felt her own pain reflected in his eyes.

'Not yet,' she said, suddenly fierce. 'Not until he's slept. And not until you've slept. You have the day off work. I know you're angry, and you can be as angry as you like with me, but what's done's done. Your head's hurting. Go back to bed and sleep it off, and let Horse sleep.'

'While you play Florence Nightingale to us both?'

'There's no need to be sarcastic,' she said, struggling to keep her voice even. 'A nurse is the last thing I could ever be, but it doesn't take Florence to see what you need. You and Horse both. I need to do some work...'

'You and *me* both.'

'Get over it,' she snapped. 'You're wounded, I'm not. So what I'm suggesting is that I bring my paperwork in here and do it at your dining table so I can keep an eye on Horse. I'll keep checking the fire, I'll keep offering Horse food and drink, and you go back to bed and wake up when your body lets you.'

'You'll check on me, too?'

'Every two hours,' she said firmly. 'Like a good Florence. Though I'd prefer you to leave your door open so I can make sure you're not dead all the time.'

'This is nonsense. I need to mend cray-pots.'

'You've got the day off,' she snapped. 'I told Hattie you were ill. Don't make a liar of me.'

'You really will look after the dog?'

'I'll look after both of you, until you wake up. Then...' She glanced down at Horse and looked away. 'Then we'll do what comes next.'

He rang Raff from the privacy of his bedroom. The Banksia Bay cop answered on the first ring. 'Why aren't you at sea?' Raff demanded. 'Hattie says you hit your head. I thought you sounded bad last night. You want some help?'

This town, Gabe thought grimly. Banksia Bay was a great place to live unless you hankered for privacy. He did hanker for privacy, but he loved the place and intrusion was the price he paid.

'And Hattie says your tenant's looking after you. Mate...' Raff drew the word out—*maaate*. It was a question all by itself.

'She hit me,' he said before he could help himself.

'Did she now.' Raff thought about that for a bit. 'She had her reasons?'

Nip that one in the bud. 'She thought I was a bunyip. She was searching for the dog. I was searching for the dog. We collided. She was carrying a poker. And that goes no further than you,' he said sharply, as he heard a choke of laughter on the end of the line.

'Scout's honour,' Raff said.

'We never made Scouts.' Raff had been one of the town's bad boys. Like him.

'That's what I mean. You need any help?'

'No. We found the dog. That's why I'm ringing.'

'*We* found the dog? You and Miss Morrissy?'

'Nikki,' he said before he could help himself and he heard the interest sharpen.

'Curiouser and curiouser. So you and Nikki...'

'The dog's here,' he snapped. 'Fed and watered and asleep by my fire. I'll bring him down to Fred when I've had a sleep.'

'You're having a sleep?'

'Nikki's orders,' he said and suddenly he had an urge to smile. Quickly suppressed. 'She's bossy.'

'Well, well.'

'And you can just put that right out of your head,' he snapped. 'I don't want a dog, and I don't want a woman even more. Tell Henrietta the dog's found and we'll take him to Fred tonight.'

'We?'

'Go find some villains to chase,' he growled. 'My head hurts. I'm going to sleep.'

'On Nikki's orders?'

He told Raff where to put his interest, and he hung up. Stripped to his boxers again. Climbed into bed. Following orders.

His head really did hurt.

She was going to check on him every two hours. The thought was...

Nope. He didn't know what the thought was.

He didn't want her checking him every two hours.

'I'd prefer you to leave your door open so I can make sure you're not dead...'

He sighed and opened his door. Glanced across at Nikki, who glanced back. Waved. He glowered and dived under the covers.

He didn't want a woman in his living room.

Nor did he want a dog.

What was he doing, in bed in the middle of the morning?

He put his head on the pillow and the aching eased. Maybe she had a point. A man had to be sensible.

He fell asleep thinking of the dog.

Trying not to think of Nikki.

It was so domestic it was almost claustrophobic. The fire, the dog, Gabe asleep right through the door.

The work she was doing was tidying up plans she'd already drawn—nothing complex, which was just as well the way she was feeling. Her head was all over the place.

Biggest thought? Gabe.

No. Um, no, it wasn't. Or it shouldn't be. Her biggest thought had to be—could she keep a dog?

As a kid she'd thought she might like a dog. That was never going to happen, though. Her parents were high-flyers, both lawyers with an international clientele. They loved her to bits in the time they could spare for her, but that time was limited. She was an only child, taken from country to country, from boarding school to international hotel to luxury resort.

And after childhood? University, followed by a top paying job, a gorgeous apartment. Then Jonathan.

Maybe she could get a small white fluff ball, she'd thought

occasionally, when she was missing Jon. When he was supposedly working elsewhere. But where would a dog fit into a lifestyle similar to her parents'?

And now...

Her job still took her away.

Her job didn't have to take her away. Or not for long. She could glean enough information from a site visit to keep her working for months. Most queries could be sorted online—there was never a lot of use stomping round construction sites.

She quite liked stomping round construction sites. It was the part of her job she enjoyed most.

It was the only part...

Salary? Prestige?

Both were less and less satisfying. Her parents thought her career was wonderful. Jonathan thought it was wonderful. But now...

Now was hardly the time to be thinking of a career change. She was good at what she did. She was paid almost embarrassingly well. She could afford to pay others to do the menial stuff.

So maybe a little white fluff ball?

Or Horse.

Horse was hardly a fluff ball. Ten times as big, and a lot more needy.

Maybe she could share parenting with Gabe, she thought. When she was needed on site, he could stay home from sea.

Shared parenting? Of a dog who looked like a mangy horse, with a grumpy landlord fisherman?

With a body to die for. And with the gentlest of hands. And a voice that said he cared.

She glanced across the passage. The deal was she wouldn't check on him every two hours as long as he kept his door open.

If he dropped dead, she was on the wrong side of the passage.

There wasn't a lot she could do if he dropped dead.

At least the dog was breathing. She watched his chest rise and fall, rise and fall. He was flopped as close to the fire as he could be without being burned. Gabe had set the screen so no ember could fly out, but she suspected he wouldn't wake even if it did.

He looked like a dog used to being hurt.

Maybe he'd be vicious when he recovered.

Maybe her landlord wouldn't let her keep a dog.

Was she really thinking about keeping him?

It was just...

The last few weeks had been desolate. It was all very well saying she wanted a sea change, but there wasn't enough work to fill the day and the night, and the nights were long and silent. She'd left Sydney in rage and in grief, and at night it came back to haunt her.

She also found the nights, the country noises...creepy.

'Because of guys like you howling on beaches,' she said out loud, and Horse raised his head and looked at her. Then sighed and set his head down again, as if it was too heavy to hold up.

How could someone throw him off a boat?

A great wounded mutt.

Her new best friend?

She glanced across the passage again. Gabe was deeply asleep, his bedding barely covering his hips.

He was wounded too, she thought, and with a flash of insight she thought it wasn't just the hit over the head with the poker. He was living in a house built for a dozen, a mile out of town, on his own. Not even a dog.

'He needs a dog, too,' she told Horse.

Shared parenting was an excellent solution.

'Yes, but that's complicated.' She set down her pen and crossed to Gabe's bedroom door to make sure his chest was rising and falling. It was, but the sight of his chest did things to her own chest...

There went those hormones again. She had to figure a way of reining them in.

Return to dog. Immediately.

She knelt and fondled the big dog's ears. He stirred and moaned, a long, low doggy moan containing all the pathos in the world.

She put her head down close to his. Almost nose to nose. 'It's okay,' she said. 'I've given up on White and Fluffy. And I think I do like dogs. You're not going to the vet.'

A great shaggy paw came up and touched her shoulder.

Absurdly moved, she found herself hugging him. Her arms were full of dog. His great brown eyes were enormous.

Could she keep him?

'My parents would have kittens,' she told him.

Her mother was in Helsinki doing something important.

Her father was in New York.

'Yes, and I'm here,' she told Horse, giving in to the weirdly comforting sensation of holding a dog close, feeling the warmth of him. 'I'm here by the fire with you, and our landlord's just over the passage. He's grumpy, but underneath I reckon he's a pussycat. I reckon he might let you stay.'

The fire was magnificently warm. She hadn't had enough sleep last night.

She hesitated and then hauled some cushions down from the settee. She settled beside Horse. He sighed, but it was a different sigh. As if things might be looking up.

'Perfect,' said Nikkita Morrissy, specialist air conditioning engineer, sea-changer, tenant. She snuggled on the cushions and Horse stirred a bit and heaved himself a couple of inches so she was closer. 'Let's settle in for the long haul. You and me—and Gabe if he wants to join us. If my hit on the head hasn't killed him. Welcome to our new life.'

CHAPTER FOUR

GABE WOKE AND it was still daylight. It took time to figure exactly why he was in bed, why the clock was telling him it was two in the afternoon, and why a woman and a dog were curled up on cushions on his living room floor.

Horse.

Nikki.

Nikki was asleep beside Horse?

The dog didn't fit with the image of the woman. Actually, nothing fitted. He was having trouble getting his thoughts in order.

He should be a hundred miles offshore. Every day the boat was in harbour cost money.

Um...he had enough money. He needed to forget fishing, at least for a day.

He was incredibly, lazily comfortable. How long since he'd lain in bed and just...lain? Not slept, just stared at the ceiling, thought how great the sheets felt on his naked skin, how great it was that the warm sea breeze wafted straight in through his bedroom window and made him feel that the sea was right here.

Lots of fishermen—lots of his crew—took themselves as far from the sea as possible when they weren't working. Not Gabe. The sea was a part of him.

He'd always been a loner. As a kid, the beach was an escape from the unhappiness in the house. His parents' marriage was bitter and often violent. His father was passionately possessive of his much younger wife, sharing her with no one. If Gabe spent time with his mother, his father reacted with a resentment that Gabe soon learned to fear. His survival technique was loneliness.

As he got older, the boat became his escape as well.

And then there was his brief marriage. Yeah, well, that had taught him the sea was his only real constant. People hurt. Solitude was the only way to go.

Even dogs broke your heart.

Sixteen years...

'Get another one fast.' Fred, the Banksia Bay vet, had been brusque. 'The measure of a life well lived is how many good dogs you can fit into it. I'm seventy years old and I'm up to sixteen and counting. It's torn a hole in my gut every time I've lost one, and the only way I can fill it is finding another. And you know what? Every single one of them stays with me. They're all part of who I am. The gut gets bigger.' He'd patted his ample stomach. 'Get another.'

Or not. Did Fred know just how big a hole Jem had left?

Don't think about it.

Watch Nikki instead.

He lay and watched woman and dog sleeping, just across the passage. Strangers seldom entered his house. Not even friends. And no one slept by his fire but him.

Until now.

She looked...okay.

She'd wake soon, and she'd be gone. This moment would be past, but for now... For now it felt strangely okay that she was here. For now he let the comfort of her presence slide into his bones, easing parts of him he didn't know were hurting. A dog and a woman asleep before his fire...

He closed his eyes and sleep reclaimed him.

She woke and it was three o'clock and Horse was squatting on his haunches rather than sprawled on his side. His head was cocked to one side, as if he was trying to figure her out. Sitting up! That had to be good.

She hugged him. She fed him. He ate a little, drank a little. She opened the French windows and asked him if he needed to go outside but he politely declined, by putting his head back on his paws and dozing again.

She thought about going back to work.

The plans on the table were supremely uninteresting. Engineering had sounded cool when she enrolled at university. Doing stuff.

Not sitting drawing endless plans of endless air conditioning systems, no matter how complex.

Gabe's living room, however, was lined with bookshelves, and the bookshelves were crammed with books.

And photograph albums. Her secret vice.

Other people's families.

Nikki had been sent to boarding school at seven. If friends invited her home for the holidays her parents were relieved, so she'd spent much of her childhood looking at families from the outside in.

Brothers, sisters, grandmas, uncles and aunts. You didn't get a lot of those the way she was raised.

Her friends could never understand her love of photograph

albums, but she hadn't grown out of it, and here were half a dozen, right within reach.

A girl had to read something. Or draw plans.

No choice.

The first four albums were those of a child, an adolescent, a young woman. School friends, beach, hiking, normal stuff. Nikki had albums like this herself, photographs taken with her first camera.

The albums must belong to Gabe's mother, she decided. The girl and then the woman looked a bit like Gabe. She was much smaller, compact, neat. But she looked nice. She had the same dark hair as Gabe, the same thoughtful eyes. She saw freckles and a shy smile in the girl, and then the woman.

After school, her albums differed markedly from Nikki's. This woman hadn't spent her adolescence at university. The first post-school pictures were of her beside stone walls, wearing dungarees, heavy boots, thick gloves. The smile became cheeky, a woman gaining confidence.

There were photos of stone walls.

Lots of stone walls.

Nikki glanced outside to the property boundary, where a stone wall ran along the road, partly built, as if it had stopped mid-construction. Wires ran along the unfinished part to make it a serviceable fence.

She turned back to the next album. Saw the beginnings of romance. A man, considerably older than the girl, thick-set, a bit like Gabe as well, looking as if he was struggling to find a smile for the camera. Holding the girl possessively.

An album of a wedding. Then a baby.

Gabe.

Really cute, she thought, and glanced across the passage and thought…you really could see the man in the baby.

Gabe before life had weathered him.

The photos were all of Gabe now—Gabe until he was about seven, sturdy, cheeky, laughing.

Then nothing. The final album had five pages of pictures and the rest lay empty.

What had happened? Divorce? Surely a young mum would keep on taking pictures. Surely she'd take these albums with her.

She set the albums back in place, and her attention was caught by a set of books just above. *The Art of Stone Walling. The Stone Walls of Yorkshire.* More.

She flicked through, fascinated, caught in intricacies of stone walling.

Gabe slept on.

She was learning how to build stone walls. In theory.

She'd kind of like to try.

She reached the end of the first book as Horse struggled to his feet and crossed to the French windows. Pawed.

Bathroom.

But... Escape?

Visions of Horse standing up to his haunches in the shallows sprang to mind. She daren't risk letting him go. The faded curtains were looped back with tasseled cords, perfect for fashioning a lead.

'Okay, let's go but don't pull,' she told him. At full strength this dog could tow two of her, but he was wobbly.

She cast a backward glance at Gabe. Still sleeping. Quick check. Chest rising and falling.

She and Horse were free to do as they pleased.

When Gabe woke again the sun was sinking low behind Black Mountain. He'd slept the whole day?

His head felt great. He felt great all over. He was relaxed and warm and filled with a sense of well-being he hadn't felt since...who knew?

He rolled lazily onto his side and gazed out of the window.

And froze.

For a moment he thought he was dreaming. There was a woman in the garden, her back to him, crouched over a pile of stones. Sorting.

A dog lay by her side, big and shaggy.

Nikki and Horse.

Nikki held up a stone, inspected it, said something to Horse, then shifted so she could place it into the unfinished stretch of stone wall.

He felt as if the oxygen was being sucked from the room.

A memory blasting back...

His mother, crouched over the stones, the wall so close to finished. Thin, drawn, exhausted. Setting down her last stone. Weeping. Hugging him.

'I can't...'

'Mum, what's wrong?'

'I'm so tired. Gabe, very soon I'll need to go to sleep.' But using a voice that said this wasn't a normal sleep she was talking about.

Then...desolation.

His father afterwards, kicking stones, kicking everything. His mother's old dog, yelping, running for the cover Gabe could never find.

'Dad, could we finish the wall?' It had taken a month to find the courage to ask.

'It's finished.' A sharp blow across his head. 'Don't you understand, boy, it's finished.'

He understood it now. Nikki had to understand it, too.

People hurt. You didn't try and interfere. Unless there was trouble you let people be and they let you be. You didn't try and change things.

He should have put it in the tenancy agreement.

Stone wall building was weirdly satisfying on all sorts of levels.

She'd always loved puzzles, as she'd loved building things. To transform a pile of stones into a wall as magnificent as this...

Wide stones had been set into the earth to form the base, then irregular stones piled higher and higher, two outer levels with small stones between. Wider stones were layed crosswise over both sides every foot or so, binding both sides together. No stone was the same. Each position was carefully assessed, each stone considered from all angles. Tried. Tried again. As she was doing now.

She'd set eight stones in an hour and was feeling as if she'd achieved something amazing.

This could be a whole new hobby, she thought. She could finish the wall.

Horse lay by her side, dozy but watchful, warm in the afternoon sunshine. Every now and then he cast a doubtful glance towards the beach but she'd fashioned a tie from the curtain cords, she had him tethered and she talked to him as she worked.

'I know. You loved him but he rejected you. You and me both. Jonathan and your scum-bag owner. Broken hearts club, that's us. We need a plan to get over it. I'm not sure what our plan should be, but while we're waiting for something to occur this isn't bad.' She held up a stone. 'You think this'll fit?'

The dog cocked his head; seemed to consider.

The pain that had clenched in her chest for months eased a little. Unknotted in the sharing, and in the work.

She would have liked to be a builder.

She thought suddenly of a long ago careers exhibition. At sixteen she'd been unsure of what she wanted to do. She'd gone to the career exhibition with school and almost the first display was a carpenter, working on a delicate coffee table. While other students moved from one display to the next, she stopped, entranced.

After half an hour he'd invited her to help, and she'd stayed with him until her teachers came to find her.

'I'll need to get an apprenticeship to be a carpenter,' she'd told her father the next time she'd seen him, breathless with certainty that she'd found her calling.

But her father was due to catch the dawn flight to New York. He'd scheduled two hours' quality time with his daughter and he didn't intend wasting it on nonsense.

'Of course society needs builders, but for you, my girl, with your brains, the sky's the limit. We'll get you into Law—Oxford? Cambridge?'

Even her chosen engineering degree had met with combined parental disapproval, even though it was specialist engineering leading to a massive salary. But here, now... She remembered that long ago urge to build things, to create.

Air conditioning systems didn't compare. Endless plans.

Another stone... This was so difficult. It had to be perfect.

'What do you think you're doing?'

She managed to suppress a yelp, but only just. Gabe was dressed again, in jeans and T-shirt. He'd come up behind her. His face was like thunder, his voice was dripping ice.

He was blocking her sun. Even Horse backed and whimpered.

The sheer power of the man...the anger...

It was as much as she could do not to back and run.

Not her style, she thought grimly. This man had her totally disconcerted but whimpering was never an option. 'I thought I'd try and do some...' she faltered.

'Don't.'

'Don't you want it finished? I thought... I've been reading the books from your living room.'

'You've been reading my mother's books?'

Uh-oh. She'd desecrated a shrine?

'I'm sorry. I...'

'You had no right.'

'No.' She lifted the book she'd been referring to. Caught her breath. Decided she'd hardly committed murder. 'I'll put this back,' she said placatingly. 'No damage done. I don't think I've done anything appalling.'

But then...he'd scared her. Again.

Shock was turning to indignation.

He was angry?

She met his gaze full on. Tilted her chin.

Horse nosed her ankle. She let her hand drop to his rough coat and the feel of him was absurdly comforting.

What was with this guy? Why did he make her feel—how he made her feel? She couldn't describe it. She only knew that she was totally confused.

'I've only fitted eight stones,' she said, forcing her tone down a notch. Even attempting a smile. 'You want me to take them out again?'

'Leave it.' His voice was still rough, but the edges of

anger were blunted. He took the book from her. Glanced at it. Glanced away. 'How's the dog?'

'He's fine.' She was still indignant. He sounded…cold.

The normal Gabe?

A man she should back away from.

'We need to make a decision,' he said.

'I have,' she said and tilted her chin still further.

'Hi!'

The new voice made them both swivel. A woman was at the gate. She was middle-aged and sensibly dressed, in moleskin trousers and a battered fleecy jacket. She swung the gate open and Horse whined and backed away.

Even from twenty yards away Nikki saw the woman flinch.

'It's okay,' the woman said, gentling her voice as she approached. 'I hate it that I lock these guys up and they react accordingly. I can't help that I'm associated with their life's low point.'

Horse whined again. Nikki felt him tug against the cord. She wasn't all that sure of it holding.

Gabe was suddenly helping. His hand was on the big dog's neck, helping her hold on to her curtain-fashioned collar. Touching hers. His hand was large and firm—and once more caring?

Where had that thought come from? But she felt Horse relax and she knew the dog felt the same. Even if this guy did get inexplicably angry, there was something at his core…

'Raff told me you'd found him,' the woman was saying. 'Hi, Gabe.' She came forward, her hand extended to Nikki, a blunt gesture of greeting. 'We haven't met. I'm Henrietta. I run the local dog shelter. This guy's one of mine.'

Horse whimpered and tried to go behind Nikki's legs. Nikki's hand tightened on his collar—and so did Gabe's.

Hands touching. Warmth. Strength. Nikki didn't pull away, even though Henrietta's hand was still extended, even though she knew Gabe could hold him.

'You want me to take him?' Henrietta asked.

No.

Her decision had already been made but she needed Gabe's consent. He was, after all, her landlord.

'I'd like to keep him,' she said, more loudly than she intended, and there was a moment's silence.

Henrietta's grim expression relaxed, then did more than relax. It curved into a wide grin that practically spilt her face. But then she caught herself, her smile was firmly repressed and her expression became businesslike.

'Are you in a position to offer him a good home?'

'Am I?' she asked Gabe. 'I think I am,' she said diffidently. 'But Gabe's my landlord. I'll need his permission.'

'You're asking me to keep him?' Gabe's demand was incredulous.

'No,' she said flatly. Some time during this afternoon her world had shifted. She wasn't exactly sure where it had shifted; she only knew that things were changing and Horse was an important part of that change. 'I want to keep him myself. Just me.' Her life was her own, she thought, suddenly resolute. No men need apply.

No man—not even her landlord—was needed to share her dog.

'I need to do a bit of reorganisation,' she said, speaking now to Henrietta. 'At the moment I'm working away...'

'I can't look after him,' Gabe said bluntly. 'Not when I'm at sea.'

'I'm not asking you to,' she flashed back at him. There were things going on with Gabe she didn't understand. He had her disconcerted, but for now she needed to focus only on Horse. And her future. Gabe had to be put third.

'I'm reorganising my career,' she told Henrietta. 'At the end of this month and maybe next, I'll need to go away for a few days. After that I won't need to.' That was simple enough. She'd hand her international clients over to her colleagues.

Her colleagues would think she was nuts.

Her colleagues as in Jonathan?

Don't go there.

Could she keep working for him?

'I might even be rethinking my career altogether,' she said, a bit more brusquely than she intended. She glanced down at the stones and then glanced away again, astounded where her thoughts were taking her. How absurd to think she could ever do something so...so wonderful.

Was she crazy? This surely could only ever be a hobby.

Concentrate on Horse. The rest was nonsense. Fanciful thinking after an upset night. 'Whatever I do, I've decided I can keep Horse,' she managed. 'If I can get some help for the first two months.'

But Gabe was looking at her as if she was something that had just crawled out of the cheese.

'You've decided this all since last night?' he demanded. 'Do you know how much of a commitment a dog is? He's not a handbag, picked up and discarded on a whim. Sixteen years...'

'We're not talking Jem here,' Henrietta said sharply.

'Jem?'

'Gabe's dog,' Henrietta told her. 'Gabe found Jem on the beach sixteen years ago. She died three months back.'

'I'm sorry,' Nikki said, disconcerted, but her apologies weren't required or wanted. Gabe's face was rigid with anger.

'We're not talking Jem. We're talking you. What do you know about dogs?'

'I'll learn.'

'You mean you know nothing.'

'You're trying to talk me out of keeping him?'

'I'm talking sense.'

'I can keep him for the days you're away,' Henrietta interjected, but she was watching Gabe. 'I run a boarding kennel alongside the shelter, so if you really are going to reorganise…'

'You'd let her keep him?' Gabe's voice was incredulous.

'It's that or put him down,' Henrietta snapped. 'Nikki's offering.'

'And if I say no?'

There was a general intake of breath. If he said no…

What would she do?

Take Horse and live elsewhere? Somewhere that wasn't here? There were so few rental options.

Go back to Sydney.

No! Here was scary, but Sydney was scarier.

Move on. Who knew where? With dog?

This was dumb. To move towns because of a dog…

But this afternoon she'd felt his heartbeat as he slept. The thought of ending that heartbeat…

Horse was as lost as she was, she thought, and she glanced at Gabe and thought there were three of them. She could see pain behind Gabe's anger; behind his blank refusal to help.

She couldn't think of Gabe's pain now. She'd do this alone.

No. She'd do it with Horse.

'He's my dog,' she said, making her voice firm.

Henrietta turned to Gabe. 'So. Let's get this straight. Are you planning on evicting Nikki because she has a dog?'

'She doesn't know what she's letting herself in for.'

'You work at home, right?' Henrietta asked her, obviously deciding to abandon Gabe's arguments as superfluous.

'Yes.'

'Fantastic. When do you need to go away again?'

She did a frantic mental reshuffle. 'I can put it off for a while. Three weeks...'

'Then you have three weeks to learn all about dogs,' Henrietta decreed. 'If at the end of that time you decide you can't keep him then we'll rethink things. So Gabe... I have a happy ending in view. What about you? You'll seriously evict her if she keeps him?'

They were all looking at him. Nikki and Henrietta... Even Horse seemed to understand his future hung on what Gabe said right now.

'Fine,' he said explosively.

'That's not what I want to hear,' Henrietta said. 'How about a bit of enthusiasm?'

'You expect me to be enthusiastic that there's a dog about to live here? With a totally untrained owner?'

'You're trained,' Henrietta said. 'I'd feel happier if you were offering, but I have a feeling this guy will settle for what he can get. If the heart's in the right place, the rest can follow, eh, Nikki?'

'I...yes,' she said weakly, wondering where exactly her heart was.

'That's great,' Henrietta said and patted Horse. who was still looking nervous. 'What will you call him?'

'Horse,' Nikki said. 'I'll need stuff. I don't know what. Can you tell me?'

'Gabe might give you a...' Henrietta started and then glanced again at Gabe. Winced. 'Okay, maybe not. Let's take your new dog inside and I'll make you a list myself. Unless you want to evict her first, Gabe?'

'I'm going to the boat,' he snapped. 'Be it on your head.'

He headed for the boat, away from women, away from dog. Away from stuff he didn't want to deal with.

He needed to sort cray-pots, mend some. He started but it didn't keep his head from wandering. He kept seeing Nikki, sorting through her pile of rocks. *His mother's pile of rocks.*

He kept seeing Nikki curled in front of the fire, sleeping beside Horse.

Horse. It was a stupid name for a dog.

What was also stupid was his reaction, he told himself. What was the big deal? His tenant had found herself a dog. It was nothing to do with him. As for the stone walling...

She wouldn't touch it again.

Why not let her finish it?

Stupid or not, he felt as if he was right on the edge of a whirlpool, and he was being pulled inexorably inside.

He'd been there before.

There was nothing inside but pain.

The cray-pots weren't hard enough.

He'd check the *Lady Nell*'s propeller, he decided. It had fouled last time out. They'd got it clear but maybe it'd be wise to give it a thorough check.

Ten minutes later he had a scuba tank on, lowering himself over the side.

He should do this with someone on board keeping watch. If there was an accident...

If there was an accident no one gave a toss; it was his business what he did with his life.

He had scores of employees, dependent on him for their livelihood.

He also had one tenant. Dependent?

If Horse decided to head for the beach again, he was bigger than she could possibly hold.

It was none of his business. She didn't need him. The dog didn't need him. No one did. Even if something happened to him, the legal stuff was set up so this town's fishing fleet would survive.

How morbid was that? He was about to check a propeller. He'd done it a hundred times.

He needed to see things in perspective.

He dived underwater. Right now underwater seemed safer than the surface—and a whole lot clearer.

Henrietta left and came back with supplies, and Nikki was set. Dog food, dog bed, dog bowls. Collar, lead, treats, ball times six... Practically a car full.

'You'll need a kennel, but they don't come prefabricated in Horse's size,' Henrietta told her. 'I've brought you a trampoline bed instead. You'll need to get a kennel built by winter. Oh, and there's no need to spread it round town that I've brought this. Normally my new owners need to show me their preparations before I'll agree to let them have the dog.'

'So why the special treatment?' Nikki had made tea. Henrietta was sipping Earl Grey from one of Nikki's dainty cups, looking a bit uncomfortable. Maybe she ought to buy some mugs.

Maybe her life was going to change in a few other ways, she thought. Her apartment was furnished with the elegant possessions she'd acquired for the Sydney apartment. Some her parents had given her. Some she and Jon had chosen together. This teaset was antique, given to her by Jon for her last birthday.

The owner of a dog like Horse wouldn't serve tea in cups like this. She hadn't thought it through until now, but maybe she should shop...

'I hate putting dogs down,' Henrietta was saying. 'Sometimes, though, I don't have a choice. I can't keep them all. And if potential owners don't care enough to commit to buying or scrounging dog gear, then they don't care enough to be entrusted to a dog. These dogs have been through enough. I'd rather put them down than sentence them to more misery.'

'But me...'

'You live with Gabe,' Henrietta said simply. 'You mistreat Horse, you'll have him to answer to. Even if he says it's nothing to do with him, he'll be watching. And that's the second thing. This place without a dog is wrong. Gabe needs a dog. If he gets it via you, that's fine by me.'

'He's not getting him via me. This is my call. My dog.'

'Yes, but you live with Gabe,' Henrietta repeated, and finished her tea in one noisy gulp. 'Living so close, you're almost family, and now you have a dog. Welcome to Banksia Bay, and welcome to your new role as dog owner. Any more questions, ask Gabe. He's grumpy and dour and always a loner but he has reason to be. Underneath he's a good man, and he'll never let a dog suffer. He treated Jem like gold.' Then she hesitated. Made to say something. Hesitated again.

Nikki watched her face. Wondered what she'd been about to say. Then asked what she'd like to know. 'Could you tell me about him?' she ventured. 'What happened to his mother?'

Henrietta considered for a long moment and then shrugged.

'I shouldn't say, but why not? If you don't hear it from me you'll hear it from a hundred other people in this town. Okay, potted history. Gabe's mother died of cancer when he was eight. His dad was an oaf and a bully. He was also a miser. He forced Gabe to leave school at fourteen, used him as an unpaid deck hand. Maybe Gabe would have left but luckily—and I will say luckily—he died when Gabe was eighteen. He left a fortune. He left no will, so Gabe inherited. Gabe was a kid, floundering, desperately unhappy—and suddenly rich. So along came Lisbette, a selfish cow, all surface glitter, taking advantage of little more than a boy. She married him and she fleeced him, just like that.'

'Oh, no...'

'I'd have horsewhipped her if I'd had my way,' Henrietta said grimly. 'But she was gone. And Gabe took it hard. He still had his dad's boat and this house, but little else. So he took Jem and headed off to the West, to the oil rigs. A good seaman can make a lot if he's prepared to take risks and, from what I can gather, Gabe took more than a few. Then the fishing here started to falter and suddenly Gabe returned. He's good with figures, good with fishing, good with people. He almost single-handedly pulled the fleet back together. But he's shut himself off for years and so far the only one to touch that is Jem.' She touched the big dog's soft ears. 'So maybe...maybe this guy can do the same. Or maybe even his owner can.'

'Sorry?' Nikki said, startled.

'Just thinking,' Henrietta said hastily, and rose to leave. 'Dreaming families for my dogs is what I do. Good luck to the three of you.'

She looked at the teacup. Grinned. 'Amazing,' she said. 'They say owners end up looking like their dogs. These cups fit poodles, not wolfhounds.' She grinned down at Horse, asleep draped over Nikki's feet, and then looked back to

Nikki. 'Poodle,' she said. 'Maybe now, but not for much longer. I'm looking forward to big changes around here. For everyone.'

Gabe slipped underwater, checked the propeller and inspected the hull. Minutely. It was the best checked hull in the fleet. Then he went back to mending cray-pots. By nine he was the only person in the harbour.

The rest of his boats were out, and he was stuck on dry land. Because of Nikki.

What was she about, removing his alarm? Telling Hattie to go without him?

He'd needed to sleep, he conceded. His head still ached.

Because she'd hit him.

It was an accident. She meant no harm.

She meant to keep the dog. Horse.

It was a stupid name for a dog. A dog needed a bit of dignity.

Dignity.

She'd have to get that fur unmatted, he thought, and getting the tangles out of that neglected coat was a huge job. Did she know what she was letting herself in for?

It was nothing to do with him. Nothing! He wasn't going near.

She was living right next door to him. With her dog who needed detangling.

He'd yelled at her. Because she'd picked up a few rocks.

He'd behaved appallingly.

Why?

He knew why. And it wasn't the memory of his mother. It wasn't the dog. It was more.

It couldn't be more. He didn't want more, and more wasn't going to happen.

It was dark. Time to head home.

Maybe he could take Jem's old brushes across to her. A peace offering.

That wasn't more. It was sensible. It felt…okay.

But when he got home there wasn't a light on, apart from the security light he kept on in the shared porch.

Were she and the dog asleep?

She'd slept this afternoon. He'd seen her, curled on the hearth with the dog.

With Horse.

They were nothing to do with him.

He glanced at the gap in the stone wall. Sensed the faint echo of Nikki. And Horse.

By his side… Shades of Jem.

He was going nuts. The hit on his head had obviously been harder than he thought. Ghosts were everywhere, even to the feel of Jem beside him. Jem had always been with him, on the boat, under his bed, by the fire, a heartbeat by his side.

Whoa, he was maudlin. Get over it.

Disoriented, he found himself heading for the beach. A man could stare at the sea in the moonlight. Find some answers?

But the only answers he found on the beach were Nikki and Horse.

CHAPTER FIVE

THEY WERE SITTING just above the high water mark, right near the spot where Horse had stood and howled last night. Gabe saw them straight away, unmistakable, the silhouette of the slight woman and the huge, rangy dog framed against a rising moon.

Maybe he'd better call out. Warn her of his approach. Who knew what she was carrying tonight?

'Nikki!'

She turned. So did Horse, uttering a low threatening growl that suddenly turned into an unsure whine. Maybe the dog was as confused as he was.

'Gabe?' She couldn't see him—he was still in shadows. She sounded scared.

'It's Gabe.' He said it quickly, before she fired the poker.

'Are you still angry?'

Deep breath. Get this sorted. Stop being an oaf. 'I need to apologise,' he said, walking across the beach to them. 'I was out of line. Whether you keep Horse is none of my business. And snapping about the stones was nuts. Can we blame it on the hit on the head and move on?'

'Sure,' she said, but she sounded wary. 'I did hit you. I guess I can afford to cut you some slack.'

'Thank you,' he said gravely. 'Are you two moon watching?'

'Horse refuses to settle.' She shifted along the log she was perched on so there was room for him as well. 'He whined and whined, so finally I figured we might as well come down here and see that no one's coming. So he can finally settle into our new life.'

'Your new life?' he said cautiously, sorting wheat from chaff. 'You really intend changing your life?'

'My life is changed anyway,' she said. 'That's what comes of falling for a king-sized rat. It's messed with my serenity no end.'

Don't ask. It was none of his business.

But she wasn't expecting him to ask. She was staring out to sea, talking almost to herself, and her self containment touched him as neediness never could.

Since when had he ever wanted to be involved?

Horse nuzzled his hand. He patted the dog and said, 'You fell for a king-sized rat?'

Had he intended to ask? Surely not.

'My boss.'

He had no choice now.

'You want to tell me about it?'

She had no intention of telling him. She hadn't told anyone. The guy she'd thought she loved was married.

Her parents knew she'd split with Jonathan but both her parents were on their third or fourth partner; splits were no big deal. And in the office, to her friends, she'd hung onto her pride. Her pride seemed like all she had left.

But here, now, sitting on the beach with Horse between them, pride and privacy no longer seemed important.

So she told him. Bluntly. Dispassionately, as if it had happened to someone else, not to her.

'Jonathan Ostler of Ostler Engineering,' she said, her voice cool and hard. 'International engineering designer. Smooth, rich, efficient. Hates mixing business with pleasure. My boss. He asked me out four years ago. Six months later we were sharing an apartment but no one in the office was to know. Jonathan thought it'd mess with company morale. So... In the office we were so businesslike you wouldn't believe. If we were coming to work at the same time we'd split up a block away so we'd never arrive together. He addressed me as Nikki but I addressed him as Mr Ostler. Strictly formal.'

'Sounds weird.'

'Yes, but I could see his point,' she said. 'Sleeping with the boss is hardly the way to endear yourself to the rest of the staff, and Jon was overseas so much it wasn't an effort. A few people knew we were together but not many. So there I was, dream job, dream guy, dream apartment, four years. Dreaming weddings, if you must know. Starting to be anxious he didn't want to settle, but too stupidly in love to push it. Then two months ago there was an explosion in a factory where we'd been overseeing changes. The call came in the middle of the night—hysterical—our firm could be sued for millions. Jon caught the dawn plane to Düsseldorf with minutes to spare, and in the rush he left his mobile phone sitting on his—on *our*—bedside table. The next day our office was crazy. The Düsseldorf situation was frightening and the phone was going nuts. Jonathan's phone. Finally, I answered it. It was Jonathan's wife. In London. Their eight-year-old had been in a car accident. Please could I tell her where Jon was.'

'Ouch.'

'I coped,' she said, a tinge of pride warming her voice as she remembered that ghastly moment. 'I made sympathetic noises. I made sure Jonathan Junior wasn't in mortal danger, I got the details. Then I left a message with the manager of the Düsseldorf factory, asking Jon to phone his wife. I told him to say the message was from Nikki. Then I moved out of our apartment. Jonathan returned a week later, and I'd already arranged to move here, to do my work via the Internet.'

'But you still work for him?'

'Personal and business don't mix.'

'Like hell they don't,' he snapped. 'I've had relationships go sour between the crew. It messes with staff morale no end, and there's no way they can work together afterwards.'

'I'm good at my work.' But her uncertainty was growing and she couldn't put passion into her voice. 'The pay's great.'

'Can you work for yourself?'

'It's a specialist industry,' she said. 'I couldn't set up in competition to Jon. I could work for someone else, but it would have to be overseas.'

'So why not go overseas?'

'I don't want to.' But she'd been thinking. Thinking and thinking. She'd been totally, hopelessly in love with Jonathan for years and to change her life so dramatically...

Why not change it more?

Tomorrow. Think of it tomorrow.

'And now I have a dog,' she said, hauling herself back to the here and now with something akin to desperation. 'So here I am.' Deep breath. Tomorrow? Why not say now? 'But I have been thinking of changing jobs. Changing completely.'

'To what?'

How to say it? It was ridiculous. And to say stone walling, when she knew how he felt...

But the germ of an idea that had started today wouldn't go away.

Putting one stone after another into a wall.

Crazy. To turn her back on specialist training...

Oh, but how satisfying.

It was a whim, she reminded herself sharply. A whim of today. Tomorrow it'd be gone and she'd be back to sensible.

Don't talk about it. Don't push this man further than you already have.

'I don't know,' she managed. 'All I know is that I need something. Woman needs change.' She hugged Horse, who was still gazing out to sea. 'Woman needs dog.'

'No one needs a dog.'

'Says you who just lost one. I wonder if Horse's owner misses him like you miss Jem.'

'Nikki...'

'Don't stick my nose into what's not my business? You've been telling me that all day. But now... I've told you about my non existent love life. You want to tell me why I can't finish your stone wall?'

'It's my mother's wall.'

'And she disapproves of completion?'

'She died when I was a child. She didn't get to finish it.'

'So the hole's like a shrine,' she said cautiously, like one might approach an unexploded grenade. 'I can see that. But you know, if it was me I'd want the wall finished. Are you sure your mum's not up there fretting? You know, I'm a neat freak. If I die with my floor half-hoovered, feel welcome to finish it. In fact I'll haunt you if you don't.'

'You don't like an unhoovered floor?' They were veering away from his mother—which seemed fine by both of them.

'Hoovering's good for the soul.'

His mouth twitched. Just a little. The beginning of a smile. 'Do you know how much hair a dog like Horse will shed?'

'He has to grow some hair back first,' she said warmly. 'He grows, I'll hoover. We've made a deal.'

'While you've been sitting on the beach, staring at the moon.'

'It's filling time. How long do you reckon it'll take him to figure whoever he wants isn't coming?'

'Dogs have been faithful to absent masters for years.'

'Years?'

'Years.'

'I was hoping maybe another half an hour.'

'Years.'

'Uh-oh.'

'And years.'

'I don't know what else to do,' she whispered.

Her problem. This was her problem, he thought, and it was only what she deserved, taking on a damaged dog...

As he'd taken on a damaged dog sixteen years ago and not regretted it once. Until it was over.

He'd had his turn. Yes, this was Nikki's dog, Nikki's problem, but he could help.

'I don't think you're doing anyone any favours by letting him stare at where a boat isn't,' he said.

'I'm doing my best.'

'Yes,' he said. 'I know that.'

She cast him a look that was suspicious to say the least. 'I didn't mean to mess with your mother's memory,' she told him.

'Yeah.' He deserved that, he conceded. Like he'd deserved the hit over the head? But she had her reasons for that. Her heart was in the right place even if it was messing with... his heart?

That was a dumb thing to think, but think it he did. Since Lisbette left...well, maybe even before, a long time before, he'd closed down. Lisbette had whirled into his life, stunned him, ripped him off for all he was worth and whirled out again. He'd been a kid, lonely, naïve and a sitting duck.

He wasn't a sitting duck any longer. He'd closed up. Jem had wriggled her way into his life, he'd loved her and he'd lost her. She'd been the last chink in his armour, and there was no way he was opening more.

But this woman...

She wasn't looking to rip him off as Lisbette had—he knew that. Lisbette, getting up every two hours because she was worried about him? Ha!

Nor was she trying to edge into the cracks around his heart like Jem had. She might be needy but it was a different type of needy.

It was Nikki and Horse against the world—when she didn't know a blind thing about dogs.

She was blundering. She was a walking disaster but she was a disaster who meant well.

'I overreacted with the wall,' he conceded. 'I looked out and saw you and the dog and that's what I remember most about my mother. Her sitting for hour after hour, sorting stones. She did it everywhere. She and Billy.'

'Billy?'

'She had a collie. He seemed old as long as I can remember. He pined when she died, and my dad shot him.'

'He shot him?' She sounded appalled.

'He was never going to get over Mum's death.'

'You were how old?'

'Eight.'

'You lost your mum, and your dad shot her dog?'

How to say it? The day of the funeral, coming home, Billy whining, his father saying, 'Get to your room, boy.' A single shot.

He didn't have to tell her. She touched his hand and the horror of that day was in her touch.

'And I hit you over the head,' she whispered. 'And Henrietta said your wife left you. And your own dog died. If I were you I'd have crawled into a nice comfy psychiatric ward and thought up a diagnosis that'd keep me there for the rest of my life. Instead…'

'How did we get here?' He had no idea. One minute this woman was irritating the heck out of him, the next she was putting together stuff he didn't think about; didn't want to think about. This was his place, his beach. He'd come down here for a quiet think, and here he was being psychoanalysed.

He felt exposed.

It was a weird thing to think. She hadn't said anything that wasn't common knowledge but it was as if she could see things differently.

She had her arm round Horse's neck and she was tugging him close, and all of a sudden he felt a jolt, like what would it feel to be in the dog's place?

The dog whined. Stupid dog.

'You want dog lessons,' he said, more roughly than he intended.

'Horse doesn't need lessons. He's smart.'

'He's staring at an empty sea,' he said.

'He's devoted. He'll get over it. Needs must.'

'Says you who's still pining for your creepy boss.'

'I'm trying to get over it,' she said with dignity. 'I'm not sitting on the beach wailing. I'm doing my best. Don't we all?'

She rose and brushed sand from the back of her trousers. With his collar released, Horse took a tentative step towards the sea. Nikki's hand hit the collar at the same time as his did. Their fingers touched. Flinched a little but didn't let go. Settled beside each other, a tiny touch but unnerving.

Settling.

Things were settling for him. He wasn't sure why.

Maybe it was watching her reaction to what he'd told her tonight, added to what he knew local gossip would have told her. His mother's death, his father, Lisbette, his mother's dog and Jem... Her reaction seemed to validate stuff he tried not to think about.

Permission to feel sorry for himself?

Permission to move on.

Towards Nikki? Towards yet another disaster?

Not in a million years. He'd spent all his life being taught that solitary was safe. He wasn't about to change that now.

But he could help her. It was the least he could do.

'Horse needs a master,' he told her.

'He's only got me,' she said defensively. 'Why are we being sexist? A master?'

'I mean,' he said patiently, 'a pack leader. He's lost his. He's looking for him; if he can't find him he needs a new one.'

'Right,' she said. 'Pack leader. Can I buy one at the Banksia Bay Co-op?'

He grinned. His hand was still touching hers. He should pull it away but he didn't. Things were changing—had changed. There was something about the night, the moonlight on the water, the big needy dog between them...

There was something about her expression. She was sounding defiant, braving it out, but things were rotten in this woman's world as well. Nikki and Horse, both needy to the point of desperation.

That need had nothing to do with him. He should pull away—but he didn't.

'Attitude,' he said, deciding he'd be decisive, and she blinked.

'Pack leader attitude?'

'That's it. So who decided to come down the beach, you or Horse?'

'He was miserable.' She sounded defensive.

'So you followed.'

'I held onto him. He would have run.'

'But he walked in front, yes? Team leaders walk in front. The pack's at the back.'

'You're saying I need to growl at him? Make him subservient? He's already miserable.'

'He'll be miserable until you order him not to be, and he decides you're worth swapping loyalty.'

'I shouldn't have let him come down to the beach?'

'There's not a lot of point being down here, is there?' he said, gentler as he watched her face. And Horse's face. He could swear the dog was listening, his great eyes pools of despair. 'He's been dumped by a low-life. How's it going to make him feel better to stare at an empty sea? It's up to you to take his place.'

'The low-life's place?'

'That's the one.'

'I haven't had much practice at being the low-life,' she said. 'I'm a follower. Dumb and dumber, that's me.'

'We're not talking about your love life.'

'We're not?'

'That's shrink territory, not mine.'

'Like your stone wall.'

'Do you mind?'

'Butt out?' She sighed and tried for a smile. 'Fine. Consider me butted. What do I need to be a pack leader? A whip? Leathers?'

'Discipline.'

She grinned. 'Really? Don't tell me, stockings and garters as well.'

He stared at her in the moonlight and he couldn't believe it. She was laughing. Laughing!

The tension of the night dissipated, just like that. Except... a sudden vision of Nikki in stockings and garters...

He almost blushed.

'I mean,' he said, trying to stop the corners of his mouth twitching, 'you tell Horse what you expect and you follow through. He's hungry? Use it. Call him, reward him when he comes. Teach him to sit, stay, the usual dog things. But mostly teach him no. He's galloping towards you with a road in between; you need to hold your hand up, yell no and have him stop in his tracks. The same with coming down here. You can bring him down here on your terms, with a ball, something to do to keep him occupied. The minute he stares out to sea like he's considering the low-life, then that's a no. Hard, fast and mean it.'

'You're good at training dogs?'

'I had a great dog. Smart as Einstein. She trained me.'

'I'm sure Horse is smart.'

'Prove it.'

'I'm not sure...'

'Henrietta's daughter takes personal dog coaching. I'm amazed Henrietta hasn't introduced you already.'

'Henrietta left a card,' she conceded.

'There you go.'

'You're not interested in helping yourself?'

'No.' Hard. Definite. He watched her face close and regretted it, but couldn't pull it back.

'I'm not scary,' she said, almost defiantly, and he thought what a wuss—was he so obvious?

'I'm busy,' he said. 'This is the first full day I haven't worked since...'

'Since Jem died?'

'Nikki...'

'I know.' She tugged Horse towards her a little, which forced his hand to let go of the collar. Which meant they were no longer touching. 'You want me to butt out. Respect your boundaries. I've been respecting boundaries for years. You'd think I'd be good at it.'

'I didn't mean...'

'You know, I'm very sure you did,' she told him. 'Tell me what to do.'

'What do you mean?'

'With Horse,' she said patiently. 'Training. What should I do first?'

'Take his collar and say "Come".' This was solid ground. Dog training. He could handle this.

'Come,' she said and tugged and Horse didn't move. Stared rigidly out to sea.

'Come!' Another tug.

Gabe sighed. 'Okay, you're on the head end. We're going to roll him.'

'What?'

'He has to learn to submit, otherwise he'll spend the rest of his life waiting for his low-life. Say "Down".'

'Down.'

'Like you mean it!'

'Down!'

'You sound like a feather duster.'

'I do not.'

'Pretend the boat's sinking. The kid at the other end is standing there with a tin can and a stupid expression. He bails or you drown. Are you going to say "Bail" in that same voice?'

'He's an abandoned dog. He nearly died. He's hurt and confused. You want me to yell at him?'

'He's hurt and confused and he needs to relax. The only way he can relax is if he thinks someone else is in charge. You.'

'You do it.'

'I'm not his pack leader. Do it, Nikki, or you'll have him howling at the door for weeks, killing himself with exhaustion. You say "Down" like you mean it and we bring him down.'

'I don't...'

'Just do it.'

'Down,' she snapped in a voice so full of authority that both Gabe and the dog started. But he had the dog's back legs and Nikki had his collar. Gabe hauled his legs from under him and rolled him before Horse knew what had hit him.

The big dog was on his back. Shocked into submission.

'Tell him he's a good dog but keep him down,' Gabe said.

'This is cruel. He's not fit...'

'He's going to pine until we do it. Do it.'

'G... Good dog.'

'Now let him up again.'

The dog lumbered to his feet.

'Now down again.'

'Down!'

Once again Gabe pushed his legs from under him. The dog folded.

'Good dog,' Nikki said, holding him down and the dog's tail gave a tentative, subjugated wag.

'Once more.'

'Down!' And this time Gabe didn't have to push. The dog crouched and rolled with only a slight push and pull from Nikki.

'Good dog. Great,' Nikki said and her voice wobbled.

The dog stood again, unsure, but this time he moved imperceptibly to Nikki's side. He looked up at her instead of out to sea.

'Now tell him to come and tug,' Gabe said, and Nikki did and the big dog moved docilely up the beach by her side.

'Good dog,' Nikki said and sniffed.

'Why are you crying?'

'I'm not.'

'You're allergic to command?'

'I'm not built to be a sergeant major.'

'Horse needs a sergeant major,' he said as he fell in beside her. 'You are what you have to be. Like me being owner of half a dozen boats, employing crews.'

'You don't like that?'

They were walking up the track, Nikki with Horse beside her, Gabe with his hand hovering, just in case Horse made a break for it. But Horse was totally submissive. He was probably relieved. He'd spent too long as it was waiting for his scumbag owner. He needed a new one.

There were parallels. Caring for Horse…

Taking on this town's fishing fleet.

Nikki was waiting for an answer. Not pushing. Just walking steadily up the track with her dog.

She was a peaceful woman, he thought. Self contained. Maybe she'd had to be.

Why the sniff? Tears?

Ignore them.

'I never saw myself as head of a fleet,' he told her. 'But when the fishing industry round here started to falter I was single with no responsibilities. I'd been away, working on the rigs, making myself some serious money. I could afford to take a few risks. But in the end I didn't need to. Fishing's in my blood and I knew what'd work.'

'But now… You enjoy it?'

'Fishing's my life.'

'It sounds boring.'

'So you do what in your spare time?' he demanded. 'Macramé?

'Dog training,' she said steadily. 'I now have a career and a hobby and a pet. What more could a girl want? What do you have, Gabe Carver?'

'Everything I want.'

They reached the house in silence. Reached the porch. Nikki opened the door and ushered Horse inside. Hesitated.

'He'll stand at the door and howl,' she said, and he looked at her face and saw the tracks of tears. What had he said to upset her?

'Only if you let him.'

'How do I not let him?'

He sighed. 'Where's he sleeping?'

'In my bedroom.'

'Not on your bed. You're pack leader.'

'I know that much. Besides, the bed's not big enough.'

'So show me.'

She swung open the bedroom door. A bed, single, small. He looked at her in surprise. He hadn't been here when her furniture was delivered so he was seeing this for the first time. It was practically a child's bed.

'You don't like stretching?'

'Not if there's no one to stretch to.'

Silence. There were a million things to say, but suddenly nothing.

The bedroom was chintzy. Pretty pink. Dainty. It made a man nervous just to look at it.

Horse whined and he thought *I'm with you, mate*. To sleep in a bedroom like this...

But at least Horse had a sensible bed. Henrietta knew dogs, and she'd provided a trampoline bed that was almost as big as Nikki's.

'Say "Bed",' he told Nikki.

'Bed.' Horse didn't move an inch.

Gabe sighed. 'Bail the dratted boat.'

'Bed!' That was better. Sergeant major stuff.

Gabe shoved Horse from behind. Horse lumbered up onto the trampoline.

'Say "Down."'

'Down,' Nikki said and the dog rolled.

'Stay,' Nikki said and stepped back and grinned as Horse did just that.

Horse looked up at her and put a tentative paw down onto the floor.

'Stay!' Her best 'bail the boat' voice.

The paw retreated.

'How about that?' Nikki said, her smile widening. 'I'm a pack leader.'

'You'll make a great one.'

'I will,' she said and turned to him. Fast.

She was suddenly a bit too close.

She was suddenly very close.

'Make sure the dog stays there,' he said, a bit too gruffly. They were by the dog's bed, so close they were almost touching. They were by Nikki's bed as well. It was just as well it wasn't his bed, he thought, the wide, firm, king-sized bed he'd bought for himself when he'd come back here to live.

He had a sudden flash of recall. Last night. Nikki tiptoeing in to check he wasn't dead, leaning over him...

He could have...

No.

But she was so close. He turned to go—a man had to make a move—but suddenly she'd taken his hands in hers, tugging him back to face her.

'Thank you,' she said. 'For coming down to the beach to find me.'

'You're welcome.' He hadn't gone down to find her, he thought, but he wasn't thinking clearly and it seemed way too much trouble to explain.

'And I can see why you don't want to get involved. I won't ask you to. I've been a nuisance. But I meant well. I mean well.'

'You do.' Big of him to concede that much.

'And your head really is better?'

'Not hurting at all.' Almost the truth.

She smiled. It was a really cute smile, he thought. He could see the tracks of those unexplained tears and it made her seem cuter. All in all...

All in all, Nikki Morrissy was really cute all over.

'Goodnight,' she said and then, inexplicably, unaccountably, she stood on tiptoe and she kissed him. Lightly, a feather-touch. Maybe she'd even meant it to be an air-kiss but he moved. Maybe he tugged her a bit closer and her lips brushed his.

Burned.

She pulled back, startled. Which was how he felt. Startled. To say the least.

'Just...thank you,' she said. Struggled for words. Struggled to find something to talk about other than the kiss. 'And...and I'm so sorry your dog died. Jem must have been amazing.'

'She was.'

'You want to tell me about her?' she said but there were limits, even if she was looking at him with eyes that'd melt an iceberg.

She was his tenant. *His tenant.*

He'd helped her as much as he could.

'Goodnight,' he said and backed to the door.

'I didn't mean to kiss you,' she murmured, but he hardly heard her.

A man had to take a stand some time. A man had to know when to retreat.

He retreated.

CHAPTER SIX

THERE WAS NO reason to get up. The sensation was so novel it had Gabe lying in bed at five in the morning thinking the world was off balance.

All but one of his boats were out. They'd left in a group yesterday morning and weren't due back until tomorrow. The one stuck in harbour through lack of crew—the *Lady Nell*—was the one needing least attention. The propeller was checked. The cray-pots were mended.

Even his dratted bookwork was up to date.

He could sleep until midday if he wanted.

He didn't want. His world was out of kilter.

Because of lack of work?

Because of Nikki.

Because she'd kissed him?

Because she'd touched him with her crazy floundering from assertive career woman to a woman who was exposed on all sides.

She'd taken in a dog as big as she was. She'd given her heart and in doing so… She'd pierced a part of him he'd protected with care for years.

And he didn't want it pierced. He had to close it off again fast, but the fact that she was living right through the wall was enough to do his head in.

He could evict her. Because of the dog?

He was turning into his father.

His window was wide open. From where he lay he could see the gap in the stone fence. He thought of Nikki's face as he'd yelled.

He'd hurt her.

Last night she'd cried and he didn't know why.

The wall was there, looking at him, as it had looked at Nikki.

He climbed out of bed and went to get his mother's books. Went back to bed. He read for an hour.

Looked at the wall.

The thought of picking up those stones, taking up where his mother had left off…

How could he do that?

How could he start again?

His mother. Lisbette. Jem. Pain at every turn.

He thought of the appalling time after Lisbette left. Realising that all she'd said had been lies. Realising the extent of what she'd stolen from him.

After Lisbette, he'd taken Jem and headed west, where his experience landed him a job on a rig supply boat. Jem was included—he was a package deal, employ me, my dog comes too. But it was no problem. Jem loved their life at sea and Gabe was good. Within a year he was captaining his own boat. He could get stuff to the rigs in weather no one else would face.

He worked hard. Crew came and went. Jem was his only constant.

The protective layer he'd built around himself grew thicker. He was okay.

Moving back here... That'd been a risk, but he'd heard stories of the trouble with the fleet. Maybe the loneliness had got to him. It wouldn't hurt to help the people who'd once been good to him; who'd tried in their way to stand between him and his father.

And that was okay, too. By the time he came home the house had lost the worst of its memories. Only the shades of his mother remained.

He'd been able to step in and maintain his distance. He and Jem.

Now, just him.

And Nikki and Horse.

Who made him think of finishing the wall...

He did not need them interfering with his solitary lifestyle.

He tossed the books aside. Pulled on his fishing gear. He'd head to the harbour.

He had to get out of here.

He had to get away from Nikki?

Away from the thought of letting down some of his carefully built defences. How could a man ever do that? And why would he want to?

Nikki and Horse sat on the wharf, watched the seagulls and watched the early morning sun glinting over the distant sea.

The harbour was deserted. Most of the boats were out. The only ones left were pleasure craft and the tenders used to take owners out to bigger boats at swing moorings.

Swing moorings. Tenders. She smiled to herself. She'd only been here three weeks and already she was learning the local lingo.

'Do you know it already?' she asked Horse. 'Were you a fishing dog?'

Horse was subdued but pliant. He'd woken at first light and whined. Nikki had taken him outside. He'd done what he needed to do and then looked longingly towards the beach.

'No,' Nikki told him in her best Leader-Of-The-Pack voice and hauled him back inside. She cooked bacon and eggs for breakfast and shared. She was fed up with Dinners For One and it was fun to cook for an appreciative appetite. Horse wolfed the bacon and nuzzled her hand in what seemed like gratitude, but then he whined and looked at the door again.

He was torn between two loyalties. Lady with the bacon or the sod who'd abandoned him.

'Choose me,' Nikki said but Horse still whined.

She needed displacement activity.

So here they were, sitting on the jetty, trying not to stare at the only decent boat in port.

Gabe's boat. The *Lady Nell*.

Big and powerful and workmanlike. Like Gabe himself.

He'd made her cry.

Not...not him, she thought. It was the mixture of all sorts of stuff.

For the last two months she'd been caught up in her own drama, her own betrayal. But so much more had happened to Gabe.

He didn't want sympathy. There was no way he'd take it, but the touch of his mouth on hers...

It made her want to take him and hold, tell him the world wasn't such a bad place; there were decent people, people who could love...

He didn't want to hear it. Neither did she.

Was she still in love with Jon?

If Jon appeared in front of her right now, told her his marriage was over, had been over for years, it had all been a misunderstanding, would she go back to him?

It was doing her head in.

She was sitting on the wharf letting her head implode.

It was still really early. Six-thirty. Uncivilised. What was she doing here?

Horse whined and turned and jerked on his lead and Nikki swivelled to see. Gabe was striding along the jetty.

Dressed for work. Fisherman's overalls with braces. Rubber boots. His shirt sleeves were once more rolled to above the elbow.

Striding purposely towards his boat, seeing her, stopping dead.

'Nikki,' he said in a tone that said she was the last person he wanted here. She flinched but Horse surged forward and was too strong for her to hold. Henrietta had provided her with a choke chain—to be used 'just for the first week or so because he's so big and there's nothing of you'—but there was no way she was using it. So Horse hauled and she followed.

Feeling foolish.

His expression said she ought to hike out of here fast, taking her dog with her.

'H... Hi,' she managed as Horse reached him and attempted to jump. Gabe caught the dog's legs, placed him firmly down.

'Sit,' he growled and Horse sat. 'Hey,' Gabe said, unable to hide pleasure. 'He must have had some training.'

'I'm worried someone's looking for him,' she ventured. It seemed as good a way as any to start a conversation with someone who obviously wanted her somewhere else.

'Henrietta kept him for ten days. Raff, our local cop,

broadcast his details to every cop, to every marine outfit, to every fisherman within two hundred miles up and down the coast. He was found with no collar and evidence of severe neglect. There's no suggestion there of a happy ending.'

'Well, he has one with me,' she snapped, because he was looking at her as if…she was stupid. Dumb for offering this dog a home?

'You can't hold him,' he said mildly and she flushed. Maybe she was reading more into his words than he intended but she was keeping this dog, regardless of what her toughguy landlord thought.

'Henrietta gave me a choke chain. I tried it on myself. That's exactly what it does—choke. There's no way I'm putting it on Horse.'

'You tried it on yourself…?'

'It's awful. You tug on it, you think you're choking.'

'You only use it while you're training.'

'Did you use one on Jem?'

'I got Jem as a pup. And I'm bigger than you.'

'I do weights,' she said, glaring. 'If I want to stop Horse, I can.'

He nodded. Grinned. Walked the few steps to his boat and leaped aboard. Disappeared into the wheelhouse and came out holding…what?

A chunk of salami.

He walked back to Horse, showed him the sausage, let him sniff, backed off and called. Waving the salami.

'Here, boy. Nice sausage. Come and get it.'

Horse lunged forward.

Nikki held with all the power she possessed and yelled with all the power in her lungs. 'No!'

She wrenched Horse back, then dived in front of him so

she was a barrier between dog and sausage. She planted her feet.

'Sit,' she said in a voice she didn't know she had.

Horse sat.

Wow.

She looked down at the dog, at his great goofy desperate-to-please expression, and once again she wanted to cry.

She glanced back at Gabe and caught an expression on his face that was almost similar. 'Wow!' His echo of her thought was so pat she found herself grinning.

'We've been practising all night,' she lied smugly, bending down and hugging Horse. 'Good dog. Great dog.'

She straightened, still grinning—and Horse surged forward to Gabe and grabbed the sausage.

She burst out laughing. Horse wolfed the sausage in two gulps, returned to her side and sat like a benign angel. Obedience personified.

'I think I'm in love,' Nikki said and knew she was.

'You've made a good start,' Gabe conceded.

'I…are you going fishing?' Stupid question. He was dressed for fishing.

'Just checking pots.'

'Pots?'

'I have cray-pots laid along the coast. I don't have a crew but I can do that myself.'

'You're taking your boat out by yourself?'

'Yes.' He swung himself on board and unlocked the wheelhouse. 'I'll be back this afternoon.'

'What about your head?'

'It's fine.'

'I read on the Internet. Forty-eight hours after concussion…'

'You're not still expecting me to drop dead?'

'I keep feeling that crunch,' she said miserably. 'And the side of your face looks awful.'

It did, he conceded. He'd looked in the mirror to shave and pretty near died of fright.

'I'm fine,' he said.

'Please don't go fishing alone.'

What else was he expected to do? 'There's no one else to go fishing with,' he said explosively. 'Since you sent the rest of my crew out without me.'

'I meant it for the best. You can't go out.'

'You're going to stop me how?'

She took a deep breath. She collared Horse and she tugged him forward.

Horse reacted almost too well. He leapt the gap between wharf and boat, and Nikki was hauled after.

She caught her foot on the safety line and sprawled. Gabe reached her before she slid into the water. Tugged her up so she was standing on the deck beside him.

Held her.

'What sort of crazy stunt...? You could drown yourself.'

'I'm an excellent swimmer,' she managed, gasping, hauling herself back from him. She felt winded and stupid, and the feel of those arms... They had a girl thoroughly discombobulated. 'And if I hadn't fallen over Horse...'

'Anyone would fall over Horse,' he said grimly, and turned to see Horse heading along to the bow, standing there like a figurehead on a bowsprit. Any minute now he'd raise one paw and lean into the wind.

'He's used to boats,' he said.

'He needs to be used to boats,' she said. 'We're staying on

board until you see sense. Your crew will be back tomorrow. It won't kill you to stay on land.'

'I want to check my cray-pots.'

'Then take someone with you.'

He glared. She crossed her arms and jutted her jaw. Tree-hugger chaining herself to a mighty oak. Or ship.

He sighed. He slipped into the wheelhouse and started the engine. Strode aft and released the rear stay. Strode forward—and their connection to the wharf was gone.

She gasped. 'What...?'

'You want me to have company?' Gabe snapped. 'Fine. Make yourself at home and stay out of my way.'

When tree-huggers chained themselves to trees they didn't expect their trees to get up and walk. Or get up and sail out of the harbour.

Uh-oh. Uh-oh, uh-oh, uh-oh.

There was a twenty-yard gap between wharf and boat. Should she jump off and swim for it?

Dragging Horse behind her?

Horse was still doing his merman impersonation at the bow. His nose was pointing into the wind, every sense quivering.

Yesterday he'd looked half dead. Now...he almost looked beautiful. If you looked past the mangy coat.

Coat.

She was wearing a light pullover. Cotton. She glanced at Gabe, who was intent behind the wheel, ignoring her. He was in his weatherproofs, dressed for work.

Her pullover was pale pink. Her jeans were a soft blue.

She was wearing her Gucci loafers.

Hardly fishing gear.

'There's a jetty at the harbour mouth,' Gabe growled, seemingly intent on keeping the wheel steady. 'I'll put you off there.'

'You've done this to frighten me.'

'I've done this because I have work to do,' he snapped. 'You're in the way.'

'I'm not in the way,' she muttered. 'It's a big boat.'

'You don't seriously want to come to sea with me?'

Deep breath. Resolution. 'If you're stupid enough to want to take the boat out by yourself, then yes, I do,' she said. 'It was me who hit you. I feel responsible. If someone else hit you, you'd be welcome to be as stupid as you want. I wouldn't care.'

'You don't have to care.'

'I told you. I hit you, I don't have a choice.'

'Get off at the jetty.'

'No.' Back to tree-hugging. She was not, however, sounding as sure as she might have been.

'You'll get seasick.'

There was a thought. Hmm.

She'd been on a couple of cruises with her parents. One with Jon. 'I don't get seasick.' Or sometimes, just a little.

'We're going around reefs, checking pots in rough water. Have you ever been on a small boat in rough water?'

'I don't care,' she burst out. 'It's you who's being stubborn and ridiculous and a totally dumb, masochistic male. Your call. If you go out, you take me with you, seasick or not.'

'Fine,' he said and shifted the wheel so instead of pointing to the jetty at the harbour mouth they were pointing to the open sea.

Um…what had she done?

She kept her arms crossed and felt stupid.

The sea breeze wasn't all that warm.

They hit cross waves at the harbour entrance and she had to uncross her arms to hold on. Whoa, cruise liners never rocked like this.

'Nikki?'

'What?' She was glowering. Trying to stay righteous and purposeful.

'Put these on.' They were clear of the harbour mouth and he'd left the wheel for a moment. He took the couple of steps to where she stood and handed her a coat even more disgusting than his.

'I'm not sure...'

'Put it on,' he growled. 'And the life jacket with it. There's a packet of seasick pills on the bench below. Take one. Then tie a safety line to Horse. Then you can watch for signs of concussion all you want, as long as you stay out of my way.'

It took half an hour to reach the reef where he'd set the craypots. For all that time Nikki sat in the bow, holding onto Horse.

She was right in his line of vision, a slight figure in a battered coat way too big for her, with Horse draped over her knees. Both of them were gazing into the wind. Horse's ears flopped about in the breeze.

Nikki's hair practically had a life of its own.

She had a pert bob, cut to sculptural perfection. It was smooth and glossy and lovely—or it had been until the first burst of spray flew over the bow.

Her hair sort of forgot about being smooth. It kinked a bit.

He watched, fascinated, as the spray and the wind did their worst. By the time they were halfway to their destination her hair was a mass of curls. She no longer looked like a smooth, professional city woman. She was enveloped in a coat liberally embellished with fish scales, her hair was a riot and she was draped in a huge dog.

She hadn't succumbed to seasickness. On the contrary, once she'd settled, once she'd forgotten to glower, she almost looked as if she was enjoying herself. When she was hit by spray she turned her face into it, even laughed. She hugged her dog, and Horse looked pretty happy, too.

She'd forgotten she was checking him for concussion, or maybe she figured as long as the boat was on course she didn't need to. She was simply enjoying the ride and Gabe, who'd practically kidnapped her, felt a pang of...

Of something he didn't know how to handle. He'd brought her with him because he was frustrated and angry and he'd wanted to teach her a lesson. *Stay out of my life.*

Now she was in his life even more, and it was making him feel...

He didn't know how it was making him feel. As if he wanted to turn the boat round and head back for harbour, dump her and run?

Yeah, as if that was a sensible thing to do.

Her hair was amazing.

'Gabe!'

She was on her feet, yelling to him. 'Gabe!'

He pulled back the throttle, alarmed, and swung out of the wheelhouse to see.

Seals.

He'd been too busy watching her, watching her crazy hair, to notice, and he didn't look for seals anyway. It wasn't that he didn't like seeing them—he did, apart from when they were after his fish—but there was a massive seal colony on a rocky island a couple of miles south of Banksia Bay, and seals were simply part and parcel of his life.

They weren't part and parcel of Nikki's life. She was gazing down at them in awe.

They were riding his bow wave.

They truly were wonderful, he conceded, trying to see them as Nikki must be seeing them. These were pups, half grown, still mostly fed by their parents so they were here to have fun. The bow wave and the wake made by the *Lady Nell* were just right for them to surf. There were dozens of them, streaming in and out of the waves, riding alongside the boat, surging ahead and slipping behind. Leaping up, leaping over each other, simply having fun. Nikki was holding the rail and gasping with pleasure.

An old bull seal pulled out of the wave, reared back, surged on ahead.

Gabe grinned. He knew this guy. Mostly the bull seals held themselves apart, but this old guy had lost his harem long since. Instead of moping alone, he'd decided to relive his youth.

He slipped back into the wheelhouse, pushed the throttle back to full power and went out again. The seals practically whooped with joy at the bigger bow wave.

'They're tame,' Nikki whispered, awed.

'Not them. They're wild and free. They know what they want from me, though. Decent surf.'

'They're magnificent. Oh...' One of the young ones, smaller than the rest, surged up, leaped right out of the water ahead of the wave, then sank out of sight. If she'd reached out she could have touched him.

She was clutching Gabe's arm, gazing down with pure delight. 'Oh...'

'They eat my fish,' Gabe growled but his heart wasn't in it. He was watching her. Where was his sleek, perfectly groomed tenant now? She was in a battered, fishing sou'wester. Her hair was a mass of tangled curls, getting more and more wild as the spray soaked her. A sliver of mascara had smudged down her cheek.

He had this really strong urge…

A wave hit them broadside, not so big to worry him—he'd never have left the wheelhouse if there was a possibility of a big sea—but it was big enough to make Nikki stagger and clutch.

He let her clutch. His arm came round her waist and held—and she didn't appear to notice.

She was totally absorbed in the seals, in the antics of the pups. They were born clowns. It was as if they were putting on their own personal show, with the old bull seal trying valiantly to keep up.

The pups were jumping the bull seal, darting round his massive body as if he was a rock and they were playing tag around him.

'He's huge,' Nikki whispered.

'Cecil. He's a local legend. He's the only seal in the known world who runs his own playgroup. Most bull seals when they're past their prime head for a lone rock and live out the rest of their lives sulking. Cecil thinks this is a great alternative.'

She chuckled, a lovely throaty chuckle that made something kick inside Gabe's gut. Something he wasn't sure how to handle.

His arm was still around her. She was nestled against him, watching the seals. Her eyes were alight with laughter, her body curved against him as if this was the most natural position in the world.

He wanted, quite badly, to kiss her.

Very badly.

Defences? Why would a man want defences?

'Nikki...'

But right at that moment one of the pups leapt up and twisted right next to where they stood, so close it almost brushed Horse's nose.

Horse had been staring over the side with bemusement, not sure what he should do in this situation.

This, however, called for action. There were some things which a mature dog should not put up with, and cheeky pups taunting him was obviously one of them.

He crouched under the side rail so he was leaning right over the side and he barked, a massive, throaty bark that said, *Oi, enough—this is my territory; you guys know your place.*

Nikki chuckled and stooped to hug him, and Gabe felt her leave his side with a wrench of loss.

Given the choice, he wouldn't have let her go.

'Hey, it's okay, they're having fun,' Nikki told Horse, and Horse wagged his tail, practically beaming, and crouched again and went back to barking.

The seals backed away a little, darted out, darted back, started leaping again.

It seemed Horse was no threat.

Horse barked on, fit to wake the dead.

'Tell him "No" or he'll deafen us,' Gabe said, half laughing himself, but still with that wrenching feeling of loss.

'No!' Nikki said and then raised her voice. 'No!'

Horse subsided.

Nikki looked smug.

He wanted to kiss her so badly...

Another wave hit them broadside and the boat rolled. He reached to steady Nikki but she'd already clutched the rail. She was fine.

They were nearing the reef; the waves were building. He needed to head back into the wheelhouse and leave Nikki to Horse and to her seals.

He did, but it was a wrench.

The desire to kiss her went with him.

He pulled up twenty cray-pots and felt as if he'd done a decent morning's work. The hold was now full of live crays. Good, big ones.

Maybe he'd cook one for dinner, invite Nikki over.

Was he out of his mind?

But a man could think about it. Resolutions were made to be broken. How long since he'd invited a woman out?

She was his tenant. It was asking for trouble.

She was adorable.

That was asking for more trouble.

She'd insisted on helping and, to his astonishment, she really could help. He explained the winch system once, and she got it straight away. It was hard winching in cray-pots by himself. The pots were set in shallow water at the back of a low-lying reef. The boat had to be held steady or they'd end up on the rocks. If he'd been working by himself it was a matter of watching the sea, then heading in during a glimmer of calm, hooking the pot and winching it up from back in the wheelhouse while he could watch the sea as it came up. Then get back to safe water before he could swing the pot over the side.

But Nikki got it. She watched him do one, she demanded

to try, she hooked the second on the third run—not bad for an amateur—and she hauled the pot in by herself.

Horse objected to the weird crustaceans in the traps but he only barked once. 'No,' Nikki said and the big dog subsided and watched.

He had a crew, he thought. A woman and a dog.

He thought of the morning he'd have had if she hadn't come, and he thought why had he not wanted to take her? She lit his day.

There was a dangerous thought.

Why was it dangerous?

With the last pot was lifted he headed back from the dangerous waters of the reef,

The water out here was calm. Nikki had untied Horse—they'd needed Horse's spot to stack the pots while they worked and he seemed settled. With the pots all emptied, woman and dog were back to watching the seal pups. Nikki was hugging Horse. She was smiling at Horse. She was smiling at the pups.

She was smiling at him.

It felt...

Dangerous.

Insidious in its sweetness.

Why was he so nervous?

Because his gut said this was a woman who had the power to mess with his equanimity.

Was equanimity such a big deal anyway?

All his life he'd been a loner, except...

Yeah, except for his mother. She'd loved him. She'd held him, cuddled him, stood between him and his brute of a father.

Left him. Not her fault, though. There was no word bad enough to describe cancer.

Lisbette. Held him, loved him, ripped him off for everything he was worth.

He'd thought he was in love. How did a man recover trust in his judgement after that?

He didn't. Why should he? Was it worth the risk?

Jem. Dogs.

Back in the wheelhouse, he glanced out at Horse and Nikki, and he thought big dogs and short lifespans. Nikki was giving her heart to a dog, and in a few short years she'd have the heart ripped out of her.

She was laughing now, watching Horse watch a couple of gulls swooping overhead. Horse was trying to figure whether they were a threat. Putting his paws over his head in case they were.

When she lost Horse she'd stop laughing.

He could be there...

Where was he going with this?

Back to port. He gunned the motor, pushing the revs, deciding he needed to be back on dry land fast. Thinking he needed to get his head together fast. Then he noticed a boat on the horizon, coming fast. Much faster than his boat.

It was a pleasure craft, he saw, as the distance between them grew smaller. A couple of yahoo guys were speeding for the sake of it, gunning their flimsy fibreglass craft to the limit. Using gas for the sake of it. Thrill-seeking. They wouldn't even see the seals, he thought, or anything else. They were only intent on speed.

They veered nearer, stupidly close, probably trying to catch his bow wave to give them a more exciting ride. They yelled and waved and veered in and out of his wake. They did a three-sixty degree turn—and then they were gone, speeding into the distance.

And before he realised what was happening...

Horse gave a long, low howl, he lurched out of Nikki's arms, out of her hold and he headed over the side of the boat and after them.

CHAPTER SEVEN

No.

'Horse!' Nikki screamed, hauled off her sou'wester, kicked off her shoes and, before Gabe could react, she was over the side and after him.

No!

They were in seal territory. Pup's playground.

Shark country.

His heart hit his boots as he hauled the boat around, headed out on deck, threw lifebuoys. His gut reaction was to jump straight in after them but a fat lot of use that would be. Three of them in the water while the boat drifted to the reef... He needed to manoeuvre his way to them fast.

He headed back to the wheel. Tried to see.

Horse was a hundred yards from the boat already. Nikki was half the distance but she was heading after him, swimming strongly.

At least she could swim.

She had a life vest on, two bars across her shoulders to be inflated with the pull of a cord. He should be grateful she hadn't pulled it off with her jacket.

She hadn't pulled the cord. She was intent on reaching the dog—who was intent on reaching the speedboat.

Which was now practically out of sight.

'Nikki, head for the lifebuoy,' he yelled, his voice hoarse with panic, but she was still heading for the dog.

Stupid, stupid, stupid.

Panic would achieve nothing. Stay cool. Think.

He gunned the boat, heading after her. He cut her off from the dog and hit neutral.

'I can reach him,' she yelled, changing direction to go round the boat.

'*We* can reach him,' he yelled back. 'Get back in the boat. Now!' He hauled one of the buoys back into the boat and threw it again so it was just in front of her. 'Hold on and I'll pull.'

'Let me go. I can…'

'Get back in the boat or I'll cosh you with the gaff and drag you in.' And he meant it.

They were in seal pup territory. Great White Sharks fed round here, cruising the waters for easy pickings. Pickings like injured seals. The locals knew never to dive near the seal colony. A human in the water, creating a splash, looked just like an injured seal.

He knew the dangers. She didn't. She had to get out of there.

'Horse…' she yelled, sounding desperate. Not as desperate as him.

'We'll get him.' He couldn't manoeuvre the boat closer. It was too big; he risked her being sucked under the propeller. 'Grab the buoy. Now! I mean it, Nikki. Get back on the boat.'

She cast him a look that was half fearful, half angry—and grabbed the buoy.

He hauled her to the side in seconds. Reached down and pulled.

Tugging a grown woman from the sea was no easy task—he'd had guys go overboard before and he'd had to use a harness. Not Nikki. They said women could lift the weight of a car if their child was trapped underneath—that was what this felt like. He lifted her straight up, clinging to the lifebuoy, and he didn't even feel her weight.

He felt nothing until she was on the deck, all of her, whole, fine, safe.

'Horse…' For a nanosecond she clung but she was already pulling away, swivelling to search. 'Horse…'

She was in love already, he thought. She loved the great mangy mutt who was swimming steadily to the horizon.

How…?

'We use the lifeboat,' he snapped. 'There's no way he'll cling to a lifebuoy and we won't be able to grab and lift him from this height. I'm gunning the boat to cut him off. Get up on top of the wheelhouse, haul the ties off and slide the lifeboat down to the foredeck. Go!'

He was back at the wheel, hauling the boat round so he was heading out past Horse. Veering round him in a wide arc. Heading to a spot between the dog and where the speedboat had headed.

So Horse would be forced to swim past.

The sick feeling in his gut was growing with every moment. He knew the odds. He'd seen sharks here before. Often. Please…

At least Nikki was safe.

She wouldn't thank him if he didn't get the stupid dog.

Only the dog wasn't stupid, he conceded, as he manoeuvred the boat into position and hit the winch controlling the anchor. The dog was crazily devoted, still loyal to the lowlife who'd abandoned him. He was somehow associating the speedboat, the thrill-riding idiots, with his previous owner. He was desperate to find those he'd given his heart to.

Giving your heart... It was the way to destroy yourself.

The lifeboat slipped down over the glass in front of him onto the deck. Nikki clambered down after, water streaming from her soaked clothes, her dripping hair. She seemed almost calm, carefully, sensibly, avoiding blocking his view as she clambered down. She steadied the life-raft on the deck and started unhooking the cleats of the metal stays that formed the side rails.

Woman with sense. Woman who'd just jumped into the midst of a seal colony. Where White Pointers fed...

Any minute...any minute...

He had the boat in position. The dog was swimming towards them now, starting to veer because the *Lady Nell* was in his path.

Drop the anchor.

The anchor struck and held. But it wasn't deep enough for safety; the waves were short and sharp and threatening to break.

'Nikki,' he yelled. 'Come here!'

She cast him a fearful glance, not wanting to let go of the life-raft.

'Here!' he yelled in a voice that matched her dog training voice, and she abandoned the life-raft and headed to the wheel.

'Anchor chain,' he snapped, pointing to the lever that attached to the control. 'Gears. Throttle. Watch the sea.'

'I'm going after...'

'You don't know how to manage the motor on the life-raft

and you don't have the strength to haul a dog up. You watch the sea. Every moment. Not me. Not the dog. The sea. I mean it, Nikki, all our lives depend on it. Watch from the east. You see any big sea coming, anything at all, you haul the chain up, wait five seconds, no longer, just so the anchor's clear, then shove her into first gear like this, and turn her nose into the wave. You take action before you need to. Any suspicion of a decent wave, you turn her. Ride the wave, then drop back into neutral, drop the anchor again.'

'Should I just keep her in first gear?'

'No.' Because she couldn't watch the depth sounder, watch the dog, watch the sea all at once, and he didn't want to end up on the rocks. Lowering and raising the anchor was the best way to keep her in position. But he didn't have time to say it. He was already out on deck, lowering the life-raft and slipping down into it.

She saw him slip over the side and then she turned to watch the sea. The waves were coming from the far side of the *Lady Nell* to where Gabe was steering the little boat towards Horse.

Watch the sea. Do not watch Gabe.

She could just glance. Tiny glances in between fierce concentration. A wave was building; she saw the swell further out.

Up with the anchor, into first gear, nose into the wave.

Up and over.

The sea calmed again. Neutral. Drop the anchor.

Another glance.

He was almost there, almost to Horse. The swells were pushing Horse inshore; he was almost to the reef. Gabe was manoeuvring at the back of waves that were threatening to flip his tiny craft.

Watch the sea.

Gabe. Horse.

She'd forgotten to breathe.

The seals had disappeared. Dear God, the seals were gone.

He knew what that meant.

He was closing in on Horse but the dog was veering away, sensing that Gabe was intent on stopping him.

'Horse!' He cut the motor so it hardly purred, keeping just enough revs to hold the little craft on course. He was calling in a voice he was struggling to keep calm. 'Come on, boy.'

The dog veered sharply away.

A wave hit broadside. Gabe did a one-eighty, the wave almost tipped—and boat and dog collided.

He had his hand under the dog's collar before they were down the other side of the wave; before Horse could realise what was happening.

Now pull.

The life-raft was soft sided, industrial strength rubber. If Horse fought... He could tear the craft apart.

Where were the seals? What was happening under the surface?

Don't think. Just do.

He grabbed the collar with both hands, leaned backward so that if the dog came he'd end up full length on the floor rather than lurching out of the other side.

Pulled with all his strength.

The dog hauled back. Fought him.

Where were the seals?

He flicked a glance sideways. Nothing. Calm water. Not a seal.

'Come,' he yelled, and he roared the word, a deep, harsh

yell that sounded out over the reef to the land beyond. It startled the dog into stillness.

He had an instant only. He hauled as he'd never hauled before.

And the dog came, lurching up and sliding in, toppling over the top of him so he was lying full length in the back of the life-raft with a mass of quivering, sodden dog on top of him.

He had him. He was in the boat!

Look back to the sea, Nikki told herself. Concentrate on the sea.

She sniffed.

Stupid salt water. How did it get to be streaming down her face when she was in the wheelhouse?

It wasn't over yet.

Luckily, once Gabe had him, Horse ceased to struggle. Maybe it was because the speedboat was out of sight and he knew it wasn't worth it. Or maybe it was because Gabe's hand on his collar was implacable.

'You want to be shark meat? You want me to have to explain that to Nikki?'

Maybe the dog understood. Maybe he didn't. Either way, he submitted as Gabe reached the *Lady Nell*, roped the dinghy to the side, tried to figure how to get him up.

Figured he couldn't. Not here.

Nikki was still watching the sea. He'd half expected her to emerge from the wheelhouse as he approached but she had the sense to stay where she was.

She was, it seemed, calm in a crisis. Apart from jumping into shark-infested water.

'Anchor up, into first gear, nose her out into deep water. Head straight into the waves rather than broadside,' he yelled. 'Slow and steady, because we're tied to the side.'

And she did it, amazingly well for a landlubber, nosing the big boat carefully out, heading into the swells, changing course so no waves caught her broadside, which might have risked jerking the lifeboat, tossing him and Horse into the sea.

Still he saw no seals. He knew what that meant. There was no use telling Nikki that, though. She had enough to think about.

And finally they were out past the sharp inshore swells, to where the sea flattened into long, low rolls.

'Enough?' she yelled.

'Great. Anchor and help me.' He couldn't climb aboard to get what he needed, because he didn't trust Horse not to lurch over the side again and head for the horizon.

But Nikki was there, following instructions. He roped Horse, looping stays under his midriff, rear and aft, tying his collar, using rope work to fashion a sling.

Once secured, he swung himself up on board the *Lady Nell*, hooked the sling to the cray-pot winch, put the gears into motion.

Instead of a cray-pot being hauled up, a dog.

Nikki caught Horse's head as he reached the top, he looped his arms around the dog's back legs and they hauled him over the side, kneeling, tugging backwards, ending up a tangle of man, woman, dog and sea water.

And laughter. Nikki was laughing. Crying a little too, but hugging her dog as if he was the most wonderful thing she'd ever seen.

And then, because they were lying flat on the deck, side by side, under the dog, she was suddenly hugging him. Tight.

'Oh, Gabe…thank you. You were wonderful. Just wonderful.'

She turned, just a little so she could see him, but he moved at the same time, not intentionally, he'd swear, but it didn't matter because they were nose to nose. She was holding him, her eyes were inches from his, her mouth was just…there…

He kissed her. Of course he kissed her; a man would have to be inhuman not to.

She was streaming sea water. Her curls were dripping and wild. She looked like a drowned rat, only of course it was a ridiculous analogy because her eyes were huge and glowing, and her mouth was soft and full, and…and…

His mouth met hers and the world stilled.

She was cold and shivery and shocked.

She was warm and yielding and wonderful.

She'd been laughing, and for a moment the kiss was an extension of that laughter. An extension of the joy. He felt it blaze between them—shared triumph, awe of what they'd achieved, an extension of drama, shock, fear.

But only for a moment because, as his mouth met hers, things changed. Dissolved. Turned to something else entirely in the power of the link between them.

Heat.

It was like an electric current jolting between them, forging a link, surging with a power so great it threatened to overwhelm him. Her lips were full and tender and yielding, and they felt as if they were melting to him, fire to fire, merging to be part of him, a part he hadn't known was missing until this moment. A part of his whole.

She'd turned to hug him and her arms were around him, holding him close. They were lying almost full length on the deck. Horse was draped over their legs, soaking them. The boat was riding up and down at anchor and all he could feel, all he could sense, all he could focus on, was her lips.

Her mouth.

Nikki.

His arms came around her, tugging her to him as naturally as joining two pieces of a puzzle, setting two pieces where they belonged and feeling the rightness of it.

She was wearing a light sweater. The fabric seemed to have almost disappeared in the wet; he could feel the wonder of her body underneath, the soft, luscious contours of her breasts, the way her body yielded, melted, crushed against him.

Against his sou'wester. Against his fishing gear. He was holding a woman who wore almost nothing and he was dressed for wet weather. He hardly noticed except he wanted her closer, closer and his clothes were getting in the way.

Her mouth…

Nikki.

He'd never felt like this. He'd never known he could feel like this. He had everything he wanted in his life right here, right now.

Stupid? Maybe it was, but there was no way he was going to think that; there was no way he was thinking anything while she was kissing him.

Her hands were in his hair, tugging him closer, deepening the kiss. She wanted this as much as he did. It was as if a key deep within had been turned, releasing emotion he hardly knew he'd locked away. He let himself kiss, he let himself be kissed, and a well of bitterness was unleashed, flowed outward, away and disappeared into the warm salt spray over the ocean.

Nikki…

And then Horse barked.

The dog had been lying limp over their legs, a dead weight neither of them noticed, but when a dog Horse's size barked from your knees and stood and headed for the side again it was time to stop kissing and pay attention.

No matter how much it hurt. No matter that it was a wrench that almost tore him apart.

But he moved. He caught Horse's collar and held. Horse was still attached to the harness but he wasn't taking any chances. Nikki tried to help. She looked as if she was struggling back from somewhere she hadn't known existed. Her eyes held wonder.

Wonder for both of them?

Horse barked again and hauled to the side. Then whined. Gabe tugged him back and looked to see what Horse was barking at.

Something floated to the surface in a pool of crimson.

A seal. Sliced neatly, horribly, in half.

There was a flash of streamlined silver and the thing was gone, hauled down, out of sight, with only the pool of blood remaining.

Nikki's face lost all its colour. He grabbed her as well as Horse, scared she'd faint. He hadn't put the side lines back up; there was no way he was risking her falling.

He had the dog in one hand. His other arm was holding Nikki while she stared in appalled fascination at the disappearing streaks of blood.

'What...what...?' She choked on the words as if she was having trouble breathing. 'It was a seal. What...?'

'A White Pointer,' he said grimly, holding her fast. Trying not to think how close they'd come.

'A White...'

'Sharks,' he said. 'This is seal territory and sharks eat seals.'

'I could have... Horse...'

'That's why I was yelling,' he told her. It was no use lying. She lived here now. If she told anyone about Horse's escapade she'd be told about the sharks. 'Any injured seal is fair game. Sharks sense them by thrashing. Seals are sleek in the water. You guys were asking for trouble.' He motioned to the blood-stained water. 'The shark will be here because of you. He'll have circled for a bit, watched, and then I hauled his supper out of reach. So the seal was the alternative.'

'Oh...' she gasped, and choked back a sob of pure terror, then tugged away from him and stared at him in horror. 'You let me jump over the side.'

'I hardly...'

'You could have yelled "Shark".' *She* was yelling.

'You might have drowned with fright.'

'You could have...'

'What? Yell *Shark*, but nice harmless shark with no teeth? Pat-a-shark territory. Oh, but get out anyway because you might be allergic.'

She choked on something that was half laughter, half shock, then stared again down to where the streaks of blood were now dissipating, leaving a faint crimson tinge to the sea. She shuddered.

Horse whined again and she held him close, and Gabe thought, *Why not me? If you want comfort, why not me?*

It was a dumb thought. *Back away*, he told himself. *You've kissed her, do you want to take this further?*

Yes.

That was another dumb thought, but it was there and it wasn't going away.

Clothes. Practical stuff. Any minute she'd figure she was freezing and, as if the thought was relayed, she shuddered again.

'There's dry stuff in the locker below,' he said, and his voice came out gruffer than he intended. 'It might not be what you're used to...'

She rose. Wiped her wet hands on her tight wet jeans. Made a visible effort to pull herself together. 'Dry?'

'There's towels, overalls, sweaters, boots. We're used to wet. One size fits most. Or actually one size doesn't fit anyone—spares are huge; you roll 'em up, tuck 'em in, do what you can. Best I can do, I'm afraid.'

'The best you can do is awesome,' she whispered. 'I'm sorry I yelled.'

'You had a fright.'

'So did we all. And I'm still sorry I yelled. I never meant... I would never mean...'

She ran out of things to say. Instead, she reached for him, took his hands in hers, kissed him again, lightly on the lips, a feather-touch. And then she was gone, slipping below, leaving him with one sodden dog who was looking as confused as he felt.

CHAPTER EIGHT

THE TRIP HOME was made in near silence. Too much had happened. Too much was happening.

Nikki towelled Horse and cuddled him while Gabe stayed in the wheelhouse. He needed to stay in the wheelhouse. The fact that he wanted to be on the deck with them was irrelevant. More than irrelevant. There were things going on that needed careful thought.

When your foundations shifted, you didn't race to build again. You waited to see if your foundations shifted some more.

That was how he felt, he decided, as he headed back to harbour. As if the solid ground had been pulled from under him.

He didn't know where to take this. He didn't know...anything.

Horse, at least, had settled. He draped himself over Nikki, he whined occasionally but he'd stopped looking at the horizon.

By the time they reached port he was dry and starting to scratch.

Gabe steered the *Lady Nell* back into her berth. Crew

members usually stepped onto the jetty, attached stays to bollards, helped.

Nikki didn't know what crew members were supposed to do. She stayed where she was, under Horse.

Gabe could manage. He'd taken the boat out by himself a thousand times. He'd taken his boat out with crew a lot more.

Taking it out, even with a crew, seemed lonely compared with what he'd had today.

Woman and dog.

Remember Lisbette, he told himself harshly. The one time he'd let himself believe, he'd come close to losing his livelihood.

He'd been lucky. Then it had just been Gabe who'd been affected. If it happened again…if he got into financial trouble now, the fishing industry of this town could well go under.

A man needed to keep his head.

Steer clear of women.

How could he do that now? Where were resolutions when you needed them?

He roped the last stay, tightened cleats, collected Nikki's wet gear from below.

Nikki struggled to rise from under Horse. He couldn't help himself. He gave her a hand and tugged her to her feet.

Mistake. She was too close.

His hand didn't release hers.

Horse scratched. Distraction. Good.

He managed to get his hand back.

'He's spent too much time in salt water,' he said, deciding he had to concentrate on the practical. 'All that sponging I did last night has been undone. He'll scratch himself sore with the salt. There's shampoo you can buy at the Co-op. Ask Marcia. She'll tell you. Tell her I sent you or she'll sell you the expensive stuff.'

'Thank you,' she said. 'Gabe...'

'Yes?' He turned away, tugged up the hatch, showing by his actions that he was moving on.

He was thinking he should go home and help her bathe the dog.

He had crays to deal with. A man had to be sensible.

Dog. Shampoo. Bath. His thoughts were no longer sensible in the least.

Nikki.

He had to give himself time to get his head in order.

Stay clear.

Nikki was a smart woman, he told himself harshly, and Horse was docile. She could bathe the dog.

Her bath was big enough. But the thoughts wouldn't be vanquished. Dog. Shampoo. Bath. He had a clear vision of them in her bathroom, in the vast old tub, soap everywhere...

Um...no.

'You were wonderful,' she said.

'And you weren't shark meat,' he retorted, not turning back. Determined on being sensible. 'Excellent.'

'It is excellent,' she said. 'For all sorts of reasons. Come on Horse, we're going home.'

And Nikki and Horse stepped from the boat onto the wharf without him even helping. They walked away.

He concentrated on the crays.

He didn't watch their going, but it took real effort.

Nikki and Horse walked slowly home around the headland, following the cliff path so they wouldn't necessarily see anyone. She had some pride, and the oversized overalls and huge fisherman's Guernsey weren't exactly elegant.

Nor was her dog.

'We match,' she told him. Horse was plodding wearily beside her. She should never have taken him on the boat. He should have slept today.

He should be sleeping now.

He looked desolate, big and ragged and defeated. It wasn't his health, she thought. It was his heart. He'd leaped into the water to follow what he thought was someone who loved him.

They were on the dirt track in the middle of bushland leading back to the house. No one was around. She squatted and hugged him.

'It's okay,' she told him, burying her face in his salt-encrusted coat. 'You can move on. It's possible.'

Like she was moving on? By kissing Gabe instead of kissing Jonathan?

'I didn't actually do it to distract me from feeling bad about Jonathan,' she told Horse, who didn't understand at all. 'But it did distract me.'

It certainly had. She sat and hugged her dog, the sun shone on her face and she thought…she thought…

Life was full of possibilities. Exciting possibilities.

Possibilities that looked pretty much like Gabe Carver.

She'd thought she was alone, but she wasn't quite. A couple of elderly walkers strode round the bend and she had to shift so they could pass. They were stocky, sensible women with hiking poles, walking with intent.

They reached her and stopped.

Two days ago she might have cringed. Woman pulled from sea, dressed in fisherman's clothes, hugging a scraggy dog.

This was pretty much as far from her life in Sydney as she could get.

'Are you all right?' one of the women asked, and she even managed a smile.

'My dog's a bit subdued,' she said. 'We're having a wee rest.'

'That's not one of Henrietta's dogs?' the woman demanded, staring down at Horse. 'I remember him. I saw the accident when the dogs escaped. This one just bolted. Terrified. And you'll be the lady living with Gabe Carver. I saw Hen at the post office this morning and she said you're keeping him. Oh, my dear...'

'I'm not looking after him very well,' Nikki admitted. The sun was warm on her face. Horse was settling. She was prepared to be expansive.

The world felt expansive, she decided. Plus the way the lady had said it... *You'll be the lady living with Gabe Carver.* It gave her a local identity, something she hadn't had until now. She wasn't sure why, but she liked it. Maybe it was sexist. Maybe it was stupid. Whatever, but she still liked it. 'Gabe took us out on his boat this morning and we fell in.'

'You fell in?'

'Gabe took you out on his boat?'

Both women looked at her, then looked back at each other. Stunned.

'I went to help with the cray-pots,' Nikki said, the odd happy feeling not fading. 'But we were worse than useless. We caught some crays. Then Horse dived in and it was all downhill from there.'

'Horse?'

'My dog.'

My dog. That sounded good, too. It sounded great. There were things happening inside her that felt delicious.

She hadn't planned on staying out today. She should be rushing home now to finish her engineering plans. But instead she was sitting in the middle of a walking trail discussing her very exciting morning with a couple of strangers.

Discussing Gabe?

'That's his sweater,' one lady said and Nikki glanced down at the oversized Guernsey and giggled. Being caught in Gabe's sweater felt good, too.

'He had spare clothes,' she said and grinned. 'I didn't pinch his.'

'Oh, my dear...'

'Where's Gabe now?' the first lady asked.

'Unloading his crays. I'm going home to bathe Horse. He's itchy.' She hesitated. 'Though I'm not sure how. I could use my bath but I don't trust the plumbing. And how would I lift him in?'

'Gabe might help,' the first lady ventured.

'Gabe?' the other said incredulously and they both made wry faces.

'Gabe might do it,' the lady explained as Nikki looked a question. 'But he'd do it at midnight when no one was looking. He's a very private person, our Gabe. He helps. But he helps when no one's looking.'

'That's not a lot of use to me,' Nikki said. Waiting for Gabe to bathe Horse at midnight? Maybe not. 'Don't worry. I'll manage.' She had to. This was her dog. She needed to be independent.

But he was so big!

'I'll tell you what,' the first lady said. 'You take the doggy home and let him have a sleep. He looks exhausted. Maudie and I will finish our walk, we'll fetch the right shampoo for an itchy coat and we'll drive my truck around and help. I have a big plastic tub; I'll bring that. I'm Hilda, by the way, and you must be Nikki. While we bathe your dog you can tell us all about yourself.'

Nikki considered. She should bathe Horse herself.

Or wait for Gabe?

The first might be impossible.

The second?

A girl had some pride. She'd kissed him. That didn't mean she depended on him.

She'd been dependent on a man for the last four years, she told herself. If she was to be independent, the time to start was now.

But Horse was enormous. Be sensible. She needed to accept help when it was offered.

If she was going to be a part of this community she might as well start now.

'Thank you,' she said. 'That would be lovely.'

She could be a little bit dependent, she decided. She just couldn't be dependent on Gabe.

A working bee was therefore following her home.

Horse headed for his trampoline, flopped and was asleep in seconds. Nikki showered, then tried to figure what to wear for dog bathing. Her one pair of jeans was sodden, everything else was classy and she didn't want to scare Maudie and Hilda with her city clothes. Finally she simply put Gabe's clothes back on. She felt ridiculous, but oooh, she was comfortable.

She stared at herself in the mirror. Fisherman Nikki.

Her hand reached automatically to the can of product

designed to smooth her crazy curls. She flicked the power switch on her straightener—and then flicked it off.

She ran the hairdryer through her curls and they flew every which way. She looked at her reflection and she hardly recognised herself.

She grinned.

What next? She needed to stoke up for dog-washing.

She headed for the kitchen. Made herself a cheese sandwich. Considered. Made another. Sat on the doorstep in the sun and ate them. Thought about the sushi and black coffee she'd have eaten at her desk back in Sydney.

Hilda and Maudie were taking ages. While she waited, Horse slept.

She looked at the gap in the stone wall and it looked back at her.

It was Gabe's hole in the wall. Do not touch.

Find her own?

She had work to do. Air conditioning plans.

In Gabe's study, his books on dry stone walling…

Find your own.

She headed down to the pile of stones by the hole in the wall. Picked up stones, considered them, matched them, put them back on the pile. Gabe's hole in the fence remained just that.

Just practising. Just learning. Keeping an ear out for Gabe's truck so she could disappear fast.

There must be somewhere round here where she could get her own pile of stones.

Maybe there was someone to teach her.

Plans. Engineering. Her career.

The sun was too warm to think about plans.

She'd finish this set of plans, she told herself, and the next contracted job. But then...

She had enough money to be independent for quite a while. Her pay for the last few jobs had been enormous, and living in Jon's apartment had cost very little.

She'd been living Jon's life.

'This could be *my* life,' she said out loud.

Then she heard a 'Halloo' from along the road. Maudie and Hilda had arrived, bearing dog stuff.

'We're here to help,' Hilda called. 'I have the world's biggest ice-bucket as a bath. We have shampoo and conditioner and scissors and brushes and two hairdryers and six old towels. Do you think that should do it?'

'I hope so,' Nikki said and grinned. She felt as if she was stepping into a new life. Or maybe she'd stepped into it the moment she'd met Horse.

Or the moment she'd hit Gabe over the head?

There were people in his front yard. Lots of people. Seven? Eight? Ten?

They'd lit the barbecue.

When he'd asked Dorothy in the rental agency about setting this place up, she'd included a barbecue on her list.

'Put in a barbecue where your tenant can cook and see the sea. It'll almost double the rent.'

Up until now it hadn't been lit.

It was lit now. He climbed out of the truck and the smell of sausages and onions hit him like a siren song.

'Gabe!' It was Henrietta from the Animal Shelter, waving a bread-wrapped sausage. Henrietta's son was on barbecue duty. He recognised Hilda and Maudie, founding members of the town's stalwart walking group, deep in conversation with Joe, his own personal handyman.

Joe's springer spaniels were checking out Horse. Horse was snoozing on his trampoline which had obviously been brought outside so he could catch some late afternoon sun.

Nikki was deep in conversation with a lady older than Methuselah.

Aggie, Henrietta's mother. *What the…?*

'Nikki needed help bathing Horse,' Henrietta called, her voice filled with reproach. 'Where have you been?'

'I took a load of crays to Whale Cove.'

'Nikki needed help.'

'He's Nikki's dog,' he said shortly. *What was Aggie doing here?*

'It doesn't matter. We got on fine without you.' Nikki smiled and waved and he was hit by a blast of…difference.

She was still in his clothes. They were way too big for her. He'd thought until today that her hair was straight. Her hair was currently a riot. Curls everywhere.

She was sitting on the grass beside Horse. The springer spaniels were at her feet, nosing Horse, who was interested but he wasn't getting off his trampoline.

Someone had carried a chair outside for Aggie. She was about a hundred. Best guess. She'd been about a hundred ever since he could remember.

What was she doing here?

'Tell us what you think of Horse,' Henrietta demanded. 'Horse, show Uncle Gabe what you look like.'

Uncle Gabe? He had people in his backyard. He was starting to feel…

Horse stood up. It was a bit of a struggle but he managed it. His great tail wagged and something inside Gabe…

No. Don't go there. That ended with Jem.

He tried to look—dispassionately.

Horse had been worked on. Bathed. Combed. Anointed. The remnants of his coat were gleaming, knots cut or teased out, then brushed until it shone. He wobbled a little on his long legs but his crazy tail wagged, the feathering underneath waving wildly. He looked almost beautiful. He looked... almost happy.

He flopped back down on his belly. He gazed up at Gabe and his tail still waved.

So much for dispassionate. He was a sucker for dogs.

And after all, he told himself, this was Nikki's dog. Gabe could bend and scratch him behind the ears without committing himself to anyone. To anything.

But what was Aggie doing here? And all these people...

No one messed with his privacy.

Renting out part of his house had been a bad idea.

'You approve?' Nikki asked and he could tell she was anxious. She was kneeling beside Horse. Because he'd stooped to pat Horse, he was close.

Really close.

'He looks great.'

'Doesn't he?' She beamed. 'I know it looks like we've done a lot to a dog who needs to rest, but he just lay in the sun and we worked on him slowly.'

'We?'

'Hilda and Maudie.'

'And Henrietta and Joe and...and Aggie?'

'They came later, didn't you, guys?' She beamed round at all of them. 'Hilda met Joe at the Co-op and told him what we were doing. She suggested a barbecue so Joe got it working. There were spiders. Big ones. Even Hilda and Maudie suggested we needed Joe. And look at Horse.'

He was looking at Horse. It was safer, he decided, to look at Horse rather than Nikki.

'What do you think?'

Horse had draped himself back over his trampoline, three quarters on but a quarter out, as if he'd like to join in but he still needed the security of his own place.

The trampoline Henrietta had supplied was plain canvas, what a sensible dog needed, but someone—*someones* by the look of the people around him—had decreed plain wasn't enough. A soft green velveteen throw had been added. Also a couple of pillows that looked as if they were down-filled, soft and squishy. Two stuffed toys, a rabbit and a giraffe.

There was a sausage resting by Horse's nose, and a new red water bowl.

Horse looked bemused. As if he didn't have a clue what was happening to his life.

Like Gabe.

These people were barbecuing in his backyard.

Or... Nikki's backyard.

He'd strung a couple of wires on fencing posts when he'd first let the place, delineating boundaries, but until now no one had needed delineation. No one had been in the backyard.

He should have planted a hedge. Fast growing.

He still could.

Nikki was smiling up at him, standing, offering him a sausage, glowing, and he thought yep, hedge. Or back away fast. But...

'Why is Aggie here?' he asked.

Maudie handed him a beer. Aggie passed him a bowl of pretzels.

'Aggie's teaching me to make stone walls,' Nikki said and he almost dropped both.

Maybe his face froze. How did you control your face? He didn't know what he was showing but, whatever it was, it made Nikki's smile slip.

'What is it?'

'What are you playing at?'

'Sorry?' She didn't have a clue what he was talking about. Or did she? She'd seen the books. She knew about his mother.

'I taught his mother to make stone fences,' Aggie said sedately from her chair. The little old lady was wrinkled and gnarled and unfussed, unmoving. Watching Gabe thoughtfully. Watching Nikki. 'Best student I ever had. Last, too. After her, no one. No one wants to spend their days piecing little bits of stone together. Why would they?' Her voice grew sad, distant. 'They're all falling down, my walls. The walls Gabe's mama helped me build. They're built to last for generations but people knock holes in them. They use the capping stones for wedging gates open, that sort of thing. They break 'em and don't know how to repair them. Can't believe you want to learn.'

'You don't want to learn,' Gabe said flatly.

'Why not?' Nikki demanded. 'Why don't I?'

The question hung. They'd all turned to listen now, every one of them caught by the flat anger in Gabe's voice. He couldn't help it. Anger was just...there.

'I don't want my wall finished,' he growled, knowing as he said it that it made no sense at all.

'I know that,' Nikki said. 'I even understand it. Sort of. But this is nothing to do with you, or your mum, or your wall. I'm sorry I borrowed your books without asking, but you have them back now and that's as far as my interference with you goes. I told Henrietta I was bored with what I was doing, that I needed a break while I thought about what I wanted to do. I told her I'd been playing...' She hesitated and then decided to be truthful. 'I'd been playing with your stones. It feels good. I'd like to try it, as a hobby at least. I told Hen and she went to get Aggie, and Aggie says she'll teach me.'

'I don't want you to.'

The flat denial didn't even sound like him. The words were from some gut level he couldn't begin to understand. And, of course, Nikki couldn't understand either.

'It has nothing to do with you,' she retorted, sounding astounded. 'I'm your tenant, Gabe. If I go out in the morning and learn how to make stone walls instead of sitting inside drawing plans, how can that be interfering with you? Or don't you want anyone to learn stone walling ever again because of your mother?'

There was no answer to that. No answer at all. She was right; he was being stupid.

He'd seen stone wallers working since his mother died; of course he had. There were none working locally, but occasionally he'd see them by the roadside outside this area. He liked their quiet craft, was glad that stone walls were still being built.

It was just... Nikki. It was how she made him feel.

He should never have let her kiss him. He should never have kissed her.

He thought of Nikki, in the water where he knew sharks fed. Nikki, on the night she'd hit him, staring down at him with her eyes full of terror. Nikki, hugging this bedraggled, unloved dog, jumping into the water to save him, bringing this motley collection of people back to his house. To his home.

'I have things to do,' he said curtly, knowing he was being

a bore, not knowing what to do about it. Setting his beer and plate aside.

Horse whined.

'You're going to cook your own dinner on your side of the wire?' Nikki demanded with a flash of anger.

He'd hurt her. He'd hurt them all.

But what Nikki did on her side of the fence was her business. He should have climbed straight out of the truck and gone inside, closing the door behind him. Instead...they were all looking at him. Judging him.

'Our Gabe's a loner,' Hen said placatingly to Nikki, as if she was explaining the behaviour of a difficult dog. 'This is his space.'

'He's renting it to me,' Nikki said dangerously. 'I pay for this side of the boundary wire. If he'd wanted me to stay inside with the door shut, he should have written a different tenancy agreement. Gabe, these people helped me this afternoon. They're my friends. They're Horse's friends. So we will keep on with our barbecue. As I'll continue with learning how to make stone walls. This isn't about you, Gabe. This is my back lawn—my barbecue. You can accept my invitation to join us, in which case you'll be pleasant and not treat us as intruders, or you can head inside and keep your own company. Your choice.'

His choice. He made it.

He turned, stepped over the dividing fence and went inside.

She was shaking. Of all the boorish, rude, arrogant...

'Don't mind him, dear,' Aggie said comfortably. 'His dad brought him up hard and a leopard can't change his spots. Till his dad died, any kid who came here risked being horse-whipped and Gabe too, for inviting them. There's ghosts in that man's head and, like it or not, you've brought 'em out. Now, are you going to eat that sausage or not? Dry stone walling's not for sissies. If you're starting tomorrow you need to get your strength up. Don't mind Gabe; he's a good man at heart, even if he never let us close. You just stay on your side of the fence and let him be.'

Midnight. She'd gone to sleep and dreamed of sharks. And Gabe.

Horse was snoring under her bed. He grunted in his sleep and suddenly she was wide awake, staring at the ceiling.

Thinking of sharks—and Gabe.

She put her hand down and Horse nuzzled her palm. She liked it. Something warm and solid in the night.

Go back to sleep.

The sharks were still there. And Gabe.

She padded out to the kitchen, made a pot of tea, hesitated, made a cheese sandwich.

Horse padded after her. She grinned and made two.

She thought about going back to bed. Went out on the veranda instead.

The stars were hanging low over the night sky. The moonlight was glinting over the ocean.

Horse whined and nuzzled her underarm. They ate sandwiches together and watched the distant sea.

Horse settled his great head under her arm, on her knee. He sighed a great dog sigh, and she agreed entirely.

Too hard. Everything.

Gabe?

She should still be thinking about Jonathan, she thought. Was she doomed to forget one appalling man, only to focus on another?

Then Horse stiffened, whined and pulled away. Her hand instinctively grabbed his collar but Horse was swivelling back towards the house. The door opened—the porch door leading to Gabe's side.

Gabe.

He could have guessed she'd be out here. He'd heard the wuffling and thought maybe she'd let Horse outside without her. He was worried about fences. How high could Horse jump?

She had him safe. The big dog was straining towards him but she had him by the collar and she wasn't letting go.

She was wearing pyjamas. Cute pyjamas. Ivory silk with pink embroidery.

Her hair was a mass of tumbled curls. She looked…

Like a man should back into the house and close the door.

'I'm out here,' she said. 'You should back into the house and close the door. Or make me another entrance so you don't need to see me.'

'Nikki…'

'I'm sorry about your mother,' she said before he could get a word in. 'I'm sorry she died and left you alone. And about your dad, who sounds like he was a bully and a pig. But you rented this place to me. If I'm going to feel like it's home, I can't spend my time figuring whether you're likely to come through the door so you can avoid me. And,' she said, taking a breath, obviously gearing up to say something that took courage, 'you were rude to my friends. You need to apologise. Joe's sausages and onions were great.'

'Joe's not your friend,' he snapped before he could think about it. 'He works for me.'

'The two are mutually exclusive?'

'I don't want you in my life.'

Why had he said that? He had no right. He had no need. It was harsh, hurtful, unnecessary. He saw her flinch, then stand and back away. To her door.

'Gabe, what you're saying...it's nonsense.' She was starting to shake. 'You've never asked me to be in your life. I've never suggested...'

'You don't have to,' he said explosively. 'You just are. You stand there, looking at me... You make me feel...'

'How do I make you feel?'

'I don't want it. I don't do relationships. I don't want to feel—anything.'

'Then don't.'

'You're saying you don't sense it, too? This thing between us?'

'If I am, I'm keeping it under control a whole lot more than you are,' she said bluntly. 'You think I'm about to launch myself at you and dig in my claws? Of all the insulting...'

'I didn't say that.' He raked his hair. 'It doesn't make sense. What I'm feeling.'

'It doesn't,' she said, and somehow she managed to sound calm. 'I'm not Lisbette, Gabe.'

'I know that.'

'And I'm not interested in another relationship,' she added and she thought... Was that a lie? Because the way she felt...

She didn't understand the way she felt. Gabe was voicing his confusion. Hers...she'd managed to keep it internal. Anger was a great help.

But... *This thing between us...*

Gabe was right. It was there, tangible, real. It had to be ignored.

This big man was wounded, needy, wonderful. She wanted

to reach out and touch him. Heal him. Heal herself in the process.

He didn't want it. She couldn't.

'You want me to find somewhere else to live?'

What was wrong with him? Was he nuts?

The town thought he was nuts.

No. They thought he was a loner.

There was a fine line between loner and nuts, he decided, and the way Nikki was looking at him... He'd just stepped over it.

'I'm sorry,' he said heavily. 'I'm behaving like an oaf.'

'You are.'

'There's no need to agree!' He wasn't making sense, even to himself.

'Yes, there is.' She sounded wary. But also...amazingly, she sounded amused. 'You kissed me, but so what? The way you're acting... Why? There's no need to think I'm planning weddings, kids, holes from your side of the house to my side, mortgages, puppies and old age homes with rockers side by side.'

'Old age homes?' he said faintly.

'That's how you're looking. Like a man faced with the whole domestic catastrophe. It was a barbecue. Eight people, including you, plus three dogs. On my side of the dividing line. You want to go out tomorrow and buy some twelve foot high screening?'

'I said I was sorry.'

'You still look like you expect me to jump you.'

'I don't.'

'It was just a kiss. I was scared. People do stupid things when they're scared. I won't go swimming with sharks again and I won't go out on your boat.'

'I won't ask you to.'

'Aren't you the gentleman?' She hauled open the door to her side of the house. 'I'm going back to bed. Do you have anything else to say? If so, say it now. I paid three months in advance. You want to give me notice to vacate? That'll be nine weeks where we need to coordinate using this porch so you won't have to look at me. And,' she said savagely, as if this was the final straw, 'I won't even demand that you fix the pipes.'

'The pipes?'

'They still make noises.'

'Talk to…'

Joe. I know. I have. Because there's no way I'd ask my landlord to take a personal interest. There's no way he would.'

'There's no need…'

'There's not, is there? Tell me in the morning whether you want me to vacate. Meanwhile, I'm going to bed. I'm taking my dog with me. I'll lock my door after me and stay on my side of the wall… Oh, and Gabe…'

He was way out of line. He was being an oaf and there didn't seem to be a thing he could do about it. Even Horse was clinging to Nikki's side, as if he knew who his friend was.

'Yes?' He couldn't even find the words to apologise again. He was appalled at his own behaviour.

'I *am* learning to make stone walls,' she said. 'Aggie's teaching me, starting tomorrow. We're working on restoring a wall out the back of Black Mountain, so if the idea offends you you'd better steer clear.'

'I'll be at sea tomorrow.'

'Hooray,' she said. 'You can head for the horizon and never think about us again. Come on, Horse, it looks like our peace in the moonlight is over.'

* * *

She walked inside with as much dignity as she could muster. Horse sidled in with her.

She stood with her back to the door and she shook.

Horse was shaking, too.

She was scaring the baby.

With something between a sob and a laugh, she knelt and hugged the big dog. He licked her face.

Ugh. It was as close as a girl could come to having a shower. A warm shower.

The urge to sob subsided. She sank so she was sitting on the floor with Horse draped over her.

They both stopped shaking.

She'd managed to make her escape with dignity, but it had been a near thing.

'He's just a bore,' she told Horse. 'He's a guy who's been brought up with no manners. A woman-hating, dog-fearing hermit.'

His crew liked him. Joe liked him. The town made excuses for him and they wouldn't do that if he wasn't a good man at heart.

Was it just her?

Was he reacting that way because she'd kissed him?

'I can't take it back,' she told Horse. 'I don't even want to.'

Drat him—he had her thoroughly confused. And Nikki was a girl who didn't like being confused.

'I'm straightening my hair again tomorrow,' she told Horse, but he didn't seem impressed. She wasn't sure if she was either.

'But I *am* going to learn dry stone walling. It'll be a great job for a dog to come along and help. You want to do that?'

She got another lick for her pains. Grinned. Pushed herself to her feet and headed back to bed.

'Coming?'

Horse looked at her. Looked at the door. Whined.

Was he wanting the beach? Or Gabe?

Gabe or beach?

'Neither,' she said, tugging Horse to her bedroom with her. 'If it's your low-life owner, get over it, your future's with me. And if it's Gabe...exactly the same.'

He felt about two inches high. Justifiably. What had she done to deserve the lambasting he'd given her?

She'd borrowed his books? She was trying to learn how to make a stone wall?

She'd twisted his heart.

There was the problem. Heart-twisting. It made him feel as if he was wide open, vulnerable to a woman. Vulnerable to Nikki.

He'd been nuts to ever rent the apartment out.

But if he'd met Nikki any other way he'd have felt the same, he thought. It wasn't that she was living next door. It wasn't that she was dragging him into her life. It was just that she was... Nikki.

A man'd be mad not to want her.

He wanted her.

It was a hunger so fierce it made him feel his world was no longer stable.

He'd get it stable again, he thought. Maybe he already had. Even if he was to let weakness prevail, after tonight he'd burned his bridges. The way she'd looked at him...

He deserved nothing less.

Maybe it was just as well.

The fleet would be in at dawn. He'd help sort the catch and he'd be out again. Deep sea fishing, he decided. Out for four or five days.

He could rotate the crews so he could be out for weeks.

Great.

Or not great.

Nikki was just through the door. He'd hurt her.

So knock and apologise?

He'd already done that. Not one of his finest moments.

He had to do something. He couldn't just leave.

That was exactly what he intended.

She heard his alarm through the wall. Five a.m.

Horse whined and hauled himself up beside her. Her bed was ridiculously small. What sort of masochistic streak had made her buy a single bed? No matter, she wasn't pushing her new pet off.

'Gabe's going fishing,' she told him. 'It's just as well. He's...unsettling.'

Unsettling or not, when she heard his truck disappear she felt...she felt...

Like she had when Jonathan left—but worse.

She hadn't needed Jonathan.

She didn't need Gabe.

Liar.

How can you need him? she demanded of herself. You don't know him.

But she did. It was like...meeting a part of her that had been missing.

They were alike, she thought. Hers had been a barren childhood. Gabe's had been worse but something in him resonated with her, touched her at a level she couldn't begin to explain.

Nonsense. Sentimental garbage.

But then she heard his truck return. Footsteps. A heavy thump on the porch. Her heart twisted.

Nonsense or not, if he knocked...

He didn't. Receding footsteps. The truck's engine restarting. He was gone again.

Horse headed for the door, barking, sounding excited. She hopped out of bed and opened the door with caution.

An ice tub was on her back step.

Crayfish, prawns, mud-crabs, oysters, mussels were arranged to perfection on a massive tub of ice. A bottle of champagne was wedged on the side.

She recognised the champagne label and gasped. Even Jonathan would have been impressed.

A note:

Apologies. I'm not used to being social. Make yourself at home. I don't even mind if you go onto my side of the fence. Take care of Horse. Give him an oyster or six.

The ice tub was lavish. She should be touched by such a gift. She should at least smile at his note.

Instead? Desolation.

Expensive food. Champagne. Things.

Jonathan used to give her gifts when he left her.

She wouldn't waste this. She'd share, and not just with Horse. She had friends now.

But she wouldn't share with Gabe. Gabe, who couldn't apologise in person.

Did she care?

'I'm a woman of independent means,' she said out loud to the world in general, but she didn't know what she meant.

Independence...

Horse nuzzled her leg.

She wasn't independent at all. Luckily, she had Horse, and he was a dog she could lean on.

'Want an oyster?' she asked. 'Because I don't.'

CHAPTER NINE

A GIRL HAD to have a passion. If it couldn't be Gabe—and it couldn't—then the next best thing was stone walling, and at least there her passion was uncomplicated.

Quite simply, walling felt as if a lost piece of her had been reinstated. Sitting on the edge of a paddock, dirty, sometimes damp—Aggie paused for rain but not for showers—watching her wall grow, stone by stone, Nikki felt as if she'd found her home.

Aggie was a fine teacher, happy with nothing less than perfection. Her walls were built to withstand livestock, age and weather. Knowing she had a teacher who could give her those skills was a source of satisfaction Nikki couldn't begin to explain.

Aggie was content as well. 'If you knew how much it hurts to see walls I've built be damaged and no longer be fit enough to fix 'em… If you really love this, girl, it'd be my pleasure to teach you. And don't fret about an income. Farmers love these walls. They get the stones out of their paddocks, they get walls that'll last for a hundred years and they look great.

It's win win. They even get grants for repair—they're heritage, you know. We can charge almost what we want to fix 'em and build more. If you're serious…'

There was no doubting she was serious. She worked and worked, and every minute she loved it more. Horse lay beside her as she worked. Dog paradise. Two weeks into lessons a rabbit stuck its nose from behind the fence. She'd tied Horse to Aggie's chair—even though they weren't in sight of the sea, she was taking no chances. But, 'Let him off,' Aggie said as Horse nearly went crazy on the end of his lead.

'Really?'

'Really.'

So she did and Horse spent the afternoon chasing rabbits, more rabbits and more rabbits still. He never came close to catching one, but every time one escaped he zoomed back to her, almost as if he needed to tell her about it. His big body practically vibrated with exhilaration.

She took him home that night as filthy and as happy as she was. She had a rabbit-chasing dog. She wanted to tell Gabe.

Gabe wasn't home. Again.

She'd barely seen him. He came home only to replenish supplies and leave again. Solitude was his life since his father had died; since the woman called Lisbette had screwed him for everything he had. She understood—but it still felt bad when she turned into the driveway and Gabe's truck wasn't there; when she flicked open the curtains before she went to bed and there was no light in his window.

She was being dumb. Needy. Adolescent, even. She shouldn't be twitching the curtain to see if he was at home. She shouldn't care.

She didn't.

What a lie.

* * *

He'd spent so long at sea he was starting to see fish in his dreams.

He loved his work. He took pride in his fleet, in the men and women who worked for him, in their skills and endurance. He also loved Banksia Bay. After Lisbette he'd left, swearing never to return, but he'd left his house, his boat, the two things he'd salvaged from Lisbette's financial raid. So maybe he'd never intended to let it go completely, and when the fleet was in trouble he'd been glad to come home.

The sea was the same.

But, in truth, the last few years had even seen him tire of the endless sea. As Jem had aged he'd spent more time on land, reading in front of the fire, taking the old dog for gentle walks around the cliffs, cooking. Settling.

When Jem had died he'd headed back to sea. It was the only place he knew how to…be.

A man knew where he was at sea. Especially if the work was hard.

So now he moved from crew to crew, ostensibly to spend time with each of his skippers, to work through problems with each of the boats, but in reality it was because when he was on board the crew worked harder, and he could work to match.

If he worked, then he slept. Mostly.

He couldn't stay at sea for ever.

How long until she grew tired of playing with stones and took herself back to Sydney?

How long before a man could put her out of his head?

She finished the tail ends of her contracted work—the last part of her life as an engineer. She needed to make one last trip to Sydney and that part of her life would be over. She could make it a day trip.

She didn't want to leave Horse with Henrietta. Even though Hen was lovely and her boarding kennels were great, Horse still shook when he saw her.

She'd like to leave him with Gabe.

Fat chance. Gabe was never at home.

'Leave him with me,' Aggie said diffidently. 'My cat won't like it but it's time he had a spot of excitement. And you needn't worry. The walls around my place would keep a herd of elephants in.'

So she left Horse with Aggie and drove to Sydney. She'd checked Jonathan wouldn't be in the office. She left her final work on his desk—and her letter of resignation.

She walked out feeling not one shred of regret.

She wanted to ring Gabe and tell him.

How dumb was that?

Instead, she headed to a specialist work-wear firm. She bought heavy duty overalls, leather gloves, sturdy boots, goggles and a bright yellow jacket so she could be seen if she was working by the roadside.

Bright yellow, like Gabe's sou'wester used to be before he wore it in.

Gabe.

Her thoughts shouldn't always turn to Gabe.

They just did.

There was nothing left to do in Sydney. She'd left at dawn, thinking she might need to spend time in the office, but her former colleagues were cool. She'd dumped more work on them. There was no suggestion of socialising. The work gear had taken all of half an hour to buy so she was back in Banksia Bay by three. At Aggie's, Horse greeted her with joy.

'He's been sitting by the door all day, pining for you,' Aggie said. 'I've been fearful to let him out. I had to let him chase the cat to cheer him up. Mind, that might be the last time I can take care of him—if you bring him back, my poor old cat might leave home for ever.'

Nikki grinned. She hugged her dog and loaded him back into her car, resolving to buy Aggie's cat some gourmet cat food. Thinking she wouldn't need to leave Horse again anyway. Who needed Sydney? What more could a woman want than what she had right now?

Gabe.

Stupid or not, she wanted Gabe.

And he was at home.

Aggie's normal working day was nine to five. It was barely four when Nikki turned into the drive and Gabe was on the veranda. She could tell by his face that he hadn't been expecting her.

Her heart...quivered?

This was nuts. She was behaving like a moonstruck adolescent. The tension between them was a construct that could and should be eliminated. Now.

'Hi,' she said, pretending cheeriness. Horse, however, didn't need to pretend. He headed up to the veranda, leaped to place his huge paws on Gabe's shoulders and Gabe only just managed not to fall.

Adolescent or not, she wouldn't mind putting her arms there either. Holding.

Stupid. She was a mature woman approaching her landlord. Her rude, hermit-of-a-landlord who wanted nothing to do with her. Or her dog.

He was hugging her dog.

She turned her back on the pair of them and started hauling stuff from the car. Carrier bags labelled 'Grey's Industrial Work Gear'. Cool stuff.

She lugged her bags up the porch steps. Gabe—and Horse—stood aside to let her pass.

'Work gear?' Gabe queried, and she flashed him a suspicious look. The way he'd said it...

'Get over it,' she said. 'You don't have a monopoly on wearing overalls.'

'You've bought overalls?'

'Four pairs. Serious stuff.'

'Aggie's still teaching you, then?'

'I imagine you've heard. Five days a week. I went back to Sydney today to drop final plans off and to resign. Then I went and bought overalls.'

'You've resigned?'

She sighed. 'Yes.'

'You can't be serious.'

'What on earth does it have to do with you?' she demanded. 'Just because your mother made stone walls, is that a reason no one else can?'

'Only you.'

Only you. The two words hung. She didn't know what they meant, but she did know they were important.

'What is it about me,' she said at last, 'that makes you think I can't be a stone waller?' *That makes you think I'm threatening?*

'Nothing.'

Horse had sunk to all fours and was nosing Nikki's packages. They were interesting. They were tools for her new life.

She was not going to let this man interfere with it.

Get it onto a normal plane, he told himself. Forget about... *this thing between us.* Move on.

'Come and see what we're doing,' she heard herself say, surprising herself by the dispassionate tone she managed. 'We're working behind Black Mountain on Eaglehawk Road. We'll be there tomorrow from about nine.'

'I'll be back at sea tomorrow.'

'Only if you want to be. You're the owner of the fleet. You can decide.'

'I can't make money unless I go to sea.'

'Maybe you have enough money,' she said gently. 'That's what I've decided. I've been doing a job that fills my head and my bank account, but not my heart. Horse and I are moving on.'

'I give you three months tops before you're bored.'

'How long did your mother build for?' she asked—and then regretted it. The look on his face…

He had demons, this man, and she didn't want to make them worse.

'You don't need to answer,' she said, softening. 'I had no right to ask. Don't come and see what Aggie and I are doing—I'm sure you're not interested and if it reminds you of things you'd rather forget then it's not worth the pain. Let me pass now, Gabe. I'll see you next time you're on shore.'

He stared at her for a long moment. His face was blank and still.

He wanted to say something, she thought, but he didn't know what. Or he didn't know how.

He was a big, silent man with demons. She wanted, quite suddenly, quite desperately, to hold him. Just hold him until the demons disappeared.

This wasn't an adolescent crush, she thought. There really was some intangible link…

'Gabe…'

'I'm holding you up,' he said and moved aside so there was no danger of her brushing against him. 'You have things to do.'

'Unpacking,' she managed, trying to sound cheerful. Trying to sound unconcerned. 'I've been shoe shopping. I have steel capped boots. They'll be eating their hearts out on the Paris catwalks.'

He smiled but only just, and the smile didn't reach his eyes. 'Sensible,' he said gruffly.

'That's me. Sensible.'

'Can you get your job back when you…?'

'I don't want my job back!' Enough of cheerful. Enough of sympathy. She practically yelled the words. Glared.

'Happy stone walling, then,' he said grimly.

'Thank you.'

There was nothing else to say. She walked straight by him. Horse cast him a doubtful glance and then followed his new mistress home.

Why couldn't she get Gabe out of her head? Why was he messing with her equilibrium? Why?

He was damaged goods. He made no effort to be friendly. He didn't want anyone close.

She was forging her own life. She was making friends. She could live happily ever after.

She could buy her own little house, she decided, with a big backyard for Horse. Then she wouldn't have to see Gabe except in occasional passing, one resident of Banksia Bay to another.

She had enough money for a decent deposit. She could start searching straight away—before she annoyed Gabe so much he evicted her.

She should be proactive in her dealings with men.

In her dealings with Gabe.

That was sensible.

But there was a part of her that was refusing to be sensible. Even if Gabe didn't make her feel…like she did…she kind of liked living next door to him.

'It's safety. It's because he's the size of an oak,' she muttered to Horse, but she knew it was much, much more.

She stalked into the kitchen, put on the kettle, picked up one of her pretty china cups.

Looked at it with care.

'That's what Gabe thinks I am,' she told Horse. 'Tomorrow I'm buying mugs. Can you buy industrial strength mugs as well? And I'm changing into my new stone walling gear now.'

She'd invited him to see what she and Aggie were working on. Wanting to go was irrational, but he couldn't stop thinking of it.

It was as if there were chisels wedging themselves under the armour he'd spent thirty years building.

Why?

She was his tenant. She was learning to do dry stone walling with Aggie. Both of those things were unthreatening; neither should pierce his armour.

They did.

He had to get used to it. The new normality was that Nikki was his neighbour, his tenant, the local stone wall builder.

He would go and see one of her walls, he decided. He could behave rationally, it was simply that he hadn't until now.

The forecast for the next few days was for bad weather. He knew the crew would prefer to stay in—he'd been working them all too hard. The grass around the house needed mowing. He'd do that tomorrow—and then in the afternoon he'd casually drive around the back of Black Mountain and see where Aggie was working.

Both Aggie and Nikki.

The day was warm and blustery. 'We'll be in for a storm tonight,' Aggie said, settling down with her folding chair and her Thermos. The old lady was supremely content. Her body was failing her, she could no longer handle the stones, but she could watch Nikki with a gimlet eye, ordering Nikki's hands to do what Aggie's longed to.

In Aggie, Nikki had found a world-class stone waller, and a world-class teacher. She realised that as she worked, as Aggie's eyes found the perfect stone in seconds while Nikki would have searched an hour, as Aggie decreed a fit Nikki thought perfect was appalling— 'It'll blow a gale through the cracks; take it out and start again.'

The work was physically demanding but satisfying on a level Nikki had never guessed she needed. The farmer whose property they were working on came often to inspect, and his pride and pleasure added to hers.

'I never thought I'd get this fence fixed,' he told them. 'It's been here since my great-great-granddad's day. I've been filling the gaps with wire but now Aggie has a student... Lass, you'll have your life's work cut out for you.'

It felt great.

Horse agreed. When Nikki moved, so did he. He was becoming hers, Nikki thought with even more satisfaction.

This was her perfect life. Except for the small niggle of Gabe.

Who turned up mid-afternoon.

She was having trouble fitting a stone. Aggie assured her

it'd fit; she just needed to rotate the stones above and behind. She was figuring whether she'd have to chip a bit off the stone—a process Aggie regarded with scorn as there was always the 'right' stone—when suddenly Horse was on his feet, wagging his shaggy tail and barking with delight.

'Look who the cat dragged in,' Aggie said, her voice full of pleasure as Gabe climbed from his truck.

He was wearing jeans and T-shirt, not as rough as usual. He'd shaved.

He still looked big and dark and dangerous.

He still made her heart flip.

'To what do we owe this honour?' Aggie demanded, and Nikki thought thank heaven for Aggie because there was no way she could think of anything sensible to say.

'I decided I'd come and see if she's as good as my mum,' Gabe said and smiled at her, and her heart did a backward somersault. *As good as my mum...* What sort of statement was that?

A statement without anger. A statement of a man accepting things as they were.

'She's got a long way to go but she's going to be better,' Aggie said roundly. 'Your mum had distractions. Husband. Baby. A working girl needs to focus.'

'So Nikki's focusing?'

'Yes, she is. Don't you distract her.'

'I wouldn't dream of it.' He hesitated while Nikki found another stone and tried to fit it. It was nowhere near the right size. Funny, maybe her mind was somewhere else.

'You coped with distractions,' Gabe told Aggie mildly. 'I seem to remember a husband, kids, a farm and a fishing boat. And world-class stone walling medals.'

'My Bert supported me,' Aggie growled. 'He was one in

a million. He'd spend the night fishing, sleep for a couple of hours, then if I was on a rush job he'd come out and sort stones for me. They don't make 'em like Bert any more.'

'What did you do with the kids?' Nikki asked, fascinated.

'Playpens,' Aggie said. 'They don't hold with 'em any more, do they? But I had 'em corralled while I worked, then, as soon as they were big enough, they sorted stones. Can't figure why none of them wanted to stone wall for a career.'

'I can't imagine,' Nikki said faintly. She caught Gabe's eye and laughter met laughter.

He made her toes curl.

'Can I help?' he asked and there was a statement to take her breath away.

She didn't need to answer. Aggie was way before her.

'Sure you can,' she said, beaming. 'Nikki's got a way to go to get those muscles strong enough to set the base stones. There's a good twenty yards where they've been moved out of alignment. Some moron decided to drive cattle through here, can you believe that? They pushed a bulldozer through the lot of it. Twenty yards when two would have done. How fat's a cow? At least Frank wants it fixed now, so we just need you to dig along the line, flattening a trench and I'll tell you what stones to put in. Spade's in the back of my truck. What are you waiting for?'

The laughter was still there, Nikki thought. It was suppressed—there was no way Aggie would concede anything she said was funny—but it flashed between Nikki and Gabe and it warmed something she hadn't known was cold. It made her feel...

'If you stare at that stone for any longer it'll grow teeth and bite you,' Aggie snapped. 'We're wasting time. With

Gabe to help us, I reckon we can get a couple of yards done by dusk. Get to work.'

'Yes, ma'am,' Nikki said and Gabe saluted and grinned and went to get the spade.

It felt weird.

It felt excellent.

Hard physical work—and it was hard, as hard as hauling in nets, as heaving crates of fish.

Digging along the trench. Setting the lines so he could pack straight. Then heaving rock after rock into the trench, following Aggie's orders, moving, shifting, discarding, trying again, until he had the perfect line.

Normally an afternoon like this he'd be frustrated, stuck at home, itching to get to sea again.

He was having fun. Being bossed by one tyrannical old lady.

Listening to Nikki being bossed.

Watching Nikki take pleasure in her stones.

He remembered his mother. 'There's nothing like it, Gabe, when you find the perfect stone and it fits like it's meant to be there. When you know that's its place.'

She'd never locked him in a playpen or ordered him to help, but he had helped, and the pleasure of it returned to him now.

He'd never remembered his mother without pain, but this afternoon…watching Nikki…

His mother seemed to be there. And Jem.

Horse was lazily watching, and it seemed the ghost of Jem was with him as well. There was a peace here he hadn't known was missing.

The armour was peeling back.

He worked on. Little was said, but when Aggie got vocal, chastising them for fools, idiots, anyone could see that stone was way out of line, he flicked a glance at Nikki and their shared laughter grew.

And something else.

Something that had nothing to do with his mother. Or Jem. Or anyone or anything else.

It was something about the way Nikki knelt, intent, her crazy curls—how long since she'd abandoned that sophisticated straight cut?—flying in all directions. It was watching her sorting, fitting, rejecting, choosing another, listening to Aggie's criticism, sitting back, surveying what she'd done and finally, finally accepting that she'd found the right stone and the right place.

She'd give a tiny sigh of happiness as the stone slotted in and, as each stone fitted, she'd turn and hug Horse and tell him how clever he was for helping.

Horse wagged his tail, accepting praise with decorum.

Dog and woman looked totally, gloriously happy.

She was a city girl. A highly trained specialist engineer. This wasn't her world.

It looked as if it was her world.

He thought back to the woman he'd met the day she'd moved in. She'd worn a sophisticated outer skin. Now it seemed she'd shed it and she was who she truly wanted to be.

She was beautiful. Dirty, bedraggled, windblown, totally absorbed, she was the most beautiful woman he'd ever seen.

He turned a little and found Aggie was watching him. Bemused.

'A worthwhile project,' she said and grinned, and Gabe figured he'd never blushed in his life and he wasn't about to now.

'It'll be good when it's finished,' he said.

'She's beautiful now,' Aggie said and she wasn't looking at the wall. Her grin broadened but then a sudden gust of wind slapped around the slight shelter their partially made wall was giving them, and Aggie's hat sailed off her head, a woollen beanie. Gabe retrieved it, Aggie sighed, shoved it on her head and pushed herself out of her folding chair.

'That's it. The hat barometer says it's time to call it a day.' She shoved her chair into the back of her disreputable truck. 'I drove Nikki here, but you can take her home. Can you fit that dog in as well?'

'Sure,' Gabe said and glanced at Nikki—and the laughter was gone.

Replaced by uncertainty? Fear, even? Just because he'd agreed to drive her home?

He'd been an oaf.

He had a lot of ground to make up.

They drove in silence. He wasn't sure where to start, and maybe she thought the same. But it was up to him, he decided as he pulled up at his house. At *their* house.

'I need to apologise,' he said, and she twisted in her seat and looked at him. Horse was at her feet, his great head on her lap. She'd been stroking him. Her hand stilled.

'I thought you already had.'

'Not properly.' He hesitated. 'I've been a git,' he said at last. 'My dog died four months ago. It threw me. I know it's dumb to get emotional about a dog, but I didn't want to have another around the place.' He raked his hair. Tried to figure where to go from here. 'Horse is your first dog?'

'Yes,' she said, brisk and cool. 'And I hope he lives for

ever. But the way you reacted to me... It's not all about Jem, is it?'

'No.' He shook his head, trying to figure it out. 'You remind me of my mother.' It was trite. It was barely true. There was so much more, but he couldn't begin to put it into words.

'That's so what every girl wants to hear,' she retorted but, amazingly, she grinned. 'Woohoo. But I'll take it as a compliment. After a day with Aggie, I'll take any compliment I can get.'

'You're serious enough to cope with Aggie's criticism?'

'I've never been more serious. If I can make a go of it...'

'You will.'

'I intend to try.' She reached for the door handle but Gabe reached over, caught her hand and held.

'I haven't finished apologising.'

'You've said you were a git. And you gave me crayfish.' She looked down at his hand holding hers and she couldn't quite stop a tremor entering her voice. 'That'll do nicely. Plus you've dug my trench, which I would have had to do tomorrow. It would have taken me all day and it took you two hours. So apology accepted, thank you very much.'

'Can I cook you dinner?'

She stilled. Looked down at their linked hands. 'You don't want me on your side of the wall.'

'I might have changed my mind,' he said. No. That wasn't enough. He had to say it properly. 'I was nuts. I do want you on my side of the wall. There's nothing I'd like better than to cook you dinner.'

'Can I bring Horse?'

A woman and a dog on his side of the wall. In his sitting room.

Nikki and Horse.

Suddenly Jem was right by him, egging him on.

The measure of a life well lived is how many good dogs you can fit into it.

Did that go for love, too?

He'd never truly loved. He didn't know how.

He could try.

He stir-fried prawns, Thai style, with chilli, coriander, snap peas, lime juice. He served them over rice noodles that melted in her mouth.

They ate on the veranda looking over the sea. Looking out over the hole in the stone wall. Looking out at the world.

'Where did you learn to cook?' she asked. She'd eaten at some wonderful restaurants in her time. What she'd eaten tonight was right up there.

'I've cooked since my mum got sick. It's fun.'

Fun. The word hung between them.

Fun, she thought.

Fun wasn't a concept that sat easily with this man.

'Do you cook on the boat?'

'Life's too short for a bad meal,' he said simply. 'I'll take you to sea one night and cook you calamari straight from the line. There's nothing in the world to beat it.'

I'll take you to sea one night... It was a promise.

She felt as if she were standing on the edge of a precipice.

He brought out panacotta then, so creamy it was to die for, with brandied segments of mandarin and slivers of chocolate on the side.

'When did you do this?' she demanded.

'This morning. Before I came to find you. When I decided the fleet would stay in port, I had the whole day to kill.'

So he'd planned dinner, and then he'd come to find her.

She wasn't sure what was happening. All she knew was that Gabe's grim face had disappeared. He was shedding something. Opening himself.

Horse was between them, stretched under Gabe's chair. Gabe was rubbing his belly with his boot. Horse was practically purring.

Horse, too, had eaten prawns for dinner. Life was looking good from Horse's angle.

From Nikki's as well.

Every night she came home from work with aching muscles. Tonight she wasn't feeling an ache.

'Can I ask if you and Aggie can schedule in finishing my wall?' Gabe asked and the night stood still.

'Do you really want that?' she asked, breathless.

'I do.'

'Gabe…'

'Mmm.'

'You're not just doing it to be nice?'

'I'm not,' he said, and his tone was suddenly back to being grim. 'I'm doing it because I've lived with ghosts all my life. They've controlled what I do, and now I've decided it's time I was doing the controlling. The ghosts can come along if they want—and maybe they will—but they can watch what I do rather than dictate.' He rose. 'Come and tell me what needs doing.'

He held out his hand, imperious, and she looked at it for a moment, considering.

But there was nothing to consider. This was Gabe. Gabe, whose outside armour held a man she was…wanting to love?

The concept was frightening, but not as frightening as ignoring the hand, turning away from the need.

She laid her hand in his and let him tug her up. She came, a little too fast. Ended up a little too close.

He smiled and kissed the tip of her nose. It was a gesture of laughter and friendship, surely nothing more, but it brought back the memory of that first kiss.

Of her need.

She tugged back a little—but she didn't let go of his hand. He smiled ruefully.

'Slow,' he said. 'I have the sense to be slow. The way I'm feeling...'

There was enough in that statement to take her breath away all over again.

But she kept breathing. A girl had to do something as he led her off the veranda and down to the pile of stones and the gap in the fence. Breathing was all she could manage.

Horse followed. They stood on the dew-wet grass and gazed at the pile of stones. The moon was just starting to rise over the sea. The wind was from behind them. The long, low house provided them with shelter. The night was...perfect.

'Where do we start?' Gabe asked.

'Where your mother left off. Did your father never want it finished?'

'My father loved my mother in his fashion,' he said simply. 'He didn't show it. She loved me and she loved her walls. After she died...he hated us both.'

'That's appalling.'

'Yes, but it's past time I made my peace.'

'By finishing the wall?'

'By more than that.' He hesitated. She could feel things breaking inside him, two sides warring. One side winning? The side she was starting to ache for.

'By letting go of my ghosts,' he said softly, his voice almost a whisper. Intimate and wonderful. 'By moving into a future where life isn't grim and harsh. By seeing what's in front of my eyes.'

And his eyes were all on her.

She thought about that for a bit, standing in silence, her hands in his. It felt momentous. But also... It felt simple.

As simple as falling in love?

That was what it felt like. Right now, she was giving her heart.

She thought of the convolutions of falling in love with Jonathan, the sophistry of his courtship, the elegant dinners, opera, amazing weekends in exotic places, horizon pools, butlers, champagne breakfasts.

The lies, deceit, heartache.

For years she'd thought she loved. And yet, here it was, hands linked, nothing more. Nothing to be said while something grew.

He'd made no promises. But this was a start, she thought. And if he was prepared to start...

Her heart wanted to leap into the breach, declare what she was feeling, move forward right now. But there was still wariness in his eyes, as if he expected things to implode.

He was hoping it wouldn't. Hope was wonderful.

She turned into him and tugged him to her. Wanting him close. Just...close.

Nothing more. She held him, her breasts against his chest, feeling her heartbeat merge to his.

The feeling grew. Something huge.

'I don't know how to do this,' Gabe said simply, holding her close. 'I've never learned to...let go.'

'You've been married.'

'Not married. Joined by a contract to someone I didn't know. And you?'

'I felt like I was. It was a lie.'

'Same with me. Nikki…'

'Mmm?' She tugged away a little, looked up at him in the moonlight. Saw trouble.

'I don't want to hurt you.'

'I don't think you can.'

'If I don't know that myself…' Hesitated. 'My dad… He did love my mother. He wanted all of her. I'm afraid…'

'That you're like your father?'

'Yes.'

'You're not,' she said simply. 'I know.'

The wind was rising, swirling around either end of the house, closing in again in the trees beyond. They had this one triangle of peace.

One fleeting moment.

She suddenly shivered, a premonition. He felt it, held her close, tugged her harder against him.

'There's so much I need to learn,' he said.

'Me, too. But if I can learn about stone walls, I can learn about you.'

She tilted her chin and pushed herself up on her toes. He caught her face in both hands and kissed her.

Wonderfully.

She felt loved.

That was what his kiss told her. She felt the heat, the aching need, the longing, the sheer want.

The tenderness and the passion, leashed, held under control but only just.

The smell of him…the taste…the feel…

Gabe.

The kiss lingered, stretched out, filled her. She was falling...falling...and it was so easy.

So easy to fall in love.

It was done. Just like that. If he wanted to take her...

No. Not right now. Indignant for lack of notice, Horse whimpered and pushed his great head between them. Gabe released her and Nikki thought...was there a touch of relief in the way he put her aside?

He'd committed, but only so far. There was still reserve.

Ghosts.

'No further,' Gabe said and she could have wept with frustration but he was right. If he wasn't sure...

She was sure.

'Of course not,' she said with as much dignity as she could muster. 'I... I need to go to bed. I have stone walls to build in the morning. It's all very well for layabout fishermen, taking every tiny excuse of a wee bit of wind to stay in port...'

'We've a gale predicted by morning.'

'Pussycat,' she teased and stepped back.

Go slow.

She didn't want to go slow.

And suddenly the muscles she'd forgotten about...ached.

'You know what I want to do?' she asked.

'What?' He still sounded wary.

'Have a bath,' she said. 'I haven't been brave enough. My pipes gurgle.'

'Your pipes...'

'Joe tried to fix them,' she said with patience. 'He hit them with a spanner. But they still make the most horrific gurgle. You want to come and hear?'

And she saw him withdraw, right there.

Okay, it had been a ruse. She didn't want to go inside and calmly close the door on him. Come inside and see my etchings? Come inside and listen to my pipes?

Corny.

Unwise.

'I don't think that's wise,' he said, and she shrivelled a bit. Felt…stupid.

She'd kissed him. He'd kissed her back and it was wonderful, but the next step was up to him. His face said it.

This relationship would be on his terms.

Like her relationship with Jonathan. He called the tune.

She felt…a little bit ill.

'Sorry,' she managed. 'That was dumb.'

'Nikki…'

'No, you're right, standing in my bathroom listening to pipes there's every chance I could jump you. That'd be dreadful.'

'I didn't mean…'

'Of course you didn't,' she managed but she thought, bleakly, Gabe had his demons, but so did she. Standing back and waiting for him to decide…

Like she'd stood back and let Jonathan decide for years.

Pushing would get her nowhere. Do damage. Crush a bud that'd had no chance to unfurl.

The problem was that her bud had unfurled and was wide open. She wanted this man in her arms. In her heart.

In her bed?

He'd just said no.

He'd said no to her pipes. Not to bed.

They both knew it was more.

'I can manage without a bath,' she said with as much dignity as she could muster.

'I'll check them in the morning.'

'That's big of you.'

'Nikki...'

'No, that was uncalled for. I'm sorry.' She lifted her hand and ran her fingers down his jaw, a feather-touch. 'I didn't mean to snap. You're being wise for both of us, and that's good. Tomorrow you can call the plumber. Not Joe but not you. You can come to my bathroom when you're ready but not before.'

There was still doubt. She saw it in his eyes.

He wanted her—she could see it, she could feel it, she could almost touch it. But he was...afraid?

'You're not like your father,' she said as evenly as she could. 'But I'm not Lisbette, either.'

'I know that.'

'You don't,' she said. 'Otherwise you'd check my pipes for me, right here, right now. Trust me, Gabe.'

'I do.'

'No, you don't. And whether you can learn... You can't open yourself a little and protect the rest. That's what Jonathan did. That's what I'm used to and I've moved on. I think... I think I love you, Gabe, but I'm not going to love a man who spends his life protecting his boundaries.'

She stepped back. Hoping he'd stop her.

He didn't and she felt sick.

Feeling bad was dumb. She should give him space.

She had to give him space.

Like she'd given space to Jonathan?

'Goodnight, Gabe,' she said as firmly as she could. 'Thank you for a wonderful dinner. Horse and I loved it. See you... see you tomorrow. Come on, Horse, bed.'

***

Why hadn't he taken the next logical step? No, the next instinctive step. The step every part of him except one tiny last shred of pathetic armour was screaming at him to take.

He was every kind of fool.

He'd wanted to pick her up and take her to his bed. As simple as that.

She'd have come. She'd yielded, every sweet part of her pressed against him, wanting him as much as he wanted her. But that scrap of residual armour was screaming that it was way too fast.

He was a loner. A man didn't give away a lifestyle in a heartbeat.

He headed out to the edge of the garden, staring into the dark where the sea was starting to rise in the wind. He was staring into an abyss.

He remembered how he'd felt when his mother died. When he'd realised why Lisbette had married him. When Jem had ceased breathing.

How many times could a man expose himself to that sort of pain?

He wouldn't be exposing himself. This was Nikki he was wanting. Nikki he was falling in love with?

He'd been a loner for most of his life. Why stop now?

Because of Nikki.

But to let that sort of hurt in…

He could be sensible. One step at a time, he told himself. Take it as it comes, don't rush it, leave it so you can back out any time you want.

He had backed out. He'd refused to enter her house, to check her pipes, to do something so simple.

But he knew if he'd walked into her side of the house he'd have stayed there.

In her crazy bed?

A woman like Nikki needed a king-sized bed.

He needed a woman like Nikki.

Not tonight.

Yes, tonight.

No.

She'd walked away and closed her door. She was giving him space and he appreciated it.

He didn't. A man was a fool.

She was probably already running the bath. The thought of her…

He closed his eyes. He was falling…

Step away from the edge.

Tomorrow, he thought. Tomorrow.

How could he learn to trust—to shed that last vestige of protection from pain and gather her against his heart?

If he was wrong… If he hurt her… If they self destructed as his parents had…

It was one step forward and he didn't have the courage to take it.

'I don't want another Jonathan,' she told Horse, sinking onto the hall floor to give him a hug. 'Oh, but it's hard. How to make him trust me?'

If he didn't trust her there was nothing she could do.

Trust. It was throwing your heart into the ring. He worried that he was like his father. She'd told him he wasn't. She was sure of it.

Because she trusted him.

Maybe she was a fool. Maybe she was heading down the Jonathan path all over again.

Her whole body felt as if it was sensitised, every nerve tingling.

She knew what she wanted.

Not happening.

What to do?

She glared at the wall dividing her place from his. He was so close—and so far.

'Toerag,' she muttered but she didn't believe it.

But why couldn't he trust her? It hurt.

She felt exposed and vulnerable and a tiny bit stupid.

Okay, a lot stupid.

What to do? Go calmly to bed? Look forward to a nice polite good morning in the porch tomorrow?

Great.

She wanted, quite suddenly, to throw something. Hard.

How immature was that?

'Forget the pipes,' she told Horse. 'I'm having a bath. It's the only thing I can think of. A nice hot soak and see if I can get my body to behave.'

And her mind.

Bath. Instead of Gabe.

What a substitute.

'No matter,' she told Horse and climbed resolutely to her feet and marched into the bathroom.

Don't think of Gabe.

The bath ran beautifully, despite the gurgle. See, who needed a man?

And then…it didn't run beautifully at all.

* * *

He walked slowly back to the house, hands thrust in his pockets, deep in his thoughts. Glanced up at the house...

Nikki burst out of her door with Horse behind her and headed across the porch to his door. She thumped on his door as if she wanted to break it down.

She was wet to the skin. Soaking.

She was wearing a dripping bathrobe. She was carrying her purse.

She was carrying her car keys.

Horse was wet as well.

'What the...? What's happened?'

She swivelled and faced the darkness, trying to see him. Her glare made him take a step back.

'Ask Joe,' she snapped as she focused. *Snapped?* Maybe that was the wrong word. Yelled might be a better description. 'Don't you ever come onto my side of the house,' she mimicked. 'Because I might jump you. Instead, you send Joe and he comes and thumps my pipes with his spanner. Sooo useful. Not!'

'Nikki...'

But she'd barely got started. 'I ran a bath,' she said, spitting fire. 'It ran beautifully, even if it did make weird noises. So I hopped in and tried to relax even though I was smouldering. Smouldering, Gabe, and why would I be smouldering? Because someone round here doesn't trust me enough to check my pipes. And the water wasn't hot enough so I wiggled the tap with my big toe and suddenly the whole wall burst. I'm guessing the pipe behind the wall disintegrated.'

'Uh-oh,' he said. He couldn't think of anything more... wise.

'Uh-oh is right,' she snapped and he decided saying anything at all had been stupid. Really stupid. 'Or maybe you can think of something worse to say. I surely can. Because there's water shooting out all over the bathroom, but that's not all. The bath backs onto my bedroom and that wall burst, too. So my bed's soaked. And my wardrobe, and my dresser. Everything. So I've rung Aggie and I'm going there. You'll have to care for Horse tonight. Aggie's cat doesn't like him. Take his keep out of the amount I intend to sue you for. So it's over to you, landlord. Walk over my threshold and do something about it or phone Joe. Tell him to bring a bigger spanner, and my nine weeks' notice starts now.'

'Nikki, come in and we'll dry you,' he said, struggling not to laugh. She was a flaming virago, soaked to the skin.

But she wasn't seeing the humour.

'You'll dry me?' she demanded, barely getting the words out. 'What, with towels? Close? How do you know I won't jump you? You don't even trust me enough to check my pipes. What would happen with a naked woman and a towel? Get out of my way, Gabe Carver. I'm going to Aggie's. All by myself.'

He needed to gather her up, carry her soggy person into his side of the house, take charge. But he was…gobsmacked.

She stalked across the yard and flung the gate open, all flaming temper and outraged beauty. He was stunned to immobility.

By his side, Horse whimpered and Gabe agreed. He needed to fight the desire to laugh. He needed to…

But she was already in her car, moving fast.

Maybe she'd sensed the laughter.

'Nikki…' he yelled but it was too late.

Her car wheels spun on the gravel. She turned out of the gate and disappeared into the night.

And Horse lunged after her.

'Horse!'

He was too late there as well.

Nikki was gone and Horse had followed.

CHAPTER TEN

ANYONE BUT AGGIE might have been surprised. Aggie, however, had a husband who'd fished and her sons still did. Wet didn't shock her, and when she opened the door to a dripping, seething Nikki she merely stepped aside and said, 'Bathroom's that-a-way—use the yellow towel. Yell at Gabe in the morning—get dry first.'

'How did you know it was Gabe's fault?'

'Has to be someone's,' Aggie said. 'You're looking hopping-mad. Gabe's closest. Male. Why look further? You want pyjamas, or something to sit up in and seethe a while longer?' Then the phone rang and Nikki was left to dry herself while Aggie went to answer it.

A minute later Aggie was back and an armload of clothes was handed round the bathroom door. Oversized trousers, a fisherman's sweater, thick socks, boots.

And Aggie's voice had changed. 'They're too big, but it don't matter. Get dressed fast.'

'Why?'

'Word is Horse chased after you. The road to Gabe's place hits the cove at the bottom of the hill, then rounds the bend.

Horse didn't reach there before you disappeared so he must've figured you went the way of the last scumbag who owned him. He's headed out to sea. Phil Hamer noticed your car turn into here. You know you can't do anything round here without being noticed—he was on his way home from stocking the supermarket and wondered about me getting visitors late at night. Then he met Gabe further on, heading for the cove. He stopped to help but there was nothing he could do. Horse's already out past the breakers. Gabe's headed for the harbour to get the boat. Phil figured you'd want to know. If you head straight for the jetty at the entrance you might catch him. Otherwise, he'll be heading out alone. Filthy weather—he'll need all the help he can get. You're wasting time, girl. I'd come with you but I'd only hold you back. Go.'

He'd run, but Horse was on a mission and wasn't to be stopped. By the time Gabe reached the cove Horse was already in the surf.

He yelled, desperate. 'Horse!' No response. Of course not. Horse wanted Nikki.

'She's in the car, not out to sea,' he yelled and that was dumb as well because Horse wasn't listening. He'd seen Nikki disappear and he knew where people who disappeared went. He gave one long, low, despairing howl and swam for the horizon.

Gabe swore and swore again. Headed into the surf after him. Hoping he'd be washed in.

Maybe he would. Maybe he'd have the sense to realise he couldn't swim against the current—but the undertow was fierce. Gabe stood chest-deep in water, fighting the undertow, hoping the dog would turn.

Nothing.

The tide was going out. It'd be impossible to fight.

There was no sense trying to swim after him. Gabe knew he didn't have the strength to fight that sea.

He stood thigh-deep as the waves battered him, as he forced himself to think.

Outgoing tide. Northbound current. Big sea.

What hope of finding him?

Zero.

He felt sick to the stomach.

He was vaguely aware of Phil Hamer, the fussy little supermarket manager, uttering sounds of distress at the water's edge. Trying to give comfort.

There was no comfort to be had if he lost Horse.

He waited for as long as he dared, hoping against hope Horse could fight his way back. But even if he'd wanted to return... Once he was out the back of the surf the current would take him further.

He'd take the boat out. Try to find him.

He was a stray.

He was Nikki's dog.

He was Horse. He had to try.

But on a night like this... To take the boat out alone... It would be worse than useless.

He couldn't ask for help. To ask his crew to put to sea in the face of an oncoming storm for a stray dog...

'What can I do?' Phil bleated, immeasurably distressed.

'Nothing, mate,' he said bleakly. 'I'll head out and do what I can, but I need a miracle.'

She left the lights on in her car, shining straight out over the entrance. She stood out on the jetty at the harbour entrance, putting herself deliberately in the path of her car light, so whoever was in a boat heading out to sea could see her.

So Gabe could see her.

The wind was fierce and there was no moon. Water was washing up over the ancient timbers.

For an awful moment she thought she'd missed him. She stood in the rising wind on the tiny jetty and felt sick.

But then the *Lady Nell* emerged from the darkness and she started yelling. 'Gabe! Gabe!'

He couldn't miss her. Hysterical woman screaming at harbour mouth. Waving as if she were drowning.

He didn't veer in.

'Gabe!' She put everything she possessed into that scream and the boat turned. Came alongside.

'It's rough. You can't...' he yelled but he'd come close enough for her to jump and she jumped.

Possibly a distance an Olympian would be proud of.

She staggered, grabbed the handrail, lurched sideways.

But Gabe had her before she could fall, grabbing her, hauling her roughly against him and half dragging her back into the wheelhouse.

'What the...? You could have been killed. Of all the stupid...'

'Why didn't you come closer?'

'You weren't meant to jump. You weren't meant to be here. There's a storm coming.'

'You were going out without me? *To find my dog?*' Hysterical didn't cut it. She was screaming.

'I lost him.'

'He's my dog.'

'It's dangerous.'

'He's my dog!' She couldn't get any louder if she tried.

But with that last yell… The adrenalin of dressing, driving way too fast to reach the entrance, thinking she'd missed him, jumping. Knowing she'd lost Horse… Something gave.

She folded and he caught her and held her hard against him.

She let herself crumple against him, taking mute comfort in the size of him, the strength. The boat was heading out to sea. He wasn't taking her back.

'I can't let you risk…' he muttered.

She thought about that. Got incensed. Anger helped. She hauled back and thumped him hard on the chest. Started yelling again. 'What gives you the right to say who risks?'

'I lost…'

'You didn't. Horse lost himself. He's a crazy mutt who hasn't figured out for himself where his heart is. It's my fault. I shouldn't have left him. I shouldn't have lost my temper.' She thumped him again and it was like striking oak. 'So don't you dare say we can't share. We're finding him together.'

He folded her against him again, her thumps totally useless.

'We won't find him,' he said. Facing facts. Bleak as death.

'We can try. But we do this together.'

'It'd be better if you let me do it alone.'

'Better for who? Are you out of your mind? We love him to bits. We both love him and we both do this. Both or no one.'

Aggie watched Nikki leave and turned to the phone. No one could expect an old lady to calmly go back to bed when Horse was at risk.

Banksia Bay was a tight-knit community. Gabe employed half the fishing fleet, and their families and friends encompassed the town.

The dog community was big, too.

All she had to do was rally the troops.

She rang Henrietta first. 'Ring round, let people know. Skippers of the other boats. Crews.' She hung up as she heard Hen yelling at her son to get off the Internet, to come and help.

Then she rang Raff. The local cop and Gabe were mates. She had Raff onside in a heartbeat.

'I'll ring Whale Cove,' Raff said curtly. 'Harry at North Coast Flight Aid owes me a favour or six. If the chopper's free…'

But… 'It's a filthy night. Raff, this is for a dog,' Aggie faltered, thinking she should just remind him.

'This is for *Gabe's* dog,' Raff said. 'This town's been wanting to help Gabe for years and he doesn't let 'em close. You think we'll miss a chance now?'

'It's Nikki's dog.'

'Same thing,' Raff said curtly. 'He mightn't think so but the rest of us do.'

He knew the currents. Gabe knew the vague direction where Horse might be swept, but in the darkness in a storm-tossed sea…

The thing was hopeless.

He had to try.

He had, he thought, two hours maximum before the storm closed in and he had to take Nikki home. He hated that she was out here. He hated having to share this risk.

To risk Nikki…

She was out on the deck, watching desperately as his floodlights lit the sea.

His heart twisted in pain for her. And for him.

Horse was out here somewhere because he thought Nikki had headed to the sea. Three weeks of Nikki, and Horse knew where his heart lay.

Whereas he...

Tonight he'd backed off. He'd sent her to her side of the house alone. Then, when she'd appeared at her door, a drowned rat, a flaming virago, he'd stood like a great idiot while she yelled and handed over her dog and headed away.

Away from him.

He wanted to hold her, right now, desperately, but he had to stay in the wheelhouse and she had to search.

They needed more eyes.

Call for help?

Sure. Call the town, say, *Come out guys, risk the storm sweeping in early, to save a dog.*

This was his pain.

No. It was Nikki's pain. Shared.

This was what he didn't want to happen. This awfulness. Grief was to be faced alone. To make others share it was appalling. Worse than suffering it yourself.

He watched Nikki's rigid frame at the rail and he felt ill.

Her eyes didn't leave the sea. He was making parallel runs from behind the breakers to out where Horse could conceivably be swept.

So much sea.

Hopeless.

But then...

A helicopter came, sweeping in fast and low from the south. Searchlights flooded the ocean.

The radio. Raff...

'Gabe, that's Harry up there. Signal him that he's focused

on the right boat. He'll pick up your frequency from this conversation.'

Harry—North Coast Flight Aid. What the...?

He signalled upward and Harry banked the chopper, heading into the cliff. Starting parallel runs of his own.

There'd be a crew in the chopper. More eyes.

'There's more boats coming out,' Nikki yelled, her voice cracking, and Gabe turned to glance at the harbour entrance.

This wasn't one or two boats. It was a flotilla, heading out into the storm.

What did they think they were doing? It was only just safe now. In another hour or two...

'We're thinking we have a two-hour window,' Raff yelled through the radio. 'Keith's back at base working out currents, search paths. He's allocating runs. You're furthest out, you do the north most run. Straight from where you are now into the back of the breakers and back again. You've only got one pair of eyes, so Nikki does the north lookout. *Mary Lou*'s got you covered; Tom has four aboard so he'll search your south side and his north, then the next boat takes over where his limit is. The chopper goes closer to the reef. Any questions?'

'I can't ask...'

'Who said anything about asking?' Raff snapped. 'Let's find this dog and get home.'

They were one of a pack.

Searchlights were playing over the water. Boats were everywhere—the flotilla was making parallel runs, heading into the cliffs, as close as they dared, then along, then out to the maximum distance the current could take a dog.

The helicopter was above, sweeping as well, so the whole

surface of the sea was lit. They needed the moon, but with the approaching storm they had nothing.

They needed luck.

Nikki hadn't moved since they'd left the harbour. She'd hardly registered the approaching armada. She watched and watched.

Maybe she prayed as well. Gabe hadn't prayed since he was a kid. He prayed now.

One dog in a huge sea.

He might well already be drowned. He'd been near death three weeks ago. Three weeks wasn't enough to get his strength back.

He watched the sea and in between he watched Nikki.

What had he been thinking?

He'd tried to keep his distance.

He glanced around at the flotilla who'd set out in filthy weather to save one dog.

No one was keeping their distance this night.

And with that knowledge...something was breaking within him. The armour he'd built with such care...

He'd told himself he needed no one. He depended on no one.

Not true. It had been an illusion. It had taken one crazy dog and one loving woman to make him see the truth.

Plus an army of Banksia Bay dog-searchers.

Where was his illusion now? Gabe Carver, who walked alone, had ceased to exist.

For Gabe Carver was breaking his heart for a dog, breaking his heart for a woman, and there wasn't a thing he could do about it.

And the town, his crew, his friends... They were breaking their hearts for him.

A tiny flotilla in an approaching storm, searching the sea for one stray dog.

Where was the use of armour here? He tossed it aside and he knew it was gone for ever.

Horse.

Nikki.

The people surrounding him.

His heart was wide open.

Please...

There was no fast find here.

Back and forth. Back and forth.

Twelve-thirty. One.

The wind was rising, the sea steadily growing. Soon the helicopter would have to call it quits, and also the smaller boats.

Back and forth...

The chopper was making parallel runs ahead of the fleet, moving further out, making sure of the boundaries.

Slow, methodical sweeps.

Then, suddenly, as one of the smallest boats notified Gabe reluctantly that it was time to turn back, the helicopter banked and turned and hovered.

The down-draught flattened the sea close to the cliff.

The boats hadn't gone so far in. It was too close to the cliffs, too shallow, dangerous.

The chopper was hovering over a reef—Satan's Lookout. A shard of granite reached from the sea, further out than the bulk of the reef. A trap for unwary shipping.

The radio crackled to life. Harry from the chopper, yelling into his headset. 'He's down there. We can see him. He's clinging to the lee side of the reef. If it was a person we'd drop a harness but there's no way we can pick up a dog of that size. I'm not sure even you guys can get him off there.'

The good news? Horse was alive.

But Horse didn't do things in halves, Gabe thought. Swimming with sharks. Satan's Lookout. How many lives did one dog have?

Nikki was beside him, clinging. She must have seen his face change as he listened to Harry. 'What's happening?' she asked and if her face lost any more colour she'd disappear entirely. She was probably seasick, Gabe thought, and she hugged her stomach and he knew he was right.

What to do? Rough seas and shallow water. There was no way they could take the big boats close. They'd have to take a lifeboat.

But to steer close to the rock and lift Horse... They'd need two people to pull it off, Gabe thought, feeling sick himself. Usually he had Frank and Hattie as crew, both experienced. Tonight he had Nikki.

Nikki would never be competent enough to cope in the life-raft. Could he leave her at the wheel? Could he do it on his own?

No.

But to ask it of others...

The radio crackled into life again. 'Boss?' It was Bert, skipper of the *Mariette*. 'We're all lowering lifeboats. Mick and Mike'll go in ours. Sara and Paula are doing the same from *Bertha*, and Tom and Angie are coming off *Mary Lou*. That's three boats to look after each other. *Mary Lou*'s lifeboat's the most solid, so Angie and Tom'll try and get him off. There's backup to pick up the pieces if needed, and we'll use harnesses and link to each other. This dog doesn't bite, does he?'

'No, but...' His crew had obviously talked on another frequency. This was being taken out of his hands. What he couldn't ask was being offered.

'So he's a pussycat?' Bert demanded.

'A great hulking, sodden pussycat.' But his mind was racing. For others to risk their lives to save his dog... Nikki's dog... 'But I can't ask...'

'You're not asking, we're telling,' Bert said and there was even a note of humour in his voice. 'Takes a bit of getting used to, don't it? Accepting help. You just keep your nose into the wind and keep our Nikki from jumping over the side. We'll get her dog back to her in a trice. Or maybe in more than a trice but we'll get him back. Right, guys.' He was linked to the communal radio—obviously they'd changed frequency to hatch their plan but they were back on common frequency now. 'Let's go fish ourselves a dog.'

So Gabe was forced to wait, to stay idle, to depend on others, while men and women put themselves in danger over a dog he'd been stupid enough to let go.

He should have crew with him so he could do this himself. He should at least help. But there was no way he could ask Nikki, a seasick landlubber, to take over the *Lady Nell*. She had no skills.

But she did have skills, he conceded as he watched the lifeboats be launched. Different skills.

Changing direction and following her dream? Turning her back on her past?

Giving her heart?

She'd gone back to the rail. She was sick and cold and frightened.

He wanted to hold her.

He had to stay at the wheel. This sea was rough and getting rougher. It took experience and skill to keep the *Lady Nell* steady.

He had to depend on others.

He needed others.

He needed Nikki.

His armour was gone. He was no longer bothering to cling to remnants, no longer thinking about what he still needed to protect.

There was nothing to protect. What he needed was outside the armour.

Nikki. Horse. And these people—his crew, his town.

He felt terrified. Totally exposed. If one of those boats capsized...

They didn't.

There were three small boats with three magnificent seamen in charge. The chopper stayed overhead, flattening the water, lighting the scene like day. They all wore lifelines. If someone fell in, Harry would have someone down with a harness in seconds.

The biggest fear was right at the rock.

Horse was clinging to the lee side—sensible dog. But still, for a boat to get in there...

Angie was in the bow of the biggest lifeboat. Like him, Angie was born of a fisher-family. She was older and more experienced than he was, but she had three teenagers at home. What was she thinking?

She was going whether he permitted it or not. He was no longer in charge.

The focus of the community was saving a dog.

Please... It was a muddle of a prayer.

He should be where Angie was.

He had to stay at the wheel. He had to depend on others.

They were at the rock, Angie and Tom. Angie was wearing a headset. Harry was watching the sea from above, giving her instructions. Watching the sea from on high.

Nikki was clinging to the rail, watching every move as if she could guide them by sight.

He wanted to hold Nikki.

His job was to hold the wheel and wait. And to depend on others.

And feel his foundations shift under him. He'd never felt such fear.

Depending on others.

They were twenty feet out from where Horse clung now. They were watching, waiting, waiting.

A lull. *Go.*

Did he yell it? His ears rang, maybe every skipper had yelled it in unison over the radio.

They were already there, surging into the rock. Angie stood to reach...

Horse had to let go.

'Let go of the bloody rock.' It was Angie, yelling into the radio headset like she boomed to the other boats over the water. It was a voice to wake the dead, to shock the unshockable, to make Horse release his grip.

And Angie had Horse around the midriff, dragging him back.

They were in the boat but they were still in danger. The next wave...

Tom had the tiller, the boat swung, hit the wave head on, rode through it—and they were safe.

The lifeboat headed for the *Lady Nell* rather than back to the *Mary Lou*. They figured Horse needed Nikki.

Still Gabe couldn't help. It nearly killed him, but he had to hold the *Lady Nell* steady so there was a modicum of shelter on the side they were boarding.

They made two runs before they got a patch of clear water. Angie heaved the big dog up as Nikki reached down.

Then Horse, almost flaccid until now, looked up and saw Nikki. His great paws found purchase on the side and Angie no longer had to heave. Horse launched himself at Nikki as if it were she who'd been drowning. Nikki and Horse subsided onto the deck, one sodden tangle of woman and dog. Together.

Tom and Angie hauled themselves up onto the *Lady Nell* as well. Tom tied the lifeboat behind. They'd try and tow it back to harbour but even if they had to let it go it was safer than risking the run back to the *Mary Lou*; another boarding.

The chopper was still overhead. The rest of the boats surrounded them.

The chopper's floodlights lit the scene—woman and dog reunited.

A happy ending.

No, Gabe thought, looking out at the sea of people surrounding him. The sea of people who cared. It was a happy beginning.

These were his people. He belonged.

He and Nikki and Horse…they'd come home.

'Tom,' he called, because he was the head of this fleet and a man had to take a stand some time.

'Yeah?' Tom was watching Nikki hugging Horse, grinning and grinning.

'Come and take this wheel,' Gabe growled. 'There's a woman and a dog I need to hug.'

'I didn't think you did hugging,' Tom said, grinning even more, and Gabe managed a grin back.

'I do now.'

CHAPTER ELEVEN

THE PROBLEM WITH depending on others was sharing. Every single person wanted a piece of happiness.

The boats streamed into the harbour and it seemed half the town was there to greet them—the half who hadn't been out on boats.

Women were fussing over Nikki, hugging her, saying, *Oh, it's a sign that the dog's been saved—you're meant to stay here, dear.*

Henrietta and her troop of dog-lovers were fussing over Horse. Drying him, warming him, giving him warmed feed to settle his stomach. Maybe Nikki needed some of that.

Aggie was there, beaming and beaming.

And the men were fussing over Gabe. Okay, not exactly fussing—Banksia Bay's fishermen didn't do that. They gripped his hand, one after the other, grinning, exultant at their shared triumph. 'Pleasure, mate,' they said almost universally as he tried to thank them, and he knew it was.

This *was* a shared triumph. Sharing. It was a concept he needed to embrace.

But... How soon could he get Nikki alone?

'You want us to whisk you back to Whale Cove?' Harry asked. He'd set the chopper down in the unloading dock and come to share the happy ending. He and his crew were delighted. Without the chopper, they'd never have succeeded.

Without any of these people...

'I hear there's a great honeymoon suite in the Sun Spa resort at Whale Cove,' Harry said reflectively. 'We could whisk you there right now. I'm not sure if they take dogs, though.'

Maybe he'd been looking at Nikki a bit too long, Gabe thought. Maybe what he needed was plain for all to see, for Harry gripped his shoulder and grinned. 'Another one bites the dust. I thought you were a confirmed bachelor, like me. Oh, well, can't win them all. Good luck, mate, welcome to the other side.'

He left, still chuckling.

Others were going, too. Reluctantly. It was after two in the morning.

'You want me to take Horse back to my place and take care of him for the night?' Henrietta asked, and Nikki, a whole six inches from Horse, tugged him closer.

'No. Thank you but...no.'

'Just thought,' Hen said airily. 'Just saying. If you guys need space...'

'We don't need space,' Gabe said and Nikki glanced up at him and he thought...uh-oh.

A man needed to tread warily. He was, after all, the guy who'd refused to fix her pipes—the guy who'd lost her dog.

'I'm hoping we don't need space,' he said.

'You still want to stay the night at my place?' Aggie asked Nikki, and Nikki looked at him—really looked at him. And something changed in her eyes. Something...

'Thank you,' she said. 'But no. Thank you all. You've been absolutely wonderful, but Horse and I need to go home.'

He took her home.

Her side of the house was still sodden. Water was running down her walls. It had been running since they'd left.

There'd be one nightmare of a mess to clear up later, but now...they turned off the water to Nikki's side of the house and let it be.

Who needed two sides to a house anyway?

Nikki was shivering. She hadn't stopped shivering. He whisked her into the bathroom. His bathroom. Ran the bath, good and hot, propelled her in.

'H... Horse...' she muttered.

'I'll take care of Horse,' he said, and it nearly killed him to leave her but he needed to warm the house.

He stoked up the fire. Made it blaze. Dried Horse with warm towels and more warm towels.

Horse looked devotedly up at him from the fireside. Like: *I'm sorry I caused you trouble but I needed Nikki.*

He and Horse both.

They sat by the fire. Waited.

Nikki came out, wrapped in a towel.

He stood and she walked straight into his arms. He held her close and he knew... This was his woman, his heart, his life.

'I need you,' she whispered and it was an echo of his own heart.

'I've gone about this all the wrong way,' he said into her hair.

'What do you mean?' Their breathing was synchronised. Their heartbeats were synchronised.

'I should have welcomed you with pleasure, cut down

the dividing fence, shared Horse, helped with the barbecue, loaned you my mother's books, been proud of you.'

'Nah,' she said. 'I probably would have thought you were wet.' She hesitated. 'Come to think of it, you are wet. I'm warm and dry. You need dry clothes.' But she was still against his heart.

'Not yet. I'm still apologising.'

'There's time to make amends,' she said. 'You can hug me with pleasure, cut down the dividing fence, share Horse, help with any future barbecues—and I think we should have one soon to thank everyone for tonight—lend me your mother's books, be proud of me. Do you think my apartment's underwater?'

'What's a little water? Nikki, I love you.'

She stilled.

She didn't speak. She just…melted.

He was holding her tight, feeling the warmth of her. Accepting the reality that he was holding the woman of his dreams, right here in his arms.

'I don't suppose you'd consider marriage,' he said and he hadn't known he intended to say it; it was just there.

It shocked them both. She almost dropped the towel. She grabbed it just in time. Made a recovery. Sort of. Took a step back.

'Marriage,' she whispered.

'Just a thought.' He tried to figure how to say all the things that were in his heart and couldn't. Made a bad joke instead. 'It'd make Horse legitimate. You'd be Mum and I'd be Dad.'

She choked. 'You'd marry me—for a dog?'

'I'd marry you for you.'

'You're grumpy.' She was eyeing him with caution now, as if he had the poker.

'Only when hit on the head. I'll try not to be grumpy for anything less.'

'I still want to learn stone walling.'

'I love that you still want to learn stone walling.'

'You go to sea thirteen nights out of fourteen.' She took a deep breath. 'I've learned tonight… I do get seasick.'

'I won't go to sea in rough weather.'

'Promise?'

'Not very rough.'

'Thirteen nights out of fourteen?'

'I'm the fleet owner. I can decide. How about only when I must? And if you were home in my bed…there'd hardly be a must.'

'Of course there would. First hint of a barracuda and out you'd go.'

'Not if you were in my bed.'

'You have a bed on the boat.'

'So I do. But…'

'Then I guess I could take pills and come with you,' she ventured. 'If you'll dig my trenches.'

'Is this business we're talking?'

'I like things to be clear.'

'You want me to find pen and paper and we'll sign stuff before I kiss you?'

'You want to kiss me?'

'More than anything on earth.'

She sighed, a long, drawn-out sigh where things seemed to be let go.

'If I kissed you back I might drop my towel,' she said, smiling and smiling.

'You want to risk it?'

'Horse would be shocked.'

'I believe,' he said softly, in a low, husky growl because that seemed all he was capable of right now, 'I believe our Horse is asleep. Dead to the world.'

'Don't say dead.'

'Alive,' he said, smiling down at her. Smiling and smiling. 'Like I am. I feel more alive right here, right now, than I've ever been in my life. You want to risk the odd towel?'

'I'd risk more than that,' she said, stepping forward, stepping into his arms. 'I'd risk my heart. Or wait…maybe I can't. Maybe my heart's no longer mine to risk.'

It took a while to plan a wedding, mostly because the tiny church on the headland on the far side of Banksia Bay was surrounded by a crumbling stone wall. No one was marrying in that church, Aggie decreed, until the wall was mended, so instead of planning wedding dress, bridesmaids, flowers, Nikki sat on the headland overlooking the sea and fitted stones into a wall that would last for another hundred years.

She loved it—and there was no problem that her attention was focused on the wall, for she had others to do the 'tizzy bits' for her wedding. Aggie and Henrietta and Angie and Hattie and Hilda and Maudie… So many friends.

Her day would be splendid, they decreed, and so it was.

In the end the church was too small. In the end the day was perfect so Gabe stood under frangipani, with the sea as his backdrop, while all the town clustered close by to wait for his bride.

Nikki's parents were here, astounded, bemused, and in the end even confusedly proud that their daughter knew so definitely where she was going, what she was doing.

'She can charge a lot more than she's doing,' her father decreed of his daughter. 'With a skill like this…'

'I can't believe he didn't go to university,' her mother said of Gabe, but they were here, they were smiling, and they'd accepted her new life.

They had no choice, for this *was* Nikki's life. This place. Banksia Bay. Gabe.

A bagpipe sounded, a blast of triumph, and Aggie squeaked in triumph herself. This was her wedding gift, her son the bagpiper, whether Nikki willed it or not.

Nikki did will it. She'd grinned when Aggie had told them. 'Bagpipes,' Gabe had said faintly.

She'd tucked her arm into his and said, 'I won't have it any other way.'

Nikki. His bride.

The bagpipes meant she was here.

Horse was lying beside him, groomed, gleaming, almost handsome. The big dog understood it now, that Gabe and Nikki were one—equals. He'd stay with Gabe or he'd stay with Nikki, but he was only truly content when they were together.

Which was great because that was exactly where Gabe and Nikki intended to be.

Bagpipes. Nikki.

Horse lumbered to his feet and Gabe held his collar. Someone had put a garland of frangipani round Horse's neck. How corny was that?

He loved it.

Then Raff was elbowing him aside, taking Horse's collar firmly in his.

'Priorities, mate,' he said. 'Bride first, dog second.'

He didn't need to be told, for Nikki was here, and he only had eyes for Nikki.

His bride.

Her gown was gorgeous, white silk with an exquisitely beaded bodice and a deceptively simple skirt that draped and flared as if she were floating. She looked as if she was tied to her father's arm to stop her rising. Her hair was beautiful. She'd never again tried to straighten it. Angie had tucked frangipani into her curls.

But Gabe wasn't looking at her hair. He wasn't looking at her gown. He looked only at Nikki. Her smile. Her lovely, lovely smile as she met his gaze, at the shared laughter that was always there. Laughter and love.

He was truly loved.

There was momentary drama. Horse tugged away from Raff and Raff was dumb enough to let him go. But Horse didn't go far. He trod sedately down the carpet they'd laid for the bridal approach, and he greeted his mistress with quiet dignity. Then he turned and walked calmly back to Gabe, preceding the bride.

He glanced around at the congregation as if to say, *See, I know what a real dog should do.* Then he sat beside Gabe to watch.

And watch he did, as his Nikki married her Gabe.

As his mistress found her home.

As life truly began for them all.

* * * * *

Mardie And The City Surgeon

Marion Lennox is a country girl, born on an Australian dairy farm. She moved on—mostly because the cows just weren't interested in her stories! Married to a "very special doctor," Marion writes for the Harlequin® Medical™ Romance and Harlequin® Romance lines. (She used a different name for each category for a while—readers looking for her past romance titles should search for author Trisha David, as well). She's now had more than seventy-five romance novels accepted for publication.

In her non-writing life, Marion cares for kids, cats, dogs, chooks and goldfish. She travels, she fights her rampant garden (she's losing) and her house dust (she's lost). Having spun in circles for the first part of her life, she's now stepped back from her "other" career, which was teaching statistics at her local university. Finally she's reprioritized her life, figured what's important and discovered the joys of deep baths, romance and chocolate.

Preferably all at the same time!

Books by Marion Lennox

CHRISTMAS WITH HER BOSS
MISTY AND THE SINGLE DAD*
ABBY AND THE BACHELOR COP*
NIKKI AND THE LONE WOLF*

*Banksia Bay

Other titles by this author available in ebook format

To John and Joy, for giving life to my books,
as well as saving calves at midnight.

CHAPTER ONE

It was a dark and stormy night. Lightning flashed. An eerie howl echoed mournfully through the big old house.

The lights went out.

She *had* to stop watching Gothic horror movies, Mardie Rainey decided, as she told Bounce to cut it out with the howling and groped to the sideboard for candles. She especially had to stop watching horror movies on nights when a storm was threatening to crash through her roof.

Bounce, her twelve-month-old border collie, was terrified. Mardie was more irritated than spooked. The vampire had been sinking his fangs when the power went off. Now she'd never learn what happened to the fluff-for-brains heroine who would have been a lot more interesting with fang marks.

What a night. The wind was hitting the chimney with such force it was cutting off the draw, causing smoke to belch into the room. She was down to a few candles and a flashlight.

There was a leak in the corner of the room. She'd put a bucket underneath. Without the sound of the television, the steady plinking was likely to drive her crazy.

She should go to bed.

A crash, outside. A big one.

Bounce stared at the darkened window and whimpered. The hairs on the back of his neck stood up.

'It'll be one of the gums in the driveway,' she told him, feeling sad. She loved those trees. 'That's for tomorrow and the chainsaw.'

There wasn't a lot she could do about it now.

Bounce was still whimpering.

She took his collar and headed for the bedroom. 'It's nothing to worry about,' she told him. 'We don't have trees close enough to hurt the house. Lightning and thunder are all flashy show, and I warned you about watching vampires.'

Bounce whimpered again and pressed closer. So much for guard dogs.

Normally he slept in the kitchen. Not tonight.

It really was a scary night.

Maybe she did need vampire protection, she conceded as she headed for bed. Bounce might be a wuss but the only alternative was garlic. A girl couldn't sleep with garlic.

'Bed's safe,' she told him. 'The sheep are in the bottom paddock and that's protected. The house is solid. Everything's fine. At least we're not out in the weather. I pity anyone who is.'

Blake Maddock, specialist eye surgeon, should have stayed the night in Banksia Bay, but he wanted to be back in Sydney. Or better still, he wanted to be back in Africa.

He'd wanted to leave Banksia Bay the minute he'd discovered Mardie wasn't there.

What sort of stupid impulse had led him to attend his high school reunion? Wanting to see Mardie? That had been a dumb, sentimental impulse, nothing more. As for the rest, he'd turned his back on this place fifteen years ago. Why come back now?

Nothing had changed.

Or...it had a little, he conceded as he drove cautiously through the rain-filled night. But not much. There'd been births, deaths and marriages, but the town was just as small. People talked fishing and farming. People asked where he was living now, but weren't really interested in his answer. People asked did he miss Banksia Bay.

Not so much. He'd left fifteen years ago and never looked back.

Three miles out of town was his old home—his great-aunt's house. He'd been sent here when he was seven, to forget Robbie.

Ten years ago, sorting his great-aunt's estate, he'd found a letter his father had written to her after Robbie's death.

> We don't know where else to turn. His mother never warmed to the twins, to boys. Now... They were identical, and every time she looks at him she feels ill. She's drinking too much. Her friends are shunning her. We need to get the boy away. If we can tell people he's gone to relatives in Australia so he won't be continually reminded of his brother, the pressure will ease. Can we send him to you, for however long it takes until his mother wants to see him again?

And underneath was the offer of a transfer of a truly astonishing parcel of shares of the family company.

How much had his parents wanted to get rid of him?

He knew now, how much.

So a bereft seven-year-old had been sent to the other side

of the world, to a reclusive great-aunt who'd run away herself, years before, after a failed romance. Who'd been kind according to her definition of the word, but who'd lived in the shadow of her own tragic love affair and never spoke about Robbie.

No one spoke about Robbie. No one here knew.

'Don't tell people about your brother,' his father had told him as he saw him onto a plane. 'Least said, soonest mended. I know it wasn't all your fault—your brother was equally responsible. Your mother will accept that in time. Meanwhile, get on with your life.'

His life as a kid no one wanted. His life in Banksia Bay.

It was dumb to have come tonight, he conceded. This had been his place to hide, to be hidden, and he had no need of that now.

And Mardie hadn't even attended.

Mardie had been in the year below him at school. His one true thing.

He remembered the first day he'd attended Banksia Bay School, dropped off by his silent great-aunt, feeling terrified. He remembered Mardie, marching up to him, littler than he was, all cheeky grin and freckles.

'What's your name? Did you bring lunch? I have sardine sandwiches and chocolate cake; do you want to share?'

How corny was it that he remembered exactly what she'd said, all those years ago?

It was corny and it was dumb. It was also dumb to think he might see her tonight. He hadn't thought it through.

He wasn't actually in a frame of mind where he could think anything through. He'd flown in from Africa exhausted. Dengue fever had left him flat and lethargic. It was four more weeks at least before he could return to work, he'd been told.

What work?

Bleak thoughts were all over the place. He'd stayed at his great-aunt's apartment in Sydney, the place she'd kept for shopping. He'd kept it because it was convenient, somewhere to store his scant belongings. It was the only place he could vaguely call home. Listlessly he'd checked mail that hadn't been redirected since he'd been ill, and found the invitation to the Banksia Bay reunion.

And he'd thought of Mardie. Again.

For some unknown reason, during this last illness Mardie had strayed into his thoughts, over and over.

Why? She'd have forgotten him, surely, or he'd be a distant memory, a blur. Theirs had been a childhood friendship, turning into a teenage romance. She'd be well over it. But... he wouldn't mind seeing her.

Could he drive to Banksia Bay and back in a night?

The question hung, persisted, wouldn't listen to a sensible no.

He'd decided years ago that Banksia Bay, the place where his parents had abandoned him, the place where he'd been sent to forget, was a memory he needed to move on from. But now, with his career uncertain, his focus blurred by illness, the reasons for that decision seemed less clear.

And his memory of Mardie was suddenly right back in focus.

Two hours there, four hours for dinner, two hours back. Okay, he'd be tired, but he didn't want to stay in Banksia Bay. Doable.

So he'd put on his dinner suit, driven from Sydney, sat through interminable speeches, too much back-slapping and too many questions. All on the one theme. 'Isn't it wonderful that you're a doctor—have you ever thought about coming home?'

This wasn't home. It was the place he'd been dumped after Robbie.

And of course Mardie wasn't at the dinner. He hadn't realised it was a reunion for just the one class.

He'd left as soon as he could. He should have gone straight back to Sydney.

But the thought of Mardie was still there. He'd come all this way...

Could he casually drop in at ten at night?

Um...maybe not.

The trees on the roadside were groaning under the strain of gale-force winds. The windscreen was being slapped with horizontal sleet.

Mardie's farm was right here. If it was daylight he would be able to see it.

Why did he want to see her?

She'd been a kid when he left Banksia Bay. Sixteen to his seventeen. She was probably married with six kids by now.

The impossibility of dropping in was becoming more and more apparent. On a moonlit night, maybe. If he'd rung ahead, maybe. He knew her phone number—he'd had it in his head for twenty years. As he'd left the reunion he'd thought he'd see if her lights were on and then he'd ring, and if she answered, he'd take it from there.

Only of course he'd forgotten there was no cellphone reception out here. Or maybe he'd never known. He'd left practically before cellphones were invented.

Enough. He needed to get back to the highway, put sentiment aside and focus on sense.

Focus on the road.

A blind bend. Darkness. Rain.

Mardie's house was a couple of hundred yards from the road. No lights. So that was that. Maybe she'd moved.

Of course she'd moved. Did he expect her life to have stood still?

And then...a dog, right in the middle of the road.

He hit the brakes, hard.

If it wasn't wet he might have made it, but water was sheeting over the bitumen, giving his tyres no grip.

His car skidded, planing out of control. He fought desperately, trying to turn into the skid, trying...

A tree was in front of him and he had nowhere to go.

Bounce was quivering beside the bed, flinching at each clap of thunder. Growling at the weird shapes made by lightning.

'You're starting to spook me,' Mardie told him as she snuggled under the covers. 'One more growl and you're back in the kitchen.'

The next clap of thunder sounded almost overhead and suddenly Bounce was right under the duvet.

Farmer with working dog. Total professionals. Ha! She hugged him, taking as well as giving comfort.

'We're not scared,' she told Bounce in her very best Farmer-In-Charge-Of-The-Situation voice.

Thunder. Lightning. The house seemed to tremble.

Another crash.

This one had her sitting up.

Uh-oh.

For the last crash was different. Not thunder. Not a falling tree.

It was the sound of tyres screaming for purchase, and then impact. Metal splintering.

And then?

And then it looked as if she was braving the elements, like it or not.

He wasn't hurt. Or not much. There was a trickle of blood on his forehead—the windscreen had smashed and a sliver of metal or glass must have got past the airbags. But he'd hired a Mercedes. If there was one thing these babies were good at it was protecting the occupant.

One of his headlights, weirdly, was still working. He could see what had happened. The trunk of the tree had met the front of the car square on. The whole passenger compartment seemed to have moved backward. The windscreen seemed to have shifted sideways.

The tree was about a foot from his nose.

Rain was sheeting in from the gap where the windscreen had been.

He ought to get out. Fire…

That was a thought forceful enough to stir him from his shock. He was out of the car in seconds.

A dog met him as he emerged, knee height, wet, whining, nuzzling against him as if desperate for reassurance from another living thing.

The dog. The cause of the crash.

He should kick it into the middle of next week, he thought. Instead, he found himself kneeling on the roadside, holding it, feeling shudders run through the dog's thin frame. Feeling matching shudders run through his.

They'd both come close to the edge.

He tugged the dog back a bit, worried the car might blow, but it wasn't happening, not in this rain. Any spark that might catch was drenched before it even thought about causing trouble.

The sparks weren't the only thing drenched. Thirty seconds out of the car and he was soaked.

What to do? He was kneeling beside his crashed car in the middle of nowhere, holding a dog.

He was four miles from Banksia Bay, and Banksia Bay was in the middle of nowhere. It was a tiny harbour town two hours from Sydney, set between mountains and sea. He'd already checked for phone reception. Zip.

He had a coat in the car. He had an umbrella.

It was too late for coats and umbrellas. He was never going to be wetter than he was right now.

The dog whined and leaned heavily against him. A border collie? Black and white, its long fur was matted and dripping. The dog was far too thin—he could feel ribs. It was leaning against him as if it needed his support.

He put a hand on its neck and found a plastic collar, but now wasn't the time to be thinking about identification.

'We're safe but we're risking drowning,' he said out loud, and he stared through the rain trying to see Mardie's house.

Dark.

Still, it was the closest house. It was over a mile back to his aunt's old home which, someone had told him tonight, had become a private spa retreat, but was now in the hands of the receivers. Deserted. After that... He couldn't think.

The trees around him were losing branches. He had to get out of the weather.

Did Mardie still live here?

How ironic, after coming all this way because he'd stupidly assumed she'd be at the school reunion, to end up on her doorstep like a drowned rat. Waking her from sleep.

Crazy.

His head hurt.

He had no choice.

He turned towards the house and the dog plodded beside him, just touching.

'Mardie and a husband and six kids?' he asked the dog. 'Or a stranger.' And then, despite the rain, despite the shock, he found himself grinning. 'I came all this way to find Mardie. It seems fate's decided I'm still looking.'

The phone was dead.

There was no mobile reception here ever, but she did have a landline. Not now. The lines must be down.

She was on her own.

A car crash.

This was worse than vampires. Much worse.

She hauled on her outdoor gear at lightning speed, her sou'wester with its great weatherproof hood, her waterproof over-pants and her gumboots. She grabbed her most powerful flashlight.

Bounce refused to come out from under the bedcovers.

'Watch the house, then,' she conceded, thinking she'd be better without him anyway. She'd like the comfort of his presence but if it was a disaster…

She'd need an ambulance, not a dog.

She felt more alone than she'd ever felt in her life.

'It's you or no one,' she said savagely to herself and hauled open the door.

To be met by Blake Maddock.

* * *

How could you not see someone for fifteen years and know in an instant that you were looking at the same man?

She did. She was.

At seventeen, Blake Maddock was the best-looking guy in grade school. He was tall, dark and drop-dead gorgeous. He had deep black hair and skin that seemed to tan without the sun. At seventeen he'd needed a bit of filling out, but not any more.

This was Blake Maddock all grown up.

The grown-up version of Blake Maddock was wearing a black dinner suit, black bow tie, white shirt and silver cufflinks.

His jet-black hair was dripping. His suit was sodden.

Blake.

She must be dreaming.

But it didn't pour with rain in dreams, or she didn't think it did. This wasn't an apparition. Blake Maddock was standing on her veranda.

'Mardie?' he said, and she figured he couldn't see her. She was in the hallway and of course it wasn't lit. The lightning was almost continuous now though, and whenever it forked it lit the veranda as bright as daylight. She could see him, over and over again.

Blake.

'H...hi,' she managed but she stuttered the word. She tried again but the stutter got worse.

'It is Mardie?' he said, trying to see.

'Y...yes.'

She caught herself and stepped outside. The wind practically knocked her sideways.

A black shadow moved from Blake's side to hers. It leaned against her legs as if seeking refuge.

Blake Maddock and dog. What the…?

Her mind stopped whirling. The night slid away. Blake Maddock was right in front of her—Blake, her very best of friends.

She grabbed his hands and held on, and he stared down at her and attempted a half smile. She stared up at him, incredulous. His smile twisted, self-mocking, and it was the smile she remembered. Blake…

His smile faded. He stared down at her in the weird light provided by lightning—and then he tugged her into a bear hug.

She let herself be tugged. He was soaked to the skin. He was bigger than she remembered, taller, *harder*.

She let herself be crushed against his chest. Right this minute, all she could feel was joy.

'Blake.'

It was barely a whisper. Her past had returned. Her past was dripping wet on her veranda.

Her past was hugging her as if he'd missed her as much as she'd missed him.

Another crash of thunder, deeper, longer. This was no night for standing in the sleet, hugging. He put her at arm's length, but still he held her, hands gripping hers. As if holding on to reality.

'I've crashed my car,' he said and she thought…she thought…

She didn't think anything. She was too flabbergasted.

'Where…? Why…?'

'I've come from the school reunion.'

The school reunion. Things settled. Just a little.

She'd heard what was happening—a reunion for the class above hers from fifteen years ago. Tony Hamm, the local butcher, had been organising it. Her friend Kirsty had told her about it when she was in the local store this morning.

'They're so excited. But dinner suits... That's only because Jenny Hamm wants to wear the dress she bought for her sister's wedding. You should hear the complaints.'

Tony's class.

Blake's class.

She'd thought then...

Yeah, she'd thought, but she hadn't said. She hadn't asked: *Is Blake Maddock coming?*

Obviously he was. Obviously he had.

He was on her veranda.

He'd said he'd crashed his car. There was a trickle of blood on his forehead. She struggled to get her confused mind to focus.

'There's blood...' she managed. 'Your head...'

'A scratch. I'm fine.'

'Really?'

'Really.'

She was getting her breath back. She hadn't seen this guy for fifteen years. There were so many emotions in her head she didn't know what to do with them.

'Get into the hall,' she managed. 'Out of the wind.' She pulled away, then stood aside and ushered him into the entrance porch. As if he was a casual acquaintance.

'Is anyone else hurt?' Her voice sounded funny, she thought. 'The other car...'

'Only me,' he said, and his voice astonished her. Deep and rich and growly. All grown up. 'I hit a tree.'

'A tree?'

'I'm not drunk,' he said, and he truly was Blake, his voice touched with the lazy humour she knew so well. 'I've been to the reunion dinner. They served Tony Hamm's home-made beer and Elsie Sarling's first attempt at making Chardonnay. It wasn't a struggle to stick with water.'

Her lips twitched in return, smiling back. Tension eased. An old school friend in trouble. She could do this. 'So the tree?' she said cautiously.

'It jumped out and hit me.' He sighed. 'No. The dog jumped out. I managed to miss the dog. I hit the tree instead.'

He'd hit a tree. A car crash, late at night. Blake.

So many emotions…

Priorities. 'Is the car blocking the road?' she managed and was absurdly proud of herself for sounding so sensible.

'No. I was aiming to miss the dog and I made a good fist of it. It's well off.'

That, at least, was a plus. She didn't need to get the tractor and drag a wreck from the road to stop others crashing into it.

She could focus on Blake.

Or actually…not. Focusing on Blake made her feel weird, like stepping through the wardrobe into Narnia, into another world. The world of fifteen years ago. Concentrate on the dog, she told herself. The dog seemed far less complicated.

It was a border collie, mostly black, with touches of white. It, too, was wet to the bone. She felt it shudder against her legs, and it was a far deeper shudder than Bounce's vampire-and-thunder-induced shudder.

If there was one thing that could touch Mardie Rainey's heart, it was a dog. A wet and obviously frightened dog was always going to hit her heart like an arrow. It even distracted her from Blake. She knelt down to see, to pat.

'Hey, sweetheart, where did you come from?'

But then she felt its collar, and she knew.

A ribbon of plastic.

She knew this collar.

'Oh, no.'

'Not yours?' Blake asked.

'No. This is a pound dog.' She fingered the collar, feeling ill. 'The local Animal Welfare van crashed last week and dogs escaped. Stray dogs are turning up everywhere. This collar says this is one of them.'

But this was a border collie.

Farmers round here valued their dogs above diamonds. Border collies were natural workers. For one to end up in the pound didn't make sense.

But she could only concentrate on the dog for so long. The dog was distracting, but not distracting enough.

She had Blake Maddock in her front porch.

'Mardie, I'm in trouble,' Blake said above her. The momentary emotion that had given rise to the hug had faded, leaving manners. 'Would your mother object if I came in to dry off and ring for help?'

Would her mother object?

Memories of the last time she'd seen Blake flooded back. Blake in this house, in this kitchen. Blake kissing her senseless.

'Come to Sydney,' he'd said urgently, holding her close. 'You're smart. You could get a scholarship. There's stuff we can do, Mardie. We can make a difference. Come with me. You can't be happy here.'

She remembered her whole body melting as Blake kissed her so deeply she thought she surely must say yes. She remembered his hands slipping under her blouse, and she remembered the hot, aching need.

But she was sixteen and her mother was suddenly there, confronting them with anger. Her mother was so seldom angry it jolted them both.

'Blake, it's time for you to go home. Mardie and I need to be up early, to draft the sheep ready for crutching.'

And, as she'd spoken, Mardie had seen fear.

Her mother had heard what Blake had said. She'd heard him asking her to go to Sydney.

She'd known, even then. At sixteen, the weight of this farm was on her shoulders.

You can't be happy here... Why not?

She loved Banksia Bay, and she loved farming. She'd also loved Blake, with every shred of her sixteen-year-old being.

But Blake couldn't wait to be off. He was heading to Sydney to do medicine.

She could get a scholarship? To do what? Something to make a difference? What was he talking about?

She loved her art, she loved making things, but even then she'd known Blake saw her passion as not to be taken seriously.

Even then she'd known they were moving in different directions.

'Write,' she'd told him, feeling desolate.

'Follow me to Sydney. Finish school and apply to the same university. I'll wait for you.'

She still remembered the desolation. 'I don't think I can. Blake, please write.'

'And just be friends?' he'd demanded, incredulous. Her mother was waiting stolidly for him to leave. She moved into the living room, out of hearing but not out of sight. 'We've gone too far to be just friends.'

She thought of that statement now. It had been an adolescent ultimatum: follow me to Sydney, move in my direction or cease being my friend.

All or nothing.

It had to be nothing.

She'd watched him go and her sixteen-year-old heart felt as if it was breaking.

And now he was back—grown, changed, but still Blake. He was watching her face, reading her warring emotions as he'd always been able to read her emotions. 'Is your mother...?' he started.

'Mum's fine,' Mardie said.

'She's asleep?'

'It's midnight.' She hadn't seen this man for half a lifetime. Use your head, she told herself. There was no way she should tell this...stranger...that she was home alone. Let him think her mother was still sleeping in the front room.

Even if he had hugged her.

Even if he was Blake.

'Did I wake you?' he asked. 'I'm sorry.'

'I was still awake. A tree came down and then I heard the car crash. I was coming to find out.'

'If you could turn on a light...' Blake ventured.

'No power. But come in anyway. Are you...are you really okay?'

'Shaken, not stirred.'

And at that...she smiled.

James Bond movies had been their very favourite thing. That last year together, a new movie had come out. She remembered persuading her mother to take them to Whale Cove. Dressing up. Standing hand in hand in the queue, waiting for tickets. She'd looked as glamorous as a sixteen-year-old on limited means could manage. A home-made dress, all slink and crazy glamour. Stilettos from the second-hand market. Blake had worn a dinner suit, probably not even hired. Money was never a problem for Blake. He'd looked a fairly adolescent Bond, but at sixteen she'd thought he'd looked a Bond to die for.

Shaken, not stirred.

Right now she was stirred.

She stood aside to usher him into the house. His body brushed hers as he passed.

There was no way she could feel him through her waterproofs.

She felt him. Every nerve in her body felt him.

This was weird. A teenage love affair, long over.

It was the night, she told herself. Her fear from the crash. The appalling storm. A boy she'd once loved.

A man, she told herself sharply. A stranger. She needed to be practical, sensible, and together.

'The dog...' he said.

'Dogs are welcome in this house.' Even stray and sodden ones. Maybe especially stray and sodden ones. 'Go through to the kitchen,' she said. 'It's warmer. I'll find towels and shed my coat.'

They were operating by flashlight. She lit a candle on the hall table and handed it to him.

The lightning outside was almost one continuous sheet. The house went from dark to light, from dark to light...

'This isn't James Bond,' he said. 'It's Gothic Horror.'

Gothic Horror... Her thoughts exactly. He'd always been on the same wavelength. The thought was...unsettling.

Unsettling but good. As if a part of her was suddenly restored.

There was a crazy thought.

'If you've grown fangs since I last saw you, I'm heading into the night right now,' she muttered. 'Kitchen. Go. Now.'

The dog whimpered and pressed closer against her.

'Leave her with me,' she said as he hesitated.

'She's my responsibility.'

'You brought her to me,' she said. 'One dog doesn't add very much to what I take care of.'

'Mardie…'

'Just go.'

After fifteen years, Blake Maddock had walked back into her life.

For some stupid reason, her head felt as if it was exploding.

Blake. A childhood friend. A teenage boyfriend. Nothing more.

Focus on the dog. Nothing else.

She headed for the linen closet and the dog stayed with her, its body still just touching her leg. She crouched in the dim light and ran her hands over the sodden coat and the dog whined a little and pressed in closer.

A female. Full grown. Trembling without pause.

There was no obvious wound. She didn't seem tender to touch.

She needed to get her into the light. Into the kitchen, where she had a bigger store of candles.

Back to Blake.

Not quite yet. Her head wasn't near to accepting the weird way her body had reacted to his presence.

She gathered towels. She thought about Blake; how she could get him dry. His clothes were soaked. Towels?

Something more.

She hesitated, told herself she was stupid, fetched a bathrobe.

The dog stayed with her, sticking close, a feather-touch of contact.

This dog had done it hard, she thought. The Animal Welfare van had crashed over a week ago. Where had this dog been since then?

Mardie's heart wasn't hard at the best of times. She could feel it stretch right now.

'Yeah, I'm a sucker for dogs,' she told her. 'Especially beautiful dogs like you. But there must be some reason you were at the pound in the first place. Were you in for sheep-killing?'

That was the most common reason a farm dog ended up discarded. A dog got a taste for blood. It was tragic, but once a dog started killing sheep there was little that could be done.

Most farmers quietly put them down. If they were too attached, though, they'd take them to the pound, hoping some townie would take them on, someone with a contained yard with not a sheep in sight.

It hardly ever made for a happy ending. A working dog wasn't meant to be contained. They pined, they made trouble for their new owners, they ended up being put down anyway.

So…she now had a stray dog, probably a sheep killer, and she had Blake Maddock.

A girl should have some protection.

A clap of thunder shook the house so loud the windows rattled.

She thought of Bounce under her bedclothes. Until the storm ended there was no way Bounce was moving.

She was on her own—but what else was new?

Having Blake Maddock in her kitchen was new.

You've faced worse than Blake Maddock, she told herself.

And…it was Blake. The thought made something inside her shiver, and it wasn't fear.

Hormones?

Nonsense. Hormones were for a teenage romance. Get over it. Be practical.

It was good advice. She took her armload of towels and her bathrobe, she took her courage in both hands—and went to see if she could follow it.

CHAPTER TWO

THE GREAT THING about a wood-burning stove was that a power outage couldn't mess with it. Cutting wood was a pain, but Mardie had learned to enjoy it, and the stove more than paid for itself with comfort. In the small hours after a difficult lambing, when she was cold and wet, the fire was a warm, welcoming presence.

It was the heart of her home.

Blake was standing before it now. He'd put the kettle on the hob. He'd opened the toasting door so he could see the flames; so he could hold his hands out for warmth. He had his back to her.

He was so...large.

She'd known he'd become a doctor. Someone had been to a graduation ceremony in Sydney years back and had seen him.

She hadn't heard of him since. And now, here he was, big and handsome and rugged, wearing a dinner suit, a city doctor in city clothes.

She had a city doctor in her kitchen.

She had Blake in her kitchen.

See, there was the anomaly. Blake was from another life.

Blake no longer fitted here, yet there was part of him that was... Blake.

And he didn't look like a city doctor, she thought as he turned to face her. In truth, he looked more weathered than most farmers. He looked tanned and muscled, and the creases of his eyes were etched deep, as if he constantly faced harsh sun.

He also looked a bit...gaunt? That'd be the crash, she thought, but then she decided it looked more than that. She sensed deep-seated strain, and he looked too lean for health. He looked as if he might have been ill—or maybe he simply worked too hard.

City surgeon, making millions? More millions. She knew little about Blake's parents other than they'd been killed in a light plane crash when he was twelve, but she did know they were wealthy. His great-aunt had money, too.

Blake obviously had moved on in the same mould.

'I hear you're a doctor,' she said cautiously, and he nodded.

'Yes.'

'Congratulations.'

'On being a doctor?'

'Of course. You've cut your head. How bad is it?'

'It's nothing.'

'Have you hurt anything else?'

'No.'

'Promise?'

'Yes.'

'Let me check the cut for glass, then. Sit.'

'Still bossy?'

'Always.'

He sat.

He used to argue. Always.

Maybe he was hurt. Maybe he...

'I had six airbags,' he said. 'I was almost suffocated but not hurt. This has to be superficial. But I would be grateful if you could check.'

She checked. She filled a bowl with warm water, she washed his face with care, she used the flashlight to check for glass.

It was an ugly scratch. There were a couple of metal slivers, embedded. She found tweezers, tugged them out. She put on antiseptic and a plaster.

Touching him was weird. Touching him felt...shivery.

Get over it. He was the one who should be shivery, not her.

Concentrate on need.

'You need to get dry,' she said, trying to keep her voice steady. 'There's a bathrobe here that's wool and warm. Dry yourself and put it on.' Deep breath. 'I think you need to stay the night. I'd drive you into town but you've already proven it's not safe to be out. I don't see that you have a choice. You want to change now, while I towel the dog? Take a couple of candles upstairs. Same bedroom you always had. I keep the spare beds made up. You don't have a choice.'

How had that happened?

One minute he was deciding to turn back to Sydney. The next he was standing in Mardie's attic, hauling on her dressing gown.

No. Not hers. It was soft brown cashmere and it was huge. A man's.

Her father's?

He remembered Mardie's dad with huge regret. Bill was a big, genial countryman, deeply contented with his wife, his farm, his daughter. As kids, Blake and Mardie had trailed after him like two adoring puppies, helping, messing around, being with him.

Bill had died of a massive heart attack when Mardie was barely in her teens and he'd felt as gutted as Mardie. He'd felt little emotion when he'd been told his own parents were dead—he hadn't seen them for years—but Bill...

If this was Bill's bathrobe...

He smiled, remembering Bill, remembering this place as it had been.

Why had he never come back?

He knew why. Because of Mardie.

Mardie...

She'd grown up, of course she had, but she was still the same Mardie. She was short, blue-eyed, freckled and compact. Her honey-blonde curls were still tied into braids. And her eyes...

He'd always loved how they'd creased into laughter in an instant. Time had now etched those laughter lines to permanent.

Tonight she was wearing tattered jeans and an old woolly jumper. Bright red socks with a hole in one toe.

Years of tending sheep, of living on this farm meant she was wind-burned, sun-burned, cute as a button.

She was a farmer.

She could have been so much more...

No. It had been stupid to demand that of her fifteen years ago. It was stupid to think it now.

So get this over with, he told himself. Don't let your emotions get tangled up. Get in there, be courteous and thankful, accept her offer of a bed for the night, call for a tow truck first thing in the morning and get out of here. You've seen her. That was what you wanted. Now leave.

Because?

Because Banksia Bay seemed threatening, and Mardie seemed even more threatening. He didn't know why, but she was.

Or maybe he did. Maybe he was old enough to see it.

Mardie was comfort, fun, loving. She was a refuge, as she'd always been his refuge.

Mardie was all the things he could never let himself have.

What was keeping him? She towelled the little collie as dry as she could, encouraged her to lie in Bounce's dog basket, then started making toast.

The collie whined and headed back to her, once more just touching her knee.

She made toast and the dog kept contact all the time.

'What's wrong?' she asked, and offered her a piece of toast.

The dog didn't take it. As if she didn't see it was being held out.

She moved it a little closer.

The dog sniffed, sniffed again—and then delicately took it from Mardie's hand.

What the…?

She'd been working by candlelight. She flicked the flashlight back on and looked. She really looked. And in the better light…

No.

She plumped down on the kitchen chair and drew the dog to her.

'Oh, sweetheart. Oh, no.'

Blake walked back into the kitchen and stopped short.

The dog's head was resting on Mardie's knee. Tears were sliding unchecked down her face.

'Mardie...'

She looked up at him, and all the tragedy of the world was in her face.

'She's blind,' she whispered. 'She was tipped out of that van a week ago and she's blind. How's she ever survived?'

Blind.

Things fell into place.

The dog standing motionless in the road, not registering his oncoming car.

The dog touching him, staying by his side, following him here by touch.

The dog moving to Mardie, whose clothes would smell of farmyard, of the familiar, then not leaving her. Just touching.

'How do you know?' he asked, but already he knew it for truth.

'Look at her eyes.' She flicked on the flashlight.

He looked.

The dog's eyes were opaque, unfocused, unseeing. Cataracts covered both the eyes entirely.

She'd be seeing vague shapes, light and dark through thick white fog, he thought. Nothing more.

'It'll be why she was in the pound,' Mardie whispered. He'd walked back into the kitchen absurdly self-conscious of wearing a great woollen bathrobe but Mardie was oblivious to anything but the dog. 'She's only young. I'm guessing four at the most. And she's smart and so polite. She's skin and bone. She must be starving, yet she took the toast like a lady. Oh, sweetheart.'

She sniffed and sniffed again. She ran her fingers through her hair, a gesture he remembered, Mardie under stress. She'd obviously forgotten, though, that she'd tied her hair into braids. Her fingers caught one of the bands and her hair fell loose, a cascade of honey curls.

One braid in. The other free. Tear-stained, messy, freckled... She didn't care. She was totally oblivious.

Something kicked him, hard, deep inside. Something that hadn't kicked him for a long time.

'Let me see,' he said, more roughly than he intended. He knelt on the floor, cupping the dog's jaw in his hand, looking at her eyes.

The dog let him do as he willed. She was totally trusting, or maybe she'd gone past trust. Maybe she was at the point of: *Kill me now, nothing can get worse than this.*

Definitely cataracts.

If it was the same as humans... Cataracts sometimes came with age. Sometimes they were caused by illness or injury. These, though...

'Sometimes they're genetic,' he said, thinking out loud. 'She seems a young, otherwise healthy dog.'

The dog let her head lie on his palm and sighed.

Mardie sniffed again.

'Years ago, one of my neighbours' old Labradors, Blacky, got cataracts,' she muttered. 'Roger said the cost of having them removed was too huge to consider. Blacky was a pet, though, old, fat and lazy at the best of times. He was content to live out the rest of his life in front of Roger's fire. But for a young working dog... If she can't work she'll be miserable, and useless to whoever owns her.'

She fingered the plastic collar.

The flashlight was still on. They read the collar together, Blake absurdly aware of honey-blonde curls tumbling to her shoulder only six inches away. Absurdly aware of a ragged sweater.

Mardie...

'She has a name.' Mardie seemed unaware of his distraction and Blake looked where she was looking. There was a number written in black on the collar, followed by rough script.

Bessie. Owner: Charlie Hunter.

'It's worse and worse,' Mardie said, and her face said it was.

'Charlie Hunter?'

'You must remember Charlie. He's a farmer up on the ridge. A nice old guy, keeps to himself, almost ninety. He used to be the best dog-trainer in the district. Brilliant. When he won All Australian Champion I made him...'

But then she faltered. Bit back what she'd been about to say.

'I guess... I guess whether I know him or not doesn't matter. But he had a stroke eight weeks ago and he's had to go into care. I'm guessing this is his dog.' She took a deep breath, and when she continued her voice cracked with emotion. 'So this is Bessie. He kept her even though she was blind, and when he could no longer keep her he put her in the pound. I wouldn't have thought... It would have been kinder to put her down.'

And she rose and walked out of the room.

Bessie sniffed his hand and he patted her, stroking her silky coat. The kettle whistled on the stove.

The roof was leaking in the corner, into a bucket. A steady trickle. The bucket was almost full.

He took a candle and checked the living room, the matching corner. Another bucket.

The way they were filling, it'd be a twenty-minute roster to empty them, all night.

He made tea and then Mardie was back, with another collie by her side. Bigger. Younger. Having to be towed.

'Bounce,' she said sternly, hauling him into the room whether he liked it or not. 'Get over the thunder. You're needed. Meet Bessie.'

Bounce was clearly cowed by the storm. Another low rumble filled the night. His ears flattened and he whimpered.

Bessie whimpered back.

Bounce's ears forgot about flattening. Another dog, in his kitchen? This clearly took precedence over thunder. He launched himself forward, stopping abruptly two inches from Bessie's nose. He sniffed.

Bessie sniffed back.

The procedure was repeated from different viewpoints.

Bounce gave his tail a cautious wag.

'Basket,' Mardie said.

At the side of the woodstove was an ancient dog basket. There'd been dogs in that basket ever since Blake could remember. There were never less than three. He'd been vaguely surprised not to see dogs in there tonight.

The family was down to one dog?

'Basket,' Mardie said again. Bounce gave her a *Must I?* look but turned and headed where he was meant to go.

Bessie went too, just touching.

Bounce turned in two circles, sighed, flopped.

Bessie flopped, too. Closed her eyes. Was asleep in an instant.

Bounce stared up at Mardie, doubtful as to this new order.

'Stay,' Mardie said gently, and Bounce sighed again, but he wriggled until his body was curved around Bessie's. He settled.

'That's great,' Blake said, feeling immeasurably cheered. 'Another dog...they have ways of figuring they can trust.'

'They'll both relax,' Mardie said. 'Bounce wasn't finding me the least bit reassuring against the gods of thunder but an older one who's not scared is just what he needs.'

'And tomorrow?'

'Tomorrow I'll call Henrietta, who runs the pound,' she said bleakly, sitting back down at the table. Hauling her mug of tea close and holding it, as if needing the comfort of its warmth. 'But one step at a time. Would you like toast before bed?'

She was suddenly businesslike. Brisk. Putting emotion aside.

There were still tracks of tears on her cheeks.

He found her absurdly...or not absurdly...

'I don't need anything to eat,' he said, a bit too abruptly. 'I've just had a reunion dinner.'

'So you have. You're sure your head's okay?'

'It's fine. Thank you.' She was seated right by him. So close... Instinctively he reached out to touch her hand. It was a gesture of gratitude, nothing more.

She flinched.

It was as much as he could do not to flinch in return.

'I'm staying up to eat toast,' she said, carefully focusing on her mug of tea and not him. 'Sleep well. There's a bit to face in the morning, so get some rest.'

'Mardie?'

She did look at him then, with all the distrust in the world. His heart twisted.

'When I left... I never meant to hurt you,' he said.

'You did hurt me,' she said, flat and definite. The emotion

of that instinctive hug was gone; remembered hurt was back.

'I wrote to you. I worried about you. You never wrote back.'

'I needed…to protect myself.'

'Then that's all right,' she said stiffly. 'All explained.'

'I was a kid. I was stupid, not to keep in contact with my best friend.'

'We were teenagers,' she conceded. 'Sensitivity isn't a teenager's strong suit. Forget it. Go to bed.'

'Sensitive or not, I've regretted it. More and more as I grew older.'

'It doesn't matter.'

'It did to me. It does. I am sorry. That's why I came tonight. I wanted to see you. It's what I wanted to say.' And before he could think it through—because if he had he never would have done it—he stooped and he kissed her. His kiss was light, a brush of his mouth against her forehead. It was a kiss given because he couldn't bear not to. A kiss of apology.

It was a dumb gesture. She pulled away as if he burned.

'That's enough of sorry,' she told him brusquely, harshly. 'It was all a long time ago. It doesn't matter any more; just go.'

'Are you planning on bucket-emptying all night?'

She sighed. Looked at the buckets. Didn't look at him. 'They'll be okay.'

'They'll flood.'

She'd been thinking that, in the fraction of her mind that wasn't taken up by him. An hour ago the leak had been a drip. The drip was becoming a trickle and the trickle was threatening to turn to a gush.

'I'm sure it'll be fine.' Some things weren't worth worrying about. No way was she getting up on the roof in this weather.

'It'll be the corner of the roof, where the spouts meet,' he said. 'The water's banking up; there's too much for the drainpipe to cope with.'

'How do you know?'

'I've coped with more than floods over the last few years. Once upon a time your dad let me up on the roof with him. I can remember the set-up, and I know down-pipes.'

'You understand plumbing?' She was incredulous.

He grinned. 'Hey, I'm a doctor. Plumbing's half my med training. Plus my work has been practical in more ways than one. So now, not only am I offering my professional opinion, I'm proposing surgery. Though I'll need to put my dinner suit back on. There's no way I'm getting Bill's robe wet.'

She wasn't listening to the end of his statement. She was too intent on the first. 'You can't get on the roof. Are you out of your mind? Have you seen the lightning?'

'I have,' he agreed, grateful that here was something concrete he could do, something to lessen the emotion. 'It's sheet lightning, not fork. Fork's bad. Sheet's not great but we also have trees, much taller than the house. Plus there's two chimneys, both of which would be hit before the house itself. I'm not proposing to stand on the roof acting as a lightning conductor. I'm proposing to stick a ladder against the corner of the house while you hold the bottom, then climb up and disengage the down-pipe. I might need a hacksaw. Do you have a hacksaw?'

'I...might,' she said, flabbergasted.

'Excellent. With just a hole instead of a pipe, the water'll stop banking up under the eaves.'

'How do you know?' she said, suspicious, and he grinned.

'Trust me, I'm a doctor.'

She didn't grin back. 'You'd go outside again—into the

storm?' She was still hornswoggled. 'Plus you have a lump the size of an egg on your head.'

'Hero material, that's me,' he said, trying to make her smile. 'But I'm not too heroic. The lump's already subsiding and I know what I'm doing. But I do need my sidekick—that'd be you in your sou'wester.'

'I wouldn't need to get up all night,' she said, dazed.

'There's my board and lodging paid for. What about it, Mardie? Deal?'

She struggled to shut her mouth. Stop being flabbergasted. 'You're proposing we brave the tempest?' she managed. 'With a ladder? I don't mind a bit of rain. Rainstorms are when most of my lambs seem to be born. But you... You'll need to put that disgusting dinner suit on again.'

'It's not disgusting.'

'If it's not yet, it soon will be,' she said darkly. 'But this is an offer I'm not refusing. Okay, Superman, you're on.'

He fixed the leak, by the simple expedient of climbing the ladder, hacking the drainpipe out of the spout, clearing the worst of the banked-up leaf litter and letting the water gush free. He even managed to do it so water didn't land on Mardie's head as she held the ladder below. It seemed simple, except she couldn't have done it. Balance in the rain and handle a hacksaw as if accustomed to it. Balance while not noticing the lightning.

He was steady and sure and fast.

She felt...

She felt...

She had no idea how she felt.

He came down the ladder. Brushed against her, which made her feel...as if she didn't know how she felt. Grinned, a triumphant small-boy grin she remembered. 'Flood averted,' he said. 'Much better than a finger in the dyke, don't you think?'

'Much,' she said faintly, because she couldn't think of anything else to say.

When had he got so big?

When had he got so…male?

They stowed the ladder, they came back inside and he dripped in the hall.

'Would you…' she started and then she stopped. She simply didn't know what to say next.

'Would I like another towel? Yes, I would. And then bed.'

'I… Thank you.'

'Enough of the thank yous. Let's call it quits.' He touched her lightly on her cheek—and she flinched and his smile died.

She got him his towel. He nodded his thanks and headed straight for bed. Up to the attic where he'd stayed when he was a kid.

She headed back to the kitchen. She'd told him she was staying up to eat toast.

She'd lied.

She was staying up to think about Blake.

Blake Maddock was in her attic.

Blake Maddock had fixed her plumbing. Blake Maddock had kissed her.

Blake Maddock had touched her cheek, a gesture of farewell, and her cheek still burned.

For this was a new Blake Maddock; the grown-up version. He was a guy who'd pulled away her flooding down-pipes as if he coped with manual labour every day of his life.

That was what he looked like.

Whatever he'd been doing for the past fifteen years, it

hadn't made him soft. He was lean—almost too lean—but his muscles made up for it. And his body... As he'd come back down the ladder, his soaked clothes clinging, he'd looked... he'd looked...

A girl shouldn't think how he'd looked.

And he'd kissed her.

So...what? He'd kissed her for the first time when she was six years old and she'd given him her sandwich. She'd giggled and her friends had said 'kissy kissy'. They'd all giggled then. She and Blake were best of friends.

Not any more. They weren't even minor friends. Friends would have sat up for an hour or so, catching up on what had happened through the years.

He didn't want to catch up. He was stuck here because his car had crashed. He'd fixed her down-pipe because he felt sorry for her. He wanted to get the night over and get back to Sydney.

So why had he kissed her?'

'Because he's arrogant and he has more money than anyone has a right to. He thinks he's aristocracy.' She said it out loud but it didn't make sense.

He'd never acted rich. All the time she'd known him, he acted as if his family's money was something he didn't want to know about.

He never talked about his parents, then or now. Everything she knew, she knew from scant town gossip.

Tonight...she should have asked what he'd been doing. She'd assumed he was a city doctor, but he looked so weathered...he must have been doing something else.

Neither had asked the important questions. Neither had told.

She should have told him her mother wasn't here. He could have slept in the front bedroom.

Would he be able to sleep in the tiny attic bed?

It didn't matter, she told herself, sticking bread in the toaster without thinking. Their friendship was over. She hadn't seen him for fifteen years and after tonight she wouldn't see him again.

She shouldn't mind.

Quite suddenly, quite fiercely, she minded.

What would her life be if she'd gone to Sydney with him?

Maybe she'd be a doctor's wife. A rich doctor's wife. They'd have a gorgeous house, a couple of kids, piano lessons, midweek tennis. Society functions. Ladies' lunches.

Um...how about that for a stereotype?

She could have gone to university as he'd wanted her to. She'd been smart enough. Maybe she could have been a doctor, too.

A doctor? Her favourite subject at school was art, and she still remembered the adolescent Blake's disparagement. 'It's all right for a hobby but not for a career.'

He'd had ambition. She didn't, or not ambition as he saw it. She'd never wanted to leave Banksia Bay.

Apart from Blake. She'd wanted, desperately, to go wherever Blake went.

At school he'd been quiet about his future, telling no one, even hugging his desire to study medicine to himself. He kept lots of things to himself. Even to her, his best of friends, he'd seldom talked of his family, his future, or his past. Maybe that was wise. His family's wealth made him different from most kids in Banksia Bay. The eccentricity of his great-aunt made him different. The fact that he had fabulously wealthy parents who never came near made him really different.

He was still...different.

He probably had a wife, she thought suddenly. He might even have cute, piano-playing kids.

He wasn't wearing a wedding ring. She'd noticed.

'Don't go there,' she told herself, and ate the toast without thinking about it.

Bounce opened one eye and watched with hope. She gave him a crust, then offered another to Bessie, but Bessie didn't stir.

She was a smaller dog than Bounce. Sweet.

Blind.

'Don't think it,' she told herself, but she knew she was thinking it.

She couldn't. It'd be cruel to keep a blind working dog. It'd be sentimentality at its worst.

'And it's not as if there's any spare money to spend on operations.' She was still talking out loud. 'Even if it's possible.'

A thunderclap rolled across the night and made her shudder. Instead of heading behind her legs, Bounce simply nestled closer to Bessie.

Bounce had a new best friend.

Which left her alone.

Bed. Alone. Without even Bounce.

'That's a dumb, sad thing to think,' she told herself. 'Ooh, who's feeling sorry for herself? Go to bed and enjoy listening to the thunder. And don't keep thinking of Blake. He's nothing to do with you and he's out of here, first thing in the morning.'

He should have sat up and talked.

He lay in the dark and counted bruises to distract himself. The crash hadn't left him completely unscathed. His head ached. Something had thumped his shoulder and that ached, too.

He'd been barely civil downstairs. He hadn't asked anything of her life for the past fifteen years. How dumb was that?

She'd think he was just using her.

He *was* using her. This was the closest place to stay out of the storm. Even if they'd been strangers he would have asked for shelter, and she might have been kind enough to say yes.

Of course she would. This was Mardie, still feeling sorry for strays after all these years.

What had she been doing all this time? Married? He should have looked for a ring.

Surely not. A husband would have made himself obvious.

Her mother? Etta hadn't appeared either, but Etta had suffered from appalling arthritis fifteen years back. She'd occasionally been bed-ridden even then. How was she now?

He should have asked.

He should have asked lots of things.

Once upon a time he'd known all there was to know about Mardie. They'd been lone children on adjoining farms. When his parents had sent him here, seven years old, deeply traumatised, he'd missed his twin as if part of him had been ripped away. Mardie had helped fill that appalling void. They'd spent their childhood together. Best friends.

And then... Six months before his final exams he'd suddenly seen Mardie differently.

Theirs had been a fumbling teenage love affair, as painful as it was sweet. But it meant, for the first time, he saw a possibility for sharing the load into the future, of having someone by him as he carried his burden of guilt and grief.

How unfair was that? He'd never even explained—how could he? *Help me make up for my brother's life?*

He'd said simply, 'Follow me to Sydney,' and she'd said no. 'Write,' she'd said.

He'd thought at first that he could, but what he hadn't realised was how much it hurt. Those first months in a huge, anonymous university college, away from anyone he knew... Losing Mardie... It had been like losing Robbie all over again.

But he had to leave. Banksia Bay was where he'd been dumped. It had become a refuge but he'd always known he had to leave.

'Stay there until we all forget,' his father had said. Even at seventeen he'd known forgetting was never going to happen. Staying in Banskia Bay seemed like a long, continuous betrayal of memory.

So he had to leave, but if he'd phoned Mardie, if he'd heard her voice, if he'd made any contact at all, then he risked crumbling. And how could he do that?

Robbie, his ghost, his shadow, was driving him.

Behind Robbie... His parents, running through inherited money as if it was water, squandering their lives, losing Robbie in the process. Consciously forgetting their son.

His great-aunt, floundering after an ill-advised love affair, locking herself away in Banksia Bay, as far from what she thought of as civilisation as she could get, using her inheritance as a shield from the world. Consciously forgetting her lover.

So many lives, wasted. Including Robbie's.

For Robbie's sake, the squandering would stop. The forgetting would stop.

So he'd decided that contacting Mardie would simply keep the wound open. Then, by the time he was settled, by the time the ache eased, it seemed too late to rekindle friendship. He'd burned his bridges, and now he had to pay the price.

The price was that tonight she'd welcomed him almost as a stranger. He'd kissed her and she'd backed away. He'd touched her and she'd flinched. And he'd gone to bed without even asking about her mother.

They'd have time to talk in the morning, he thought. He'd ask...and then he'd leave.

Again.

He stirred uneasily. The spare bed always had been too small, too hard. He ached.

The storm kept on, unabated.

He lay awake and thought of Mardie. Of a life long past.

Of a seventeen-year-old who was desperate to save the world, to do *something*, but who wanted to carry Mardie with him.

Why remember it now? Theirs was a childhood friendship, faded to nothing. He shouldn't have come.

It was just...the invitation to the reunion had seemed almost meant. He wasn't sure why he'd kept thinking of Mardie during this last long illness, but he had.

The Mardie of his childhood.

The problem was, he decided as he drifted towards sleep, it wasn't the Mardie of years ago he was thinking of now. It was the Mardie of now. Mardie hugging him joyously in that first instinctive burst of surprised welcome. Mardie in her vast sou'wester, holding the ladder as if this was the sort of work she did every day of the week. Mardie, as she was, but a thousandfold more.

Why had he returned?

Sleep was nowhere.

The night had no answers, and neither did he.

CHAPTER THREE

BLAKE FINALLY SLEPT—and he woke to the sound of singing.

For a moment he thought he was dreaming. He was in a tiny attic room. Whitewashed walls. A narrow bed.

For that instant he was back in his childhood, and then he was wide awake. The events of the night before flooded back.

Mardie was outside, somewhere below his bedroom window. Singing.

He glanced at his watch. Silly o'clock.

He swung himself out of bed and winced. Yes, the airbags had saved him from injury but he was still battered.

He also still suffered aches from illness. Haemorrhagic dengue did that to you. He stretched cautiously. Ouch.

The singing went on. It was something operatic, ridiculous, sung at the top of her lungs. Mardie at full caterwaul.

He found himself grinning, remembering early grade school. The whole school had been learning Christmas carols for the annual concert. An ambitious music teacher had listened to each child in turn. Divided them into sections. Soprano, alto, baritone, tenor.

She'd listened to Mardie, grimaced and given her a section of her own.

'You can be the drum,' Miss Watson had decreed. 'Stay at the back and boom along to the beat. Just sing "Pum Pum Pum Pum Pum."'

But what Mardie lacked in talent she made up for in enthusiasm. The night of the school concert, Mardie's ear-shattering "Pums" had practically drowned out the choir, and the audience had dissolved into delighted laughter.

Mardie had laughed as well.

He grinned at the memory, his aches receding as he pulled open the shutters and looked down.

She was milking the cow. One cow. This was sheep country, not dairy. She'd be milking for personal use.

Or not. One cow made a lot of milk.

Who was living in this house with her?

The house was silent. The storm of the night before was past. The early-morning sun was glittering on the wet paddocks.

Mardie was sitting in the little open shed at the back gate, calmly milking the cow in the wooden bail he remembered climbing on as a child.

This place was a time warp, he thought. All the things he'd done in the past fifteen years...

He'd seen the world. His work in Africa...

She'd stayed home and milked the cow.

'Rather than stand and stare, make yourself useful,' she yelled up at him. 'There's bacon in the fridge. Start cooking. I'll be inside in five minutes.'

Had he been so obvious?

'Is there anyone else home?' he yelled back.

'No.' Short and to the point. 'Except the dogs and they're not moving. I think they're in love.'

'Mardie...'

'Bacon,' she yelled. 'I'd like four rashers, two tomatoes, four slices of toast and I'll cook my own eggs when I get in. Or you can milk the cow. Take your pick. By the way, the pool of water under the downpipe's practically a swimming pool. If you hadn't diverted it, it'd be in my house. You deserve four rashers as well.'

His dinner suit was still sodden. Of course. Clothes were an issue. Why hadn't he brought spares? Feeling...weird...he donned Bill's bathrobe again and headed downstairs.

The kitchen was warm and welcoming and smelled of damp dog. Or a bit more. Bessie's week of being a stray had left her distinctly on the nose. But if there was one thing Blake's work in Africa had equipped him for, it was working with smells. He might bathe her before he left, he thought.

Or maybe not. Maybe he should leave fast.

Depending on Mardie.

Both dogs rose as he entered, heading out of their basket to greet him. Bessie came side by side with Bounce. Just touching. She'd learned this mechanism to cope, he thought—finding something trustworthy and sticking like glue.

She touched his hand with her wet nose and he felt his gut twist.

A blind working dog...

Don't get involved, he told himself, but he already was. He was thinking of bathing her but he was thinking much more.

Breakfast first.

He knew this place backwards. Little had changed. The

kitchen had been repainted, though. Sea blue. Nice. The big old woodstove was still the centrepiece.

There were a couple of extraordinary enamelled paintings on either side. Abstract. They looked like wildfire under glass. Even when the woodstove wasn't lit, these paintings would give warmth to the room, he thought. Mardie always did have an eye for good art.

Breakfast.

The vast frying pan, black with age, seemed an old friend. The bacon was a slab rather than pre-cut rashers, just like it'd always been when he stayed here as a kid. He cut it thick, tossed rashers into the pan, and dog smell was immediately replaced by cooking bacon.

The dogs wiggled with hope, and he cut more. It was a special morning. Bacon all round.

He was halfway through making toast when Mardie appeared. She was wearing another ancient sweater with holes in the elbows. She'd pulled her gumboots off at the door and her feet were covered with bright yellow socks. No holes this morning. Sartorial elegance at its finest.

She'd done her hair, braiding it and coiling it high. It made her look a little more sophisticated than last night, but not much. Nothing could ever make this woman sophisticated, he thought. She was carrying a bucket of milk, the quintessential dairymaid. She looked…

Incredibly sexy.

That was a dumb thing to think. Since when had faded jeans, torn sweater and a bucket of milk made a woman sexy?

But there was no denying, Mardie was…sexy.

And it seemed the admiration worked both ways. 'I'm glad you've put on the bathrobe,' she said as she heaved her bucket onto the bench. 'Have you been working out? I can't remember all those muscles. Standing at the attic window showing them off... I would have thought a bit of modesty would be appropriate.' Then, as he started to feel discomfited, she grinned. 'I know. It's bad manners to comment, but manners were never my forte. And while I'm commenting... You're too thin. You want a glass of milk? Guaranteed non-pasteurised, non-homogenised, organic, still warm from its own personal milk heater, Clarabelle Cow.'

She dipped a ladle into the bucket and poured two big glasses. Handed him one.

How long since he'd drunk milk straight from the cow?

He thought of the hospital food he'd endured over the past awful weeks. Thought he should have just come here.

That was a bad idea.

He put down the glass and she smiled. 'Milk moustache,' she said and handed him a tissue. 'Nothing changes.'

Something had. They used to wipe each other's milk moustaches. That had started when they were knee high to a grasshopper. The fact that she'd handed him a tissue...

Now they were practically strangers.

It behoved a man to remember it.

'Why the cow? Can you drink a bucket a day?' he asked.

'I make cheese with a friend. Lorraine's a local potter—we help each other in all sorts of ways and we make cheese on the side. We have one cow each. It works well because if either of us is busy we do the other's milking. And we're good. We sell it at our farmer's market. You have no idea how much we can charge, and it's fun.'

Fun. For some reason the word threw him.

Mardie, with her milk moustache, having fun.

'How long have you been up?' he asked, moving on with an effort.

'Dawn. I went round the sheep to make sure none got hit by lightning, but the Cyprus hedge is a great shelter and they're fine. The gum's down across the drive, though. You had to go round it last night?'

'Yeah.' His mud-covered shoes on the veranda testified to the scrambling he'd had to do to get here.

'I'll get the chainsaw onto it. That's my after-breakfast job. Oh, and I believe your car's a write-off.'

'You've seen it?'

'I've seen it,' she said grimly. 'How fast were you going?'

'Obviously too fast.'

'You're so lucky you're not dead.'

And there was something about the way she said it... The lightness suddenly disappeared. Her words were flat, with a faint tremor beneath.

There was something about the way her face changed.

He knew this woman. He hadn't seen her for fifteen years but he knew...

'Who else has been killed in a car crash?' he asked, and it was a question and a statement all in one.

'I...' She stopped. She shook her head but he knew her denial was a lie.

'Your mother?' He felt sick. *He should have asked.*

'My mum's in Banksia Bay Nursing Home.' She concentrated on fetching eggs from the pantry, refusing to return to car wrecks. 'Her arthritis cripples her. I bring her out here whenever I can. She sits on the veranda in the sun and tells me all the things I'm doing wrong.' She smiled again then, starting to crack eggs into the pan. Moving on. And he couldn't push. *He had no right.*

'But you know something?' she said, still inexorably changing the subject. 'She's happy. She doesn't need to stay here. All these years we fought to keep her independent, she finally gave in and now she's surrounded by friends. She plays bridge, she watches old movies, she reads. She doesn't need her daughter to do the humiliating things. She comes out here and enjoys the farm but she's always ready to go back to her comfy bedroom with her music and her books and the local nurses who make her feel loved. I don't feel bad about it at all.'

'So you're here completely by yourself?'

There was a moment's hesitation. Then... 'Yes.' It was almost defiant.

'You should have gone to university.' It was an explosion.

She paused, mid egg break. Stiffened. Then she calmly went on breaking eggs. Four. She scooped bacon fat over them so they cooked sunny-side up. Slid them onto two plates. Sat at the table and loaded her plate with bacon.

'I've never regretted it,' she said at last. 'Not for a moment.'

'Look at you.' Why was he feeling so angry? Why was he feeling...that it had all been a waste? It wasn't fair to attack her, her lifestyle, but...the idea that she'd been *mouldering* here was suddenly killing him. 'I go away for fifteen years, I get myself a medical degree, a career. I've done so much. And you...'

'Have you been happy?'

'Happiness isn't the point.'

'What else is the point?' she demanded, buttering toast. 'My mother's arthritis started when she was thirty. When she was thirty-eight she lost her husband. Yet she's happy. She had the choice. Miserable or happy. She chose happy. She still chooses happy. Pass the marmalade, please.'

'What did she do with her life?'

'She made us all happy,' she snapped. 'Including you. Don't you dare say that's a waste. Marmalade!'

'Where are you putting all this?' She was about five feet two. She was little and wiry and compact. She was eating enough to keep him going for a full day.

'Work makes you hungry,' she said evenly, and her anger had been carefully and obviously put away. 'You've been lying in bed letting your calories sink languorously anywhere they want. My calories have been bouncing all the way down to the bottom paddock on the tractor, into the bails to milk Clarabelle, over to see your car and the ruined tree, and they're all used up. Speaking of your car…' She glanced at her watch. 'I'll ring Raff, the local cop, at eight. And Henrietta.'

'Henrietta?'

'The lady who runs the pound.'

'No.'

It was an explosion, and the word stopped them both short.

Mardie paused, her bacon midway to her mouth. She gazed at him, calm and direct. 'No?'

From their basket, the two dogs watched. Or one dog watched and the other watched by proxy. Bounce had been declared Bessie's eyes.

'No?' she said cautiously. 'Are you offering her a home?'

'I can't.' That was practically an explosion, too.

'Neither can I.' She met his gaze square on. Knew what he was asking. Rejected it. 'Don't ask it of me.'

He needed to make some phone calls before he talked about the next option. He needed to know his facts. But for now… 'Why not?' he asked.

'She's a working dog. Look at her. She's beautiful, young, energetic, aching to run. She's bred to work. I've seen injured working dogs before. Without their work, they pine. Look at how thin she is. Charlie Hunter is a kind old man and he would have loved her to bits. He'll have fed her whatever she'll take. When he went into the nursing home he'll have handed her over to Henrietta at the pound, and Hen loves dogs. She'll have hand fed her if that's what it took to get her to eat. But she's still stick-thin. I know a depressed dog when I see one. She's blind and she's miserable.'

'So you'd put her down?'

'Like it's *my* decision?' She glared. 'That's unfair and you know it. But as for keeping her... Bounce would be out every day with me, working the sheep. He'd come home and Bessie would smell him, would know what we'd been doing. Border collies have arguably the highest IQ in the animal kingdom. They're not content to be lapdogs. It won't be safe for me to have her where sheep might kick her, where blind doesn't work. She's not meant to spend the rest of her life in a basket by the fire and I won't do it to her.'

'Cataracts are removable.'

'Maybe.' She spread marmalade on a second piece of toast, looked at it and then set it aside. 'I read my veterinary guide after you went to bed last night. Cataract operations in dogs are problematic. There's a high chance of failure and the cost per eye is astronomical. I couldn't even think of going there. Putting her though that...'

'But if you wanted her...'

'You found her,' she said, and her voice was back to harsh.

'She could never stay with me.'

'What's the difference between staying in a city apartment while you work all day, or staying by herself here?'

'I don't work in Australia,' he said.

'You don't work in Sydney?'

'My great-aunt had an apartment there. I'm clearing it out.

From now on I'll be based in California. I really can't take on a dog. But I didn't mean to make you responsible.'

'But you did,' she said, suddenly savage. 'You're making me feel all sorts of things I don't want to feel.'

He raked his hair. 'I'm sorry.'

'Good. Excellent, in fact. Let's get you out of here.'

That was surely the best option. He glanced down at his bathrobe. Winced. Thought about his still-soggy dinner suit.

She'd followed his glance. 'I'll run into town when the shops open and buy what you need.'

'I need to get back to Sydney.'

'There's a bus this afternoon.'

'I don't…'

'Want to use the bus? You have no choice. Otherwise you're stuck here for the weekend and this house is too small. You know it is. Now, if you'll excuse me, I have work to do.'

'What needs doing?'

'I told you. I need to attack the tree across the drive with the chainsaw. Otherwise I can't get into town to get you clothes. I also need to move the sheep back into the outer paddocks. The Cyprus run's restricted—it's my safe paddock but there's not much feed. I either have to move them or hand feed them. So if you'll excuse me… Every minute you keep me here is a minute more before I can run into town to get clothes.'

'You expect me to sit in your father's bathrobe while you work?'

She stilled. 'My father's bathrobe?'

'I assumed…'

'Don't assume,' she snapped. 'My father never wore a bathrobe in his life.'

'Whose…?'

'Stay out of it.' Her anger was palpable. Any minute she'd throw something at him.

'Mardie, I need to help you,' he said, feeling his way through what seemed a minefield.

'You can help by staying out of my way.'

He rose, angry himself. 'I'm not useless.'

'You're useless in a bathrobe or a dinner suit.'

'I did fix the spouting.'

She glowered. 'So you did. I'm trying to remember it.'

'Are you punishing me for walking away fifteen years ago?'

Whoa. There was a moment's deathly silence. Her face lost colour. She closed her eyes and when she opened them something had changed. Anger had been replaced with pure ice.

'Are you out of your mind?' she demanded, speaking slowly, each syllable dripping with frost. 'You think I've been longing for you for fifteen years? Doing nothing? Grazing a few sheep, pining after my long-lost love, playing lovelorn little hayseed?'

'I didn't say...'

'You didn't have to say. What you're thinking is like a huge placard over your head.'

'All I said was that it was a waste...'

'To stay here? To live where I love to live?'

'A hundred sheep...'

'I'm a craft therapist, Blake Maddock.' She was practically yelling. 'And an artist. I did my training part-time, an art course in Whale Cove, going back and forth for almost four years. I work in the local nursing home, organising outings, craft, music, fun. I also practice my art and I'm good. It gives me huge pleasure, and I'm starting to sell. I've sold off acreage because I can't run this farm as a full-time commitment but I still love it. My sheep make me happy. I love my work in the nursing home. I make the best cheese in the district. My mum still loves coming out here. I don't earn enough for luxury but I love everything about my life. And in case you think I've been pining for you... You think you're wearing my dad's bathrobe? I bought that for Hugh. For my husband. Hugh was killed in a car accident two years ago, the week before Christmas, the week before I gave it to him. For some reason I kept it and I loved it. So you're standing there in my husband's bathrobe, accusing me of having no life, of having lived in a time warp since you left, of doing nothing. And you kissed me last night like you were doing me a favour!'

There was no *practically yelling* about it. The last sentence was truly a blast. The dogs backed to the far end of the basket and cringed.

Blake felt like doing exactly the same.

'Mardie...'

'I'm not listening to another word. If I listen to any more, you risk getting a bucket of milk thrown at you. I'm going out now. I'm going to cut the tree away from the driveway and I'm moving sheep. Then I'm going to drive into town, fetch you some clothes that aren't Hugh's and buy you a bus ticket. I believe it leaves at two. I'll drive you to the bus station and it'll be pure pleasure to see the back of you. It was lovely to see you but now it'll be lovely to see you go. So now... Take care of the dogs while I'm out. And thanks for cooking the bacon. I'd eat some more but I feel like choking.'

She stomped out of the kitchen. Bounce leaped after her and she slammed the door.

He was left with Bessie.

He was left with what he'd done.

* * *

Bessie whimpered, nosed her way across to him and lay her head on his knee.

The little collie was doing it for her own need, not his, he told himself, but he took comfort anyway as she rubbed her head under his palm.

Mardie was a widow. She'd trained as a craft therapist.

Fifteen years and he knew nothing of anything. It was a great black hole.

He should have kept in touch.

Walking away from Banksia Bay had been a no-brainer. From the moment Robbie died he knew he'd have to do something. He remembered the announcement of his final-year marks, the letter offering him a place at medical school and the relief of finally knowing he had a plan.

But then he remembered telling Mardie and watching her face pale as it had paled a few moments ago.

He'd been exuberant, exultant. 'I'm going to Sydney. I can finally do something with my life.'

He glanced out of the window at the rain-washed world, at the undulating paddocks, the vast, spreading gums lining the driveway, the shimmer of the sea in the distance.

He and Mardie had spent a magical childhood in this place. Wandering the farm, the beaches, the harbour. Surfing, rabbiting, messing round with boats, nothing to contain them.

But he needed to work. In Africa he'd made a difference. No more.

He glanced out of the window again. Mardie was heading up the drive on the tractor, towards the shattered tree. Chainsaw on the back. Bounce running along behind.

A husband, dead. A mother cared for.

A wasted life?

It was unfair. He needed to apologise.

He already had. There was nothing more to be said. She wanted him to leave.

He couldn't leave yet. He'd work with her one last time. He'd make amends if he could.

Bessie stirred on his knee, her blind eyes staring at nothing, white clouds of fog.

'Maybe we're both blind,' he told her.

Me, me, me. Wrong attitude. To be feeling sorry for himself when this dog was in such need.

Self-pity helped no one. He needed to help Mardie. He needed to sort the fate of Bessie. He needed to make some phone calls.

And then he needed to leave.

CHAPTER FOUR

THE TREE HAD spilt straight down the middle. The scorch marks from the lightning formed a vicious slash down the side of the trunk still standing and the ground around the base was scorched black.

She loved the trees down the driveway, a sentinel of mighty gums a hundred years old.

She felt like crying.

Not just for the tree.

What was he doing, walking into her life again with his stupid, hurtful judgements? What crazy twist of fate had him crash his car where hers was the closest house?

Seeing him stand in her kitchen…in the bathrobe she'd bought for Hugh…

It made her feel tired and old and ill.

And also immeasurably sad. Her first sensation on seeing him again had been joy. Then, as she'd stood in the rain last night, holding the ladder while he fought her drainpipe, the joy had turned to something else. Something inexplicable.

A resurrection of what she'd once felt, or something more?

It didn't matter what she'd felt. She didn't need his judgement.

Work was her salvation. If she worked hard enough she didn't have to think. This tree would take weeks to clear, but she'd do enough now to clear the drive.

She attacked the smaller branches first, slicing them free and dragging them clear. After chopping the main branches for firewood, she'd be left with a pile of leaf litter. She'd use it eventually for mulch, but first she had to get it into a clear space so at the height of summer she didn't risk fire as it rotted and heated.

It was heavy work, heaving branches onto the trailer on the back of the tractor, but work was what she needed to defuse anger.

Work had always been her salvation. When her mother grew sicker. When Hugh died.

When Blake left.

How could she put Blake leaving alongside her grief for her mother, for Hugh?

She'd been sixteen. It couldn't have hurt as much.

She still remembered it though. Blake walking away.

She wanted to cry.

She didn't.

It was just…him walking back. Reminding her of what she'd lost.

She hadn't lost anything. She especially hadn't lost Blake. She'd never had him.

The chainsaw sliced through a protruding branch. She stepped back smartly as it crashed from the broken trunk.

It was hauled away before it hit the ground.

She turned, and Blake was there.

He was back in his dinner suit. Or most of his dinner suit. Trousers and shirt and shoes. His trousers were still soaked. His gorgeous dress shoes were muddy. His white shirt was damp, the top buttons were undone and the sleeves were rolled up. Everything clung.

Don't look. He made her feel…

Don't feel.

He grabbed the branch and dragged it across to the trailer.

'You'll ruin your suit,' she managed.

'I can afford it.'

Of course he could. Money had never been an issue.

The old stories seeped back. Miss Maddock, Blake's great-aunt. She'd arrived here in her thirties, so gossip said, cashed up, buying the lonely house out on the headland, doing it up almost as a mansion, but seeing no one. There was money to pay for upkeep, money to keep her isolated, money enough to snub the district, take a shopping trip to Sydney once a month, be as eccentric as she liked.

Mardie was too young to remember when Blake arrived but she knew the gossip about that, too. 'His mother's ill. His parents have more money than they know what to do with. The aunt's agreed to look after him until his mum gets better, heaven help him.'

Then, as he was about to finish junior school, more gossip. 'They're dead in a plane cash in Italy. Blake'll have to stay on with the old lady. Word is the parents were really rich. It's in trust for the kid. Though how he can use it, stuck here with her…'

The town heard a little about the plane crash, learned Blake's father was a wealthy gambler who spent his life between casinos, learned his mother had been 'ill' for a long time, learned nothing else. The aunt shut up and told the town to mind its own business.

Past history. She hauled her thoughts back to now.

Don't feel.

She cut the chainsaw motor and the silence stunned her.
'Thank you,' she said.

'It's the least I can do,' he said shortly, heaving the branch with a strength that put hers in the shade. 'After offending you just about every way I can think of, I need to make amends. You want me to keep going with this while you move the sheep?'

'Chainsawing's a skill.'

'Hey, I'm a surgeon,' he said, sounding miffed, and suddenly she found herself smiling.

And how could she not look? How could she not feel?

He was standing in the early-morning sun, dressed in the remnants of his dinner suit. His hair was rumpled; he obviously hadn't stopped to worry about personal grooming. He'd grabbed another branch and was about to heave.

'A surgeon,' she said, cautiously. 'So that makes you a chainsaw expert?'

'You're saying I'm not capable?'

'If you've been practising chainsawing on your patients for the last fifteen years, heaven help them.'

He grinned. It lit his face, making him look younger. It made him look like the Blake she remembered.

She felt her smile fade. Blake…

'Mardie, I'm sorry.' He wasn't coming close; there was half a ruined tree between them. 'I barge back into your life, I make stupid assumptions, I insult you, I try and land you with a blind dog…'

'Plus you didn't make the bacon crispy,' she retorted. 'I can forgive anything else.'

'I didn't…'

'Whatever you've been doing in the last fifteen years, it's not been cooking. Are those clothes very uncomfortable?'

'They're fine.' He paused, looked down at his sodden trousers, gave a rueful grimace. 'Okay, they're appalling.'

'I could lend you…'

'I don't want any more of your husband's clothes.'

'You didn't appreciate the bathrobe?'

'The bathrobe's excellent—although dry jocks would add a little something, even to the bathrobe.'

Dry jocks…

She blushed.

How long since she'd blushed? Her blushing used to kill her as a teenager. She thought she was over it.

She wasn't. She blushed. Over the mention of jocks. What, was she thirteen again?

'Hey,' Blake said, and suddenly his attention was no longer on her. Which was just as well. The blush was taking a while to subside. He stooped and peered at the slab of trunk that had peeled away. 'Look at this.'

She looked—and she blushed some more.

At ten years old, before she had any idea of vandalism, of desecration of trees, maybe before she had any sense at all, her dad had given her a pocket knife for her birthday. It had neat little tools on the side. It had her name engraved on the hilt. She'd loved that knife.

It hadn't always been a force for good—as displayed by what Blake was looking at.

The carving was at the base of the tree, practically in the dirt so only she knew it was there. It was cut into the bark and it had scored deeper and deeper as the tree grew.

M.R. xx B.M. A heart.

Blushing didn't begin to describe what was happening right now. She was about to go up in flames.

Blake was grinning.

'So I was dumb,' she snapped and reverted to chainsawing. Really loud. Loud was her salvation.

Would her blush never subside? She cut the lowest branch free, right through the middle of the initials.

M.R. xx...nobody. A heart all by itself.

He didn't comment.

They worked on, Mardie sawing, Blake carting timber.

Her blush and her head gradually cleared, and so did the driveway.

It would have taken her half a day to do this herself, but in an hour they had the driveway clear. The rest could be done over time. Not this morning, when she had Blake to get rid of.

She was so aware of him...

Stupid, stupid, stupid.

'Sheep?' he said, as she tossed the chainsaw onto the back of the tractor.

'Yep. I'll take the trailer off and head down and get them. I'll need Bounce.' She gave a man-sized whistle and Bounce came flying to her side.

Bessie emerged from the house. Reached the steps. Stopped.

'Can you stay with Bessie?' she asked, but Blake was already striding back to the house. Instead of going inside, though, he lifted Bessie down the steps, set her down and then headed back, Bessie at his side.

Mardie was removing the trailer from the tractor. Trying to block Blake out. She needed to head down the paddock and move the sheep—without a city doctor and a blind dog.

'It's rough going down there,' she said. 'I don't think...'

'Let her come,' he said gently. 'She's breaking her heart. She could sit at your feet on the tractor. There's room.'

'And when I get down there? I need to work. I can't...'

'I'll come with you.' Then, instead of waiting for her to

agree, he climbed onto the running board, set Bessie at Mardie's feet and hung on himself. He looked down at Bounce, who was quivering all over, anticipating adventure. 'Sorry, mate, you're going to have to run behind.'

'He wouldn't have it any other way,' Mardie managed. And stupidly she felt like blushing again.

He was far too close. He was right...there. His shoulder was brushing her waist.

He expected her to calmly drive the tractor with him standing on the running board?

A woman could crash.

What were her hormones thinking?

Whatever they were thinking, they had nothing to do with her, she told herself. Her hormones could go take a cold shower. This guy was rude and insulting and an echo from her past she could do without.

It was just that he was so...close.

He'd ripped his shirt. He had a smear of mud down his face. He obviously had no shaving gear with him. His five-o'clock shadow was dark and...okay, and *sexy*.

She thought suddenly of her teenage James Bond fixation. Blake as James Bond at seventeen? Not even close.

Blake now...

He looked a lean, mean James Bond, she thought. And he was right by her side. She and James, off to face adventure with their two sleek adventure dogs.

Or off to move sheep with one silly pup and one blind stray.

'We should have brought the Lamborghini,' Blake said, and she glanced up at him in amazement.

They'd always had this. The ability to read what the other was thinking, to laugh even before the other was laughing.

She couldn't stop herself smiling.

'You want me to gun this baby?' she demanded. 'In fourth gear I reckon we can hit ten miles an hour. Three minutes tops from nought to ten. Who'd look for Formula One when we have my old tractor?'

He chuckled.

She loved his chuckle.

She loved Blake.

Huh?

No! She was old enough and sensible enough to stop herself right there. Once upon a time she'd loved Blake, with all the passion of her sixteen-year-old self, but even then she'd been sensible, knowing she couldn't follow him.

Now the sensible side of her kicked in again. She'd loved a seventeen-year-old Blake, but that wasn't who was standing on her running board. This guy must be what, thirty-two? He'd lived more of his life without her than with her. He had another life somewhere she knew nothing about.

He'd made all sorts of judgements about her, and she wasn't about to do the same to him.

She didn't know him any more.

'Are you married?' she asked suddenly. He was gazing out over the paddocks towards his aunt's old house, his eyes following the route they used to travel on their bikes, sometimes half a dozen times a day.

'Why do you want to know?'

'Because it's all been about me,' she said, exasperated. 'You've got my back-story, even down to the colour of bathrobe I hoped my husband liked. I know nothing.'

'You know I studied medicine.'

'And you know what I did. Snap. Now marriage. I've shown you mine, you show me yours.'

'Was yours happy?'

'Blake!'

He grinned at that, a trifle rueful. 'Yeah, I know. Unfair. It's just...' His voice trailed off.

'You did get married?'

'No,' he said. 'I was engaged for a bit. It didn't work out.'

'Oh, Blake...'

'Old history. I'm over it.'

'Another doctor?'

'Yes.'

'That makes sense.'

'What's that supposed to mean?'

'You wanted someone to share your life.' She hesitated. 'No. It was more than that. You needed someone to incorporate into your life. A marriage was never going to work on that basis.'

Silence. Her words had been mean, she thought. She should apologise. She did in her head but not out loud.

For some reason barriers were needed. She didn't need to get any closer to this man than she already was.

She needed him to get off the tractor. She needed him to stop touching her.

They reached the gate into the Cyprus paddock. 'Leave this one open,' she said.

He jumped down, and she was jolted by the sense of loss. How dumb was that?

He swung the gate wide, waited till she was through and then jumped up again. It was a prosaic action, done a score of times a day in her life, but she could tell... His face was revealing more than he could possibly know.

There were all sorts of sensations crowding in. The sensory experience of morning on a farm after rain... Something she almost took for granted but he'd lost fifteen years ago.

He hadn't lost it. He'd set it aside.

The Blake she knew was still in there.

The sheep were grazing near the Cyprus hedge. She'd used this paddock a few times recently and pickings were lean. The sheep headed towards the tractor as soon as they saw her coming, hopeful for hay.

'You're going to have to work for it,' she told them, turning thankfully to practical and prosaic. 'There's plenty of feed in the back paddocks, so you need to move.' She jumped down from the tractor—on the far side of Blake because there was no way she was brushing past him—and whistled to Bounce.

'Away to me,' she called. Firmly. Hopefully.

Eventually Bounce was going to be a brilliant working dog. He was desperate to please, and fiercely intelligent. Right now, however, he was just a bit too eager. Full of potential and hope.

He headed clockwise round the back of the pack as per order but he rushed, he went too close to the sheep and they startled. They started scattering before he could get to the back of the mob, spreading out in bleating sheep hysteria.

She'd have to run herself to get on the other side of them. She took off...

And suddenly Bessie was beside her, like a shadow, running in tandem, keeping pace.

The sheep reacted differently with the dogs. With her they were likely to run past, spread out, but Bessie's presence gave them pause. They fell back, uncertain. Bounce finally got round the back—and they started heading the way she wanted them to go, to the open paddock gate.

'Way back,' she yelled to Bounce and he streaked further back.

He barked.

And then Bessie was gone from her side, flying across the paddock to join Bounce at the rear, but on this flank.

She had two dogs at the back.

Bounce barked again and Bessie moved further back. She was well out of reach of the flock but they knew she was there.

How had she done that? *She was blind.*

There was no time to think about it now. Mardie sprinted towards the gate to stop them veering along the fence instead of through. But Blake was already there.

James Bond in his dinner suit, herding sheep.

The sheep crowded towards him, saw the open gate, hesitated.

Bessie barked.

Bounce crowded them behind.

James Bond held the gate.

They rushed through, a steady stream of non-panicked sheep, and the thing was done.

With just Bounce that might have taken her half an hour. They'd done it in minutes.

Blake swung the gate closed. 'How easy was that?' he demanded, grinning in satisfaction. 'Two good dogs...'

Both of them looked at Bessie.

As the sheep had flooded through the gate she'd paused, stopped. She'd have followed movement, light and sound. Now, things would simply be green again.

She sat, waiting for some sensory cue to move again.

Bounce headed to her side and sniffed. Rubbed himself against his new friend. Touched Bessie as she had touched him.

The start of a canine love affair?

Oh, for heaven's sake... She really was operating on hormones this morning. Mardie whistled. Bounce ran towards her and Bessie came with him.

Wagging her tail.

Wagging her whole body.

Border collies worked for pleasure. Herding sheep had been bred into them for generations.

This dog was seriously good.

She'd kept her distance from the flock. It was a bright morning and the sheep were washed clean with the rain. White against green...it had been possible for her to help.

And if she could help blind...

How much would it cost...?

'I'll pay,' Blake said and she blinked.

'Pardon?'

'I can't keep her,' he said. 'I know it's not fair to ask you to keep a dog I found, but you've always had more than one dog. I remember three.'

'I don't think...'

'She's born to work,' he said. 'She's almost as good blind as Bounce is now.'

'Bounce will get better,' she said, distracted and loyal. 'He's a work in progress.'

'And Bessie's a work of art. You know she's good. You could use her. I can afford...'

'It doesn't always work,' she said shortly. She'd thought this through it morning, with her face against Clarabelle's flank. It was the time she did her best thinking, but the conclusions she'd come to this morning were bleak. 'You think I'd do that to her? Send her to the city, two operations, each one risky. Weeks in a strange place, strange kennels, knowing no one. She's done that already. She's been in the pound since Charlie went into care. She's been thrown out of the Animal Welfare van when it crashed and she's been wandering lost for a week. You want me to put her through more trauma?'

'Yes,' he said bluntly. 'She could take it.'

'She can't.' Mardie squatted, clicking her fingers, and the gentle little collie came to her. 'She's had enough, Blake,' she said. 'To put her through operations with no guarantee of success...'

But he wasn't accepting what she was saying. 'It would succeed,' he said, just as firmly. He hesitated. 'Okay, there's never a hundred per cent guarantee but it's close. She's a young dog. These cataracts haven't been present for all that long. I've had a good look. They're full, fluid-filled, not old and shrinking. That means less risk of scarring. Underneath, her eyes should be fine. There's a small risk of retina detachment with the operation, but with the best aftercare the risk is tiny.'

'How do you know?'

'I do the same operation all the time on humans,' he said simply. 'That's what I am, it's what I do—ophthalmology. There's a vet in Sydney who spent time with me while we were training. He's a personal friend and, Mardie, I know he'll do this for me. I'll pay all the expenses and at the end of it you'll have a fine working dog. I know she's my responsibility; I'm not asking you to take her on as a favour. I know she'll be a fabulous dog. I know she can be cured.'

She stared up at him, stunned. 'But the cost...' She couldn't think of anything more sensible to say.

'You know money's not an issue.'

Of course it wasn't. Somehow she forced herself not to

look at Blake, to look only at Bessie. To think only of Bessie. So many things... To take this next step...

'I'd... I'd have to talk to Charlie,' she managed.

'Charlie?'

'The guy who owned her.'

'He put her in the pound.'

'He didn't have a choice. He was hospitalised himself.'

Bessie was being licked now by Bounce. Her week of escape had left her with interesting smells, and probably interesting tastes. Both dogs seemed deeply content.

Bessie and Bounce... Growing more devoted by the moment.

Hormones. Leave them out of this.

'How long would she need to stay in Sydney?' she asked, cautiously. Forcing herself to think past Blake. Beginning to think...maybe.

'Maybe a week. A few days before for tests and a few days after.'

'You'd be doing this because...'

'Call it thanks for the night's accommodation.'

'Then we'd be square again,' she said, a bit too harshly because suddenly...suddenly that was how she was feeling. Harsh. 'It wouldn't do to be in my debt.'

'Mardie...'

'I'm sorry, that's not very gracious.' She rose, reaching a decision. Regrouped. Tried very hard to put harsh behind her.

'Okay, so I don't want charity, but this is Bessie we're talking about. So that'd be it? You'd take her to Sydney, fix her eyes, give her back to me, no strings attached?'

'What do you mean—strings?'

'I'm not sure,' she said. 'It was only...that kiss. Blake,

dumb or not, I don't want to go down the friendship path again. One cured dog, that's all this would be.'

'I never suggested anything else.'

She didn't reply.

She was being dumb.

He'd never suggested anything else. Of course he hadn't. So what...*else* was she thinking?

He hated not knowing what she was thinking. He'd always known.

He didn't know now.

He gazed around him, at the farm, at the sunlight on the wet grass, at the great crashed gum in the distance.

The shattered timber...

A friendship finished.

It wasn't about the kiss, he thought. It was about much more.

'I should have written,' he said softly into the morning stillness. 'I'm sorry I didn't. I was young and stupid and I didn't know how to handle my own grief at leaving.'

'You weren't sad to be going. You were jumping out of your skin.'

'I was,' he said. 'But I was sad to be leaving you. Gutted.'

'You didn't show it.'

'If I'd shown it,' he said simply, 'I never could have left.'

Then the outside world arrived. A police car pulled up out on the road, and Raff, the local cop, strolled across the paddocks to meet them. Someone had obviously reported Blake's crashed car.

'Hey,' Raff called. Blake knew Raff—he'd been part of the pack of local kids and he could see Raff recognised him in turn. Raff greeted him with warmth and a trace of relief. 'I heard you were at the reunion last night. When Gladys Mitchell called and said a Mercedes was wrapped round a tree I thought it must be you.' He grinned as he took in Blake's battered clothes. 'New fashion for farm work? Give the place a certain style, eh, Mardie? So what happened?'

He listened as a good cop should, but when he was told about Bessie his cheer slid away.

'Dogs,' he said bleakly. 'They're all over the place, and this one... At least Henrietta will be thankful she's found. You want me to take her back to town?'

'I'm keeping her,' Mardie said, and Raff looked from the dog to Mardie and back again.

'She's blind, Mardie,' he said, as if Mardie might not have noticed. 'I don't know how to say this but...'

'Blake says he'll fix her for me. He's an eye surgeon. He knows about cataracts. He'll take her back to Sydney and cure her.'

Raff whistled, stunned. 'You'd do that?'

'Yeah,' Blake said, feeling suddenly defensive. There was surprise in Raff's voice—amazement that an outsider was offering to help in what was essentially the town's business?

He'd never been part of this community, he thought. He'd been the rich kid. The kid who lived with the weird old lady. Now here he was, still on the outside, a guy in a dinner suit, offering charity.

But the charity, it seemed, was acceptable. 'Hen'll offer you her kingdom,' Raff said. 'Mind, her kingdom consists of lost dogs so I'd run a mile. But what about you, Mardie? Can you afford to keep another dog?'

Afford...

Were things so tight, then, that the cost of even keeping another dog would be a consideration?

'Of course I can. And she's good, Raff,' Mardie said. 'Great with sheep. I'll go in and talk to Charlie.'

'Charlie?'

'Her collar said she's Charlie's dog.'

Raff whistled at that, too. 'Of course. I remember... She'll be great, then. Charlie's been amazing,' he told Blake. 'In his day he's been the best dog-trainer in the district. Took every championship going.'

And Blake suddenly remembered.

Just before Mardie's dad died he'd taken them to the local sheepdog trials. They'd seen an elderly man in a battered coat and wide-brimmed hat take all the awards going. Charlie. Charlie's dogs had moved sheep so skilfully they might as well be attached to them by leads. The dogs simply looked at the sheep and the sheep jumped to obey.

'I'll learn how to do that,' Mardie had declared, and he couldn't help himself—he looked at Bounce. Who was still sort of...bouncing.

'He's a work in progress,' Mardie repeated defensively, and he grinned.

'I can see that. Taking a while to settle.'

'Bessie'll teach him,' she said. 'When she's better.'

'So you are serious?' Raff asked Blake. 'Will you take her to Sydney with you now?'

And Blake got that, too. This guy was interested in practicalities and he was also protecting his own. He wasn't having Mardie landed with a blind dog and a half-promise to fix her. Maybe Raff knew, as Blake did, that once Mardie took Bessie on, she'd keep her, regardless.

Once Mardie gave her heart, she didn't take it back.

And that was a kick in the guts, too.

She'd married?

What was she supposed to have done? Had he expected her to stay loyal to him for fifteen years? Pining for a memory?

He'd moved on. So had she.

'I need to contact my vet friend,' he said, but he was speaking to Mardie. He was thinking of Mardie, feeling bad. Okay, he'd let her down in the past, but on this at least he could make good. 'I don't know when he could fit her in. And I'll need to get her there. I imagine I'll need to take the bus back to Sydney and come back once I've organised a car.'

'I'll take you back to Sydney,' Mardie said.

Silence.

Mardie, driving him back to Sydney.

It was little more than a two-hour drive.

Why not?

It was just that...

He saw the corners of her mouth twitch. Uh-oh. She'd guessed his errant thought. His dumb thought.

'I'm guessing Blake's worrying that Sydney's a big, big city and I might rightfully be scared,' she told Raff, her eyes suddenly alight with laughter. 'But I hear there's folk who've visited and come out alive.' She snagged a blade of grass and started chewing. Country hick personified. 'Ain't that right, Raff?'

'He's right in that there's perils aplenty,' Raff said gravely, cop-like, catching on in an instant.

'Like what?' she said and put on an anxious face.

'Restrooms,' Raff drawled back. 'Fearsome places. They teach us in cop school. If you use a city restroom, don't sit on the seat—city germs'll kill you before you can put your shopping on the floor. And don't put your feet on the ground or you'll be hit by a syringe from under the stalls. White slave traders,' he said, his voice loaded with doom. 'You'll wake up in a harem in Bathsheba. You reckon you can risk that, our Mardie?'

Mardie grinned. At Raff, not at him.

'I reckon I'll take my chances. Lorraine'll look after my place for a while. Mum's happy right now. The forecast for the weather's settled. It'll do me good to have a few days away.'

Whoa, Blake thought. A few days? She was coming to Sydney as in...*coming to stay*?

'My aunt's apartment only has one bedroom,' he said before he could stop himself.

Mardie's grin widened. She and Raff were still enjoying their joke. 'Not a harem, then?'

'Um...' He managed a limp smile. 'No.'

'Too bad. But I have somewhere I can stay in Sydney,' she said quite kindly. 'In Coogee. I can take Bounce there. It'll be easier on Bessie if Bounce is close; a semblance of normality. Is Coogee close to where Bessie will need to be looked after?'

'Yes.' As luck would have it, the next suburb to Central Vets.

But... How come she had a place to stay in Sydney? The way she and Raff were laughing...she went often?

There were a million questions he wanted to ask.

He was an outsider. He had no right to ask.

'I'll catch the bus back to Sydney,' he said, not knowing what else to say. 'I'll let you know about Bessie's operation and you can come as soon as it's scheduled.'

'Organise it now,' Raff said, laughter giving way to cop in charge.

'You don't trust me?'

'I don't want Mardie landed with a blind dog.' Raff's smile died. 'You haven't been near the place for fifteen years. Why should I trust you? Sorry, mate, but my job's looking out for this community.'

'I keep my word.'

'I trust him,' Mardie said.

It needed only that—that she gave him a reference as well as everything else. But he glanced at her and she met his gaze and he saw...

It was more than words. She was meeting his gaze head-on, her eyes clear and steady, and he knew that a decision had been taken.

He'd lost something fifteen years ago. A tiny part of that was being given back.

He smiled at her, and she smiled straight back, a wide, cheeky smile that was almost daring.

He'd forgotten how lovely that smile was.

Or maybe he'd always remembered but he'd locked it away in a corner that had stayed locked; a corner that held things that hurt too much to take out and examine.

A corner that held Robbie?

'You have a change of clothes somewhere?' Raff asked, watching them both with a bemused expression. It was a cop expression, giving nothing away but maybe understanding more than they wanted.

'No, I...'

'There's nothing in the car except your laptop and brief-case,' Raff said. 'I searched it. I also wasted a few minutes searching in case you were dead. You might have phoned, Mardie.'

'The phone's down.'

He swore. 'Sorry, that's right, a tree crashed on the lines

between town and here. It should be up by lunchtime. Okay, moving on, you need to organise the dog and then you need to organise something to wear. You go out in public like that and I'll have calls to arrest you for indecent exposure.'

Raff was right. He was indecent. His ripped shirt was hardly there.

Both Mardie and Raff were gazing at him. Raff with speculation. Mardie with...something else.

She started to smile and then...suddenly her smile turned again into a blush. He watched as she fought, but failed, to keep her colour under control.

It wasn't just a blush. It was sheer, breathtaking beauty.

Mardie...

'I'll take him into town and buy some gear,' she managed, trying to sound practical despite the blush. 'If he can organise Bessie's operation for this week I'll take them both to Sydney tomorrow.'

'Excuse me,' he said. 'Is this about me? And I can take the bus.'

'Don't look a gift horse in the mouth,' Raff said shortly. 'If Mardie's happy to take you... Sunday's the soccer bus. You don't know what you're missing.'

'I can't stay here another night.'

'There are bed and breakfasts in town,' Raff said. 'Though most of your reunion lot are staying for the weekend. You'll be lucky to find anywhere.'

'Don't be dumb,' Mardie said. 'You can stay and help me get rid of the rest of the tree.'

'Organise the vet first,' Raff said.

'I told you, Raff, I trust him.'

'Yeah, you'd trust anyone,' Raff said and handed Blake his radio. 'Satellite,' he said. 'I can get signal anywhere. For emergency cop stuff. Or, in this instance, emergency dog stuff and protecting-Mardie duty. If Mardie's putting you up for the weekend and you're imposing a dog on her, it's the least I can do. Mardie might trust you. I want proof. Ring your mate and see if you can get this operation organised. Now.'

CHAPTER FIVE

COLIN COULD DO IT. 'For no one else,' he said, 'but for you, yes. I leave gaps for emergencies. Cataracts don't usually rate but in this case I'll slot her in. I'll need her here three days beforehand for tests and eye-drops. If everything's good then I'll schedule surgery for Thursday. She'll need careful monitoring afterwards but you should be able to do that yourself.'

He'd worry about aftercare later, Blake decided, relaying the part about surgery and tests but not the aftercare. He knew it'd be complicated, and things were complicated enough.

Raff left, promising to send a tow truck for the car. Promising to let Henrietta know about Bessie.

He left grinning.

He'd backed Blake into a corner. Instant dog surgery.

He'd backed him into staying another night with Mardie.

Staying with Mardie was the biggie. He felt... It felt...

As if he was out of control, and Blake Maddock was a man who didn't like being out of control.

The trip into town made him feel even worse. Mardie had offered to buy clothes for him, but that seemed weird.

What he hadn't thought through was how weird it would be to walk into Morrisy Drapers and have every person in the shop recognise him.

They already knew what had happened. Of course. Banksia Bay was like that. He was wearing his battered dinner-suit trousers and Raff's spare jacket with cop insignia. Inconspicuous R Us.

He felt like a flashing neon.

'Oh, you poor boy.' Mrs Connor, who ran Morrisy Drapers, was a gusher. 'We hear your car's a write-off. But Raff says it's a rental car so that's lucky. But you were even luckier you weren't killed. And all for a stray dog. My old dad says never swerve for animals. They're not worth losing your life over.'

'Bessie's lucky he did,' Mardie said roundly. 'How could he not try to miss her? And he didn't risk his life. He was driving a tank.'

'A Mercedes isn't a tank,' Mrs Connor said, shocked, as she handed clothes over the counter. 'A tank's what you drive.'

'My truck's not a tank. It's practically luxury,' Mardie retorted. 'Isn't that right, Blake?'

Blake glanced outside to where they'd parked the truck. It was an ancient Dodge, built, he suspected, to withstand the Huns.

Definitely tankish. Though most tanks didn't have rust.

'Um…pure driving pleasure,' he managed and he was rewarded by Mardie's smile. It was a truly gorgeous smile.

It always had been a gorgeous smile. He hadn't realised how much he'd missed it.

'It's definitely classy,' Mardie declared, eyeing Blake's pile of sensible clothes with approval. 'Like these. Jeans and T-shirt, pure class. What about boots, Mrs Connor?'

'Work boots or nothing,' Mrs Connor said.

'Excellent,' Mardie decreed. 'We have twenty-four hours before we head to Sydney and I intend to put him to work. You want to change here, Blake, before we head to the nursing home?'

'We're going to the nursing home?' He wanted to go straight back to Mardie's. Actually, he wanted to go straight back to Sydney but it wasn't happening. It was Mardie who was giving orders. He was on her turf, doing what she wanted.

The nursing home it was. Her mother, Etta.

'I need to see Mum,' she said. 'I need to organise a few days away, and we also need to see Charlie, to explain that you found his dog and you're going to save her. Mum will love to see you.'

'It might be better if you go alone,' he said diffidently, and she looked at him as if he was crazy.

'Better for who?'

'For your mum.' Etta had been so good to him. He should have kept in touch. Why make her remember what a stupid kid he'd been? 'I've been no part of your mother's life for a long time now,' he said, almost to himself. 'It's best to leave things as they are.'

She looked at him for a long, considering minute. Looked as if she was about to say something and then thought better of it. Reconsidered.

'Fine,' she said at last. 'Stay in the truck. Stay nice and uninvolved, like you have for fifteen years.'

Mardie checked in at the nurses' station first. She worked here three days a week. She needed to organise time away.

Liz, the nurse administrator, greeted her with unconcealed curiosity. She was practically vibrating with her need to know. 'So the rumours are true. Blake Maddock's back.'

'I hate this town.'

Liz giggled. 'We're fast. I hear he's hot. You guys were such an item...'

'Fifteen years ago,' she retorted. 'Will you cut it out?'

'You're not the least bit interested?'

'No!' That was a lie, but the guy was sitting out in the truck being uninvolved. It'd pay her to be uninvolved as well. Very uninvolved.

'Yet you're going to Sydney with him.'

'I really hate this town. Yes, but I'm not staying anywhere near him. I'll stay at Irena's. He's organising the operation on Bessie's eyes, that's all.'

Liz's smile faded. 'Bessie. Raff told Henrietta you found Charlie's dog. You really think the operation will work?'

'Blake's an eye surgeon. He says it will.'

'It'll be the best gift you could give to Charlie. Did you bring her with you?'

'I wasn't sure if I should.' She hesitated. 'Would it be kind?'

Liz considered and then grimaced. 'Maybe not. He gave her to the pound, and it nearly killed him. If the operation doesn't work... For him to say goodbye again...'

'You think I shouldn't tell him we're trying?'

'He already knows she's been found. This is Banksia Bay, after all. Tell him what's happening, but it might stress him too much to see her. Operations sometimes fail, regardless of what your Blake says.'

'He's not my Blake!'

'Regardless of what *anyone's* Blake says,' Liz retorted, her smile returning. 'Get her better and bring her in then. Meanwhile, don't worry about your mum; you know we'll look after her. And even though we love your craft classes, we all know how long it's been since you've had a break. Take a real holiday. Have some fun. If anyone deserves it, you do.'

And then she paused. Someone was strolling past her window.

Her eyes widened. 'Oh, my...'

Mardie followed her gaze.

Blake.

Jeans. T-shirt. Work boots.

Body to die for.

'Oh, my,' Liz repeated, mocking fanning herself. 'If I'd known he was going to turn out like this I would have snagged him in grade school. Only, of course, you got in first.'

'I did not!'

'You did, too.'

'Yeah, well, if I did it's all in the past,' Mardie said hotly. 'He wiped Banksia Bay from the map when he left.'

'Yeah, but a woman could forgive a lot of a guy who looks like this.'

'Not this woman,' Mardie retorted. 'I have a long memory.'

'Boyfriend-girlfriend fights from fifteen years ago?' Liz chuckled. 'With that package in front of me I'd get over it fast. People change.' But then Liz held up her hands as if in surrender. 'Okay, sweetie, if anger's needed to keep you safe, then stick to your anger. But don't let it mess with fun. Say goodbye to your mum and then go to Sydney—and you keep an open mind.'

Then she glanced again at Blake and fanned herself some more.

'A very open mind,' she repeated. 'A girl'd be a fool not to.'

Mardie's mother was playing solitaire. She glanced up as Blake opened the door and her eyes grew huge. She recognised him in an instant.

'Blake Maddock. Oh, my boy…' Somehow she pushed herself stiffly to wobbly feet and held out her arms.

It took a moment to respond. He stood in the doorway, looking at the woman who'd been practically a mother to him. She'd been far more a mother than his own.

She'd been burdened with arthritis for all the time he remembered, but he'd never seen anything but cheer. She'd lived surrounded by chaos, the radio always on, her kitchen table always laden with her next creation. Her cooking trials had been truly scary. He and Mardie would appear for lunch, Mardie's dad would be looking terrified and Etta would be saying firmly, 'You can eat it or not, there's always eggs on toast, but give it three bites first.'

Chocolate pudding with chilli. Duck à l'orange, only: 'We can't afford duck so I shaped a duck with mince instead. Do you think it looks like a duck?'

Crazy stuff.

Wonderful. Fun.

He'd loved it.

He'd loved Etta. And Bill.

And Mardie.

He should have stayed in touch. He'd been a stupid kid, he'd long accepted his reasons for leaving, but still he felt bad.

Regardless, here was Etta, wobbly on her feet, standing with open arms. Tears were slipping down her cheeks and she was smiling and smiling. 'Blake,' she said again and he walked forward and hugged her.

Mardie walked in the door and her mother was hugging Blake. No, her mother was being hugged. She'd been lifted right off her feet, and she was crying, laughing and railing against him, all at once. 'Put me down, you silly boy. You'll do yourself a damage. Ooh, put me down.'

Blake and her mother...

She stopped short in the doorway and she felt as if the earth had shifted.

Her mother adored Blake. From the time he'd first been allowed past the boundaries of his great-aunt's property, Etta had welcomed him with open arms.

'You ring your aunt and ask if you can stay for lunch,' she'd say, and Blake would look at the crazy experiment on the kitchen table and jump right in.

'Yes, please. That looks...really yummy, Mrs Rainey.'

Now... It was as if she was welcoming home a long-lost son. But Mardie had watched her mother wait for news from Blake, as she herself had waited. She wasn't feeling so welcoming.

If she let herself be as welcoming as her mum... Dangerous territory. She felt as if she were teetering on the edge of some kind of abyss and she needed to step back fast.

She needed to be happy. Bouncy. Impersonal. She pinned on a smile and forced her voice to brightness. 'Isn't it great he's here? Did he tell you he crashed his car last night?'

'No!' Her mother sank back into her armchair, looking at Blake with such an expression...

How could Blake walk away and come back and still be loved? Mardie thought.

He hadn't expected it. He didn't want it. She could read Blake's face and she could see regret and dismay.

He didn't show it in his voice. Instead, he told Etta about the crash, making it funny. He told her about Bessie, making the story sad but hopeful. By the end Etta was demanding they bring her in.

'We can't,' Blake said and told her about Charlie.

'Oh, of course. So you'll fix her and bring her back to visit him all better?' Etta's eyes were shining.

'We'll fix her and then Mardie can bring her in.'

'You come in,' Etta said, suddenly stern. 'I bet Charlie remembers you. He'd love that.'

'My life's in Sydney. And overseas.'

'People only go overseas for visits, and Sydney's a two-hours drive away. If you can go overseas you can come here.'

'Bessie will be Mardie's dog,' he said, gently but inexorably. 'I don't have a place here any more.'

'There's a place in Mardie's spare room, any time you want,' Etta said with asperity. 'That's fine with you, Mardie, isn't it?'

Maybe not. But Mardie didn't say so. She gave her mother a reassuring smile, she said of course Blake could always stay, and she knew that Blake intended nothing of the kind.

He'd walked away. He was home by accident, but it wasn't his home.

He couldn't wait to get away from Banksia Bay. Nothing had changed.

They left Etta, and walked silently to Charlie's room.

Blake was feeling disoriented, as if shadows of the past were reaching out to touch him. Mardie was silent by his side.

She'd been angry with him—she was angry with him. He'd forgiven himself, he thought. He'd figured why his teenage self had acted as he had. Justifying it to Mardie seemed harder.

Justifying it wasn't necessary. He didn't need to tell Mardie…

Maybe he did. Maybe that was the whole reason he'd come home.

Not home. Banksia Bay.

Regardless, now wasn't the time.

Charlie Hunter had once been a big man. No longer. He'd shrivelled with age, and his last stroke had left him paralysed down his left side. He lay motionless, surrounded by memorabilia. Trophies and ribbons. Photographs of dogs. A gorgeous enamelled plate showing Charlie—with dogs. Leads, collars, framed Australian Championship certificates. A lifetime of dogs.

'My Bessie,' he whispered as Blake told him what had happened, what they hoped to do. He could barely get the words out.

'If you don't want...'

But where there'd been apathy and defeat, suddenly there was fire. 'Are you dreaming?' he demanded. 'If I'd had the money, her eyes would have been fixed two years back.' Charlie's words were distorted with paralysis, but he said them loud and strong so they couldn't be mistaken. 'But these last two years, since my first stroke...well, a blind dog wasn't what I needed. It wasn't fair on her, though. She spent her life at my feet, never whining, just there for me. But when she was a pup...the joy of her...'

He paused and fought for breath. Fought for strength to go on. 'It would have been kinder to put her down,' he whispered. I just...couldn't. So finally I sent her to the pound instead. What a cop-out. If you could cure her...'

'No promises,' Blake told him. 'But we'll try.'

'You're a good lad,' Charlie whispered. 'I remember my Hilda talking about you, saying she had no idea how such a miserable old grouch as your aunt deserved a kid with such a good heart. And happy. You were happy as a kid.'

Happy. There was that word again. It caught Blake like a faltering of the heart.

Happy was for childhood. Not for now. Now was for keeping promises.

Without going back to Africa?

It wasn't the time to think of that now. Get out of Banksia Bay and then think it through.

'Bessie'll be back here soon,' he told Charlie. He was sounding too brusque but there was nothing he could do about it. 'Mardie will bring her in as soon as she gets back from Sydney.'

'That's a promise,' Mardie said and he caught another edge of anger. Fair enough. He was promising Mardie's time. He was promising Mardie would see things through.

She would, though. She was the dependable one.

She was the one who stayed at home while he moved on.

Mardie had things to do for the rest of the day. It seemed leaving the farm for over a week involved organisation and she didn't want his help.

'Find a book and give your head a rest,' she told him. 'Lie by the fire and think how lucky you were last night.'

She headed out to see someone called Lorraine, who'd look after the place while she was absent.

He was left with the dogs.

He *was* tired.

He picked up a copy of the *Farmers Weekly* and tried to read.

The dogs lay in front of the fire and tried to settle.

They were all doleful.

Enough. Yes, his head was aching; yes, there were bruises which hurt; the aches from dengue were still with him but lying around made him think of them more.

He had proper clothes now. He could do proper stuff.

He put on his boots and both dogs were alert and at the door in an instant. Together they had it figured; Bounce maintained contact with Bessie as if he realised how much she needed him.

Smartest dogs in the world. Bonding with each other while he watched.

It'd be a joy to give Bessie back her sight, he thought, a joy for Bounce as well as for Bessie.

It'd also be a joy for Mardie. A gift he could leave her with.

The thought was a good one. He headed outside, a dog at each heel, feeling better.

He intended to go for a walk over the farm. He did for a bit. Things looked the same. There was a new shed out the back, seriously big, that had him intrigued, but it was locked.

Was this a guy's shed, he wondered, locked after Hugh died? The thought of Hugh left him feeling strangely empty. Sad that he hadn't kept in touch. That he hadn't been here for her. That there was a part of Mardie he didn't know?

He didn't want to walk any further, he decided. He didn't want to end up at his aunt's crazy mansion which, according to the guys he'd talked to at the reunion, was now boarded up, after the spa operators who'd bought it had gone bankrupt.

Despite the hour, he was tired. Dengue had left him with residual fatigue that was taking months to recede.

But to sleep seemed impossible. Instead, he headed for the massive pile of ruined tree.

They'd cleared a path down the driveway, but heaped on either side were mounds of splintered timber yet to be moved.

How long since he'd played with a chainsaw?

This was a man's job. Fatigue receded in the face of a plan. He grinned and practically felt his chest expand. 'We can do this,' he told the dogs and he felt their quiver of excitement, responding to his enthusiasm. Man with chainsaw.

'So chainsaw, tractor, trailer. I hope she's left the keys. Let's see how much we can get done before she gets back.' It was a small enough token of his thanks, he thought.

Chainsaw. Excellent.

He found the chainsaw in the unlocked shed by the house. On close inspection it seemed a truly excellent power tool. He'd been frankly jealous of Mardie wielding it this morning. 'Nothing to this,' he told the dogs, who both gave rather dubious wags of their tails.

'Okay, you guys can stand back,' he told them. 'You count the logs as I stack 'em for firewood.'

Bounce looked at Bessie and whined. She moved in close and both dogs headed off to the bottom paddock.

Getting some exercise, or abandoning the *Titanic*?

'Dumb dogs,' Blake said. He heaved his chainsaw across his shoulder and headed for the tree.

She hadn't meant to be away for so long, but Lorraine was aching to show her a vase she'd created and to demonstrate a technique she felt could take her in another direction.

Lorraine was a potter. Mardie was an enameller. Together they'd just invested everything they owned and a bit more into a state-of-the-art kiln—a kiln to die for. They could both do so much now they had it.

Lorraine's enthusiasm was infectious, and at home was…

Blake. It was worth talking enamelling, talking potting, so she didn't have to go home to Blake. Blake, whose mere presence had her discombobulated.

But she couldn't stay away for ever. Finally she said goodbye to Lorraine. She headed home.

She turned into the drive and slowed.

They'd cleared the driveway this morning, but there'd been a mass of timber left on either side.

Blake must have worked like a man possessed. The pile of logs beside the woodshed was four times what it had been this morning.

And the remains of the trunk… She was close enough to see. Close enough to…

No!

For what was left of the trunk, still standing tall this morning, had now crashed to the side of the driveway.

And worse…

Behind the massive trunk she could see… Blake on the tractor, slumped over the wheel. Unconscious?

She was out of the truck before she knew it, screaming without words. Or maybe there were words, just the one.

No. No. No.

Running.

'Blake…'

She was clambering across fallen branches, stumbling, ripping branches aside. Feeling cold, empty terror. 'Blake!'

She thought…she thought…

'Blake!'

He lifted his head from the steering wheel. Pushed himself up. Spoke.

'Mardie?'

Alive…

Her heart kick-started again. Just.

Blake. Alive.

He sounded dazed. Half asleep? 'I got it down,' he said. 'The whole thing.'

There was even a tinge of pride in his voice.

He got it down.

Terror receded, leaving a void where things didn't make sense. She was struggling to take it in.

She was in the middle of a crush of timber.

Blake was alive.

'I thought you were dead,' she said stupidly, not believing what she was seeing. 'I thought…'

'I went to sleep,' he said apologetically. 'I cleared the branches that fell, and then I thought I could get the rest of the trunk down. It took more than I thought.'

Asleep.

'I thought…' she said and then stopped.

He'd seen her face now. She knew she wouldn't have a vestige of colour left.

'I had dengue fever,' he said apologetically. 'It takes it out of me. I really wanted to get it down. Then I brought the tractor and trailer close to clear the mess but I thought…' He gave her an apologetic smile. 'The sun felt great. I thought I'd take a quick nana nap.'

A nana nap. He'd been taking a nana nap while she thought he'd been brained by a tree.

She gazed around her, taking great gulps of air. Maybe she'd forgotten to breathe.

He'd cleared half a tree.

Then he'd had a nana nap.

'I might have been slightly ambitious,' he conceded. 'I had

this idea of clearing the lot before you got home, and it's a great chainsaw.'

'It...it is,' she agreed. Paused. Took a few more breaths. Then had to say it out loud. The thing that was hammering in her head. 'You could have been killed. I thought you had been.'

She started to shake.

She couldn't stop.

She couldn't...

And suddenly he was stomping across the pile of crushed wood and leaf litter until he reached her.

He held her shoulders and he held her tight.

'Mardie, it's okay. Nothing's hurt. I knew what I was doing. The tractor and I were on the other side of the driveway when it came down. It only looks bad because I brought the trailer in close to start clearing up.'

She couldn't hear. His words were a buzz.

The events of the past, surging back. Moments that had transformed her life.

Her father, folding as he walked in from out in the paddocks. Dead in an instant.

Hugh. One stupid moment, stupid kids in a too-fast car, and his life was over.

And again... The instant she'd seen the fallen tree and Blake slumped over the wheel.

Reaction took over, leaving her no choice in how she responded. She tried to shove back from his hold and she yelled, as she'd never yelled in her life.

'You stupid, stupid moron. You used a chainsaw when no one was home. Don't you realise the first rule, *the first rule*, is to have someone with you when you use big power tools? You just chopped. Macho, macho stupidity. You've given me half a winter's full of chopped wood and what good would that have done if you were dead?'

'You'd have been warm,' he said cautiously. Still holding her.

She wasn't responding to humour. She couldn't. 'It's cold in the cemetery.' She was still yelling.

'Yes, but it's me who'd have been there, not you. But it didn't happen. Mardie, it didn't happen. It was never going to happen. Believe it or not, I knew what I was doing. I'm sorry I didn't finish clearing it. I wanted to. I'll pay to...'

'*Pay?* I don't care about payment.' She was still hysterical. 'I'm not in this for money. I'm not the one who walked away to make money.'

And suddenly it was about more than the tractor. More than this moment. Much more. She was out of control and she was saying it like it was. Years of hurt, welled up and finally released.

'I walked away to make money?' he said cautiously.

'You never looked back,' she said, still out of control. 'Not once. You and your aunt and your stupid, rich family who couldn't even look after a kid, and your stupid money making. If you'd been killed now it'd be no less than you deserve. Of all the stupid things...' She caught her breath on an angry sob. 'I could have lost you again. And now you've brought down the rest of the tree and we'll have to clear this and all you can think of is paying.'

She'd almost lost him again.

She heard her words echo, reverberate. They'd come straight from her heart.

They both knew it.

She was shaking as if she'd stepped out of an ice box.

Her teeth were chattering so hard she could hardly get the words out.

There were tears tracking down her face. The night Hugh died... The day her father collapsed...

The day Blake left.

The dogs moved close to the base of the mess of tree and whined, worried by her yelling. *She* was worried by her yelling. She didn't get out of control.

She was out of control now.

She was still in the middle of the leaf litter. Blake was still holding her.

The branch under them sagged.

And suddenly Blake was in charge. He took her by the waist and lifted her free, tugging her down to solid ground. He set her in front of him but didn't release her.

He held her round the waist as she trembled. Holding her tight. Not saying a thing. She tugged away, but not very hard. Not enough to succeed.

'What...what do you think you're doing?' she managed.

'Waiting until you get over the shock. Trying to reassure you that it's okay.'

'It isn't.'

'Tell me what happened, Mardie,' he said softly. 'The car crash. Was that how your husband died?'

'I... Yes.' There was nothing else to say.

'Here?'

She didn't want to tell him. She never talked about it.

She told him.

'We were driving home from Lorraine's, up the road. A Christmas barbecue.' Her voice was still shaking. Her world was still shaking. 'Six o'clock on a warm Sunday night. A carload of kids came round a blind bend on the wrong side of the road and that was...that. I ended up with a fractured pelvis. But Hugh...my gentle, loving Hugh who'd give me the world, who gave me the world, was gone in an instant. And the dogs. All our dogs. They were in the back.' Another sob. The urge to yell was back, but she couldn't raise the energy. She felt desperately tired. 'And you...you play with chainsaws as if it doesn't matter one bit. You just...risk...'

It was too much. She choked on a sob, her knees gave way from under her and he drew her into him.

For a fraction of a moment she resisted, holding herself rigid. He could feel her anger. He could feel her fear.

But he could feel her shaking and it was the shaking that killed her resistance. She crumpled and he gathered her against him and held and held, as if there was nothing more important than to hold her against his heart and let the world go on without them.

Nothing was more important.

The dogs stood beside them, silent sentinels. Neither moved, as if both realised this moment couldn't be interrupted by a wet nose; it couldn't be interrupted for the world.

He simply held her.

Had she had someone to hold her when Hugh died? he wondered. Two years ago.

Had Mardie buried her husband and come home to an empty house?

The dogs...

He thought of them now. Minor in the scheme of things, minor compared to a husband, but still...

Every time he'd been to this place there'd been a dog pack. 'You need generations of dogs, training each other.' He remembered Mardie's father saying it. 'You lose a dog, it's a heartbreak. You lose all your dogs...' He'd shrugged. 'I don't know how a man could go on without them.'

Bounce was Mardie's only dog, and he was only about twelve months old. That meant it must have been twelve months before she could even bear to get another dog.

He'd have been in Africa. He scanned Australian news on the internet, but never in such detail as names of car crash victims. If he'd known...

The shaking was starting to subside. She tugged away a little and he released her to arm's length, no further.

'Tell me about Hugh,' he said softly, and she managed a ghost of a smile. Realising he was trying to haul her from shock. Trying to respond.

'He was from Whale Cove. Practically a foreigner.'

He smiled, straight into her eyes. It was a smile he couldn't remember using before. Or maybe he had. It was a smile just for Mardie.

'You met him at Whale Cove?'

'That's where I did my art course. He was a paramedic, an ambulance driver. He was gentle, kind, loving...all I ever wanted in a husband. We were friends for ages, were engaged for two years, married for three.'

'He lived with you here?'

'There was Mum.' She was recovering a little but her voice was still shaky. 'We couldn't leave her, and Hugh was happy to transfer to Banksia Bay. Then, when she finally decided to move to the nursing home, Hugh said he loved this place as much as I did. It would have been a great place for our children...' She broke off. Closed her eyes.

'Enough,' she said. 'We have stuff to organise.' She stared at the driveway. 'This to clear, for a start.'

'No.'

'No?'

'I think,' he said apologetically, 'that neither of us should use the chainsaw for a while.'

'You want me to come home to this mess?'

'I've fixed that.'

'It doesn't look fixed.' Indignation was returning. Indignation versus shaking? He almost smiled. Indignation any day.

'That's what I was talking of when I mentioned paying,' he said. Whether or not the shaking had stopped, he was still holding her and she was still allowing herself to be held. 'I rang Raff. He gave me the name of a guy who chops wood for a living. Tony Kennedy'll be here at eight on Monday to clear the mess.'

'But you're already covering the cost of Bessie's operation,' she managed, sounding stunned.

'You know I can afford it.'

There was a moment's silence at that, drawn out, tense, loaded with something he didn't recognise.

'I don't…take charity,' she said at last.

'I don't believe I'm offering charity. I'm responsible.'

'You're not responsible for Bessie.'

'I'm not paying for Bessie for you. I'm paying for Bessie for me. But, regardless, I owe you.'

'Why do you owe me?' she asked in a strange, tight voice.

That, at least, was easy.

'You and your parents made my childhood bearable,' he said simply and firmly. 'I owe you a debt I can never repay. I should have been here for you two years ago. That I wasn't…'

He let the sentence hang.

Silence. More silence. He wasn't sure what to say next. How to begin to make things better?

There was no way.

Mardie was watching him. Her face was calm. Assessing. Very calm. And suddenly he thought…it was like the eye of the storm.

He could almost feel the other side.

'Do you think I needed you?' she asked, almost diffident.

'I assume…'

'Assume nothing.'

'Sorry?'

'Do you think I spent the last fifteen years pining for you?' she asked, still in that strangely calm voice.

'I know that's not true.'

'You do,' she said cordially. 'Yes, at sixteen you were my boyfriend. I wept for weeks when you left. But weeks, Blake Maddock, not years. And then you know what? I got angry. And then I got over it.'

'Good for you.'

'Don't patronise me,' she snapped, and the storm moved closer. With the potential to build. 'Of all the…'

'I didn't mean to patronise.'

'Yes, you did,' she said. 'You do. You're sorry you weren't here for me two years ago. As if somehow, magically, you could have made it better.'

'I never meant that.'

'Good,' she said. 'I'm glad you didn't mean it. Because it wouldn't have made one whit of difference. Do you know how surrounded I was?'

'No, I…'

'I was loved,' she said. 'I *am* loved. Don't you dare think of me as poor, lonely Mardie, facing the big bad world because heroic Blake Maddock wasn't here to take care of her. This place is my home. I'm loved. When people are in trouble here, we help. I had a broken pelvis and my husband was dead but I had my community to surround me. My freezer still contains so many home-cooked meals that I could live on tuna bakes for years. My sheep were cared for, my fences fixed, my house painted. My garden was replanted so that I've had veggies and flowers ever since. I have a friend who came and stayed for two months—Irena. I was cosseted to bits. And here you are saying you're so sorry you weren't here for me, as if it would have made a blind bit of difference.'

She took a deep breath, the calm façade cracking wide open. 'And you know what? It's great that you've organised this tree to be cleared, and I accept with pleasure. But I don't depend on it. If I'm in trouble, I have a town full of people who'll help. If I rang up a few friends and said I can't cope with a fallen tree I'd have a working bee here in minutes. You know…'

Another breath.

'Last winter I got the flu. I didn't let anyone know because I hate fuss, only then I ran out of wood. The place was cold, and I was too tired to get out of bed and chop some. Then Liz arrived. She's the administrator of Mum's nursing home. I'd rung and said I had a cold and couldn't come in, but Liz thought she'd check anyway. She practically called out the army. An hour later the house was a furnace, there was food, fuss, heat packs, every home remedy known to man. I was so coddled I had no choice but to get better.'

'That's…great.' It was a pathetic comment but what else was he to say?

But she hadn't stopped. She'd barely paused for breath.

'And you know what?' she snapped. 'It all happened without you. And now… I love it that you're helping with Bessie. I'm grateful you've organised the tree. But don't you dare think I'll fall in a heap without you. I spent a few weeks in tears as a lovesick teenager and then I moved on. Now, if you don't mind, I have things to do to get my life in order before I leave. And, believe it or not, I can do all those things by myself.'

CHAPTER SIX

THE POWER CAME ON.

Mardie headed down the paddocks to do one last run around the sheep before dinner.

He suspected she didn't need to. He suspected she didn't want to be in the house with him.

The tow-truck driver arrived and shook his head over the Mercedes. Blake had already rung the hire-car firm; insurance would sort it from here. He retrieved his laptop and briefcase, watched the wrecked Mercedes be towed away, and then went back to the house and set up his laptop in the attic.

It might be wise to lie low for a while, he thought. Leave Mardie to settle down.

He was due to speak at a fund-raising dinner on Monday. It was his first foray into public speaking since his illness.

He read his prepared speech and frowned. Surely he could do better.

He thought of Mardie and he thought…passion. The world could do with more passion. So could his speech.

He squared his shoulders and pulled up a blank document.

Try again? He couldn't quite match Mardie in the passion stakes but he'd give it his best shot.

The sheep were as safe as she could make them. They had feed and water, the hens were happy, the place was secure.

Back in the house, she looked—tentatively—for Blake and was relieved when she realised he was upstairs. She could hear him on his computer. Working.

Good. He was out of her hair.

He wouldn't have the internet up there. She should have offered him access to her computer.

She might make the offer, she decided, but not until after dinner. She hauled a tuna bake from the freezer. A nice easy fix. Plus it would underscore what she'd yelled at Blake. Excellent.

She picked a lettuce and a couple of tomatoes from the veggie patch. Practically gourmet. Blake Maddock would be used to five-star restaurants. How would he react to defrosted tuna bake?

She really had yelled at him.

Maybe she'd overdone it, just a little.

She should call him down. Have a drink before dinner.

Maybe not. She was, she discovered, still seething.

She should check the weather forecast. She hit the internet and confirmed there was not a storm in sight. Excellent.

She went to close the computer and then...

A thought.

She just happened to type *Blake Maddock, Ophthalmologist*.

She'd never searched for him. For all these years, she'd never enquired. She hadn't wanted to know.

She wanted to know now.

Blake Maddock, Ophthalmologist. Enter.
She entered Africa.
She stared at the screen as if it had grown two heads.
For Blake was right in front of her, but not the Blake she knew. This was the face of some major foundation, Eyes For Africa. Blake as a professional.

Blake working in desperate conditions. Blake, surrounded by queues of kids. Blake operating. Blake standing in the background as a nurse removed bandages from a little boy's eyes. A clip of a documentary describing Blake's work.

On the front of the website there was a blurb for a black-tie dinner this coming Monday in Sydney. *Head of Eyes For Africa, Dr Blake Maddock, will be addressing...*

She'd known nothing.

This town knew everything there was to know about everyone. Surely...

No. Banksia Bay knew everything there was to know about its own, and Blake no longer belonged. His aunt had scorned the town, and when Blake left that was the end.

She read on, her head spinning as she flicked through screens of information.

He'd headed to Africa almost as soon as he'd finished his specialist training. His work there was groundbreaking.

He'd said he worked overseas. But... Africa? *All this time...*

'I guess you know all about me now, too,' Blake said from behind her and she froze. She didn't turn. To say she was dumbfounded would be an understatement.

'Africa,' she whispered.

'It's where I keep my harem. Stocked by my white slave traders.'

She managed a smile but it didn't reach her eyes. This was too astounding for humour.

'You work for charity,' she said, finally spinning to face him.

'Yes.'

'You're not rich.' It was…an accusation?

'I am,' he said diffidently. 'My family made a fortune in tin mining—I still own shares. My great-aunt had extravagant taste in home renovation but for the rest she was miserly. My parents died before they could spend their inheritance. I can afford to pay for a dog and a bit of tree clearing.'

'That's not what I meant,' she said, thoroughly confused. 'I thought you studied medicine to make money.'

'Why would I do that, when I already have far more than I need?'

'I don't know,' she said miserably. 'How would I know? Blake, why?'

The question was almost a wail.

'Does there have to be a why?'

'Yes,' she managed. 'There does. I thought I knew all about you. Then I thought I didn't know anything. Now…' She shook her head. 'Sorry. It has nothing to do with me, what you do. I don't have the right to ask.'

She closed her eyes. She counted to ten because she didn't know what else to do.

Opened them. Thought of a long-ago question.

Asked it.

'Who's Robbie?'

The question hung.

Robbie.

'Why—' he found it hard to speak '—why do you ask?'

There was a long silence. The question hung.

And then she told him, 'There was someone called Robbie.' It was a statement, not a question, and it left him winded.

There was someone called Robbie.

Not according to his parents. Or his great-aunt. No one.

There was someone called Robbie.

'Yes,' he said. 'How did you know?'

'It's the only thing I've been able to think of,' she said, sounding unsure. 'When you left… I thought I knew everything about you, my best of friends. But that last night… You were so excited about leaving, about studying medicine. But you'd never said what you wanted to do until then. It was like there was some part of you you'd kept hidden. I couldn't figure it out, but after you'd gone and I was trying to make sense of it… Robbie was the one thing I couldn't ask about. He was the one thing I didn't know.'

He tried to think of something to say. He couldn't.

'How…?' he managed again at last.

'When we camped out in the tent on the back lawn,' she said diffidently. Unsure. 'As kids. You cried out in your sleep. Nightmares. Stuff like "Robbie I can't… Robbie, don't…" I got Mum and she brought us both inside and cuddled you back to sleep. Then, another time when you were sleeping over, I heard you crying, "Robbie, Robbie", and I knew Mum went up to you. I asked you once, "Who's Robbie?" and you said no one. I asked Mum, and she said kids who lived alone often have friends in their head. She said if you didn't want to tell us then I wasn't to ask. But I thought… Whenever you had the dream…you sounded terrified. I heard Mum tell Dad once, "That boy has demons". For some reason when you left I thought… I thought the demons might be Robbie.'

Robbie.

For all these years he'd done what his father told him.

'Don't tell people about your brother. It makes your mother ill.'

And then, when he couldn't stop crying, he'd been packed off to Australia, to an aunt who barely said Blake's name, much less his twin's.

Robbie...

The sound of Mardie saying it was a release all by itself.

The demons might be Robbie. It was suddenly unbearable that she thought that a moment longer.

'Robbie was my brother,' he said, and the words sounded strange, as if they were coming from some dark recess that had been locked for years. They were.

'Your brother?'

'My twin.'

She was on the swivelling computer chair. The chair wasn't moving. She was totally motionless, her eyes not leaving his. Trying to read him.

'He died?'

'Before I came here.'

'How old?' It was scarcely a whisper.

'When I was...when we were seven. We were living in a beachside mansion in California. My mother's birthday. A party, so many people. It was hot, we couldn't sleep so we decide to go for a swim.'

'Night?' she whispered.

'Midnight. It was a stupid time to go for a swim, but there was so much noise...'

'Your parents let you go for a swim at midnight?'

'They didn't know. We were supposed to be sleeping, but it was hot. And the nanny...' He shrugged. 'I don't know where she was. Anyway, we crept down the back stairs. The noise... I remember one woman was laughing like a hyena. Robbie copied her. He was giggling.' He paused. 'And then he dived into the pool, into the shallow end. His neck...'

He broke off. How to go further? He couldn't. Even to Mardie.

'Enough,' he said. 'It's ancient history. My parents never talked of him, didn't want me to talk of him. My aunt didn't speak of him either. That was fine by me. It hurt, so I didn't. But it seemed... When I got into medicine...'

'You did that for Robbie?'

'I did it for me,' he said savagely. 'To stop the hurting. I thought...if I could help kids...' He raked his hair. 'Sorry. I'm not going to burden you. Robbie's my shadow, and he's always with me. Working in Africa helps, makes up in some way for Robbie having a life. I know now that trying to forget him made it worse. It seemed a betrayal but I had no choice. I was a kid and decisions were made for me that were bad. I've moved on. Or maybe I'm still moving on.' He hesitated, regrouped, somehow hauled his thoughts back to now. 'Can I smell fish?'

'Tuna,' she said, looking stunned.

'Tuna bake?'

'Y...yes.'

'Excellent,' he said. 'My favourite.'

'Liar.'

'I don't lie,' he said and then he smiled. 'Okay, maybe I'm stretching the truth a little when it comes to tuna bake. How long is it that it's been frozen?'

They ate dinner in near silence. Tuna bake. What's not to like? Mardie thought, though maybe it was time she did a bit of freezer-clearing. Time had made the noodles crystallise, and even though they'd reheated looking fine, they tasted...well, cardboard might be a good way to describe them.

Even Bounce and Bessie seemed a bit dubious.

Thinking about clearing freezers was okay. Thinking about dogs was okay, too. If she thought about a seven-year-old called Robbie, her head might explode.

'You know, I reckon the dogs need to get used to these tuna bakes,' Blake said as he helped her clear. 'How many more do you have?'

She smiled, but absently, circling the subject of Robbie. Knowing she should go back to him. Thinking she couldn't.

She was feeling as if this man beside her was suddenly who she'd thought he was—a part of her. It was a dumb feeling, but there it was.

Blake... How she'd felt... How she was feeling... It was muddling into emotional turmoil.

She wanted to put her arms around him and hug him.

She wanted...

No.

'The internet said you're in Australia fund-raising,' she managed at last, cautiously.

'Yes.'

'When are you going back?'

'I'm not sure.'

'You're not...?'

'Is there anything else that needs doing? If not, I should get some work done before bed.'

She was finding it hard to speak. She'd known this man so well, once upon a time. How strange that Robbie, Africa, these two great unknowns about him, were making her feel that, at some deep level, he was still...hers?

He'd always kept his inner thoughts to himself, but she'd guessed stuff. She'd even guessed that someone called Robbie was important, but she'd accepted her mother's explanation.

And when he'd left? Hormones had messed with how she'd reacted, she thought. She'd been too busy seeing her needs, her loss, that she hadn't begun to probe what he needed.

Okay. She attempted an inner regroup. She did know this man. Pressing him for answers would never work. She needed to come at him sideways.

He'd asked her if anything needed doing. She met his gaze then, and for the first time she really looked at him. Really saw him. She was looking for the boy behind the man, the Blake she knew. She'd been disconcerted by his size, his deep, sexy voice, his dinner suit, his crashed Mercedes.

Now she just saw Blake.

And she saw the strain. Something lost. Something more than a long-ago grief.

He'd tell her in time, she thought. If she could regain a little of what was lost.

Okay, moving sideways... She looked down at her feet to where two dogs were slumped side by side. Alternate universe. Dogs.

'Bessie smells,' she said.

Blake looked startled. 'Sorry?'

'She's been lost for a week. Before that she was in the pound. Tomorrow we're taking her to Sydney. My truck's a four-seater so she can sit in the back with Bounce, but it's going to be a pretty pongy journey.' She managed a grin. 'If it was Bounce I'd wait until a warm day and put the hose on him. Bessie, though, needs tenderness. That means warm water in the tub in the wash-house, towels and my hairdryer. You just asked if you could help. Here's your answer. I'm not sure how Bessie feels about personal hygiene but if she's anything like Bounce, heaven help us both. You hold and I'll wash. Let's go.'

* * *

The wash-house was a lean-to bathroom-cum-laundry at the back of the house. The bath was huge.

Mardie filled the bath, and Blake tried lifting Bessie in.

A lot of farmers never washed their dogs. They either made them stay outside or in some cases they were so used to smell-of-dog in their living room they didn't notice. Fleas were dealt with by dumping the dogs in the sheep dip.

Maybe that was all Bessie had known. It was certainly all she wanted to know. When Blake lowered her into the water she responded as if this was death-by-drowning.

'It's okay, it's okay, it's okay,' Mardie said, frantically soothing, but frantic and soothing didn't go together. Bessie opted simply for frantic. She lurched upwards, managed to get her paws onto Blake's shoulders and heaved.

Blake was suddenly prone, backwards on the floor, with sodden collie all over him.

Mardie tried hard to keep a straight face.

She failed.

'Oh, dear...' she said, convulsing.

'You try,' Blake said, staggering upright. Glowering. Dripping.

Mardie grinned. Excellent. Blake might be a highly trained eye surgeon, but this was her territory. She could wrangle a ram if she must. A gentle collie...

Nothing to it.

There was, actually, something to it. She ended up as soaked as Blake, but pride was at stake, and Bessie stayed put.

'Shampoo,' she said bracingly to Blake. 'You soap her.'

'I'm wet enough.'

'Wet doesn't stop the smell. Pull yourself together. A bit of willpower.'

'Right,' he said and staggered back to the fray. Laughing.

Things had changed. Something about wetness and laughter and a shared challenge. The tension of the past few hours peeled away.

Blake and Mardie and a dog. Two dogs, for Bounce was cautiously out of range, anxiously supervising as his new love was turned into a sudsy mop.

Things were suddenly okay again. Or more okay than they'd been.

They were back to...

Friends?

By now Bessie had figured they weren't trying to drown her. She'd figured suds meant no harm. So she settled. Except for the shaking.

She wasn't shaking from terror. She was shaking as an intelligent dog got rid of water. No matter how hard Mardie held, she sent suds flying all the way to Bounce at the door.

Blake was doing his best to massage the suds. Every time she shook he got coated.

Every time she shook Mardie subsided into giggles.

'It's fine for you; you have a change of clothes,' Blake retorted, massaging on with grim determination.

'I have a clothes dryer,' she said. 'It's not great for dinner suits but it's fine for work gear. You can go back into the bathrobe while I clean your clothes.'

'Domesticity at its finest,' he said dryly—and then chuckled.

She loved his chuckle. She loved... She loved...

Bessie chose that moment to shake again, which was just as well. Because suddenly Mardie wasn't sure what she loved. Or where the boundaries were.

The boundaries were deeply scary.

* * *

They dried Bessie as best they could in the sodden bathroom, then took her into the living room. They towelled her in front of the fire and Mardie fetched her hairdryer.

There was a moment's alarm from Bessie; hairdryers were also something she'd never met. But the warmth of the fire, Mardie's reassurances, Bounce's presence—Bounce knew what a hairdryer was and was intent on sharing the hot air himself—was enough to make her relax.

Mardie and Blake were wet but the room was warm, and what was a little damp between friends? They sat by the fire, with Bessie draped over their knees, Mardie drying and combing, and Blake cutting tangles.

They worked in silence, but the silence wasn't tense. It was as if they were getting to know each other all over again.

Coming together. Merging.

They swapped ends and worked on.

Bessie relaxed completely. She was warm and cared for and the safest she'd been since she'd been put in the pound. She practically purred.

'I hate the thought of taking her to Sydney,' Mardie murmured. She was drying her tail, a lovely feathery black-and-white wag machine. 'Uprooting her again seems cruel. I just want to let her settle.'

'She can't get what she needs in Banksia Bay.'

'Same as you?'

'This was never my home,' he said simply.

'So where's home now?'

No answer. She didn't press.

They finished drying. Bounce gave Bessie an encouraging lick, as if to say, *Job done, wake up, your place is with me now.*

Bessie heaved herself to her feet. Bounce waited until she was steady, then headed for the sofa.

The living room sofa was forbidden to dogs except on the rare occasions when Mardie needed comfort, or when a dog could sidle in unnoticed and curl up before Mardie saw…

Bounce edged to the sofa, Bessie by his side. He glanced nervously at Mardie—and then he was up, Bessie with him.

The two dogs were practically grinning as they dived between cushions. They wriggled under, and hid. Not very well.

Mardie should yell.

It was all she could do not to laugh.

'I take it by Bounce's demeanour that the sofa's forbidden,' Blake said, smiling with her.

'It certainly is. I'm sure Bessie knows it, too.'

She must. Both dogs had nosed under cushions, determined on invisible.

Mardie giggled. She felt…

As if she was standing on the edge of something momentous. Huge.

How she felt about Blake.

'We're both wet,' Blake said, sounding regretful. 'I need to get these clothes into the dryer.'

That'd mean going to bed. They both knew it.

Neither of them moved.

The fire was crackling, sending out gentle heat. They weren't cold. Wet or not, staying right here seemed an excellent option.

She was like the dogs, Mardie thought. She was blocking out the world, revelling in comfort, hoping she wouldn't be noticed.

She was taking comfort from Blake's presence, hoping it wouldn't end.

'Tell me what Hugh was like,' Blake said softly and it had ended.

Or…not, she thought, confused. It should hurt, telling this man about the man who'd been her husband, but suddenly it didn't.

It seemed right.

'Hugh was my friend,' she said softly. 'He was ten years older than me. He was big and quiet and solid. He laughed when I did. I loved him.'

'Would I have liked him?'

'He wasn't like you.'

'That's not what I asked.'

'No.' She considered.

Hugh. A man supremely contented with his lot.

He was the youngest of seven brothers. He'd been brought up tough.

He didn't have an ounce of toughness in him.

He had the best smile.

'Yes, you would have liked him,' she said and she knew it was true. And then she thought…if Hugh could see her now, curled up by the fire, covered in dog hair, smelling of dog shampoo, talking to her friend from childhood…

'He would have liked you, too,' she said. 'He'd be glad, for me, that you're here. I used to tell him about you. He liked it. He didn't have all that happy a childhood himself and he was hungry for happy.' She hesitated. 'He would have been really interested in what you do. "Tell me," he'd say. So that's what I'm saying. Tell me about Africa.'

He hesitated. Unsure. 'I suspect you've read all you need to know,' he said diffidently.

She thought about that, of the countless documentaries

she'd seen, of the wildlife, of the humanitarian crises, the sheer scope of human tragedy.

Yes, she'd read about it. But to be there...

'What does it smell like?'

'Smell...'

'Smell. First impression.'

'Dry and sparse and wind-blown,' he said, frowning. 'I used to stand on the cliffs here and smell the salt. In Africa I smell the sand. The wind... The locals call it *arifi*, meaning thirst, a wind that scorches with many tongues. It rips the heart out of a man. It doesn't give a smell, it takes it away. It leaves you sucked dry. And the people...the kids...the damage...' His voice died. 'There's no point thinking about it.'

'You're doing something about it.'

'Not any more.'

'You're not going back?' she asked, astounded all over again.

'Not,' he said harshly, feeling the frustration build. 'I can't. I might be forced to go back to something like you're doing.'

'Um...' she said cautiously, stunned by his sudden anger. 'Are we back where we started? Mardie Rainey, born in Banksia Bay, headstone for the local cemetery ordered at the same time as my birth certificate?'

'I didn't mean...'

'I'm sure you did mean.' She might be shocked into sympathy but she wasn't letting him get away with this. 'You're summing up my life as worthless?'

'I didn't...'

'Yes, you did,' she said, but she wasn't angry. She was simply sad. 'How do you think that could make me feel?' she said, meeting his gaze square on. 'Seeing my husband die and watching my mother fade. Living here by myself, in my childhood home, and then opening the door to my ex-best friend who tells me what a waste my life has been. You're right, I haven't saved a single African child. We all can't.' Deep breath. 'Why do you keep trying to hurt me?'

'I'm not.'

'I believe you are,' she said steadily. 'I thought… I thought I didn't know you any more but it seems I do. I remember when Mum used to try and hug you, you'd turn yourself rigid, pushing her away. It took her ages to be able to hug. I think you're doing exactly the same thing now. Why?'

'Are you trying to hug?'

'I'm not trying to hug,' she said simply. 'I'm asking what's wrong. One friend to another. You've told me about Robbie. Now tell me about the next big thing. The thing that's put the strain behind your eyes. The thing that's making you want to lash out.'

'I…'

'Just say it, Blake,' she said softly. She put out her hand and touched his—and she waited.

For however long it took.

The fire crackled in the grate. Bounce started snoring. Bessie wuffled and nudged cushions so the two dogs were closer.

She waited.

And finally he closed his eyes and said it.

'I can't go back to Africa,' he said, and he tugged his hand from hers, as if he no longer had the right to the contact. 'It seems I'm taking my frustration out in all sorts of inappropriate ways. It seems hurting you is one of them.'

'Why not?' she said at last.

'I've had dengue fever three times. They tell me three strikes and I'm out. I've had my three strikes.'

'You can never go back?'

'Nowhere there's dengue'

'Or you die?'

'I know the odds. I believe them.'

'So what will you do?' She managed a half smile. 'Unless you're serious about running sheep?'

He shrugged, not returning her smile. 'Who knows? Feel sorry for myself. Go to school reunions. Hurt my friends.'

'There's three strikes,' she said. 'You've done them all. Now you're out again. So the next thing is...'

'I have no idea.'

She thought for a little. Thought about touching his hand again. Thought better of it.

The fire did some more crackling. Bounce did some more snoring. Bessie just seemed to...listen.

There was no hurry for what had to be said.

'Burying yourself in anger would be the fourth thing,' she said at last. 'When Hugh died, I yelled at trees, at rocks, at my friends, at the kids who crashed into us, at anything. It didn't help.'

'Neither did anyone telling you to get over it.'

She smiled at that, wryly. Agreed with a vengeance. 'All that did was make me want to slug someone even worse. Like I wanted to slug you when you criticised me.'

'So now it's you who's angry?'

'Maybe I am,' she said. 'Why wouldn't I be angry? You're judging my life as worth less than yours. You're saying if you can't go to Africa you're nothing. But you can't see what I get and what I give.' She met his eyes, challenging. 'I like my life, and I do good things. I make people happy. I make me happy and I don't need to defend myself to you or to anyone.'

'I know you don't.'

'Then stop beating yourself up about something you can't

change. You do the best you can. No one should expect you to do more than that, including the ghost of Robbie, including yourself.' She hesitated. She wanted, quite badly, to take his face in her hands and kiss him. As comfort?

If it was only that, she thought, she'd do it in a heartbeat, but there was that between them…

'Go to bed, Blake,' she said instead. 'Relax. Think of all the excellent things you can do in the world. There's lots, I'm sure there are, in places where there isn't dengue. Figure it out.'

She pushed herself to her feet.

He rose with her. Came too fast.

She was too close.

His hands came out and steadied her.

And the need grew.

A need from fifteen years ago?

That night in the kitchen…a kiss interrupted. It was between them now, a tangible thing. Fifteen years and a kiss unfinished.

Fifteen years of need.

A need that was as great now as it had been then. More so.

A need that seemed a compulsion, an aching void that had to be filled.

Two halves of a whole, meant to be together.

The fire hissed at their feet, sap catching, making tiny explosions, fizzing to nothing.

A need so great…

'Do you want me to kiss you?' Blake asked, and the world held its breath. The world including Mardie.

'Properly?' she asked.

'With your mother not watching.' He was smiling, a smile that turned her heart.

'I've spent fifteen years figuring out how that kiss should have ended,' she whispered, trying to keep her voice steady. 'I wouldn't mind knowing...'

She wouldn't mind knowing what?

He had no chance to find out because he was no longer listening.

A prophecy carved in a ruined tree. *M.R. xx B.M.* Carved when she was ten years old.

Finally happening.

And fifteen years were gone, just like that. They were a man and a woman grown, but at some basic level they were still who they'd been, friends who'd spent half a lifetime together, who'd grown from boy and girl to man and woman, and who'd moved to this, the next and natural level.

It felt natural. It felt inevitable and it felt right.

Her lips melted against his. Her body curved into his, and she moulded into his hold, tilting her chin, taking as well as giving.

He tasted her kiss.

He tasted her mouth.

He tasted her body and he loved her, as he always had, as he always would.

She smelled of dog shampoo. In truth, maybe she tasted of dog shampoo.

She was wonderfully, miraculously perfect.

She was Mardie. His friend. His home.

She was too great a temptation to resist. She was too sweet to think of pulling away.

She was too much his Mardie to do anything but kiss her.

For this moment he surrendered absolutely. He let himself hold her as he wanted to hold her, to be in this place, by her fire with her dogs nearby, to have her in his arms and to feel her loving him.

Mardie of the loving heart...

He'd fallen in love in the school playground all those years ago and he'd never fallen out. He loved her with every shred of his being.

Forget the dog shampoo. She tasted of nectar, ambrosia, more. She tasted...

Of Mardie

Mardie. His Mardie.

He hadn't known he was off centre but he knew it now. Mardie. His centre.

She was on tiptoe, deepening the kiss, demanding as well as giving. Surrendering but besieging. Wanting as much as he wanted.

She wasn't close enough. He was tugging her against him, her breasts were curved into his chest and she felt as if she was melting into him.

He wanted her closer.

Part of him.

Her hands were in the small of his back, clinging. He was still damp. The fabric between them felt as if it was nothing. There was only a vestige of decency.

The vestige of sense...

He couldn't think that.

But...he had to think it or he'd sweep her up and take her to bed, this instant. It was all he wanted to do. For it felt so right, so meant. After fifteen years, finding his home.

Her hands were slipping to his hips. Tugging him closer still.

Sense.

All he wanted was to take her. All he wanted was to give.

Sense!

Somehow he found the strength to pull away, to break the contact, and heaven knew it broke more than that.

He did it. He held her by her shoulders, at arm's length, gazing down into her dazed and bewildered eyes.

'Blake...' she whispered and her hands covered his. 'You don't want...'

'I did want,' he managed in a voice he scarcely recognised. 'I do want. But I should never... I can't have.'

'Why can't you have?' There was suddenly a trace of indignation in her voice, the feisty Mardie surfacing under the lover. 'It's not as if I'm unavailable,' she said. 'Is it the thought of Hugh?'

She was suddenly glaring at him. Self-sacrifice, it seemed, wasn't in her vocabulary. He wanted to smile.

He didn't.

He'd wanted to kiss her and he had, but now...he felt as if he was at the edge of a deep, sweet vortex, being tugged inexorably into its unknown centre.

Away from everything he'd worked for.

'I'm not giving up,' he said, hardly aware he was speaking. 'I can't. To escape back to Banksia Bay... I no longer need to escape.'

She tugged back so his hands could no longer hold her shoulders. She looked confused. But then his gaze locked on hers and there was anger behind the confusion. Anger growing.

It seemed she was waiting for an explanation. It was as if he'd kissed her under false pretences.

Suddenly she was practically tapping her foot.

So explain. If he could.

'Mardie, my parents sent me here after Robbie died because it made my mother ill to look at me,' he said, trying hard to make sense of what he hardly understood himself. 'My great-aunt took me in. This place had been her refuge for years and it became mine. My parents were...dysfunctional, to say the least. My great-aunt was little better, but once I met you, and your parents... This was safe as I'd never been safe. It was home as nowhere had ever been home. Even after ten years here I still felt overwhelming thankfulness that I'd found you. I could have stayed. But I had things to do, my Mardie-girl. I still have things to do, and I can't do them here.'

'Don't call me Mardie-girl.'

Mardie-girl.

He hadn't meant to.

Her father had called her Mardie-girl, and in private, as they'd grown older, it had started slipping out. Mardie. His Mardie-girl. No. She was right. Its use now was inappropriate.

And it had rekindled anger.

'I'm only Mardie-girl to people I love,' she snapped—but then she flinched and she closed her eyes. 'Though that's dumb,' she whispered. 'Because I do love you. You know I always have. Though not...not like this. Not like tonight. What I had with Hugh was real and wonderful, and the thought of you didn't get in the way for a moment. But we've always... meshed. Only I never saw myself as a safe harbour. An escape. I saw myself as an equal. A friend. Fun, happy, silly, sad—you and me, mates.'

'We were. I hope we are.'

'Then why are you spouting nonsense about escape?'

'I don't know that, either.' He raked his hair and raked it again for good measure.

'Then I guess that makes two of us not understanding,' she said, more mildly now. 'I thought you wanted to kiss me. It seems I was wrong. Okay. You've stopped kissing me, so let's leave it at that. You need to strip off and put those clothes in the dryer. You can't do that with me around. I might get the wrong idea. No. That's nuts. It's all nuts. I'm confused, you're confused. So let's focus on what we know for sure. We have two happy dogs, one of whom needs medical help. Tomorrow we're going to Sydney. So tonight I'll leave you to your convolutions and your plans for the future, which doesn't include kissing, and I'll go to bed. Goodnight, Blake. Happy plans.'

And that was that. She clicked her fingers for the dogs and she headed out of the room and down the passage to her bedroom.

She walked inside, the dogs following her—side by side, Bounce glancing back at him with what looked like reproach—and she slammed the door behind them.

She left and he stood by the fire until it died to embers.

Once again he'd hurt her. He should walk away now.

She was driving him to Sydney. She'd have to put up with him the whole way. She'd see him during the week as they cared for Bessie. Then...

Did he really want to walk away?

No. But what was between them...

It wasn't friendship. It was so much more.

That she'd guessed about Robbie left him winded. That she and her parents had respected his privacy, had guessed he was hurting, had let him be...that left him awed.

They'd loved him.

Love. It was a strange concept.

In medical school he'd met a girl as committed to aid organisations as he was, passionate about saving the world.

They'd studied together, worked together, become lovers almost as a side issue. Become engaged.

Six months later she'd met an African aid worker and fell hopelessly, helplessly in love. 'I'm sorry, Blake, it's the way he makes me feel. I really love him.'

They were still friends. But...love?

The way a heart twisted?

The way he makes me feel...

The way he felt tonight, when he'd held Mardie.

No. Stop, right now. This is Banksia Bay.

Banksia Bay was never an option.

He didn't think Mardie's life was worthless, of course he didn't, but...could he imagine himself working here? Taking care of coughs and colds? Playing with sheep on the side?

Being with Mardie-girl.

Just Mardie, he corrected himself. Not his Mardie-girl. What had once been granted to him with love, had now been withdrawn.

He couldn't pursue it.

Because of Robbie? He'd forgiven himself years ago for Robbie's death. One seven-year-old could never be held responsible for another's moment of risk-taking, regardless of what his mother had thought and said. But still that sense remained, to do something worthwhile, to somehow compensate for the waste that was his brother.

He should be able to walk away from it. See a shrink. Move on.

But it had been with him for too long, was too great a part of his life. He had no hope of ever moving on.

And that meant walking away from Mardie? He knew it did.

The door swung open, almost of its own accord. He

glanced across and it was Bessie. She'd managed to push past the loosely hinged doors. For some reason she was nosing her way across to him, following his scent. Finding him. Putting a paw up, as if asking for a pat.

As if offering comfort.

He'd always wanted a dog. He'd always been so jealous of Mardie and her dog pack.

If he stayed here...

No.

'You don't belong with me,' he told Bessie, more roughly than he intended. 'Bounce is just down the hall. So's Mardie.' And before he could think further about it he led her out of the room, down the passage.

Mardie's door was open. Bessie must have pushed it wide again.

He could just call...

He didn't.

He propelled Bessie silently into the room and closed the door after her.

And went up to bed without saying a word.

She heard him return Bessie

She heard him close the door.

She lay awake and thought.

About two little boys swimming at midnight. About Blake's parents. Packing him off to Australia. Loading him with guilt. The legacy they'd given their son...

Anger was no use.

That was the problem. Nothing was any use. What had been done was done, and Blake was living with the consequences for ever.

It was doing her head in. Anger, sorrow—there was even a touch of humiliation tossed in there as well. She had it all.

She thought and thought, until sleep finally gave her release.

She dreamed of twins.

She dreamed of Blake.

She woke to the sounds of chopping.

Blake. Doing his manly thing again. Sigh.

At least it wasn't the chainsaw, she thought grimly, throwing back the covers and heading for the window.

The first weak rays of dawn were barely filtering over the horizon. Even Clarabelle wasn't at the gate yet.

Blake was chopping.

He was back in his jeans, but he was bare to the waist. He was lifting the logs he'd sectioned yesterday, putting them on the block beside the woodshed and attacking. The axe came down over and over, with strong, rhythmic strokes.

The wood was green. It took three, four strokes to strike each log through.

He didn't falter. One after another. Stacking the pieces and moving to the next. No pause.

She should call out that she had enough wood to last her for the winter. She wouldn't be burning it green anyway, and next winter it'd split with half the effort.

But she knew without being told that he needed the physical effort.

Demons. Her mother had surely been right.

Not demons. Robbie.

He didn't look up. Every ounce of energy went into smashing the axe into the wood.

She wanted to walk out and take the axe from him. She wanted to hold him, just hold him, the child inside the man.

She couldn't. Whatever harm his parents had caused had gone so deep she couldn't touch. His harm would just hurt her.

Fifteen years ago he'd walked away and she'd lived without him ever since. She could do it again.

With demons like his, there didn't seem a choice.

CHAPTER SEVEN

THE JOURNEY TO Sydney was made mostly in silence. The truck had an excellent radio, for which Mardie was profoundly thankful. She tuned it to a discussion on nineteeth-century circuses. She tried to be fascinated.

For Blake had gone somewhere she couldn't reach. He was silent and grim, hardly speaking at all.

'Hitchhikers are supposed to entertain the truckies who pick 'em up,' she said at one stage.

'Would you like me to talk?'

'I'd like you to tell me about Africa,' she suggested. 'More than it has a truly appalling wind.'

'You don't want to know.'

'Fine, then,' she said, grittily cheerful, and went back to her circuses.

When they reached the city she needed facts. 'Where's your apartment? Where can I drop you off?'

'It's on the harbour,' he said shortly. 'But you don't want to be caught in city traffic, and we need to take Bessie to the vet clinic. We'll go to your place, dump your stuff and take her straight there.'

'Yes, sir.'

'I didn't mean...'

'To be brusque? Of course you did,' she retorted. 'But I like brusque. Least said, soonest parted. Let's go.'

Least said, soonest parted... He wouldn't have put it like that, but then he wouldn't have put it at all. He was simply doing what he needed to do.

If he told her what he thought of the pompous historian spouting circus stuff, if he joined in, he might relax, and if he relaxed then they'd end up where they were last night and he'd end up hurting her. Hurting her more.

Shut up and move on. Do what needs to be done. Leave.

To go where?

He'd figure it. Eventually.

'This is Irena's,' Mardie said, pulling up outside a tiny weatherboard cottage overlooking the cliffs of Coogee. 'She has cats. Bounce is used to them. Let's see how Bessie reacts.'

He climbed from the truck as Mardie negotiated the garden path and rang the bell.

Irena's house. A friend of Mardie's. If he'd thought about it, he'd probably have guessed Irena to be a Banksia Bay local who'd moved on.

Country girl made good?

That was the kind of thinking that was getting him into trouble.

It might also be a little bit wrong.

For the woman who opened the door was...magnificent. Fiftyish. Six feet tall. Black leggings, high black boots, a purple sweater that reached mid-thigh and a tiny skirt. Strings of amethyst and topaz. Oversized earrings.

A Cleopatra haircut.

She greeted Mardie with a cry of delight, enveloped her in a hug and Mardie practically disappeared.

The hug over, Mardie was held at arm's length and inspected.

'Look at you.' It was a cry of dismay. 'If you haven't brought anything decent to wear...'

'I have brought clothes but I don't want to get dog on them. Irena, meet Blake Maddock, the guy I was telling you about. Blake, Irena's my agent.'

Her agent?

'How lovely,' Irena purred, and smiled a totally bewitching smile that said she knew exactly what personable men were made for and she knew exactly what to do with them.

Mardie giggled. 'You're scaring him,' she said.

'Not him. He's a big boy.' She grinned at Blake and turned back to Mardie. 'Did you bring them?'

'Yes, but...'

'I want to see them. Now.'

'We need to get Bessie to the vet's.'

'Colin's not expecting us for another hour.' Blake was fascinated.

'An hour's great,' Irena said with satisfaction. 'And you said it's right by here. Excellent. Bring them in.'

'The dogs...?' Blake ventured.

'Bring them in, too,' Irena said with ill-concealed impatience. And then she gave a rueful smile. 'Sorry. Your dog's why we're getting the plates early and I should be grateful. I am. So I'll take Bounce inside, and the memory box—is it in the tray? Mardie, you bring Bessie and introduce her to the girls. Blake, you bring the plates.'

'The plates?'

'It's the box on the back seat,' Mardie said, taking pity on him. 'The memory box is the big one in the tray. The plates are smaller. But please be careful. If you drop them I'll have to shoot myself.'

'You and me both,' Irena said. 'And Cathy.' She glanced at her watch. 'I hope you don't mind but she's been desperate to see. She should be here... Oh, great, here she is now. Come on in.'

And then they were in Irena's huge kitchen, which seemed to take up half the house. There were two Siamese cats, circling the dogs with care. Bessie seemed cautious but not overwhelmed. She stuck close to Bounce and seemed fine.

It was Cathy who looked overwhelmed.

Cathy was a middle-aged woman, mousy, wearing a twinset and a tweed skirt, looking scared. She'd received one of Irena's hugs as well, which could, Blake thought, overwhelm anyone.

'Blake doesn't know what's happening,' Mardie announced, looking bemused. 'Sorry, Blake, I should have told you.'

'You didn't tell him about the memory wall?' Irena demanded. 'It's only the most beautiful thing you've ever done.'

'Blake and I have been too busy for chat.' She was opening what Irena was calling the memory box. Tugging out assorted...things.

A battered seaman's cap. A container of model trains. A box of fishing flies. Photographs. Letters. Boots. An ancient pair of scuffed slippers.

A rat-trap?

What the...?

'Cathy's husband was drowned when a pilot boat tipped at the harbour mouth twelve months ago,' Irena told him and Cathy flinched as all eyes turned to her. She reached out and took the rat-trap, and held it as if it were a shield.

'I'm so sorry,' Blake said, because there was nothing else to say. 'What happened?'

'It was an awful night,' Mardie explained, as Cathy hugged her rat-trap like a talisman. 'An oil tanker was threatening to flounder on the rocks past the heads. They sent tugs and pilot boats out. They saved the tanker, but one of the tugs and one of the pilot boats were lost. Six men and two women were drowned. Cathy's Bernard was one of them.'

'Bernie was a crewman on the pilot boat,' Cathy whispered. 'He went out…and he didn't come back. It's been awful. But now…we're going to have a memorial wall, at the harbour where their boat used to be tied. Mardie's making plates. Nine plates for each one lost. Seventy-two plates in all. Mardie asked me to choose things that were important to Bernard, things the kids and I want him remembered for. Funny things. Silly things. Like the rat-trap.'

'Why the rat-trap?' Blake was totally caught in the emotion in the woman's face. The grief. The pride.

'We were friends at school,' she whispered, and pride prevailed. 'One day I told him there'd been a rat in my bedroom and the very next day Bernie brought me a rat-trap. We were both fourteen and I went to bed that night with my trap under the pillow. No way was I using it for rats.' She hesitated. 'Isn't it dumb, to have kept a rat-trap. Did…did you use it, Mardie?'

'I surely did,' Mardie said. 'Can you unpack the plates?' she asked him. 'Each panel's on individual padding.'

He lifted the plates free, one after another.

Nine enamelled plates.

He couldn't believe their beauty.

Each one was about twelve inches square.

The first was a portrait, glass, fired onto a copper base. A seaman.

It wasn't exactly a portrait, he thought. It was slightly abstract, an impression, but it was wonderful. The strength of the man came through—a battered sailor, his face creased against the weather, the sea behind him.

Cathy choked back a sob. She let the rat-trap fall to take it. She just...looked.

He lifted the next plate free. It was like a collage. A thing of exquisite beauty, but built from images of ordinariness. Here was the rat-trap. A football. Fishing flies.

A second plate was trains—a whole panel of trains Bernard had obviously loved. The real trains, the models, were spilling from the memory box, but their image on the plate was just as real. Bernard's face was on this plate again, as a faded background, a man watching with pride as his trains circled a track of crimson glass.

The colours were extraordinary. The depth of field, the layering of objects upon objects. Each one was saying this man had such depth...

Nine plates, representing a man's life.

Cathy was crying openly now, moving from plate to plate, touching them with awe, with reverence and with love.

'You guys need to get Bessie to the vet,' Irena said, a bit more roughly than she needed to, sniffing a bit, but Blake wasn't ready to surface yet.

He turned to Mardie—who was watching Cathy. Smiling a smile he'd never seen before.

'You did all these?' he managed.

'I've done seven sets,' she said. 'Sixty-three plates. I have Robyn Partling's story left to do. Another month and I'll be finished.'

'You should see where they're going,' Cathy whispered. 'They've made a wall at the harbour. Every person will see my Bernard. They'll see he loved trains. They'll see that letter he wrote to the paper about the turtles. They'll even see my rat-trap.'

She choked, and Irena put a bracing arm around her.

'Whisky,' she decreed. She turned to Mardie and Blake and sent them a silent message. Go. 'I'll dry Cathy up, but I suspect she'll like to be alone with these. So off you go and save your dog. Cathy and I will phone the harbour master. He's the one organising this. The other six have blown him away. This one will be no different.'

It took ten minutes to drive to the vet's. It took almost that long for Blake to catch his breath.

He remembered the plates over the fire-stove and knew now where they'd come from.

He'd seen the plate in Charlie's nursing-home bedroom and knew it was Mardie's as well.

Brilliant.

They pulled into the car park. Mardie went to get out of the truck but he caught her hand. There were things he needed to get clear.

'I always knew you could draw,' he said slowly. 'I never dreamed...'

'That I'd do enamelling? There you go, then. And I never dreamed you could be a doctor in Africa.'

'You never said...'

'You knew I loved drawing.'

'Yes, but not like this,' he said explosively. 'These plates... I'm not an expert but...with your skill you could make a fortune.'

'I do make money,' she said diffidently. 'But not with these. My friend Liz is a nurse I work with. Liz's brother, Mike, was one of the men who died that night. I came to the memorial service. I saw Liz clutching an old fire engine Mike loved when he was a kid and I thought… I could do something.'

'But you've been enamelling before?'

'For years. I run the sheep to keep the grass down. I work three days a week at the nursing home because I love it. The rest of the time I do this.'

'Raff said you were broke.' He was trying to get things clear. 'You couldn't afford to help Bessie. I assumed…'

'There's a lot of that about,' she said. 'Assumptions. You always saw my art as my hobby, not the passion it is. While I had no idea you were striving for medicine and why.'

'So you've been enamelling since school?'

'It's what I do,' she said gently. 'I don't make millions but I do make a living. The problem is the cost. There's always something. For these plates I needed a bigger kiln, a good one. You need an even temperature over the entire surface or the glass cracks. Lorraine's a local potter. She and I went halves but it still cost a fortune.'

She turned to Bessie and Bounce on the back seat, moving on with decision. The two dogs were sitting bolt upright in their harnesses, both looking nervous. 'Okay, Bessie, you're next. Do you think we should take Bounce in?'

'I think we should,' Blake said, because a man had to say something and that was all he could think of.

Concentrate on the dogs.

Anything else was too difficult.

Colin was waiting for them, a big, confident vet who oozed professional competence. In the veterinary clinic, with its strange smells, Bessie reacted with even more nervousness.

Colin, however, was amenable to Bounce staying beside her. He could see that together they were settled.

A bond was growing between these two dogs that was starting to seem a tangible force.

Like me and Blake, Mardie thought, and scared herself by thinking it. Glanced at Blake and thought…for once, don't know what I'm thinking.

Luckily, both Colin and Blake were intent on Bessie's eyes. Colin was cautiously optimistic and once he examined her he became even more so.

'It's looking good. We'll need blood tests, scans, the works, and I need to start her on anti-inflammatory eye-drops. Can you leave her with me today, pick her up about five?'

'Can Bounce stay with her?' Mardie asked, and Bounce looked up with sudden distrust. 'I know, smarty-boots,' she told him. 'You understand. But today you're the sacrificial lamb. If I could hop into the cage with Bessie to comfort her I'd do it in a heartbeat, but I suspect I wouldn't fit.'

Everyone laughed

They left the dogs and walked out into the sunshine.

Laughter died. Silence.

No dogs. Nothing.

Sunshine, beach, nothing.

Without speaking, they headed towards the beach. Found themselves on the sand. Just walking.

Just walking.

There was something about Bessie and Bounce…

Togetherness. He hadn't felt like that even when he was engaged to be married.

Maybe that was why he was no longer engaged. He didn't know how to do it.

So what was the problem with that? He'd always been an outsider.

Except when he was with Mardie.

He was with Mardie now.

The difference was, Bessie and Bounce connected. They belonged together, in a way he and Mardie never could. Mardie had been his escape from reality. Banksia Bay. Mardie. They were part of his past, the part that had been used to 'get over Robbie'. Neither were part of his real world.

He could, Blake realised, walk away right now. He could pay Colin's bill. Take a cab into the city to his apartment. Leave Mardie with Irena, with her life that didn't include him.

No. There was a growing part of him that was denying his outsider tag, that was hungry to come in.

'I'd like to talk over what Colin says this afternoon,' he said diffidently. 'I have this fund-raising dinner tonight...'

Don't go any further. A voice was raging in his head. Don't! To be an outsider was the life he was accustomed to, the life he'd chosen.

A life where the pain of losing Robbie could never be repeated.

'Talking to lots of strangers,' Mardie said sympathetically. 'Ugh.'

'Would you like to come?'

He couldn't believe he'd said it.

He'd said it.

'It won't be all that interesting,' he said. 'Corporate money, politicians, people wanting to look charitable while contributing as little as possible. But...' He hesitated. 'You did ask about Africa.'

'So I did,' she said. 'You'll be talking about Africa?'

'Yes.'

'Then I'll come.'

Just like that. She glanced at him and their gazes locked—and then they looked away. A step taken…

Regretted?

'I'd like to be there, but inconspicuously,' she said hastily. 'Can you arrange for me to slip in at the back?' She ventured an uncertain smile. 'But, as for coming… It's only fair. You've seen my plates; I wouldn't mind seeing your work.'

'Great. I'll pick you up at…'

'No,' she said, suddenly definite. 'I have a truck. You have a mangled Mercedes. And, besides, I'm not coming as your partner. I'm coming as me. If you could organise a ticket I'll collect it at the door.'

'And you'll wear beige and blend into the wallpaper.'

'Something like that.'

'You're not an inconspicuous woman.'

'I am, too,' she said. 'Five feet two in socks. Favourite footwear, gumboots. Favourite perfume, wet dog.'

'In this crowd that'd be conspicuous,' he said and grinned. Feeling suddenly absurdly happy. Not knowing why but suddenly not caring. 'Would you like to have lunch now?' he asked before he knew he was going to.

But she was shaking her head. Looking a little…scared? 'Irena wants me to talk to the harbour master,' she told him. 'And I imagine you have things to do as well. If we need to discuss Bessie… Ring me in the morning if you don't get a chance to speak to me tonight.'

'Of course I'll get a chance.'

'It doesn't matter if you don't,' she said softly. 'We live in different worlds, Blake. They've collided today and it's lovely. But, apart from this one collision…we both need to get on with our lives.'

* * *

He did have things to do.

There was the small matter of insurance and a crumpled Mercedes. That took most of the afternoon.

He checked the cost of hiring another. Crashing hire cars did appalling things to premiums.

He gave up, found a car yard and bought one.

He headed back to his apartment. Ran through his presentation.

Passion.

He rewrote and rewrote. Thinking of Mardie.

Tell me about Africa...

What was she doing now?

She was due to pick the dogs up at five. She had a cellphone. He'd ring...

She answered on the second ring, and he thought: how easy was that? He could have rung her any time over the past fifteen years.

Why hadn't he?

He knew why.

'We're on the beach.' She was yelling into the wind. 'The dogs have spent all day in a cage. They have energy to spare.'

He wanted to be with them. Badly.

Not happening.

'How's Bessie coping?'

'She's running with Bounce, still just touching, but they're going as fast as each other. They look fabulous. I think they're in love.'

Love.

Don't go there.

Mardie would look fabulous too, he thought. Her hair

would be flying every which way. She'd have bare feet, he guessed. Jeans, T-shirt, freckles, curls...

He was standing in his great-aunt's faded apartment.

He wanted to be on the beach with Mardie.

'What did Colin say?' he managed.

'He'll have the results of the blood tests back on Wednesday. There's a couple of other things, but he's really optimistic.' She hesitated. 'He's willing to do both eyes at once, if you'd like.'

'It's not up to me.'

'It is, because you're paying.'

'So pros and cons?' His emotions were all over the place. He seized on the professional with gratitude.

'It's cheapest to do one eye only,' she said. 'Dogs manage well with one eye.'

'They manage better with two. But if there's infection...'

'He said that. He said if he operates on two at once there's a tiny chance of cross infection; that something going wrong with one can mess with the other. But he says the chances are minuscule; he's almost willing to guarantee success in a dog as young and healthy as Bess. And here's the thing. He also says it wouldn't put her under additional stress. She'd have it done, it'd be over, I could take her home and she never need come here again.'

Excellent. But why did that make him feel...wrong?

'So that's that, then,' he said, more harshly than he intended. 'Two eyes. Decision made. Are you still coming tonight?'

'I... Yes, if it's okay.'

'I've organised a ticket.'

'I'll come just as the dinner ends,' she said. 'I'd like to hear you speak but you don't need to pay for my dinner.'

'Speeches are through dinner. There's no choice.'

'Then can I have a nice quiet seat down the back where I can sneak away?'

'It's all arranged,' he said. 'I'll see you then.'

'Then I'd best go and get the sand out from between my toes,' she said. 'Oo-er. And I just bet Irena will make me put on a frock.'

The dinner was formal. Very formal.

If Mardie had known how much the tickets cost, she'd never have agreed to come, Blake thought, as he greeted what seemed like the complete *Who's Who* of Australia. Politicians. Celebrities. There were a few professionals who were here to learn, like the doctors from North Coast Rescue—a division of the Australian Flying Doctor service—but they were in the minority. Most people were here to see and be seen.

Maybe he should have warned her. Even sneaking into a dark corner, she wouldn't want to look like a country mouse.

She *was* a country mouse.

She was also one of the most brilliant artists he'd ever met. Mardie.

He felt like shouting it to the rooftops. Hey. The Mardie I knew... The Mardie I disparaged... She's kind and loyal and clever—and she's talented beyond belief.

She was nothing to do with him.

One of the most eminent politicians in the land was waiting to be introduced. He needed to get a grip. Work the room. Remember why he was here.

'I'm very happy to meet you, ma'am. We certainly appreciate what you've done for us. Let me tell you about Sharik. She's five years old—here's her photograph. Through your funding, she can now see. If I could just tell you about the rest of the children in her village...'

She hadn't thought this through.

They had fund-raising dinners at Banksia Bay. Yes, she knew it'd be a bigger deal than that, but this... This was breathtaking.

The venue was right on Sydney Harbour. There were queues of cars lining up. Rollers. Bentleys. Porsches. A Lamborghini!

Maybe there was something else on in the same building, she hoped nervously, thinking it was just as well she'd caught a cab. Imagine driving up in her truck.

A security guard was at the entrance. 'Your ticket, ma'am?'

'I... Dr Maddock said he'd leave a ticket for me at the entrance.'

'You're Miss Mardie Rainey?'

'Yes.' *Aargh.* Was it too late to cut and run?

It *was* too late. The man took her arm. 'Take over, Pete,' he called to his colleague. 'Miss Rainey's arrived.'

Had she decided against coming?

The head table needed to sit first. Guests of honour were seated before the riff-raff—if you could call two-thousand-dollar-a-head ticket holders riff-raff.

Regardless, Blake was being ushered to his seat and Mardie wasn't here yet.

'Sir...'

He turned and the security guard was guiding her forward.

Mardie.

But different.

She took his breath away.

He thought suddenly of the night years ago, of the premiere of the James Bond movie in Whale Cove. Etta had made Mardie a dress they both thought was the last word in sophistication.

This, though...

Every woman in the room was gowned in sophisticated splendour. Gowns that clung, satin, silks, sleek this-year's fashion.

Not Mardie. She was dressed...as Mardie.

Her dress did cling. And yes, maybe it was silk, but that was where the comparison ended.

It was tiny, deceptively simple, and it was breathtakingly lovely.

It was a sheath of shimmering fabric that resembled nothing so much as a jewel box straight from the Ottoman Empire. Crimsons, purples, deep pinks, with threads of gold. Simple yet exquisite. It fitted her from breasts to just above the knee as if it was a second skin. It was as if she was wearing a perfect jewel.

She wore a dainty filigree choker around her throat, embedded with stones to match the dress. Enamelled? A Mardie Rainey original? He guessed it was.

Her legs were in shimmering silk stockings. Her stilettos made her legs look as if they went on for ever.

Her curls tumbled over her shoulders, arranged with simplicity and a style that made every other woman's hairstyle seem overdone.

She smiled a greeting to him and he realised everyone in the room had stopped talking.

Why would they not, in the face of this smile?

Mardie...all grown up. Not a country mouse at all.

Mardie, grown past him?

'I'm so glad you could come,' he managed, and the politician's wife he'd been speaking to gave a delighted cry.

'It's Mardie Rainey. Oh, my dear, your work's divine. Are you here with Blake?'

'She is,' Blake said promptly, before Mardie could confirm or deny, and he stepped forward and took her hand.

'Hi,' he said and smiled. He felt like keeping on smiling. Not letting go of her hand.

'Quiet corner?' she said.

'Top table's the quietest.'

'You didn't…'

'I hate going to these functions as a singleton. It messes with the seating plan. The organisers were relieved.'

'Blake…'

'So you've saved the day. Where did you get that dress?'

'I made it.'

Of course. His breath was taken away all over again.

And…these people knew her?

The politician's wife did, at least. 'I've been trying to have Mardie make me some jewellery,' she said. 'Like the choker… Oh, my dear, it's to die for.'

'I'm caught up at the moment,' Mardie said.

'With the memorial wall for the pilot tragedy,' the woman said. 'Yes, but it won't make you money. I'm prepared to pay…'

Mardie smiled politely, made some air promises, turned once again to look at the two empty seats at the top table.

'They're waiting for us,' Blake said.

'I can't believe you did this.'

'You don't enjoy sitting between the gov…'

'No. Don't tell me who they are; I don't want to know,' she

said. 'The only way to survive this is to spend dinner telling myself everyone's ordinary.'

He smiled, ushering her to her place. His hand touched the small of her back as she sat. It felt... It felt...

'Blake?'

'Mmm?'

'Remember that time I let you try my bath-boat on the dam?'

'I... Yes.' He did remember.

Back to being eight years old. A wide dam in the back paddock. An ancient bathtub.

Mardie's method of getting from one side of the dam to the other was to seal the bath's open plughole with clay and paddle like crazy. She'd offered to let him try. She hadn't actually told him that the clay plug disintegrated and time was of the essence.

He therefore paddled to the middle and paused to see if there were tadpoles.

The next moment he was neck-deep in tadpoles.

Her lips twitched as she watched him. 'You can remember,' she said.

'I might just...'

'I'm just thinking,' she said, softly but surely. 'Top table, huh? Is this revenge? I'm thinking there has to be an even better fate for you than tadpoles.'

She ate a magnificent dinner, feeling more than a little overwhelmed. Feeling a bit...as if she was pleased she'd dressed up. Initially she'd gone for simple, but when she'd emerged from the bedroom Irena had sent her straight back to change.

'You go anywhere near a guy like that wearing a little

black dress, you're out of your mind. You have clothes that could knock his socks off.'

'I don't want to knock his socks off.'

'Then there'll be other women who do,' Irena said bluntly. 'Would you be happy to see him head off into the night with someone else?'

Of course she would. She had no claim on him.

But she'd changed anyway, and she didn't regret it.

She was being treated as Blake's partner. He didn't have time to spend with her. Most of his attention was taken by the Very Important Persons on the far side of him. But every now and then he glanced at her, their eyes met, and it was enough.

He was still Blake. Her friend.

The guy she'd dressed up for.

The people around her—politicians, celebrities—were making small talk. Inanities.

Boring.

So... So why not help? Blake was here for a purpose, she thought suddenly, and she'd been given a free ticket. So why not work the room as Blake was doing?

'I've come to Sydney this week to have my dog's eyes operated on,' she told the guy beside her, slipping the words neatly into a pause in the conversation. 'Cataracts. It's the most marvellous operation. My collie will be back to herding sheep, running on the farm, doing all the things she loves. It's such an amazing operation. And did you know how little it costs in Africa, for a person? Compared to here, it's tiny.' She'd read this on the foundations's website. She knew her facts.

'How awesome would it be?' she said softly. 'To make a blind person see? To give the gift of sight...? How great must it feel to be able to give that gift?'

She sensed, rather than saw, Blake's body stiffen beside her. Whatever he'd been expecting, it hadn't been her taking up the cause.

But she was getting little response. The people around her were hardened to appeals.

The politician's wife was still looking at her choker with longing.

Okay, go sideways. Ignore Blake's stiffening. Do what seems right.

She thought of the pictures of Blake in Africa. The work that could be done...

'My next piece of jewellery...' she said, thinking out loud, eyeing the wife of the Very Important Politician, 'is a choker like this one. If I sell it, I'm thinking that might raise enough for thirty eye-operations. Or more.'

'I'd buy it,' the woman said. 'In a heartbeat.'

'I'll pay more,' the woman opposite said.

'Raffle it,' her partner said, looking amused.

'You'd get more if you auctioned it,' another man said. 'If you're serious?'

'I... Yes.' And she discovered she was.

'How long would it take you to make one?' the politician asked, pushing inexorably forward. 'My wife's been looking at it since you walked in. If I covered the basic cost...'

'I'm donating it,' Mardie said.

Conversation at the far end of the table had stopped. Blake put a hand on her arm. A warning? 'Mardie...'

'I know what I'm doing,' she said. She returned to the politician doing the dealing. 'I need to complete a project I'm working on, but I could easily have the choker made by November.'

'Deal,' the guy said. 'Blake, it's time for you to tell us

what we need to know. I'm thinking your lady's offer comes afterwards.'

'Knock 'em dead,' Mardie said and managed to give Blake a smile.

This was what she'd come for. *Tell me about Africa.*

The people around her faded to nothing. She wanted to know.

He'd never been much of a public speaker at school. Was he nervous?

She was nervous on his behalf.

He smiled back at her. Then he touched the choker lightly, a feather touch, and his finger just grazed her neck. Sending a shiver… 'This is to do it justice,' he said and that was exactly what he did.

And she needn't have worried, for this was a Blake she'd never met before.

He greeted his audience with ease, he made a wry observation about the day's political events which made everyone smile—and then he took them to Africa.

Tell me about Africa.

She'd asked and he'd been curt to the point of rudeness. But not because he didn't care. Not because he couldn't tell it.

Because it was a part of him?

He had a screen behind him, a half-hour documentary where a cameraman had filmed Blake treating children's eyes.

Sound had been recorded along with sight, and the moment the video started the sound of the wind echoed through the room.

They were working in a makeshift tent under a canopy of half-dead trees. The wind sounded appalling. What had he called it? *Arifi…*

It made her shudder. She could feel it through the flimsy fabric of the children's sparse clothing. She could sense it, blasting sand into those vulnerable eyes.

She watched as Blake and his assistants fought to keep the equipment clean, fought to keep the sand at bay, fought to help.

The people...the kids...the damage... That was all he'd said to her when she'd asked. It was practically all he said here. His words were an aside to what was happening on the screen—simple explanations, nothing more.

The cameraman was focusing on the children's faces, and then closer. To eyes that were so damaged...

Blake's commentary was a word at a time, saying what was necessary. Nothing more.

'This is Afi. She's better now, practically a hundred per cent vision in her left eye. Moswen's not so good. Look at the scarring. We're hoping for funding for complex surgery for her but we're not holding our breath. Here's Tawia. Four years old. We caught her early, but where she lives...the flies... She gets infection after infection...'

She was, she discovered, crying. She groped for a tissue and the politician's wife handed her one. The woman had a handful and was using them herself.

Blake was touching these people—influential, wealthy people who could make a difference.

This was Blake fighting for what he was passionate about.

How could she ever have thought he'd gone to medical school to make money?

The presentation finished. Every person in the room was still in Africa.

Blake cleared his papers from the rostrum. Prepared to step down.

A thought...

There was this one moment before people turned back to their wine, their social conversations, before they returned from where they'd been taken.

She slipped the choker from her neck and pushed it to the man who'd asked if it was for sale.

'Take this,' she said simply. 'I should have thought of it. Auction it now.'

'What are you doing?' Blake demanded.

'What I want to do.'

There was no better time...

If these people left, their world would catch up with them. The dinner itself had raised money. Blake's presentation would raise more. But if she could find an outlet for the distress in the room right now...

'There's more where that came from,' she told Blake. He looked as if he'd protest and she reached out and took his hand. Linked her fingers in his.

'Hush,' she said. 'I want to do this.'

So he hushed. They both hushed, while a small and beautiful choker, of copper and semi-precious stones, maybe three hundred dollars of materials and a week of Mardie's work, was sold for an amount that took her breath away.

For Africa.

'And there's another for the losing bidder in November, if she wants it,' she whispered to the auctioneer as the room applauded. 'The same but different. I'm happy to consult on colour and style.'

Bemused, the auctioneer made the offer and the woman accepted, signing a cheque on the spot.

Leaving Mardie hornswoggled.

She'd just sold jewellery for a sum she could scarcely comprehend.

Only Blake's hand was holding her to earth.

'So...so you think we did all right in the fund-raising department?' she managed.

'We did.'

'You were wonderful.'

'Not as wonderful as you,' he said softly. 'But now... You're minus jewellery. I'm thinking... Mardie, would you be interested in a diamond to take its place?'

'A diamond...?'

'Mardie, you are my very best friend. I can't believe what you've just done. To marry you... It would be my honour.'

Her world stilled. He was...proposing? Where had that come from?

He'd taken her breath away.

He'd taken his own breath away. She met his gaze and realised he was as shocked as she was.

Had he meant to say it?

In this crowded room... *A proposal?*

'I don't think...' she said and then found courage. Also a certain amount of indignation. 'No. I don't need to think. Diamonds aren't my style.'

'Not?'

'Hugh gave me the only diamond I want,' she said and she met his gaze squarely. She glanced down at her left hand and it lay there still, her tiny solitaire.

Her armour against future hurt.

'I'm guessing yours would be bigger,' she said. 'But it would come with strings.'

She took a deep breath. Regrouped. She knew his proposal

had been instinctive, a spur-of-the-moment response to current emotion. One of them had to be sensible.

'Blake, you asked me once before to become part of your life. That couldn't happen then and it couldn't happen now. For if you were serious—about giving diamonds—I'd be asking you to give yourself. And I don't think you know how.'

'I didn't mean...'

'I know you didn't mean.' Indignation was great. Indignation helped. 'Forget it.'

And then the world took over. The woman who'd bought the option on the second choker came surging forward, twittering her excitement. People needed to speak to Blake. Chequebooks were coming out. He had to work the room.

They glanced at each other and, by mutual consent, turned back to what was important.

His work. Africa.

The work he was doing was breathtaking.

He'd just asked her to marry him?

Be part of his life?

All or nothing. Just as it had been fifteen years ago.

It was surely a mistake. An aberration. He looked as shocked as she was. She concentrated on staying social, doing some ego-massaging, trying to make those chequebooks produce more.

Wondering how soon she could get away.

Blake was mid-negotiation with the head of a huge airline corporation. Something about transport for children who needed specialist care...

One of the Outback doctors was waiting to talk to him.

She could slip away. She must.

She needed to get back to her dogs. Ground herself.

She rose and slipped to the Ladies, then, instead of returning to the crowded dining venue, she just happed to edge outside.

There was a cab rank just...

'Where do you think you're going?'

Blake. Of course. He had eyes in the back of his head, and he'd always been a mind-reader.

She didn't look back but waited for him to come up to her.

'I'm going home.' She fought to sound commonplace. As if he hadn't just asked...*about marriage*? 'I'm worried. Irena's out for the night and I have two dogs locked in her too-small laundry. I need to give them a run.'

'I'll take you.'

'You're needed here.'

'There's no more to be done,' he told her. 'I've organised to meet people from the Outback Medical Service on Thursday—something about mutual knowledge sharing—but they were pushed for time tonight and couldn't stay. The rest is duelling chequebooks. Tonight was every fund-raiser's dream. One person donates on such a grandiose scale—i.e. for your choker—and no one can be seen to be outdone. Even the corporates. It was brilliant. If you knew how many eyes tonight will save...'

'I'm glad.'

'Then let me take you home.'

'The diamond...' she said tentatively.

Their gazes met. Locked. A silent message. *Don't go there.*

'The diamond was a mistake,' he said firmly, as if it really was. 'Said on the spur of the moment because I thought you were wonderful. I still do think you're wonderful, but of course you have Hugh's.'

'Of course.' Why did that make her feel desolate?

Because that was all it was. A diamond with no Hugh behind it.

Nothing.

'So can I take you home?'

'Yes,' she said, and she should have thought of Hugh—but she didn't.

CHAPTER EIGHT

ONCE AGAIN THEY drove to Coogee in near silence. There were so many words between them, but there seemed nothing to say. It was as if there was a chasm between them, with no one courageous enough to step near the edge.

'So you decided against another Mercedes?' she asked, thinking at least his choice of car was a safe enough topic for discussion.

'Do you know how much insurance premiums go up if you crash a Mercedes?' He shrugged. 'It was hired. I decided it was cheaper to buy this time.'

'And you're not a man who wastes money.'

'Are you criticising my choice in cars?'

'Who, me?'

But maybe she was. The car he'd ushered her into was an ancient model, a bit rusty, almost as old as she was.

She glanced across at the man beside her, looking absurdly handsome in yet another dinner suit. How many men had a spare dinner suit?

And drove a Mercedes, followed by a rust bucket.

And looked cool in all of them.

A man of parts.

'So you see this as a long-term investment?' she said cautiously and got a ghost of a smile in return.

'Not too long-term. I'm probably leaving Australia in four weeks.'

'Where will you go?'

'I'm thinking back to California.'

'Back?'

'That's where we used to live,' he said. 'All those years ago. My grandfather set up a charitable trust there. That's what I've expanded—the foundation. Our CEO quit last month. Given...my limitations, it seems sensible that I take on his role.'

She frowned. 'I thought you were the CEO.'

'I'm chairman, because of the family connection. Administration's never been my forte. I far prefer working in the field. I've done the occasional fund-raiser, like this one, but mostly I've left the administration to others. It'll be a good fit for me now, though.'

'Now that you can't do fieldwork?'

'Yes.' Short. Harsh. Desolate.

'You sound like Bessie,' she said softly. 'Charlie said it'd be kinder to put her down if she can't work. Is that how you feel?'

'That's melodramatic.'

'Not so melodramatic if you love your work. Like me if you took the art out of me.'

'It means so much to you?'

'I suspect not as much as your work.'

'So if you were to think of coming to California with me...?' But he said it tentatively, as if he already knew it was out of the question. As they both knew it was.

'That'd be two of us miserable,' she said. 'Why are you asking? For the same reason you asked fifteen years ago? Because you wouldn't mind a security blanket?'

'I would never think of you as a security blanket,' he said vehemently. 'What you did tonight...'

'Was fabulous,' she said, deciding—with a fairly major effort—that she needed to cheer up. Or at least sound as if she'd cheered up. 'It pays to be different. All those diamonds, all those floor-length gowns, and I walk in wearing a homemade tube and costume jewellery. I sit next to the most gorgeous guy in the room and suddenly I'm cool and my choker's desirable and the whole room wants what I'm having. But the money it produced... Can you believe it? How much money do those guys have to play with?'

'You needn't worry,' Blake said. 'Those cheques will be lodged as tax deductions, used to gain all sorts of corporate advantage. The chokers themselves are just icing on the cake. They're not as important as image.'

'That's put me in my place.'

'It was a very nice tax deduction,' he said kindly.

'Oh, the praise. I'm all a-flutter.'

He grinned and suddenly the atmosphere in the car lightened. The stupid issue of diamonds receded. 'It was more than the choker,' he said softly. 'If you knew how much of a difference your actions made...'

'To the kids in Africa?'

'Of course.'

'Do you ever think of anything else?' she ventured.

'It's what I do. It's what I am.'

'Because of Robbie?'

'I don't know any more,' he said simply. 'Yes, when I

started it was about Robbie. Now, I love what I do. I believe in it and I'll keep working towards it.'

'So no holidays?'

'Not so much,' he admitted.

'You know,' she said softly, 'maybe you should take some time off before you take on this very important job you have in California. Cut yourself some slack.'

'I don't need slack.'

'You don't do slack. That doesn't say you don't need it. Your face says you haven't done slack in a very long time.'

'I haven't relaxed,' he admitted. Hesitated again. Regrouped. 'So you'd never think about coming to California?'

'Why would I?'

'We could do good.'

'No,' she said. 'We wouldn't. We'd self-destruct. This is a dumb conversation, Blake. It's unsettling. Leave it. Once upon a time we were friends. Now we have a dog in common and nothing else. We both know it can't ever be any more than that so we might as well stop now.'

Irena was out, at the opening of an art exhibition. 'Don't wait up for me,' she'd told Mardie. 'These things can stretch out for days. Mind, if you get caught up, too...' She'd eyed Mardie thoughtfully. 'Which I hope you do. If my neighbour doesn't see my car, she'll come in and feed the cats. Shall I leave a note saying feed the dogs as well?'

'No!' Mardie had said, revolted, so here she was, back home at eleven at night, not even pumpkin hour. Home to her dogs and Irena's cats.

So much for Irena's hope. Blake hadn't even as much as suggested he'd like to...she didn't know...have crazy, hot sex? Anything.

He'd simply asked her to marry him.

Which was much easier to refuse.

Blake was standing on the doorstep with her. 'I don't like you going into an empty house,' he'd said curtly as she'd told him there was no need. 'And I need to check the dogs are okay.'

The dogs were okay. She opened the door and they practically knocked her over in their joy. Bouncing with excitement.

The cats were a picture of smouldering resentment, perched precariously on the curtain rails.

Uh-oh.

It seemed the laundry door hadn't closed properly. She gazed around in dismay at the chaos.

That lamp looked...expensive.

'You'll have to make another choker fast, to pay for this,' Blake said, his lips twitching, and she found herself chuckling.

What was it with this man? He drove her nuts. He was driven by demons she could never hope to compete with, yet underneath...

Underneath he was still just Blake. A boy she'd loved.

A man she could still love?

Should she take his proposal seriously?

Maybe he had been serious, she thought. He wasn't a man who took things lightly.

He'd asked because he meant it?

If he had...

If he had, there was part of her that ached to accept. Only of course it hadn't been a proper proposal. It was just like that invitation to come with him to university all those years ago. Come to California. All or nothing. Be subsumed by his life.

Share his demons?

She had no intention of sharing his demons. No way. She had enough of her own.

He was helping her fight down the over-excited dogs. He was too near.

How to tell him to go home?

How to tell him he was far too distracting?

'I... I need to change and take the dogs for a walk,' she said. 'I need to get rid of some energy.'

'You're not walking in the dark.'

'It's Coogee,' she said patiently. 'It'll be lit like daylight. Security patrols. The works. I've done it before. The security guys even know me—at this time of night they'll turn a blind eye if I let Bounce off his lead.'

'How often do you come down here?'

'I sell my enamelling,' she said patiently. 'I live in two worlds.'

'So you could come to California...'

'No, Blake, I couldn't,' she snapped. 'Have you forgotten my mother? Have you forgotten how much I love Banksia Bay? And have you even begun to realise how much I don't know you? Enough. You're welcome to come for a walk on the beach with me, but that's the extent of it. If you have time to wait until I put some jeans on. If you don't mind walking in a dinner suit.'

'Lately I've been doing all sorts of strange things in a dinner suit,' he said, sounding grim.

'Maybe your life's changing in more ways than one,' she said. 'Think about it. California doesn't sound like much fun to me. How about some lateral thinking?'

As if... When had this man ever changed direction? Was it possible that he ever could?

* * *

He stood and waited until she put on jeans and windcheater and trainers, and when she came back to the sitting room he couldn't figure whether he loved her more in her wonderful home-made dress or in her casual jeans.

Love...

It was a simple word but it was resounding more and more.

Mardie.

Mardie herding sheep. Mardie tackling the tree with her chainsaw.

Mardie loving her mother, loving her community.

Love.

But he didn't truly know what love was and how he was feeling now... He didn't know what to do with it. There was nowhere to take it.

He'd asked her to marry him. What if she'd said yes?

He'd make it work.

She wasn't taking the risk. She was being wise for both of them.

Beach, walk, dogs.

He tossed his jacket and tie, rolled up his sleeves, pretended to be casual.

Pretended he could fit into Mardie's world.

He knew that he couldn't.

He'd expected a stroll. He didn't get one. Mardie walked as if there was a sheep in trouble down the back paddock and she wasn't wasting time getting there.

The tide was far out. The foreshore was well lit but even if it hadn't been, the full moon made walking a pleasure. They could walk for miles on the ribbon of wet sand and on the paths around the cliffs—and maybe she intended just that. She was striding as if she meant to leave him behind.

That was okay. It felt okay that she was simply on the beach beside him.

More—it felt good.

It felt good to the dogs, too. Strange smells. Shallows to run in. Humans to herd. Both these dogs must know the sea. Bessie stuck to Bounce's side, but she seemed almost the leader, egging Bounce on.

Blake let his attention stay on the dogs. It was easier to think dogs rather than think Mardie, for every time he thought about Mardie...

Mardie tonight, glowing, sophisticated, beautiful, generous. Every man in the room watching her. His Mardie-girl...

To walk away...

Not his.

Don't think about it.

Think of Bessie.

To cure her would give such pleasure. It wouldn't feel so bad going back to California knowing he'd left Mardie with two dogs instead of one.

Why had he asked her to marry him?

He hadn't been serious. If he seriously wanted this woman to marry him, he needed to get down on bended knee and do the thing in style.

The answer would be the same. The idea was, as she'd said, unworkable.

Unthinkable.

Except he was thinking it.

Marriage on his terms?

Marriage for him; not for Mardie.

Bad idea.

'So what were you about, offering diamonds?' Mardie asked, still striding, and he wondered if she was angry. She'd never been one to sulk in silence. Bring the elephant into the room and inspect it from all angles.

'Thinking aloud,' he said. 'Wishing our worlds could collide.'

'Would you really want our worlds to collide?' she asked. 'Or is it more that in your world you don't have anything of my world? And my world feels safe.'

'Safe...'

'Why did you come back to Australia after your illness?' she asked. 'I know there was this fund-raiser, but someone else could surely have handled it. If home's in California...'

'It's not.'

'Home has to feel somewhere.'

She slowed. She'd kicked off her sandals and was walking in the shallows.

He'd been walking a little up the beach where it was drier. As she slowed he tugged off his shoes and hit the water, too. Her anger seemed to have dissipated. He flinched as the first wave hit and she smiled.

That smile... Marriage... Why wouldn't a man ask, even if the concept was impossible?

The dogs came tearing back to them, crazy circling, as if making sure their flock of humans stayed in a tight knot.

He wouldn't mind staying in a tight knot with Mardie.

Home was...

Here. With this woman.

It always had been. Ever since that first day in the playground. Sharing lunches.

Why had he come back to Australia?

It had been his refuge after Robbie died. He'd found peace here. He still thought of Australia as a refuge.

He couldn't stay somewhere because it was a refuge. He couldn't love somewhere because it was safe.

He couldn't love a woman for the same reasons.

Mardie was much, much more.

'Ooh, there's some stuff going on in that head of yours,' she said. 'For heaven's sake, Blake, let it go. Race you back to the headland. You could always beat me, but you've been sick and I've been training. One, two, three, go…'

And she was off, flying along the wet sand, her dogs hurtling along behind her. Dogs and woman…

He'd never met someone so…free.

She had her demons. Of course she did.

She chose to let them take care of themselves.

Maybe he, too…

No. Too hard. It was far too hard.

She beat him—of course she did—he'd spent the first half of the race in stupid, unproductive thought—and when he did finally catch her, she seemed angry again. They were at the start of the path up to the house. She didn't pause; she went right on up, and when they reached his car parked out the front, she fussed over dog leads and didn't look at him.

He waited until she straightened. Tried to figure what to say.

She held out her hand. A formal gesture of farewell.

'I've had a lovely night,' she said, a trifle too stiffly. 'Thank you.'

'That's… I've enjoyed it, too.'

'I can manage on my own now, with the dogs.'

'I'll be here on Thursday when Colin operates.'

'There's no need.'

'I'll be here.'

'Thank you,' she said simply. 'That would be lovely. Goodnight.'

And before he could react, before he could reach out a hand and take hers—she slipped into the house with her dogs without another word.

Tuesday and Wednesday, he didn't see her. There was no reason.

She needed to take Bessie back to the vet's for a couple more pre-op tests, but she lived close and for him to take the half-hour trip there…

As she'd said, there was no need.

He had things to do. There were always things to do.

One of the cheques for Mardie's chokers bounced. He was used to that. Guys big-noting themselves among their peers, then letting the charity cope with the consequences.

He made a few enquiries, discovered the guy did have serious money, discovered he'd tried this on before.

He made a couple of calls to the media, had a journalist do a dig story and he had a phone call from the bank within the hour.

The cheque had magically been cleared.

There was no way the scum-bag was getting Mardie's choker without paying.

He could do good, he thought, as he tallied the figures for Monday night. He could make the foundation much bigger than it was now. He could make it huge.

He wanted to work in the field.

But that was dumb. The cause was what counted. To die of dengue because he wanted to be indispensable… How would Robbie feel about that?

His twin. The guy who questioned everything he did.

How would Robbie feel about Mardie?

There was a dumb question. A dumb thought.

Put her out of his mind.

Then suddenly he thought… Irena. Irena was Mardie's agent. If Mardie had an agent then there must be more sales.

Mardie had looked him up. He could do the same. He did an internet search for one Mardie Rainey, looking for stockists. Discovered a tiny gallery that specialised in three-dimensional art.

He just happened to walk past. He just happened to walk in, expecting rings, bracelets, maybe even chokers like he'd seen on Monday night.

Instead he found tiny enamelled pictures. This then, was how she'd landed the job commemorating the pilots. Where she'd gained her reputation.

These pictures were extraordinary.

They were of…nothing. Glass on copper.

A blade of grass against a weathered fence post.

A piece of driftwood on a beach.

A raindrop.

Nothing.

Everything.

He looked at them and thought of Africa. A child's sight.

So little. Everything.

He thought of Mardie's life.

And he thought of his own.

Thursday. 'Have her here at eight. No breakfast,' Colin had decreed and Mardie had Bessie there at seven forty-five. She stayed in the truck until the clinic doors opened, hugging

Bessie, wishing they'd elected to have only one eye done today and not both. Both eyes seemed scary.

Even one seemed scary.

She'd left Bounce with Irena and the cats. Bessie had to do this alone.

She had to do this alone.

Bessie seemed bereft, and she felt exactly the same.

But then… Her truck door swung open and Blake was there. Just…there.

Deep breath. This was good. Wasn't it? Two of them could feel bad about Bessie together.

He was so close.

He'd asked her to marry him. The question had hovered in her head for two days.

Stupid.

She was so happy to see him again she could hardly speak.

'S…so tell me again why we're doing both eyes?' she managed.

'So we won't have to spend another night like last one,' he said. 'Staring into the dark thinking of all the things that can go wrong.'

'You, too?'

'I know the odds,' he said. 'Healthy dog, healthy eyes under the cataracts, great surgeon, tried-and-tested procedure—this is as good as it gets. The biggest risk is retina detachment and that's a risk no matter whether we do one or both. It'll be fine.'

'Yet you still sat up all night.'

'Yep,' he said and lifted Bessie from her arms. 'I'm a sucker for a lady with facial hair. Colin's here. All systems go. Let's get our Bessie's sight restored so she can get on with her life.'

'Blake?'

'Mmm.'

'Did you come...just to wish us luck?'

'I'll stay close until it's done. I've agreed to meet a couple of guys at the airport in an hour but that's close enough to here. If you'd like me to stick around...'

'I would.' She hesitated. She shouldn't need this man.

'I definitely would,' she said.

They stayed with Bessie until the anaesthetic took hold, but then they had to leave.

'You're not watching,' Colin told him. 'Blake taught me,' he explained to Mardie. 'If there's anything guaranteed to make my hands shake, it's my teacher watching. Take him away and don't let him come near until I've finished.'

'Fine by me,' Mardie said, feeling bad. She hugged Bessie and left. Feeling...watery.

She pushed open the door to outside with more force than necessary.

Blake ushered her through. Closed the door after her. Offered her a tissue.

Went a step further and hugged her.

'I don't cry,' she managed. Not pulling away.

'You shouldn't. Bessie's about to be cured. What's there to cry about?'

'Do you get emotional about patients?'

'Never.'

'Liar.' She knew this guy.

'I shouldn't.'

She sniffed. She managed—with a pretty big effort—to pull herself out of his arms. Blew her nose, hard.

Got a grip.

'So you want me to stay here while you have your meeting at the airport?'

'Stay with me,' he said softly and took her hand.

She gazed down at their linked hands.

Thought, inexplicably, of Bessie and Bounce. Practically Siamese twins.

She didn't pull away.

What was he doing, meeting these guys? He was wasting time.

He'd met them the night of the dinner. Riley and Harry. Doctor and pilot with an Outback Flying Doctor medical service based at Whale Cove. Squeezing the dinner in between care flights.

It seemed Harry was a friend of Raff's, the Banksia Bay cop. Raff had told them about him. They'd come on Monday night to listen. Asked if they could talk to him.

A job offer? Questions about fund-raising? Normally he'd decline but he'd been feeling...disoriented. As if he didn't know how to say no.

Now...he and Mardie watched as the light plane came in to land, a patient was transferred to an ambulance headed for a city hospital, and then Harry and Riley were free.

They didn't speak. They simply waited.

With their patient transferred, the men came over to them. Big men, tough, in the uniform of the Flying Doctor Service.

'Raff says you're looking for a job,' Riley said bluntly, straight to the point.

Raff. Banksia Bay. Of course. Everyone knew everyone.

'He has his wires crossed. I'm not.'

But it seemed Raff had done some research. He'd worked fast and he had it right. 'Raff says you've been in Africa treating eyes,' Riley said. 'He says you can't go back because of dengue. Now he thinks you're planning to be a pen-pusher. That'd be just plain dumb. We could use you, right here, right now. There's no dengue where we work, just a whole heap of need.'

It wouldn't work.

They drove back to the vet clinic and the silence in the truck was almost tangible.

Blake was staring straight ahead.

'I'm going back to California,' he said at last. 'I think I have to.'

'So you met them why?'

'I thought they might want to talk mutual fund-raising.' But he hadn't. He'd known the minute he'd met them that there was a job on the line. If he and Mardie…

No.

'You wouldn't consider it?' she ventured. 'Robbie doesn't give you that option?'

'I should never have told you about Robbie.' It was an explosion.

'I should have guessed.' She hesitated, and then went on. 'Blake, that night, all those years ago,' she said softly. 'I can only imagine. Two little boys, lying in that great big house. Following rules. But then…the joy of sneaking out to play in the pool. Two little boys having fun. And tragedy. But surely that doesn't mean you need to follow rules all your life, especially if those rules are ones you've set up for yourself. If those rules were meant to make up for Robbie, they never can. They never will.'

'This is…'

'None of my business? Maybe not. Or maybe it is my business, because you're my friend.' She took a deep breath. 'On Monday you even suggested I marry you. It was offhand, like something I wouldn't even consider, but you know something? I would.'

'Mardie...'

'Only not with your shadows,' she said, with only the faintest tremor behind the words. 'For I'm not sharing.' Another deep breath. 'Blake, have you ever talked to seven-year-old Blake?'

'What do you mean?'

'It's a thing you do,' she said diffidently. 'It's a thing I learned. When Hugh died... I was a mess and our local doctor organised a shrink to see me. You know what was going round my head? That I hadn't put the dogs in their crate. I'd cleaned it and then we were running late so I thought—why bother putting it back? So they were fussing in the back seat, and Hugh was telling them to pipe down, and the kids came round the bend. He didn't have time to swerve. If he'd had that extra split second... I thought... Well, you know what I thought.'

'It wasn't your fault.'

'Yeah, you say that. Everyone says it but you can hear it as many times as you want and not believe. You know that better than me. But the shrink... You know what he did? He made me find a picture of me from before the accident. And he said I needed to treat the hurting me as separate. The Mardie-Before and the Mardie-After. And the Mardie-After needed to talk to the Mardie-Before, talk through exactly what happened that day, tell her that what she did wasn't criminal or even stupid. He said I should give that Mardie a hug and move on. And you know what? Eventually I did.'

He didn't say anything. Nothing.

'So...could you look at a photograph of your seven-year-old self, and tell him he has to pay for the rest of his life?' she ventured. 'Or would you look at that seven-year-old and give him a hug and weep for what he's gone through already? Robbie's death. Your parents' abandonment. And then...could you tell the little boy that you were to live his life as he ought to live his life? To have fun. To do good if that's what you want, but only if that's what you want, not because you're paying back shadows. To...' She paused. Thought about it. Finally said it. 'To allow yourself to be happy.'

'I think we should leave it,' he said heavily, and she thought, yes, she should. She'd said everything she could say.

Or...not quite.

Just say it.

'And, as for Monday... As for the diamond... I would marry you,' she said simply. 'In truth, I decided when I was ten that I wanted to marry you. And it seems I've never stopped. I loved Hugh, but in a different way; he was a different man. It doesn't take away what I felt for him, what I feel for you. It seems I've loved you all the time and I guess I always will. Shadows or not. But if you can't get rid of your shadows I guess our loving will keep us at a distance. Because there's no choice. For both of us.'

They met a beaming Colin.

'I couldn't ask for better,' he said. 'Textbook perfect. It's gone brilliantly in both eyes. She's on the way to recovery. All she needs is absolute quiet, to wear the cone collar all the time, no barking, drops twice a day, total care, and in four weeks I'm thinking you'll have a magnificent working dog. Do you want to see her? She's still heavily sedated.'

They went in and saw her.

Her eyes were still closed. Colin gently lifted a lid and the awful milkiness was gone.

Mardie felt... She felt...

Good. Excellent. Dog-wise, at least, this was job done. She could get on with her life with two dogs.

Blake would go back to the US. Things would return to normal.

But, despite her tumultuous emotions, Colin's words were starting to sink in. Quiet. Cone collar. No barking. Total care...

She didn't quite have a handle on this.

'No barking at all?' she said, faltering.

'I thought Blake would have explained post-op care,' Colin said, frowning.

'Blake did mention it,' she said. 'I just thought... I can handle eye drops.' She took a deep breath. 'No. Sorry. I can handle everything. I'll take Bounce to the boarding kennels for a month. It won't kill him. If Bessie's locked inside, she'll stay quiet.'

'You're hardly ever inside.' Blake said.

'I guess loneliness is the price she pays for her sight.'

'It's not,' Blake said.

'Not?'

'I have an apartment here in the city,' he said. 'I'll be working here for the next few weeks. I do some online teaching,' he explained as they both looked at him in surprise. 'I can do that while I keep Bessie at my feet. I know she'll miss Bounce but it'll work. I'll bring her back to the farm in a month, just before I go.'

There was the solution, just like that. Easy.

Mardie looked down at the sleeping dog. Bessie.

It should feel great.

It was an eminently practical solution.

She could walk away. Go back to Irena's, collect Bounce, go back to the farm.

Blake would return Bessie to her in a month. And then... nothing.

It was a neat solution all round.

It felt...

It felt...

Not neat.

'That's great,' she said, sounding feeble. 'I... You have your car here, Blake? I can go, then. I really would like to get back to the farm this afternoon.' She put her hand on Bessie's soft head, taking as well as giving comfort.

'Take care of her,' she whispered. 'Thank you, Colin. And...and thank you, Blake. You're both wonderful.'

'I'm not wonderful,' Blake said.

'Yes, you are,' she said, gaining strength. 'Yes, you are, if you let yourself be.'

CHAPTER NINE

FOUR WEEKS WAS a very long time in the life of Mardie.

She did exactly what she'd been doing a month ago. She spent three days a week in the nursing home, helping aged fingers give pleasure to their owners, having fun. She worked furiously on her last plates, and then slowed because Robyn Partling's life refused to be told in a rush. In a month they were done and she loved them.

She could take them to Sydney this weekend and deliver them.

Or not.

This weekend Blake had said he'd bring Bessie home, and something inside her—the silly, hormonal something—was saying, *Last chance, Last chance, Last chance.*

He rang, friendly but curt. 'She's done brilliantly,' he told her. 'Colin's taken the cone off. Her eyesight's amazing. He says she's ready for farm life again. Can you be home at two on Saturday?'

'Of course,' she said simply—and then she was nervous. Really nervous.

What was she doing, thinking *last chance*? There never

was going to be a chance. He'd drop off Bessie and say goodbye and fly out to California and that'd be the end of an unsettling period of her life.

She had to settle.

Which meant...normal.

Saturday.

She went to see Charlie and told him Bessie's latest news. She told her mum.

'We'd love to see her come home,' they both said, and she thought—normal; I can do that.

Two o'clock on Saturday.

Blake was coming home.

No. Bessie was coming home. Blake was merely the delivery man.

He turned into the farm gate, expecting the old Mardie. Mardie in her jeans and an ancient sweater—the Mardie who belonged here, not the unsettling Mardie who'd blown him away in Sydney.

He wanted it to be the old Mardie. He'd take the thought of her back to the States with him, he thought, as he'd carried her in his thoughts for years. She was a warm part of his heart that had stayed safe, that was used for comfort but not permitted to interfere with what he had to do.

He wanted that part of him to stay unaltered.

He looked to the veranda and there she was, on the top step, Bounce beside her.

Bessie was harnessed in the back seat but he heard her whine.

'Home,' he told her and the word felt...

Yeah, like the word he wasn't allowed to feel. He needed to hand Bessie over and get out of here, memories intact.

He pulled up. Bounce tore down from the veranda, Mardie following a trifle more sedately but not much. She was smiling.

What cost that smile?

'Bessie.' He let her out and Mardie was on her knees, hugging, and Bounce was going wild, trying to reach his friend. He watched the group hug and felt his heart twist.

'Bessie.' It was a quavering voice from the veranda and Bessie froze. Pulled out from the group hug in an instant.

Looked up.

Really looked.

Her eyes worked fine. Her hearing was even better. She knew who was on the veranda and she was gone, flying across the yard, up the steps, reaching the old man in the vast padded hospital chair. Skidding to a stop. Not jumping. Just sitting, hard beside him.

Charlie's gnarled old hand dropped to her silky head and she quivered from nose to tail. She put a paw up, as if in entreaty. Quivered some more.

'Up,' he whispered and she needed no more persuasion. She was up on his blanketed knees, licking his face, her paws on his shoulders, doing what an untrained, out-of-control dog would do when reunited with her beloved owner.

Only this was no untrained dog. Charlie chuckled and submitted to licking, and even hugged back himself, but he was frail and he knew it.

'Enough,' he said, and Bessie was off his knee in an instant, sitting beside him, looking adoringly up at him. Charlie was smiling and smiling.

So was Blake.

And Mardie.

And so was her mother, and the nurse who stood silently behind. Groping for tissues all round.

He'd thought he was bringing Bessie back to Mardie. Instead... Here were Charlie and Etta and a nurse with a name tag that said she was Liz, administrator of the Banksia Bay Nursing Home. He was bringing Bessie home to Banksia Bay, to be enveloped once again in this all-embracing town.

'Welcome home,' Mardie said as he reached her, to him alone, and she hugged him unself-consciously, as if it was the most natural thing in the world.

Could he accept that welcome?

He thought suddenly of that night all those years ago, shut in the house, bored, tired, fed up with listening to the grown-up party downstairs. One moment's breaking of the rules. *Let's go out and swim.*

That moment felt like now.

'You want to see what she can do?' Charlie asked, his voice cracked with age and pride, and the moment when he could have hugged Mardie back was past. When he could have whirled her round and round in his arms and held her to him and declared he, too, was truly home...

It was a fantasy. A stupid, dangerous longing.

'Of course,' he managed and put Mardie aside, and heaven alone knew the effort that cost him.

'Charlie's wonderful with dogs,' Etta said placidly from her chair, looking from Mardie to Blake and back again, and Blake knew she was asking questions in her mind that couldn't be answered.

'Charlie's the best dog-trainer in the district,' Liz said. 'Half the dogs in this town have been trained by Charlie, or by guys Charlie's trained to train, and the younger dogs have reached the stage where they seem almost to have been trained by Charlie's dogs. Generations of dogs, teaching each other, courtesy of Charlie. His legacy will live for ever.'

Charlie's wrinkled face worked; he tried not to smile, tried not to look as if he wasn't moved. But he was.

Even in the past four weeks Charlie had slipped; Blake could see that.

Liz was giving him a gift. An affirmation.

As maybe in his turn Charlie had gifted each of them.

Banksia Bay. His refuge. Blake felt...

Mardie took his hand and squeezed, but it was a message, nothing more.

He couldn't feel.

The offer from the Flying Dotor... An insidious siren song.

Not as insidious as Mardie.

'I've put some sheep in the home paddock,' she said. 'You want to help take Mum and Charlie down to watch these guys strut their stuff?'

To be drawn further into this emotion?

He had no choice. There was no escaping, but did he want to escape?

Yes. He told himself that harshly.

Only not yet. All eyes were on him. He was their audience.

He was Charlie's affirmation.

So they took the two big hospital chairs across to the gate into the home paddock where Mardie had herded six sheep. They were young ones, yearlings, wild and silly, ready to run any which way.

She'd set pegs up at intervals and a tiny corral in the centre of the paddock, with an entrance about the width of a man. Or a sheep.

'Walk up,' Charlie said to Bessie and Bessie's eyes, the

eyes that had been hidden for so long, lit with excitement and pure instinctive pleasure.

'Stay,' Mardie told Bounce and Bounce quivered and stayed.

'In here,' Charlie said, his voice scarcely a whisper, but Bessie heard. 'Look back. Get back, take time, come by...'

And in moments the sheep were transformed from a bunch of silly youngsters to a beautifully controlled, collie-trained flock. Bessie moved almost without command, glancing back at Charlie every so often, a tiny glance, watching Charlie's hand. Watching each and every one of the sheep. Weaving them seamlessly through the pegs, out and back, out and back, and then into the tiny gap and into the makeshift coral.

Done.

As a display of sheer skill, of communication between man and dog, it was breathtaking.

'That'll do,' Charlie said gruffly and Bessie came flying back to his side and sat again, totally attentive, waiting for the next order.

'He's... Charlie's been teaching me,' Mardie said in a voice that was none too steady. 'Want to watch?'

So they watched as Bounce gave it his best.

He wasn't close to as slick as Bessie was. The communication between Bounce and Mardie wasn't as great. At one stage he saw Bessie half stand, as if aching to help. Charlie's hand rested on her head.

'Stay,' he said softly. 'Young 'uns have to learn.'

And Bounce was learning and so was Mardie. The sheep were eventually back in the corral and Mardie's beam was as wide as a house.

'How's that?'

'They all clapped and laughed and Bounce bounced back

to Bessie. Charlie released her, and the dogs did a wide joyous circle of the whole paddock. Not touching. There was no longer need for touch. Bessie had her eyes back. Still they didn't leave each other. Siamese twins. Touching at the heart.

Mardie's hand was suddenly in his, and this time there was no pressure. No message. It was simply because...she wanted her hand to be in his.

'Thank you,' she said softly. 'Thank you from all of us.'

He wanted to kiss her.

He wanted to kiss her more than anything else in the world.

Robbie... Don't go near the pool...

Mardie deserved more than being used as a refuge.

'I need to go,' he said and glanced at his watch. 'I... There's things to do. I leave for the States on Tuesday.'

'Of course.' She tugged back, reminded of reality. 'You can't stay for...'

'No.' Blunt. Curt. He watched Etta's face fall.

He didn't see Mardie's face fall. He carefully wasn't looking at Mardie. He'd pulled right away.

'I'll walk you to your car,' she said.

'I'll put the kettle on,' Liz said. 'You guys play with the dogs for a few more minutes,' she told Charlie and Etta. 'Mardie and I'll push you inside when the kettle boils.'

Liz had thus given them privacy. It meant Mardie could walk him back to the car and they didn't have an audience,

Mardie slipped her hand back into his as they walked.

He should pull away. He didn't.

'I'm sad you're going back,' she said softly. 'You could have made a difference with North Coast Rescue.'

'I'll make a difference with what I'm doing.'

'By sitting in an office?'

'I'm good at fund-raising.'

'Yes, but does it give you pleasure?'

'That's not the point.'

'No.' She pulled her hand away.

They reached the car. He should get in and go. Leave. Drive away and never come back.

'I should never have come,' he said.

'I'm glad you did. It's like…closure.'

'I've always hated that word.'

'Me, too,' she whispered and she turned into him. Looked up.

And he didn't get into the car.

For first there was something he had to do. Something he had no choice in, for every nerve in his body was telling him to do it.

He cupped her chin with his hands, he stooped and he kissed her.

Her lips met his. Merged.

Heat, want, need. It exploded between them, surging at the point of contact and spreading.

It was as if his world had suddenly melted, merged, fused. All centring round this one point.

This woman in his arms.

He held her, gently and then more urgently. She was on tiptoe to meet him and he lifted her, hugging her close. Melting.

Mardie. His Mardie.

Not his Mardie. He'd made his decision.

But to walk away would hurt. Why not savour this last piece of surrender, for surrender it surely was? Surrendering himself to what he wanted most in the world.

This woman in his arms.

This woman he was kissing.

This woman who was kissing him. For the roles were changing, the delineation was blurring.

A man and a woman and a need as primeval as time itself.

History was disappearing. History and pain and even sense. Especially sense.

His defences were crumbling as he held her, as her breasts crushed against his chest, as she merged into him.

Mardie.

He'd met her when he was too young to know what a woman was. She'd become part of him in a slow, insidious process that now seemed inevitable, unalterable. She was like part of him, part of his childhood, part of his teens, but... part of who he was right now.

She knew him as no other woman could know him. She'd exposed parts of him he'd hidden with years of carefully built barriers, because behind the barriers...pain.

Where was the pain now?

Not here. Not with this kiss. Not with this wonder.

It was waiting. He knew that, even as he surrendered to the here and now, to the pure loveliness of this moment. Self-recriminations were right behind him, waiting to take over. But he had this one moment. His kiss intensified, became more urgent, more compelling.

Mardie...

But she was suddenly withdrawing, just a little. He felt her body stiffen. Her hands fought to find purchase between them, and she pushed him away.

It felt as if part of himself was being torn, to let her go.

He had to let her go.

'This...this is *some* goodbye kiss,' she said in a voice that said she was shaken to the core.

'It is.' He wanted to reach out and touch her again. Gather her back into his arms.

Surrender...

Stay here. Stay safe. Banksia Bay. Mardie. Its own sweet siren song.

Staying safe couldn't last. The world was out there.

To retreat... To come home...

It wasn't his home.

'Thank you...for being you,' he said simply. 'I've loved this time.'

'No, you haven't. It's torn you in two.'

'Maybe it has,' he said simply. 'But at least now, when I walk away I know there's truth between us. Friendship.'

'Like that will help.'

'Mardie...'

'I know,' she said bleakly. 'You can't help it. You need to save the world and somehow you think you can't do it here. You can't think that I do it, that my mum did it, that Liz up there does it, that Charlie does it, too, in his way.' She paused. Closed her eyes. Took a deep breath.

'Sorry. You don't understand and you'll never understand. Off you go and save the world in your own way, my lovely Blake, and know I'll always think of you. With love. Because I can't help myself. But there'll always be a little part of Banksia Bay that's home for you, Blake, whether you want it or not. Don't forget it. Don't forget us.'

They were waiting for her. Her mother, Charlie, Liz and the two dogs.

Bessie whimpered as if she realised what she'd lost and Charlie hushed her.

Her mother held out her hand and she took it and then

stooped and let Etta hug her. Her mother's hugs... Once upon a time they'd made things better. Not now.

'He's not coming back?' Liz asked.

'What do you think?'

'Sorry, girl,' Charlie said.

There was a moment's silence while they all thought of something to say.

Then... 'That dog of yours needs work,' Charlie said roughly. 'You want a quick lesson before Liz orders us all in for scones and tea?'

'Yes, please,' she said, trying valiantly not to...well, not to stand and wail. A girl had some pride.

'Well, let's get on with it,' Charlie said. 'Time's short. We've got things to do. Get yourself together, girl, and move on.'

'You're tired,' Liz said.

'Not too tired for what she loves,' Charlie retorted. 'Never too tired for that.'

He drove back to Sydney feeling empty.

So what was new? He'd had this emptiness in his gut for ever.

Not when he was with Mardie. When he was with Mardie she filled his life.

It was a dangerous, insidious sweetness.

Why couldn't a man just give in?

And do what...?

North Coast Rescue would give him a job in a heartbeat. 'We fly clinics three days a week,' Riley had told him. 'We almost always fly north. It'd be a snap to detour through Banksia Bay—there's a light airstrip at the back of the town.

We could pick you up on the way, drop you off on the way back. Long days, but, mate, they're so satisfying.'

Three days a week. The rest… Writing? Teaching online? Doing some foundation work?

Helping Mardie train Bounce.

He'd never change the world.

He'd change a little bit.

It wasn't enough to stop this fierce, desolate drive within him.

How could he let it go?

See a shrink in the States? Come back cured?

No. He'd come back with the guilt in recess. He could never live with Mardie on those terms—she deserved so much more.

Get over it.

He thought of what he'd left behind. Mardie. Etta and Charlie. Bounce and Bessie. Sheep and hens, beach and farm.

It had been a refuge when he was a child. It had been a refuge now as he came to terms with dengue.

A man couldn't stay in a refuge for ever. He had to face his demons on his own.

He returned to Sydney.

He spent time consulting with two Australian doctors who'd volunteered to spend a year each in Africa.

He packed up the apartment, and put it on the market. It had been stupid to keep it all these years. He was never coming back.

Two more days… The loose ends were being tied.

Monday night. At one in the morning, he was staring at the ceiling, waiting for sleep that wouldn't come.

A phone call.

'Blake?'

Mardie. He was upright in an instant, flicking on the light. Her voice...

'What's happened?'

'No...no drama,' she said but he could tell by her voice that she'd been crying. 'It's just... Charlie died yesterday. In his sleep. It's...it's fine. It was his time. Liz... Liz knew he was slipping. She came out and got Bessie, and Bessie was asleep on his bed when he died. He knew she was there. He knew she was safe, and well and happy.' She caught her breath. Struggled to go on.

'It's just... I wasn't going to tell you, you don't need to know, but then I thought... I couldn't sleep so I thought I'd tell you and you can do what you want with it. His funeral's this afternoon. No one's expecting you to come. It's...it's nothing to do with you but I thought... I thought I'd let you know and let you decide whether it's anything to do with you or not.'

She shouldn't have told him.

She sat in the front pew, with her mother in her wheelchair beside her and Bessie at her feet. The Banksia Bay vicar saw nothing wrong and everything right with Charlie's dog being here, being part of the ceremony.

Charlie's coffin was loaded with every trophy, every ribbon, he and his dogs had ever won. There were photographs everywhere.

Charlie and dogs. He'd never had children but his dogs lived on.

Mardie was almost totally focused on Charlie, almost totally focused on what the vicar was saying. But a tiny part of her was aware of the door.

This one last chance...

He wasn't taking it. He wouldn't come.

'It's okay, sweetheart, you have us,' her mother whispered, taking her hand, and she flushed. Was she so obvious?

'I don't need anyone.'

'Nonsense,' Etta said sharply. 'We all need everyone.'

He came. He'd meant to go in. At the last minute he stopped himself. He still felt as if he had no place here.

Going in would be a statement he had no wish to make.

Instead he parked his car on the hill overlooking the church. Watched people go in. Watched people gather outside. Many, many people, most of them attached to…dogs?

The service was being broadcast on loudspeakers so the crowd outside could hear. The day was still and warm, and the sound carried.

He heard people talk of Charlie, with respect and with affection.

He heard Mardie. Had they asked her to speak the eulogy, then? Her voice came over the loudspeaker, true and clear. 'Charlie's dog, Bessie, is here. If Bessie has a voice, here's what she'd like to say about Charlie…'

Laughter. Murmurs of agreement, of affection, of wistfulness from the congregation.

Old hymns. Favourites he remembered from when Mardie's mum had bossed them into church.

They felt like something he missed. Like part of him, cut off.

And then a blaze of bagpipes, the ancient tune, "Dawning of that Day," signalling the end of the service.

The crowd parted so the pall-bearers could carry their burden out.

But they didn't just part.

They formed a guard of honour, all the way from the church door to the graveyard at the foot of the hill where he stood.

A man or woman or child was suddenly standing every step of the way, on either side of the path where the coffin was carried. And beside each man, woman and child...

A dog. Not just a dog, but a trained dog. Mostly working dogs—collies, kelpies, blue heelers, but the occasional poodle, spaniel, mutt.

Every dog was sitting hard on his owner's heels, rigidly to attention, eyes straight in front as the coffin passed, a last and loving respect to the man who'd spent his life training them. Who'd passed on his skills from dog to dog, from generation to generation.

Mardie was walking behind the coffin. Bessie was beside her, not on a lead, heeling beautifully, steady, sure.

Behind Mardie, others—friends, relatives, more dogs. Liz was pushing Etta's chair. Bounce was heeling by the wheelchair as if he realised the significance of this day.

A community, mourning its own.

He thought suddenly of Mardie's plates. Her skill in creating things of wonder, the pilot's wife's awe and gratitude.

He thought of Etta, Mardie's mother, her crazy cooking, the way she'd welcomed a stray little boy into her home.

He looked at Liz, who ran one of the best nursing homes he'd ever been in.

Of Raff, the local cop, who cared for this community with firmness and with love.

Love...

He thought of the children he'd treated in Africa. All those lives, altered because of what he'd done.

He thought of what he could do...

He could go back to California. Make Eyes For Africa bigger.

Others could do that. Others would do that. He could keep an overseeing role.

He could stay here and make Mardie happy.

She was already happy. She didn't need him.

He should…

No. Enough of *should*.

The procession had reached the graveyard now. Mardie was standing by the open grave, Bessie by her side. She looked…alone.

Enough.

He walked down the hillside to join her.

Not because he should. Not because it'd save the world.

He walked down to join Mardie because it was what he most wanted to do in the world.

If he could make Mardie love him… If he could be part of this community…the world would be his.

She'd been aware of him for a while, high on the hill, just watching.

He was too far away for her to be sure, but she knew. A sixth sense…

Or the fact that he was part of her and she knew her own heart.

The vicar was about to speak as he arrived, but the crowd parted to let him through and the vicar hesitated, giving Blake time to be where he needed to be.

By Mardie's side.

Holding Mardie's hand.

The vicar smiled a question—okay to go on?—and he nodded.

It was as if he had the right to be here. As if he had the right to be part of the ceremony for this old dog-trainer, a man who was loved by so many.

Charlie belonged.

As Blake finally belonged.

Mardie's hand tightened on his and he knew it for truth.

It took the rest of the day before he found some time alone with her. The wake was enormous, the pub crowded, and the day turned into an impromptu dog trial.

The football oval was taken over, hurdles, pegs, pens set up. Charlie's dogs versus Charlie's dogs.

Someone thought of a barbecue; parts of the crowd dispersed, came back with supplies. Day turned to dusk turned to dark. The stories of Charlie were legion.

Mardie moved through the crowd with Bessie. It was as if Bessie was part of who Charlie was; it was important that she stayed.

But finally only the diehards were left—old men who'd sit and remember their friend over a beer or six, Charlie's mates.

Mardie was free to leave.

Blake drove her home in her truck. His car was still up on the hill and it was likely to stay there.

There was a thumping sound in the engine. Ominous. He might need to do something about that.

He would. He'd put it on his list. His list for after he'd asked what he needed to ask.

Once again, there was silence in the truck, but it was different. Peace. Acceptance.

The beginning of joy?

He pulled up in the yard. They climbed out, the dogs jumping wearily down after them and heading straight inside, to their basket by the fire. Side by side again.

Joined at the heart.

Like him and this woman by his side.

Mardie let them in and then turned. Blake was right behind her. Close.

Watching her in the moonlight.

'I'm glad you came back,' she said simply.

'I should never have left.'

'You had to leave,' she said softly. 'You know, if you'd told me about Robbie, I would have understood. I understand now how important it was to you. How important it is.'

'It was a process,' he said simply. 'Something I had to work through. Something that started when I was seven, went full circle, then came back to you.'

She stilled, except her heart hadn't stilled. Her heart was hammering as if it might explode.

'You've come back?'

'I love you, Mardie,' he said simple and true. 'Like you... I've loved you all the time without stopping. Things got in the way. I couldn't get perspective. But now...'

'Now?'

'The funeral today,' he said. 'Hundreds of dogs, a funeral procession for one old man. A pilot's wife weeping over a plate. Raff, looking after his community. Harry and Riley at North Coast Rescue. You're all doing what you do, what you love to do, what makes you happy. But you don't destroy yourself in the process.'

'Is that what you've been doing?'

'No,' he said sharply. 'I left here when I was seventeen, and yes, I felt like a martyr then. Heading off to make up for my brother's life. But it changed. It became a passion, a love all on its own. It was only when I couldn't do it any more that shock and illness and a lack of perspective made me go back to the martyr bit.' He reached out and took her hands. 'It took one dog. One dog and one beautiful woman. It took my best friend, Mardie Rainey, to set me right.'

'So...' She was scarcely able to breathe. 'So you're set right now?'

'I have a plan.'

'A plan...'

'It's in its infancy,' he said. 'A bud of a plan. It needs work. It needs an artist to tweak the edges. But you want to hear?'

How could he doubt it? Her face must have answered for her.

'I teach online,' he said simply. 'I'd like to expand that. Medics in remote areas... I'm learning to use Skype so I can talk doctors through procedures. Video links. There's so much. If I stay in the one place, I can be connected all over the world.'

'You'd...be happy with that?'

'No,' he said. 'Not completely. So I will accept Riley and Harry's job offer. Three days a week they do their Outback clinics and they'll fly via here. I can work with them. I can still make a difference. I might,' he added diffidently, 'need to go overseas a couple of times a year, to conferences, to teaching clinics and to keep in touch with the foundation. I can still do fund-raising. And...if you wanted to...you could come with me.'

'Come with you?'

'Not to be taken up with my life,' he said. 'Not to follow my passion. But to follow your own. There'd be things you could do, techniques you could learn. We could learn together. We could...'

He paused. Thought about it.

Dropped to one knee.

'We could marry,' he said.

'Blake...' The whole world held its breath.

'I offered you diamonds,' he said simply. 'In Sydney. It was a stupid, crass thought, nothing more. And you know what? Tonight I don't even have a diamond. I've come unprepared. All I have to offer...' He shrugged. 'No. I don't have anything to offer, Mardie, but I do love you. All I have to offer is my love. I want to share your life. I want to be a part of your life. I love you, I want you, and I want to come home.'

And Mardie stared down at him and felt so much love that she must surely be dreaming.

He was waiting for her to answer. A girl had to think of something.

'So no diamond, huh?' she said cautiously.

'I... No. I can get one, but...'

'And an ancient rust bucket of a car that's still stuck on the hill overlooking Banksia Bay cemetery.'

'I guess...' He sounded confused.

'And the mere possibility—not even confirmed—of a part-time job. Part-time? Haven't you heard the saying? For better or worse but not for lunch.'

'I could... I don't know...take a packed lunch down the paddock every lunchtime. Bounce and I have some learning to do. That could be Bessie's teaching time.'

'So you wouldn't be underfoot?'

'Not very much.'

'But you want to stay here?'

'Wherever you are,' he said simply. 'That's where I want

to be, for the rest of my life.' Deep breath. 'Mardie, love, I don't want to hurry you, but this veranda's hard.'

'Is it?' She dropped on her knees before him. 'Oh, yes, so it is. You think we should put some padding on it?'

She sounded hysterical, she thought. She felt hysterical.

He took her hands in his. Hysteria faded.

'No padding,' he said. 'Just a fast answer. Yes or no. Mardie Rainey, I love you with all my heart. I want to be part of your life and I want you to be part of my life, for ever and ever. So there's no ring. I'll buy you one in the future but for now it's just me. Just me, Mardie, nothing else. No shadows. No regrets. Just us. Mardie Rainey, my love, my heart, will you be my wife?'

And she looked into his dear face, the face she'd grown with, the face she'd loved once and loved for ever.

Her Blake.

Her past and her future.

Her best friend.

Hysteria was gone. Doubts were gone—there was nothing but Blake.

'Why, yes, Blake Maddock,' she whispered, 'I believe I will.'

'He's home, too,' Blake said with deep satisfaction.

A simple ceremony on a driveway into a Banksia Bay farm. A driveway lined with ancient gum trees. A man and a woman, husband and wife, with their two dogs pressed together beside them.

The Banksia Bay vicar presiding.

Robbie's ashes had lain in a memorial wall for twenty-five years. Blake had hated them there, so now they'd brought him home, to a place where an ancient gum had once stood, a tree with linked initials, split in the storm.

Robbie's ashes were now scattered in the sunlight, on the earth around a sapling already reaching for the sky.

'No carving,' Blake said sternly to Mardie.

'Not me,' she said virtuously. 'But our children might not be into rules.'

The vicar frowned them down. This was a serious business. He read the blessing and then he smiled.

'This is a good thing to do,' he decreed as he gazed out over the farmland to the sea beyond. He'd heard the simple story and he approved. Now he motioned to the bump Mardie was proudly carrying under her smock. 'The bairn…if it's a boy, will you name him Robbie?'

'She's a girl,' Blake said, hugging his wife close. 'Already confirmed and her name's Oriane. It means dawn.'

'Lovely,' the vicar said, beaming. 'For I don't believe in looking back more than we need. Love continues. As for the rest… The past can get in the way of the future.'

Then he glanced at his watch. 'Speaking of the future, I must go.'

'So must we,' Blake said, smiling and clicking his fingers for the two dogs to join them. 'We have dog trials this afternoon. Today, my wife thinks her dog, Bounce, will beat my dog, Bessie, at the Whale Cove Sheepdog Trials. She's dreaming.'

'He'll do it,' Mardie said. 'If not this month, then next.'

'Only because Bessie needs to retire next month. We're having pups,' he told the vicar. 'Babies all over the place. But, pregnant or not, she'll still beat any dog, hands down. Our Bessie's brilliant.'

'We're all brilliant,' Mardie said. Smiling and smiling.

'Together we can do anything.' She hugged her husband and he hugged her back.

'We can do anything we want,' she said simply. 'Together we're home.'

* * * * *

OUT NEXT MONTH!

By *New York Times* bestselling author Delores Fossen comes *Tangled Up In Texas*, book one in the Lone Star Ridge series.

In-store and online June 2025

When the Jameson brothers are reunited with their childhood sweethearts, they realise that their past never faded — and neither did their passion.

Watch out for the next book in the series, *Chasing Trouble In Texas*, coming soon!

MILLS & BOON

millsandboon.com.au